CHILDREN

OF THE

VOLCANO

ESSENCE OF OHR
Book 2

PARRIS SHEETS

CHILDREN OF THE VOLCANO
Essence of Ohr – Book 2
Copyright © 2021 by Parris Sheets

FIRST EDITION SOFTCOVER
ISBN: 162253655X
ISBN-13: 978-1-62253-655-9

Editor: Darren Todd
Cover Artist: Samuel Keiser
Interior Designer: Lane Diamond

www.EvolvedPub.com
Evolved Publishing LLC
Butler, Wisconsin, USA

Printed in Book Antiqua font.

BOOKS BY PARRIS SHEETS

ESSENCE OF OHR
Book 1: *Warden's Reign*
Book 2: *Children of the Volcano*
Book 3: *Beyond the Flame*
Book 4: *The Hollow Key*

DEDICATION

To my Mother and Dad for their endless support.

CHILDREN OF THE VOLCANO

ESSENCE OF OHR
Book 2

PARRIS SHEETS

Realm of
OHR

N
W E
S

Solpate Forest

Refugee Camps

Tiot Sea

Lileth's Pass

Linde
Sea-Caves

Socren

Palace Mountains

Azure River

Rash

Coroko River

Cresthaven

Zeal

North Azure

Lake
Galen

Ashland Plains

South Azure

Hawthorne

Lake
Howell

Grayfall

Black wall

CHAPTER 1

The cold night faded. Dawn approached and with it, a brisk wind. Leaves chattered as the breeze blew across the bare shoulders of a middle-aged man.

The man shuddered and wiped a hand over his brow, plastering salt-and-pepper hair to his forehead. Sweat dripped from his temples as he placed another log on the stump. One swing, and the wood split under the honed blade of his axe.

Beyond him spanned dew-laden grass and a path of sleeping wildflowers leading to a small cottage. Moss crested the shingled roof. Like long, green fingers, a thick blanket of twisting vines threatened to overtake the log walls in its grip.

The man moved to grab another piece of wood from his pile, but something stopped him mid-reach. He cast his eyes up to the paling moon.

Something streaked overhead.

He cursed and dropped the axe, keeping his eyes on the skeletal horse as it flew above the cottage. The great beast landed at a gallop in the field.

"What are you doing?" the man barked. "You're going to frighten Evangeline."

The muscular rider flinched at the words. "I-I'm sorry, Aterus. I brought the girl, as you requested."

Aterus moved to the horse and placed his hand over the bony chest. The animal shivered under his touch. Flesh bloomed inside the ribcage, pulsing and mutating into organs. Veins and muscles slithered over the bones like wriggling earthworms, until finally, skin laced with a gleaming white coat spread across the stallion, and it was beautiful once again.

After restoring the horse, Aterus moved to the heap of auburn hair cascading down the side of the beast. "What have you done to her?"

Savairo kept his eyes on the ground as he spoke. "She was more trouble than I anticipated."

Aterus swept the hair from the girl's face and stroked the pale skin of her cheek before lifting her from the stallion's back. "I hope for your sake she isn't injured."

Savairo's jaw quivered.

"Stay here."

"Of course, sir."

Cradling the girl, Aterus walked up the flower-lined path and nudged the cottage door open. A fireplace blazed in the corner, giving light to every inch of the tiny, one-room house. With the bed at the side already occupied, Aterus laid her on a pelt before the fire.

"Sleep well, my darling." He thumbed her chin before returning outside.

"Aterus, sir, I must tell you...." Savairo had dismounted, but he clung to the horse with one hand as if unwilling to forfeit his only means of escape.

"Yes?" Aterus took up his axe and set up the next log.

"There has been a setback."

"I already know you lost the city." A smile pressed on his lips. "I heard it was quite an *embarrassing* defeat, too. Losing to your brother." A swift swing. The log fell in two and tumbled to the grass.

Savairo's mouth drooped.

"Be careful, young sorcerer. You are proving to be much less useful than I had anticipated. Perhaps I picked the wrong sibling."

"I-I have other news, too," Savairo offered.

"Better tidings, I hope." Aterus glanced back to the open window of the cabin, then kicked the split wood into a pile.

"I have found him."

"Yes, yes, I know of Risil. He'll be back where he belongs soon enough."

"He's being called Russé."

"Trying to blend in with the humans?" A smile pulled at the corner of his mouth. "He is hiding from me. Like a frightened *rat*," he emphasized the word with another drive of his axe.

"There is a boy with him," Savairo added.

Aterus turned back to him. "A boy?"

"He travels with the Soul."

"As many have." He placed the next log and drew back the axe.

"The boy set fire to the pit. He destroyed my Kayetans."

Splinters flew as Aterus' swing missed its mark and nicked a chunk off the stump. He held it there and turned his head to Savairo. "That is *not* possible. How would he—" Aterus abandoned his axe. Two steps closed the space between them. He thrust his hand to Savairo's throat, squeezed, and lifted the sorcerer from the grass. "Unless *you* had something to do with it. A coward always squeals to save his own skin."

Savairo's face purpled as he squirmed, then wheezed, "I-I swear I didn't."

Aterus tilted his head, inspecting the sorcerer writhing in his grasp, then returned him to the ground, a red handprint gathering on the assaulted skin. "I suppose not." He huffed a laugh. "A man without an army is merely a man. Insignificant. Vulnerable." Aterus peered at Savairo, who shook under the unwavering stare. "No, you wouldn't cut off your own legs. You know the consequences for such a betrayal. But if *you* didn't," his eyes grew distant as he stared into the night, "then *she* did."

"Sir?" Savairo croaked rubbing his throat. "The girl?"

"No, not the girl. My dear sister. Issira." Aterus refocused on the sorcerer. "Your loss at Socren may not be so bad, after all. The Liberation is exposed. They will be easier targets now. Let them have their victory. Let them bask in it while they can." His lips pulled down in a scowl. "Retrieve the boy. Bring him to me *alive*, Savairo. I have questions for him."

"What of the Soul with him?"

Aterus sneered. "A god without his powers is no threat."

"Maybe to you, sir, but he is strong... stronger than I can handle."

Aterus sighed. Straightening his arm, he trailed a fingernail up the tender side of his forearm. Blood seeped from the shallow cut. It lifted from his skin and floated into the air. "Take this."

Savairo produced a vial and gathered the blood, a manic lust in his eyes.

"Drink it when you face him, but be wary around the boy. I have a feeling he is being protected by the others. If he is threatened directly, anything could happen." The wound on his forearm closed, leaving smooth, untouched skin.

"Yes, sir." Savairo replaced the vial and mounted his stallion. With a nod, he rode off into the meadow as the gold sun peeked over the horizon.

Aterus stacked a pile of wood into his arms, then returned to the cottage. After tossing a log into the fire, he set the rest beside the hearth, then took a seat next to the girl. He stroked her cheek.

"Welcome home, Piper."

CHAPTER 2

Leo dragged his hand along the blood-stained stone table. It had taken the Liberation leader three days to muster the courage to set foot in Savairo's torture room. He'd ordered everyone to steer clear from this room, which his subordinates happily followed. Now, he stood at the very table where his misguided brother had murdered hundreds of people with abhorrent rituals, turning them into abominations.

Tiny holes drilled into the top of the stone slab traced the outline of a body. Beyond them lay etched runes. Sorcerer scrawl. He thumbed one that translated to "divide." Though the symbol looked familiar at a glance, added loops and lines muddled its meaning. Savairo had adjusted the old runes to accommodate his experiments. A dangerous venture. One wrong line could spoil the spell and cause ceaseless pain or even death to the user. Then again, his brother had been imbibing god's blood. Leo had seen it with his own eyes. Most likely, the risk was of little importance to Savairo.

The slab held a potent enchantment. A hum of energy raised the hairs on Leo's arm. He prodded one of the holes with a finger. A click echoed off the stone walls as hundreds of needles shot up. One nicked his thumb. Pulling away at the sharp pain, he then leaned in, inspecting his brother's contraption. A grimace settled behind his dark beard.

The oscillating needles bent inward and cut the empty air. Sparks of black energy pulsed from the magic-infused points. He imagined the screaming men, women, and children as his brother laid them on the table, restraining their flailing limbs with the cracked leather straps, which now hung loose from the corners of the torture device like discarded ribbons.

After a few minutes, the needles retracted, and Leo imagined whoever had been unfortunate enough to grace the table would be removed bloody and broken. And more important, shadowless.

This is how he made the Kayetans.

The needles would separate the shadow from the victims and infuse it with dark magic. The process took the shadow and made it into a new entity. This new creature bound itself to Savairo and did his bidding.

Leo fought back a swelling shiver, then cast his eyes to the ghastly tools strewn along the walls. Saws, shears, operative blades, and other tools that could only be of Savairo's own invention, hung from bolts crudely hammered into the cracking stone. Their metal glittered in the light of his lantern.

Nothing could have prepared him for the horrors in this room — the evil his once sweet, naive little brother had conducted in the shadows. To his own people. His own city. Savairo may have fallen far from Leo's graces, but not without help. Or rather, without the seduction of blood magic.

A soft knock at the door pulled his attention.

Vienna stood in the archway. Though he'd instructed her to take a break from her duties an hour ago, by the dirt clinging to her blonde braid, she'd disregarded orders. Her green eyes strayed from Leo and widened as they landed on the table. "What is that?"

Leo strode over, flicking his coat behind him to block the table. "What do you need?" he blurted, using a harsher voice than normal to call her attention back to him.

Vienna's glazed eyes refocused. "The children have arrived."

"Good." Leo shut the door after him and locked it, paying no mind to her curious gaze. "Have Thomas see to it they are fed, then set them up in the Estate. There is more than enough room for them there."

"Are you sure you want to give this to Thomas? My brother can—"

"That will not be necessary."

"But Thomas has been a mess," she argued. "He hasn't left Piper's room in days."

"That is precisely why I am giving this to him. He needs a distraction."

Vienna's mouth twisted, but she didn't push the matter any further. "As you wish."

Leo nodded in dismissal. When Vienna lingered, he asked, "Is there something else?"

Her face darkened. "The children have been saying odd things about the forest. The rangers, too."

"What kinds of things?"

"They brought something back." Her mouth parted as if she was going to explain, but she closed it and shook her head. "You should see it for yourself."

A jiggle on the handle to test the lock, then he followed Vienna down the stairs to the lower levels of the prison.

Leo couldn't risk anyone else setting foot in there until he'd cleared it out. Though Vienna would take up the task if he wished it, he thought it best to handle this on his own. Vienna, Felix, Thomas, even Criz and Boogy, had all been affected by the Kayetans in one way or another. Fighting them was one thing. It proved easy for the Liberation to use their anger and redirect it to the monsters responsible for murdering their families. Seeing the tools used to perform the ritual would lower morale—invite old pains. Better for everyone to keep the Kayetans out of mind. He alone would clean up his brother's mess. *That table will go first.*

Vienna led him down to the main level of the prison into one of the large rooms Savairo's guards had used as a mess hall. Initially, Leo wanted to repurpose the massive space to house the refugees coming in from Solpate. Unfortunately, few seemed keen on entering the building where their loved ones had been tortured. For now, most refugees took shelter in barns and storage facilities until a more permanent residence could be built. Ground zero of the prison served as the Liberation's new headquarters.

A rough-looking man with scraggly hair and a pronounced odor stood timidly inside the mess hall, fiddling with a hide sack in his hands. Leo recognized him as one of the citizens who had volunteered as a ranger to aid the Liberation after the rebellion. He was a thin man, which was no surprise since most of the people of Socren starved during Savairo's reign.

"Show him," Vienna ordered the ranger as she strolled in.

The man timidly peeked at Leo, his hands shaking as he struggled to open the sack. "Well, sir, I did a bit of huntin' when I went ta get the little ones like ya asked." His fumbling fingers managed to pull open the drawstring, and he withdrew a strange hide.

"What is this?" Leo took it from him.

"An elk, sir."

Leo's fingers trailed over the mossy skin. He had always been curious about the animals in Solpate.

For some reason, the creatures there looked different from the others across Ohr. They donned moss instead of fur, grew wooden antlers and hooves in place of bone and keratin, and petals substituted as feathers on the birds. But beneath the skin, the animals remained true to their kin outside the forest: flesh and bone.

This hide, though, appeared different. Coarse hairs sprouted from the base, poking through the delicate moss. The bark-like skin felt soft, covered by a thin layer of newly grown undercoat. "Is this the only one?"

The ranger shook his head. "It's the only one I got, but I seen more out there. The birds were moltin'. Looked like baby chicks, only skin and whatnot. And the ramblers...."

"What about them?"

"The kids said they haven't moved for a week."

A week. Was it a coincidence? "May I keep this?"

The ranger nodded.

Leo shook off the idea of chance. Something was *causing* the animals to return to their original state and was anchoring the walking trees. He had a hunch as to what, but he needed to be certain. "Does anyone else know about this?"

"The ramblers? Sure. Not the hide."

"Good. Keep it that way for now."

"Yessir."

"You are dismissed."

As soon as the ranger shuffled past them and out the door, Vienna turned on him. "What does it mean?"

"Just get your things."

"Sir?"

"Meet me in Lilith's pass in one hour. We are going to Solpate."

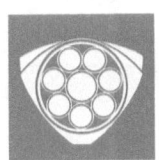

The evening sun filtered through the dense canopy onto Leo's back. Lush green trees surrounded them. They grew abnormally large compared to the ones in the city. Their trunks alone could fill the massive prison tower, and fully matured, they surpassed its height as well. The leaves seemed to mingle with the clouds.

Leo and Vienna trekked through the forest until the green leaves above turned red. Only one tree in all of Ohr held this color. The ruby of the forest sat before them. Maroon bark covered the Great Red. Scarlet leaves, perched on the edge of each twig, swayed in the light breeze, like ballooning drops of blood ready to fall from a wound. And at the base of the tree, a deep-set cavity darkened the trunk.

"This is it," Leo said, opening one side of his coat.

"I've been here before." Vienna approached the red tree in the small clearing. "This is where I hid from Idris. Kole came searching for me."

Leo's eyes flicked to her. "Kole?"

"He said he had come to rescue me." She gave a snort. Then her face grew solemn. "I guess he did save me."

"*You* needed saving?" Leo plucked a few pouches of herbs and vials from his coat pockets and dumped them onto the grass. Taking up a pouch of ash, he poured the powder along the ground, pinching the opening for a slower flow when it came to drawing the more complex runes for the spell.

"Just the once." She traced her fingers along the splintered teeth leading into the cave-like cavity. "I lost my blade. Idris had me pinned. Nothing I could do. And then...."

Leo's hand paused mid-stroke. "And then, what?"

She turned back to him. "I saw a white light. Next thing I remember was waking up in the refugee camp the following day."

"Why did you not mention this before?"

"I didn't think anything of it at the time."

He tilted his head, unconvinced.

"Well, yes, it was strange. But nothing concerning. I helped the refugees prepare for battle, and we marched on the city the next day. Things haven't exactly slowed down. Forgive me. Had I known it was something important, I would have reported immediately."

"No need for forgiveness. This past week has meant turmoil for us all." He finished the last swoop of a powdery rune. "Bring me a piece of the Great Red's trunk, please."

Vienna returned to his side, a small maroon splinter poised between her fingers. She handed it over, then waited for instruction.

"Ready?"

She squeezed his arm in response.

Palming the splinter, he focused his mind on the red tree. "Keep me in the circle. If I am gone more than an hour, destroy the runes."

"Safe journeys."

Show me what is changing Solpate. Leo drew a long breath, then poured the crushed herbs and red splinter from the tree into the vial and chugged the muddy liquid. The concoction burned its way to his stomach. He clamped his eyes against the pain as the heat flowered, extending to his hands and feet. When he opened them again, the forest had changed to the vibrant yellows and oranges of fall.

A child stood next to the red tree. In the corner of his vision, Leo spotted another figure in the distance leaning against a trunk, who seemed to be watching the child near the tree. Unable to discern anything else about the stranger from afar, Leo turned his attention back to the boy.

The child held a small, hesitant hand to the blood-red bark. As the boy's finger brushed the trunk, an explosion of light overtook the clearing. The child flew into the air, knocked back by the blast, then slammed back into the earth on the edge of Leo's vision.

As the light dwindled, a form crawled out from the red trunk. The image blurred. Leo's spell was fading. He clung onto the magic, trying to hold on until another clue revealed itself. The scene grew darker, like a veil descending over his eyes.

A green light enveloped the form crawling from the trunk. It moved toward the fallen child. Then it changed shape. Hunched back. Gray hair. Wrinkled skin.

A scream echoed around Leo, and the scene swirled like a whirlpool. Darkness swallowed him. His head hit cool grass.

"Leo!" Vienna cried. "For Soul's sake, what the hell happened?"

"Hmm?" Leo rolled to his back, stretching out the stiff ache in his legs. Stars littered the dark sky, and from the cresting moon above, he guessed he'd been out a little longer than intended. No wonder Vienna sounded so upset. "I am quite all right. A few extra hours are nothing to worry about."

"Hours?" Vienna shot back. "Leo, you were locked in the spell for two days."

"What?" Leo sat up, bringing Vienna into view.

She sat next to him, her face streaked with black powder, but even the muck couldn't hide the prominent bags beneath her eyes.

"Why did you not pull me out?"

"I tried," she said sternly, the concern in her voice switching to anger. "I've cleaned the whole bloody rune from the grass. Nothing worked. I was about to pick you up and drag you back myself."

Leo took in the scene around him, his rune no more than a smear of black on the grass.

Two days. It explained his stiff muscles. And his hunger. "I am sorry I worried you."

Vienna leaned back, folding her arms. "What did you see? It must've been something good."

"Enough to know why the forest is changing. And why our shepherds left us." His eyes trailed to the trees beyond the clearing. "I have a job for you."

CHAPTER 3

Kole blocked out the gurgling river and chirping birds. Everything sounded different here in the midst of the rolling hills. Different birds with harsher calls, scream-like compared to the tranquil songs of home. No trees stood to block the wind, which slapped cold on his cheek. Even when a breeze had managed to swell among the old ramblers, the wind had rattled the leaves like bells. Here, they sounded more like clanking bones. His new surroundings grated him.

Kole squeezed his eyes tighter, hoping it would help him concentrate, but it only aggravated his pounding headache.

"You need to relax," Russé reminded, the irritation poorly hidden in his tone.

"I know what I'm doing," Kole snapped back.

Kole had been trying to reach Issira for nearly a week, but not a single whisper or slightest brush of her presence greeted his consciousness since she last spoke to him during the battle at Lilith's Pass. After the first few days of silence, Russé figured she'd drained herself and needed time to recoup. If the Soul held concern, Kole couldn't tell; that is, until a whole week had passed with no change. Then Russé pushed him longer and harder during their sessions. Kole knew the old man was as eager as him for information of her whereabouts, but the extra work led nowhere.

At this point, he could barely clear his mind before the headaches returned. They pained him unlike any other. They started as a tingle in the back of his head, slowly intensifying until the agony compared to a hammer strike—like his skull would shatter and leave his brain exposed to the cold wind churning around him. No matter how hard he tried to push past the pain, the headaches persisted. Russé's suggested techniques proved useless.

"I can't do it." Kole tore his eyes open with a disgruntled sigh. "I feel it coming back."

Russé, sitting cross-legged opposite him, leaned away, clearly disappointed. Kole had been on the receiving side of that look too many times to mistake it. "Let me help you."

He eyed the Soul wearily, studying his former mentor. A few weeks ago, when Russé had been nothing more than an old shepherd, Kole would've taken the assistance without a second thought. The old man had taught Kole everything he knew about Solpate forest, where he'd lived since he was five. But when a Kayetan attacked and lured Russé into revealing his true identity as a god, Kole had found it hard to trust again. He kept seeing this old, hunched over, gray-haired man before him, and his mind kept falling back to old ways—seeing Russé as a friend rather than what he actually was: a god.

The reason Kole sat here, enduring this torture, solely lay on the deal he'd made. As long as Russé held up his side, so would he.

Though Russé's request may have been innocent, Kole wasn't keen on letting anyone else inside his head, where they could see his memories and read his thoughts. He already had five gods trapped in there somewhere, which seemed a bit too crowded as it was.

Russé must have sensed his hesitance because he leaned back and folded his hands patiently on his lap, as if showing Kole he would not act without permission. "I can restrain the headache so you can focus. If it doesn't work, we'll stop."

The offer tempted him. Being rid of the constant pounding, even if for a moment, gave him a sense of bliss. "Fine. I'll try it."

He flinched when Russé put a wrinkled hand to his temple. At the Soul's touch, the headache instantly dwindled. Kole waited until it completely subsided, then shut his eyes once more. *Last time. I can do this.*

Drowning out the sounds proved simpler this time. He withdrew from the world around him and let his consciousness take control.

Kole's mind resembled a map—his memories the cities and his thoughts the roads between them, linking them together. It took a lot of practice to navigate, but by now, he had a fairly good hang of it. Traveling through his own mind wasn't the difficult part but rather breaching Issira's walls.

He followed the roads to Issira and pressed into the energy blocking him out.

No give. Kole chewed his bottom lip, cursing himself for thinking it would be so easy. He took in a deep breath and pushed again.

Nothing.

Growing frustrated, he sucked in a lungful of air and with it, called on every ounce of energy left in his body. Every muscle and fiber, from his toes to his fingers, tensed. He loaded the energy outside Issira's door. Clenching his stomach, he exhaled, directing the force toward the wall. It bent and stretched. Sensing its frailty, he held out a little longer until the wall finally tore. After breaking the barrier, his head lit up with a familiar image.

A pond sat in the distance. The evening sun reflected off its stagnant surface. This time, Kole could just make out something large on the horizon. But the picture shifted with haze, like when he tried to remember a dream the morning after. No matter how much he willed it, the scene stayed dull and dim. *Come on, give me something else. Anything. Where are you?*

As if the wall sensed a foreign mind, it shoved him out and reinforced the small tear he'd entered through.

Kole opened his eyes and turned away from Russé. As soon as the old man's hand dropped from his temple, the headache returned.

"What did you see?"

"The pond."

"Anything else this time? A landmark or town in the background?"

"There was something in the distance, but...." Kole reformed the picture in his head hoping to catch something he missed. "It's too blurry. I can't tell what it is."

"A shape? A color? Anything?"

"No." Kole kicked the rocks at his feet, catapulting them into the river with a splash. "I told you I can't see it. Only a dark blob."

Silence thickened between them.

Kole stared out over the river, his frustration gnawing on him. He'd learned his shepherd skills fairly easily. Sure, he had never truly mastered them all—communing with the trees always gave him some trouble—but he managed. Even archery had come quickly to him. His impeccable aim had kept his old camp fed most nights. A great deal of things came naturally to him with a little time and practice. Some more than others. His sword skills lacked, but he blamed a lack of formal training on that. How could anyone thrive at combat with only one sparring partner and sticks as weapons? But whatever skills he'd had before... he'd lost during his encounter with the Black Wall.

The dark flames had burned every inch of his skin. The taut, corded scar tissue enveloping his body forced him to relearn the simplest things. Walking. Running. Even using his hands. Despite the difficulties, he improved day by day. He could see it—*feel* it. Yet no matter how many times he tried this whole telepathic connection thing, it felt like his skills deteriorated, which only irritated him more. The Black Wall had limited him. Crippled him. His mind remained his own—untouched by the effects of the fire—but it seemed as weak as his body when it came to these training sessions. Completely useless.

"I can't do this. I'm not strong enough. There has to be another way."

"You just need some rest. A little sleep will do us both good."

Kole snorted. "If I could get any."

"You're still having dreams? Is it Piper?"

"Every time I close my eyes, I see her and Savairo. He tortures her."

"It's not real," Russé urged.

"How do you know? Savairo's done worse. Why wouldn't he torture her? Piper probably knows the most about the Liberation save for Leo himself. If she talks...." He couldn't finish the sentence. "Maybe it'd be worse if she didn't."

"The Liberation is searching for her. I'm sure of it."

"Shouldn't we, too?"

Russé sighed. "There are other things just as important. Things only *we* are capable of doing."

"What if he's turned her into a Kayetan? Rebuilds his army?"

"That takes time. I know it's hard to accept, but if she's already been turned, there's no way to help."

Kole's head toyed with him—concocted horrid images of her being tortured for information, crying out for help with no one to hear her pleas. He shoved the thought away. It plagued his dreams enough. No need to think on it now. The Soul was right. So many things lay out of his control, even the one thing bestowed upon him: his connection to the Souls.

"I wish you could just do it yourself. This middleman thing isn't working," Kole complained.

"I wish it, too, but my connection to the other Souls is severed. You are the only way to commune with them. All you need to do is find her; I can do the rest."

"Maybe you're wrong about Issira."

Bushy gray brows furrowed. "How so?"

"I don't think she wants to be found. Why else would she make this so hard?"

"She's weak. She expended quite a bit of power on—"

"I know, I know." Kole stared into the water, pulling at his hair. When Issira had helped him during the rebellion, saved his life and given him the only clue to destroy Savairo's Kayetans, she'd exhausted her energy. "But I'm the one doing all the work here. The least she could do is give me something different. *Anything*. Does she realize this isn't working?"

"There's no way to tell. If we can't figure it out, we'll continue to follow the river."

"So we'll just check every pond and hope we get lucky?"

"It's the best lead we have for now."

"And the other Souls? Are they going to be like this, too?"

Russé's pensive gaze set on Kole. "I don't know."

"Great." Kole threw his hands up. "At this rate, Savairo could rebuild his army and take back Socren before we find *any* of them."

"We don't know what Savairo plans to do. It's better not to assume. Keep your focus on your duty. We can worry about him after."

"In the meantime, Piper might die along with the rest of the Liberation. Is that it?" Kole fumed. "It's always the Souls first to you, isn't it?"

"Kole—"

"Don't pretend it's not." He rose to his feet and turned to face him. "We both know I would've died along with Niko if you didn't need me."

"That's not—"

"Save it."

Kole left Russé on the riverbank. He hadn't meant to say Niko's name. It slipped out. Now thoughts of his friend consumed him. It wouldn't be so bad if the memories were of the good times: when they would stay up all night talking about how they'd be the best shepherds Solpate had ever seen, or when they'd sneak out after curfew just to watch the ramblers stumble around and make bets on how many would charge the camp's outer walls. He forced those thoughts into his head— tried to hear his friend's laugh. The laugh morphed into a shattering scream. Kole's mind surged to the last moments he shared with him. The feel of Niko's hands slipping through his own as they spun in the air toward the wall of black fire. Kole's skin grew hot as if it were bubbling and blistering all over again.

Urging the memory away, he clenched his jaw and cast his eyes to the horizon to distract himself. The sun hung over the rolling hills, a few hours away from nightfall, but he returned to his bedroll, eager to be done for the day. His stiff body ached; head pounded again.

Two gargantuan trees stood guard over their camp: ramblers from Solpate forest. The sight of the walking trees, even if only two, sent both a wave of ease and homesickness over him. It had been Russé's best idea yet to commandeer the pair after the rebellion. They made travel simpler and allowed Kole to focus on finding Issira rather than exerting himself from hiking. Usually, ramblers only walked at night, but having the god of nature as a travel companion seemed to have certain perks. The trees obeyed Russé's every command.

The ramblers remained anchored when they bore no riders. Russé insisted it made them look less suspicious out in the open hills, but Kole knew better. Trees four times larger than the average oak stood out like beacons, especially since the rolling hills lacked any plant life other than waist-high grass. The ramblers accompanied them for protection above all else. He only wished he could control them better on his own.

As he leaned into the furs he'd placed at the base of the trunk, he rubbed his temples. Kole turned onto his side, feigning sleep as Russé neared. He peeked out once the Soul had settled in.

The soil bulged as the ramblers arced their roots over Kole and Russé. Dirt-crusted tendrils weaved together to create a dome-like basket over top of them, hiding the two from unfriendly eyes. The good thing about traveling with the Green Soul was they never had to worry about finding a good campsite—not when the old man possessed the power to manipulate nature at will.

Shrouded in the peaceful darkness, Kole closed his eyes.

The images of the battle bubbled up. Savairo flung Piper's unconscious body over his horse, fighting back Leo and Russé with ease. Then, Piper lay on a table like the one he'd seen in Savairo's prison. The blades shot up from the stone. She screamed as they tore into her flesh, flaying her skin like a fish.

Kole flipped and turned, struggling to make the scene fade away. He homed in on the smell of the grass surrounding him. Inhaled. Exhaled. He repeated this until his body calmed. The elusive fingers of sleep caressed him. On the edge of nodding off, the screams came.

He bolted up.

The rambler roots domed around him. Russé's snores filled the small enclosure. The scream had sounded so real. His dreams had grown beyond absurd. He couldn't get a moment's peace.

Then it came again. Distant, but clear. *Real.*

He scooted to the edge of the makeshift room and pulled at the tangled roots. They loosened at his touch and wiggled away to clear an opening.

A dull, orange glow crested the top of the hill. Too late to be the sun. Fire? He remembered passing a town not long after they'd decided to settle by the river.

Russé's snores ceased. The noise had awakened the Soul.

"There's a fire," Kole said, eyes fixed on the tongue-like flames lashing up to the sky.

Russé crawled over and peered out. "Quite a bit of noise for a fire."

"We should help them." Kole sensed the Soul's hesitation. "It's just a fire."

The Soul remained quiet.

"Never mind, I forgot you're only interested in helping people who are useful to you." Kole let the resentment ooze from his words.

Russé's blue eyes flashed in the dark. "In and out. As soon as it's under control, we leave. Grab your things," he said as the rambler roots receded. Pale moonlight poured over Russé, who had already rolled his bed and shouldered his bag.

"Everything?"

"Going into the village will expose us. We'll have to leave right after."

"They're villagers. They won't even know who we are."

"Word travels faster than the wind." Russé turned around, his expectant gaze on Kole's empty hands. "Are we going or not?"

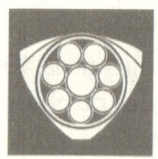

Kole hunkered down at the bottom of the hill on the outskirts of the village. He'd convinced Russé to leave the ramblers a quarter mile back. If they meant to come and go without notice, two ramblers bearing down on the village wouldn't do them any favors. He tapped his fingers on his knee, waiting for Russé, who'd insisted on scoping out the scene beforehand.

From their position, the center of the inferno came from the largest building in town square. The fire had spread to the adjacent buildings, dangerously flirting with the roofs of the neighboring structures.

He expected to see a crowd around the blazing buildings with water and buckets, but no one in the streets paid any attention to the fire. The villagers ran through the streets screaming and pushing their way into houses, behind walls, and under carriages. They were hiding. Escaping.

Then he saw it. A streak of shadow rushed between the gates of a nearby garden.

"Kayetans," Kole cursed.

Savairo had made more, just as Kole had feared. But what were his creatures doing here?

"Let's go," said Russé.

Kole pulled his hood up—half to hide his scars, half to filter the smoke—then unsheathed the sunstone blade. His fingers wrapped around the worn hilt as he stepped toward the village. When Russé pulled him the opposite way, Kole realized the Soul had meant for them to run, not help. Kole tensed and planted his feet. If Russé wanted to leave, he'd have to drag him.

"They can't defend themselves. They don't have sunstone." Kole held up the enchanted dagger he'd pilfered from the Liberation. "We can help." The grip on his arm tightened briefly before letting go.

"Stay behind me," Russé warned as he stalked across the open field.

They crouched low in the waist-high grass to a nearby corral, then followed it around the edge to a barn. The sheep inside bleated frantically, their ears twitching at the screams emanating from the village.

After a quick glance around the corner, Russé led them up the dirt road toward the town square into a fog of smoke. Kole mimicked the Soul and kept his back to the buildings to avoid an ambush from the rear, while keeping watch for any sign of another Kayetan. Despite staying low, he coughed against the thick air. The odor of burning wood stirred unpleasant flashbacks of the Black Wall. He shook it off as a man raced past, axe in hand, and fled into a house across the street. If he noticed Kole and Russé, he didn't show it.

More women and children darted by. Kole spotted a lone woman standing in the middle of the street, tears streaming down her face. Her mouth moved, but it took a moment for him to single out her voice through the chaos and roaring fire.

"Rosie! Rosie!" she called, madly looking back and forth along the street.

Kole pointed her out to Russé. They weaved their way over, dodging more scrambling villagers. It took all his will to veer closer to the flames. Even a hundred yards out, the heat touched his burned flesh.

"What are you doing out here?" Russé said to the woman. "Get inside."

She reeled. Fear flared in her eyes as she took in Kole and Russé's weapons, then it turned to desperation. "They stole her!"

"Who did?" Kole flicked his eyes between the woman and the inferno over her shoulder. The fire held his attention: ravenous flames waiting to consume him. In that moment, if she'd told them her little Rosie was stuck inside, he'd be too terrified to go after her. Despite the heat, he shivered.

"The shadows pulled her from my arms. Please, help me."

"We'll look for her, but you need to get inside where it's safe," Russé said.

"I'm not going anywhere without her," she screamed. Another wave of tears overtook her.

Before Kole could respond, a shadow streaked between the houses to the left. He pleaded for it to be a wisp of smoke from the fire, but the silhouette was undeniable.

A Kayetan shot from the alley. Its translucent form, something between phantom, flesh, and smoke, allowed Kole to see the flames of the burning buildings through the human-like silhouette. The creatures took on the outline of whoever they had been forged from. This one appeared male, slender. Two deep, sunken circles on the shadow's face stood in place of eyes. But the true tell of a Kayetan, the most dangerous part of them, was the elongated claws hanging down to their knees. Kole still found it strange such an ethereal looking weapon could cut clean through bone.

The Kayetan drew back, preparing for a swipe. Kole dove for the woman. He pulled her down, a rush of wind whizzing by his ear as the claws barely passed over him. They both tumbled into the dirt.

"Run!" Kole pushed her to her feet, then scrambled up, sunstone dagger in hand. Her steps faded away behind him as he and Russé squared off with the Kayetan. Before they could attack, it fled down the alley.

Kole straightened up, staring at the empty space before him. He'd never seen a Kayetan flee like this. The creature had become completely uninterested in them once they stood their ground. He shot Russé a curious look.

The Soul flexed his fingers over his staff. "They aren't here to fight."

"What then?"

A high-pitched cry pierced the night air. Kole flipped around. A few houses down, a Kayetan rushed by with a girl locked in its arms.

Then it clicked: Savairo required bodies for his ritual. *The Kayetans have come for the villagers.*

Kole's blood ignited in a fit of rage. He'd be damned if he let Savairo make another pile of corpses unchallenged. He bounded forward, surprised Russé already ran ahead with his staff snapped in two. The splintered edges had lengthened at the Soul's will into a pair of wooden blades.

The Soul darted after the Kayetan at a pace Kole couldn't match. Instead of trying to keep up and risk ripping his scars, he veered right and ditched the main road for a back alley. He raced past a pile of crates and shouted to villagers to find shelter.

The alley spit him out onto another road. He turned the corner. Plans to follow Russé changed when he glimpsed another Kayetan with a young boy writhing in its grip as it hauled him from a house. A last-second twist, and Kole followed. He refused to let the Kayetan take anyone unchecked. Russé could handle himself.

Cutting around the next corner, he realized the Kayetan changed course and darted for the hills. Once the shadow crossed the outskirts of town, Kole had no hope of catching up. Heart pounding as loud as his feet on the packed soil, Kole shouted to draw the kid's attention. The boy looked on him with panicked eyes. Seeing Kole must have given him new strength, because he thrashed more violently against his captor as if realizing this may be his last shot at freedom. The boy's efforts caused the Kayetan to slow enough for Kole to gain, but the creature had made it into the hills.

Kole pushed his legs to the limit, his breath coming in spurts now as he closed in. Jolts of pain shot up from his thighs, stretching too far. Praying his scar tissue would hold, he inched his stride wider.

Hoping for a clean shot at the Kayetan's heart was foolish; a miss meant hitting the boy. Kole couldn't take that risk, so he tucked his blade under his sleeve and lunged.

Bare hands proved useless against the Kayetan. They'd pass through his shadowy form, like trying to catch a cloud. The boy, though. Flesh and bone. Quite tangible.

Kole hooked his arms under the boy's shoulders and jammed his heels into the earth. Still the Kayetan pulled him along. Kole's feet bounced and twisted on the knots and lumps of soil. The tall grass swiped at him like razors. Each tug tested his grip. Kole growled as his fingers slipped on sweaty skin. He looked up into the boy's eyes.

For a moment, his vision blurred. The memories he'd kept subdued burst from the depths of his mind. The scene before him changed. Gray wind, thick with ash, replaced the rolling hills. Smoke filled his lungs. A wall of black fire loomed in the distance, its luring wind dragging him closer. The face of the boy he clung to morphed. The same fearful expression stared back at Kole, but the features belonged to his dead friend, Niko.

It's not real. The wall. The wind. None of it. But it felt real.

Niko's nails dug into Kole's forearms as he slipped away. Kole tried to hold on, to prevent the inevitable.

In the fray, the fabric hiding his disfigured face slipped off. An unfamiliar voice, full of horror and disgust, came from Niko's lips. "What are you?"

Words Niko never would've said. It shattered the fantasy and chased away the memory of the wall.

Kole took in the grassy hills once more. The Kayetan held the village boy. Except the boy's eyes held more terror than before, after glimpsing his rescuer's face.

Through with being dragged along, Kole lifted his feet. He shot his legs forward, locked his knees, and jammed his heels into the ground. Soil parted like a ship cutting through rough waves.

The Kayetan struggled against the added effort. Without warning, the shadow discarded its cargo. The boy landed on Kole, pinning him to the ground.

Free from his kidnapper, the kid rolled off and sprinted back toward the village, paying no mind to Kole lying at the Kayetan's feet.

The black, featureless face with those sunken eyes bore down on Kole.

Before his courage escaped, Kole pulled out his white-stoned blade and lashed at the creature's heart.

The Kayetan swirled away.

Kole spun, eyes searching, knowing the creature could reform anywhere in an instant. But the pitch night camouflaged any chance to spot it. Even the last row of houses blocked the light from the village fires. The Kayetan, though, thrived in the darkness.

A breeze tickled the hairs on Kole's arm. He turned.

Nothing.

Maybe it fled after losing its prey, like the other one back in the village. Still, Kole refused to let his guard down.

Something moved out of the corner of his eye. He reeled. At the edge of the village, Kole made out Russé's hunched form carrying a small body in his arms. Probably Rosie.

He let out a sigh of relief. A force caught his stomach, and he doubled over. The blow had knocked the dagger from his hand, and it landed somewhere in the tall grass. He lurched after the weapon, but claws snagged him, lifted him. Kole flailed against his captor. The village shrunk in the distance as the Kayetan carried him into the hills.

Panic welled up. Without his blade, he was useless. Fight as he may, it'd do nothing more than drain his energy. The Kayetan would let go when it reached its master and offered Kole as a fresh sacrifice for Savairo's ritual, where he'd be turned into the same sort of demon.

Kole called out for Russé, though he knew the roaring fires in the village drowned his cries. The Kayetan crested a hill, giving Kole his last glimpse of town. He fought back the rising lump in his throat. Always the prey. Always the one who needs saving. He was sick of being weak. Sick of being defenseless.

The last weapon at his disposal lay within.

With a growl, he clamped his eyes shut and withdrew from the world. Concentrated. Focused as Russé had taught him. He blocked out the fire, the villagers, the Kayetan carrying him away, and the dread shaking his body. He swept through his consciousness to the barrier blocking Issira and slammed into it. Maybe the fear coursing through his veins granted him strength, or maybe he had finally started to get the hang of this connection thing, but her defenses gave way like a breaking dam.

Once in her domain, the same image of the pond appeared. Kole knocked it away. He had no idea what he hoped for, or if it would even work, but he had to do something. If Issira denied assistance, he'd force her.

Kole imagined grasping onto her energy, encasing it in his hands. Like a handful of sand, little by little it seeped from him as he moved back to the barrier and desperately flung himself against the already hardening wall shutting him from his own mind. He charged it, willing it to break.

The wall ruptured. He fell back into the comfort of his own, familiar mind. What little of her energy he'd managed to steal flooded the open spaces of his consciousness, more spilling into him from the rift he'd left in the barrier.

As her power spread, a sudden burst of energy surged through his body. It seized control of his muscles. He ripped open his eyes. His body glowed blue—brighter and brighter until it burned white hot, engulfing every limb, every fiber.

Pain erupted in his skull. The light exploded from his skin into the night air.

The Kayetan shrieked.

Kole hit the ground. The whirl of his captor's fleeing form reached his ears.

Then, he heard her.

"Let go, Kole." Issira projected the words into his head, a wildness in her voice. *"Let go, or you will destroy yourself."*

But as she spoke, the image of the pond reappeared, except this time it came clear. He saw the pond. Black and still. The blurry outline he could never make out before now burned crisp and clear into his mind.

A cluster of hills; three in a row, identical to one another as if molded by hand. He tried to make out more details, but the pain became too much.

Kole could barely think through the agony. It seared into his skull like a branding rod. He writhed on the ground, his body shaking uncontrollably in the blue light emanating from within. Warm liquid spread over his legs, and the acrid odor of urine drifted to his nose. His mind collapsed in on itself like Issira was claiming his body for her own. Taking his mind. Taking his soul.

"Let go!" Her command came muffled as if underwater.

Kole felt his essence fade. The same energy he'd used to fend off the Kayetan turned on him. It dragged him back and corralled him into the small space where Issira once resided. Little by little, the rupture in the barrier stitched itself closed. If it sealed completely, he knew his fate: he and the Soul would be switched. Issira would have his body, and he'd be the one locked away.

"No!" Issira's voice rang through him.

He released his hold on the energy.

At his surrender, Issira pried Kole from his confines and threw him back into his body. The Soul retreated behind the barrier. When it snapped closed, the blue light extinguished, leaving Kole prone and alone in the hills.

CHAPTER 4

Piper rolled over; a veil of grogginess draped around her. Fur tickled her nose, and she jerked up with a start. A pelt lay beneath her, cushioning her against the hardwood floor. Her eyes took in the familiar house: the small table on the far side of the room, the crackling fireplace burning too hot beside her, and in the corner....

She kicked the blankets off and dashed to the bed. Her eyes stung as she stared at her mother's solemn face. A year had passed since she last saw her. It pleased her to see age had finally caught up despite her father's efforts to stop time's effects. Her skin had thinned, revealing thick, blue veins beneath, and the few wrinkles around her face had multiplied. She looked as though she'd aged ten years, at least.

Piper carefully lowered onto the bed, trailing her fingers over her mother's unfamiliar, aged face. A sad smile pressed on her lips as she smoothed the long, white locks.

"I'm home," she whispered, though she knew her mother couldn't hear her in her comatose state.

"You never should have left."

Piper turned to meet her father's eyes. "I did what I had to."

Aterus' mouth twitched slightly. Anger? Disappointment? She couldn't tell. No matter how long she spent with him, she never could read her father. Only her mother held that gift.

Aterus closed the door behind him and tossed the dead rabbit he carried onto the table. "I figured you would be hungry." He drew his skinning knife.

Focus back on her mother, Piper smoothed out the blanket, then pulled it up to her neck so it looked as though she were sleeping. "A little," Piper confessed. She didn't want his kindness, but going hungry would make her weak. Something she couldn't afford. Not here.

Her father took the legs of the rabbit and wrapped his hands around the fur.

"I won't be staying long," Piper said.

Aterus kept a steady gaze on her and twisted his hands. A soft rip filled the house as the skin broke. "You will be staying as long as I need you." After repeating the process on the other leg, he pulled back the fur, revealing glossy red skin.

Her father was a fool if he thought he could keep her against her will. She wasn't helpless like her mother. Piper kept her face still, matching her father's expression to hide her simmering anger. If he was going to play this game, so would she. "We will be leaving as soon as I've eaten."

"We?" Aterus ripped the skin from the small animal with a yank, then picked up his knife and dragged it along the belly.

"I'm taking her."

The knife slammed on the table. He leaned forward. His fingers, covered in blood, flexed as he gripped the countertop and peered across the room. "If you take her, she will die."

"She's ready to die!" Piper curled her fingers around the blanket behind her. "Look at what you've done to her. You can't keep pouring your energy into her. She is *meant* to die. You should know that better than anyone."

Aterus leaned back, focus returning to his kill, then scraped the guts from the rabbit. "Not if I can help it."

"How long are you going to make her suffer?"

"She's fine."

"Fine? When did she last wake?"

"All I need is a little more power and—"

"And what? What do you think she'll say when she wakes up to a crumbled world? When she realizes what you've done."

"She will understand." He scooped out the last of the organs.

"Mother will hate you for it."

His hand clenched around the liver in his palm. Blood oozed between his fingers. "Once I have cured her, she will understand. You, on the other hand, might not earn her forgiveness when she learns you betrayed us and left her to die."

"The world is more important than any one person. *She* knows that. What you've done... the people you've killed? She will see you as a monster. Let her go while there's still a chance to save Ohr," she pleaded.

"Is that where your heart lies now? How can this rotted piece of land mean more to you than your own mother?"

"It's only rotted because of you," Piper growled.

Aterus lifted his eyes. "You *will* help bring your mother back."

"I won't."

"If you refuse me, I will drive the Black Wall over Socren."

"What?" The reaction was involuntary. Immediately, she regretted her slip. She had to stay strong. "You wouldn't." Piper hoped he was bluffing, but it was a dangerous game to play with a Soul. Especially one with little left to lose.

Her father had moved the Black Wall many times before—a necessity, as he called it. His power was constantly divided between keeping the wall at bay and her mother on the cusp of life. When her health declined, Aterus funneled more power into Evangeline, allowing the wall to shrink the land. And from the looks of it, her mother teetered on the brink of death, which meant something would have to give. That alone made his threat all the more dangerous. Aterus had never chosen Ohr over Evangeline.

"How can you kill them without guilt? Don't they matter? Some are descendants of my mother's family."

"Your mother's family has longed passed."

"She should have gone along with them."

"Enough." He decapitated the rabbit with a chop of his knife. "You will follow orders. If not for family, then for your new allegiance to the humans. If you betray me again, or I hear word you are losing motivation," he swerved the knife over the bone with a resounding crunch, "I will kill your Liberation before you can beg forgiveness."

Piper swallowed and reached for her mother's hand under the blanket. She rubbed her thumb over the delicate skin.

No doubt Aterus would do it. His love for Evangeline had driven him mad long ago. Now he ordered Piper around, threatening his own daughter. And he expected obedience? She winced at the thought. To Aterus, she was merely an asset. Something he could use to do his work while he tended to her mother.

He would never see her as a daughter. Not in the way the humans thought of their children.

As much as Piper wanted to refuse him, too much remained at stake. "What would you have me do?"

The muscles in his neck tensed at her compliance. "Tell me about the boy."

Kole. Savairo must've told him. She debated feigning ignorance, but she couldn't deceive her father. Aterus was no Leo. She had ways to get around the Liberation leader's truth-seeing spell, but Aterus would know her intent the moment she opened her mouth. Even now, she guessed, he read her hesitance. Better to tell the truths she could. Maybe then she could earn back a bit of trust and cash it in when the time came. "He knows what Russé is. The Soul keeps careful watch over him."

"Does the boy know what *he* is?"

"No. Not fully."

"That can work to our advantage." Aterus dumped the sliced rabbit into the pot poised over the fire. "You will accompany Savairo in search of the boy and bring him to me."

She looked to her mother. "Here? But—"

"Bring him. To me."

She clenched her jaw. "What of Russé?"

Aterus poured a bucket of water into the pot and gave it a stir, then motioned to the bedside table. "Take one."

Glass vials filled with maroon liquid lined the bottom of the drawer. "I won't use it."

"You will need it when the time comes."

"I'm strong enough on my own."

His dark eyes stared through her. "You will take my blood, and you will use it."

The command made her jaw twitch. She bit her cheek to hold back the curse slithering over her tongue. Piper swallowed. The long game would play in her favor. If she kept that thought at the forefront, she could get through this—manipulate him as he did her. She forced a nod, slow and rigid, then reluctantly collected a vial.

"Good girl. Now, before you eat, spend some time with your mother. She missed you."

Piper turned her back and curled in the blankets next to her mother. The heat of her anger sent a sheet of sweat over her brow. She nuzzled her mother's nightgown.

Many of her dreams played out her most prominent fantasy of slitting her father's throat. To put him through the same drawn-out, insufferable pain he forced on her mother. He deserved it. But not even death would be enough punishment for Aterus. Thousands of lives had been destroyed because of one god.

Piper knew better than to hurt him. No use betraying him now. A weakened Aterus—an angry Aterus—meant a moving wall. Ohr couldn't take much more destruction.

She stared up at her mother, taking in the soft curve of her mouth and the deep wrinkles running down her face and neck like well-traveled roads. Being here—seeing her again—knotted Piper's stomach in a tangled mess of joy and pain. How she had missed this face. But the suffering had gone on too long. She stroked her mother's neck. *Can you even feel anymore? My touch? Do you know I'm here?* More than anything, Piper wanted to release her mother from this unnatural hold. She would do whatever it took to let her die, even if that meant playing the obedient servant.

For now.

CHAPTER 5

Something moved through the field, drawing ever closer to Kole. He kept still, forcing his breath through his nose in hopes it would be enough to go unnoticed. It had only been a few minutes since the Kayetan discarded him on the hill. He feared the thing had come back to retrieve him.

Kole's encounter with Issira had left him weak. He couldn't find the strength to stand, let alone fend off the Kayetan again, but staying made him prone to whatever hunted the hills. Sucking in a deep, slow breath, he rolled onto his stomach. No matter how gently he moved, the grass swished, like an alarm giving away his position.

Whatever stalked up the hill paused at the sound.

He held his breath, his heartbeat deafening in his ears as he strained for any clue of his stalker's whereabouts.

Stomps crunched through the grass, heading straight for him. He pushed forward, dragging his body along by his elbows. After a few seconds, his muscles gave out, and he slumped in the cover of the foliage. Cold earth caressed his cheek. He waited for his fate.

The tall grass parted to his right, and he whipped his head up.

Russé stood over him, panic set on his face.

Kole relaxed. He started to thank the Seven Souls out of habit but stopped himself.

With a heave, the Soul lifted him to his feet. "I thought the Kayetan had taken you."

"It almost did," he managed to groan. His knees buckled the moment he shifted his weight to them.

The Soul caught him before he fell. "What happened to you?"

"I don't know. I dropped my dagger. There was nothing else to use against the Kayetan so I—"

"You used Issira." A shadow cast over Russé's face, and Kole got the feeling whatever he'd done had been far more dangerous than he'd thought.

"Yeah."

When her mind poured into his, he had felt his own fade. He wondered what would have happened if he'd ignored her warning—if he hadn't pulled away. Would he have faded into nothingness? Been swallowed whole by the Soul's power? Even more terrifying was the undeniable urge to let her in. To let her stay.

"Let's get you out of here."

Kole craned his neck toward the village. "What about the Kayetans?"

"They retreated. A few villagers were taken, but there's nothing more we can do. We were outnumbered."

He didn't protest as Russé heaved him over his shoulder. Though he wished to hunt down every last one of Savairo's Kayetans—to save the villagers from being turned—even he knew when enough was enough. He could hardly stand, let alone fight.

They'd saved two. The others... as much as he hated to admit it, their deaths were already accounted for.

Russé carried him across the hills to the waiting ramblers.

As they approached, the trees slipped their roots from the soil like hundreds of wriggling earthworms and rose to their full height. One reached a long tendril to Kole. It looped around his torso, firm enough to hold him, yet gentle. The tree lifted him from the Soul's grasp and carried Kole up to the base of its trunk.

Rough bark pressed through the thin cloth of Kole's black uniform. He lay back into the trunk, dangling his feet over the ledge.

Russé had a grander way of scaling the trunk. After passing his staff off to an awaiting vine, he lifted his foot, waiting for a root to meet it. One by one, the vines drifted over. They coiled, creating a small, circular step for the Soul's foot. As he climbed, the roots came and went, creating the next step up until Russé finally reached the trunk next to Kole.

A handful of vines twisted themselves into a makeshift seat where the Soul settled in. He held out his hands. Two roots presented themselves and touched down into his open palms like reins. He peered down at Kole. "Get some rest."

After a tug on the roots, the rambler jerked into motion. Its legs below, thin and spider-like, crawled along the hills. The other, the smaller of the two, followed close behind.

The Soul ran the ramblers through the night to put as much distance between them and the village as possible. Precaution in case the Kayetans returned, Kole assumed.

The ramblers followed the Azure River southeast. Cool air drifted from the banks to Kole's face. From exhaustion and the constant bounce of the tree's stride, he slipped in and out of sleep. Only at dawn, when a familiar sight arose on the horizon, did he reach over and tap Russé's ankle, signaling him to stop.

Russé halted the ramblers, and though he'd driven all night, not a lick of darkness had manifested under his blue eyes. Alert as ever.

The Soul asked him something, but Kole missed it. The three hills in the distance preoccupied Kole's attention. The *very same* hills Issira projected to him a moment before he broke their connection. Kole pointed a shaking finger toward them. "She's there."

Russé turned. "How do you know?"

"She showed me."

Another look of worry shaded the Soul's face. "What you did back there. Don't ever do it again, you hear me? Harnessing a Soul's power like that is—"

"I didn't have much of a choice."

"You shouldn't have put yourself in that position in the first place."

"The Kayetan would've taken the poor kid."

"You put yourself at risk. I can't—" he stopped himself. "The *world* can't lose you, Kole. We've talked about this before. You need to be more careful."

Kole only stared at the hills. Though some of his strength had returned, his body felt like one giant bruise, and a fog clouded his head. He had no will to argue, so he stayed silent, dipping his head to appear remorseful. In truth, he wasn't.

The ramblers diverted their path. When they arrived at the trio of hills, Russé anchored them.

The trunk beneath Kole lowered as the roots drilled deep into the earth. Closer and closer the ground came, until the tree's trunk slammed down, leaving Kole's legs strewn over damp soil. He grunted as he heaved himself to his feet.

A small pool nestled at the base of the three hills, strange in its near-perfect circular shape. From edge to edge the body of water stretched maybe two dozen paces long and wide. Not a ripple disturbed the surface of its pitch water. Reaching the extremity, Kole peered down, unable to detect any form of fish or insect swimming in the depths. Something about the water uneased him. As he stared into it, he couldn't shake the feeling it looked back at him, gauging him just as carefully. He edged away.

Russé dropped his pack and unlaced his boots.

"You're going in there?"

"How else will we know?"

Kole shrugged, turning his attention back to the eerie water. He couldn't imagine anything living down there. Then again, Issira was the god of water. A heaviness weighed on him as Russé approached the pond, and Kole half expected something terrible to happen once he touched the surface.

The old man's bare foot slipped in. No ripple or wave broke the glass-like surface, despite Russé shuffling deeper into the water. Waist deep, he said, "I'll only be a moment. Keep watch."

Kole nodded, and Russé dove.

The black water concealed his body the moment he sunk below.

Silence.

He counted the seconds.

One minute went by. Two. Three. Four.

Russé didn't surface.

His nails pressed into his palms. No human could hold their breath that long. *Russé isn't human,* he reminded himself. How long could a Soul go without air?

Kole crept to the water's edge, eyes searching for Russé's form in the murk.

Nothing.

Then.

A cluster of bubbles broke the water. Kole stared at the spot, waiting for Russé to emerge.

Except he didn't.

Seconds ticked by. Panic rose when he realized the bubbles meant Russé did, in fact, need to breathe. If he'd let his air go, he was either swimming back up or drowning.

Should he wait? *Could* he?

"Watch my back," he shouted back to the ramblers. Their canopies rustled in response.

Kole chucked his boots off and dove headfirst into the pool. An icy blast hit him, expelling the breath from his lungs. He pawed at the water. The dark murk enveloped him—blinded him. No trace of sunlight. Nothing to tell him which way led to the surface.

A tug on the back of his shirt made him reel. Another on his waist. A third on his foot. He thrashed, but as the tugs kept coming and his hands hit nothing but more water, he realized nothing touched him at all. The *water* pulled at him.

A current flooded his nose, gagging him as another raced over his chest and forced him deeper until his back hit something firm. Kole grabbed at it. Thick and slimy. Pulling up handfuls of loose mud, he knew he'd reached the bottom.

He used his last breath to cry out for Russé, but it came out as a muffled flood of bubbles.

The cold water numbed him. His heart slowed. Seconds crept near the minute. His lungs burned, willing him to breathe.

In his panic, something soft tickled the small of his back. It snaked across his skin and wrapped around his waist. Not water. He fingered the strange tendril, but he couldn't place it. It yanked him from the mud.

Warmth hit him when his face broke the surface. The bright morning sun shone down as a root dragged him from the pool. Shivering, Kole rolled over in the mud and hacked the water from his lungs, then turned to see Russé next to him doing the same.

"What was that?" He smeared the lump of mud from his cheek.

"Issira." Russé vomited black water. The moment the liquid touched the earth, it slithered back into the pool.

"Guess we know it's the right place." Kole eyed the water, fearing it would reach out and drag them both back into its depths if they let their guard down. "You found her?"

A nod. "Trapped at the bottom. The moment I touched the tomb, the water attacked me. I think it's protecting her."

"Maybe she doesn't want to be released."

"Nonsense. The water is reacting to her power; she isn't controlling it."

Kole flipped to his back and collapsed in the grass, welcoming the sun on his skin as it slowly thawed his fingers and toes. "So, it's like the ramblers, then? Instead of walking trees, she's made murderous water?"

Russé grunted, turning over to rest on his back. "It seems that way."

"Is this how they're all going to be? The Souls, I mean."

"Possibly. We'll have to be more careful."

Kole removed his shirt and wrung it out, grimacing as the droplets darted back into the pool. "How do we get her out without drowning?"

"Drowning isn't the issue. I can attach roots to us to pull us back when we need air." Russé's brows lowered as he stared at the still water.

Kole leaned forward. "Then what is it?"

"I was unable to release her."

"We can try again. The water won't catch you by surprise this time."

"No. I anchored myself at the bottom. The water blasted me, but my roots held firm. I stayed under — tried everything I could think of. Nothing worked." Russé dipped his head in his hands, thumbs massaging his temples. "I came up and saw your shoes in the grass, and I knew you'd gone in after me."

Kole blinked at him. "You mean you *can't* release her?"

"I don't know what else to do."

Kole stared at the mud. After all this time, it had never occurred to him Russé would be unable to release his own kin. He thought back to the vision Russé had shared with him. Kole released him ten years ago. Being a child, he knew nothing about the Souls or their entrapment, and yet, *he* had been able to release Russé. If a five year old could do it, it couldn't be *that* complicated. "What are we missing?"

"Don't worry about it. You need to rest. I'll figure it out."

An hour later, Kole had filled his stomach with the last of the stale bread they'd stolen from Socren and fallen into his bedroll.

Russé sat across from him, Goren's journal open on his lap. His deep-wrinkled brow twisted in concentration as he tried once again to decipher the old camp leader's code.

It was nice to see the Soul holding up his end of their deal even though he'd been incapable of releasing Issira. That journal contained Kole's only hope at learning his past. Goren had logged everything in his books from the very first day he stepped into Solpate. Even the slightest chance it held something useful was good enough for Kole to keep trying. So far, Russé had no luck decoding Goren's strange language, but as Kole watched the Soul from his bed, the side of the old man's mouth twitched into a smile.

Kole perked up. "Anything?"

"He used the symbol."

"The Seven Souls' symbol?" Kole vividly remembered the pronged sunburst shape etched into the last page of the book. He kicked the blanket off, crawled around, and peered over Russé's shoulder.

"Here." Russé tore the page from the book and flipped to the beginning. After a moment, he pointed out a group of symbols in the middle of the page. "Red Tree...."

"The Great Red? The one you were trapped in?"

"I believe so."

"What about it?"

Russé skimmed the text. "Some sort of gift. The red gift."

"Is he talking about the tree still? He thought your powers were a gift to the forest?" Kole guessed, but the deepening lines on Russé's face suggested something more sinister.

Russé slammed the journal shut. "He's not talking about the tree."

"What is it, then?"

Russé didn't answer. He stared at the pool, lips twitching as if debating what to say.

"You know, don't you? What is it? Tell me, Russé. What is the red gift?" He folded his arms. "You promised no secrets."

But Russé remained silent, his eyes stuck on the inky water.

"We made a deal. Why do I have to keep reminding you? Hold up your end or find the Souls yourself. Why is it so hard for you to be honest?"

"Blood," Russé blurted. "The gift is blood. And it's not a gift, it's a sacrifice."

"Sacrifice?" The memory Russé had shared with him flashed in his mind. Russé had found him lying still in the grass, covered in blood. The realization hit Kole hard. What little regard he held for Goren vanished. "*I* was the sacrifice."

Russé pursed his lips.

Kole remembered his camp leader's toothless smile. The man practically raised him. And yet.... "He sacrificed me to release you."

"Yes."

A heat ignited in Kole's fingertips, flowing up his arms where it lumped in his throat. His next words soaked in disdain. "He left me to die. When I didn't... when I survived, he raised me like nothing was wrong. Like he hadn't tried to kill me." A shudder overtook him. "That sick freak."

"It was wrong."

"*Wrong?* I was five. He sacrificed a child. It was *demented.*" Kole snatched a rock from the bank and threw it into the pool. The water swallowed it without a splash. "He deserved to burn."

Kole had seen Goren every day for ten years. Every morning the camp leader greeted him with a smile. *That lying bastard.* He'd treated Kole as if he were his own. Encouraged him to enter into the Shepherd's Trials. Cheered him on. Even when the entire camp had gone to sleep, *Goren* had been the one to stay up and save Kole a bowl of soup when

Russé had him training with the trees long into the night. He'd been the only camp leader to believe in him and respect him after Kole earned his apprenticeship. Had *any* of it been real? Or had Goren been trying to lessen his guilt?

A blood sacrifice. He'd been a *blood sacrifice*. Which meant whatever sorcery Goren had done that day had been blood magic. The very same sort of magic Savairo used to rip the shadow from a person's body and turn it into one of his servants.

Kole shuddered. He felt tainted. Like somehow the magic had marked him, lumping him in with Savairo's vile Kayetans.

"Goren did what he thought was necessary."

Kole turned on him. "How can you say that?"

"Because the world was and still is dying. He believed the Souls were the only ones who could save Ohr."

"It doesn't make it right."

"No. But he chose the lesser evil."

Kole shook his head, suppressing his curses. *The lesser evil?* No matter what Russé called it, it didn't change what Goren was: a liar, and a blood sorcerer—one too similar to Savairo. For as well as he thought he'd known him, Goren might as well have been a stranger. An enemy.

"How are we going to free Issira? We need a sacrifice. Isn't that what it says? Are you going to use me?" Kole tested.

"Don't be ridiculous. There has to be a way to mimic the ritual by other means." Russé flipped to the page again. "Animal's blood may work."

Kole recognized the doubt in the old man's blue eyes. "If animal's blood worked, he wouldn't have used me. It'll be human blood." He'd never been so sure in his life. "That's the only way to free Issira. You'll *have* to use me."

Russé's finger stopped on the rune which translated to 'sacrifice.' "This is too risky."

"Goren was too much of a coward to use his own." Kole finally put the pieces together. "If anything were to happen to him, who else would free the Souls? Goren was too important to die." The words burned like bile on his tongue. "But an orphan wasn't. Who better to pick than someone no one would miss? *Me*."

If Goren had picked the *true* lesser evil, he wouldn't have let his ritual take anyone but himself. He'd been so keen on saving Ohr, he'd used the very people he sought to protect to do it for him. If they hoped to free Issira, they'd do it right this time: the way Goren should have done it in the first place.

"What would happen to me?"

"I don't know. But if it's anything like when you released me—Kole, you can't. I won't let you."

"Because you need your bloodhound alive to find the others," said Kole.

The Soul looked away at the accusation.

Goren had seen Kole as nothing more than a pawn. Now Russé did the same.

"What's the point of our hunt if we have no way to free them?" Kole asked. "We'll have to do it sooner or later, and I'd rather not sacrifice some innocent person. We keep this between us and *only* us. Use me or use nothing."

"We'll find another way." Russé returned his attention to the pages. "We don't even know what the full ritual entails. I need to read more into it." His quill scratched along the margin. As if sensing Kole peeking over his shoulder, he sighed. "You should get some rest."

Kole folded his arms. His gut reaction was to protest, but as he opened his mouth to speak, his exhaustion stole the words from his throat. Dropping his arms to his sides, he relented.

After peeling off his wet clothes and hanging them on a branch to dry, Kole slipped back into his bedroll and cautiously let his mind wander to Issira. Afraid of setting her powers loose again, he gently pressed his consciousness into hers, testing his limits. He didn't expect a response, and he received none.

The wall between them had strengthened. She'd taken extra precaution to keep him out. Kole guessed he deserved it. He *had* invaded her mind and tried to use her powers as his own. Then again, *she* had done the same in the basin not two weeks ago, forcing him to stay put and watch Russé be carried away into Savairo's custody. She'd been protecting him, he could see that now, but she had forced herself on him nonetheless. He couldn't pretend he hadn't done the same. They were even now.

Yet he longed to speak with her. Issira had been pivotal in winning the rebellion against Savairo, and he wanted to know what other secrets she held. Maybe a way to free her for starters. He formed the question in his head, letting the words swirl around the perimeter.

The moment came and went. Even if she heard him, she may be too angry to answer.

Kole didn't know if the week of restless nights had finally caught up to him or if it was some side effect to meddling with Issira's powers that made him fall straight to sleep. For the first time since the battle, when he closed his eyes, he didn't see Piper, Savairo, or his blasted Kayetans. Only darkness. Complete and peaceful darkness.

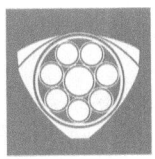

Something stirred him. Not a noise or touch. He opened his eyes. Night had fallen. How long had he slept? The question fled as he sensed a heavy gaze on his back. He rolled over.

A bloated body stood at the water's edge. Its skin a tint of blue as if chilled too long by the cold, and the black hair framing the swollen face came down to a familiar, angular jaw speckled with stubble. A face Kole would never let himself forget.

"Niko?" he sat up, squinting to get a better look in the dark.

The head lifted in recognition at the name. Their eyes met.

Kole flinched. The eyes were wrong. They weren't glassy and distant like those of the dead. Instead, bright. Alien.

Niko's ghost beckoned with a hand. When Kole made no attempt to move, Niko turned and walked into the black pond until his head disappeared under the surface.

The once opaque water now stood clear, like the gushing creeks back in Solpate. Niko looked up from the depths, inviting him to follow with another wave of his hand. Nothing in those eyes gave Kole a reason to be afraid. He sensed his ghost meant no harm, and more... wanted to show him something.

Kole hesitated at the water's edge, concerned the pool would pull him under like before. Trusting the entity, he dipped his foot beyond the surface, waiting to feel a change in the tide — anything in his body to tell him he should stop and rethink. Nothing came. He submerged himself and swam.

Now that Kole had decided to follow, Niko dove with surprising speed. Too fast for someone whose body looked as though it had been lost at sea for days. The bloated form spasmed and twitched in unnatural angles with each stroke. He led Kole to the deepest part of the pond, where a crystalline rock, pulsing with a ghostly glow, rested. Partially embedded in the mud, it resembled a bright moon half swallowed behind a cloud.

Niko hovered above the stone and reached a hand into the mud. He drew back, clutching a jagged rock in his palm.

Kole cocked his head when Niko presented the stone to him. Thinking it an offering, he reached out. But Niko pulled back and rested the sharp tip in the crevasse of his own hand.

Then he cut.

A trail of blood rose like wisps of red smoke. It mixed with the water, creating a rusty haze. Niko nodded to his hand and laid it on the glowing rock.

The moment his flesh connected, a muffled crack resounded through the water. The rock split.

Light poured out. It enveloped Niko, embracing him. His mouth stretched open, and a tiny orb of light floated from between his lips. Whatever had been within Niko, using him like a puppet, vanished. The body went limp, and he drifted, nothing more than an empty shell as the sphere of light glided inside the moon-like rock.

Kole awoke, a shiver resonating from his core. No water. His skin dry.

Russé hunched over him, fear melting from his eyes as Kole sat up, but the muscles in his neck stayed tense. "What did you see?"

The dream returned to Kole as he scanned their camp. Goren's journal lay open, pages crinkled against the grass as if Russé had tossed it aside in a hurry. The sun shone overhead. He'd only slept a few hours.

He pulled the blanket around his bare body, fending off the chill. A squirm in his gut gave him an inclination his dream had been something more, so he relayed it to the Soul. When Kole mentioned the orb leaving Niko's mouth, Russé leaned away, a sigh escaping him.

"It looks like we don't have to worry after all."

"What do you mean?"

"The ritual requires a life."

"A life? But he just used a little blood."

Russé shook his head. "That orb you saw was a soul."

"Issira?"

"No, a mortal soul. Yours. When a human or animal dies, your essence leaves you. In your dream, Niko was acting out the solution— what we need to do to release Issira. The whole dream was probably a clue from her."

"Wait, how does offering a soul help get her out?"

"I *think* the soul acts as a roadway—a connection to bring Issira back to Ohr. It makes sense. A soul for a Soul."

"I guess." Kole sunk back. Replaying the dream, he'd hoped only a little blood was necessary. He rubbed the back of his neck. One glaring problem remained. "Won't I die?"

"Well, yes. Normally giving up your soul means death, but I can control it. I can make it so it returns to you after Issira is freed. As long as I can restore it to your body quickly enough, you should come back."

Kole mulled over the words in his head. "But I'm still going to die?"

"For a brief moment. But once I return it to you, you'll be fine."

Kole stared at Russé, open-mouthed. The Soul had finally lost his mind. Dying wasn't on the table, no matter how brief or painless Russé made it sound. A little blood, sure. *This?* Too much. "What happens if you can't put it back?"

"You'd die. Permanently."

"Right. And how sure are you about this whole 'putting it back' thing?"

"Sure enough to risk it. But I know our deal means I have to be completely honest with you, so I will disclose... I've never done it quite like this before."

"*Quite like this?*" Kole repeated. "Meaning...."

"I did something similar years ago when you released me. I came out of that tree and found you dead, but I was able to return the essence to you before death could fully set in. This will be trickier with Issira involved. The timing of everything. I need to be sure she's out before reviving you. Then there's the blasted water." Russé shook his head in dismissal. "In theory it will work."

"Well, that's reassuring," Kole mumbled and pulled the blanket tighter around his shoulders. "And if *I'm* being completely honest, I'm going to need a little more convincing than that."

"I can do this. You have my word that you will be entirely safe."

"Except for the dying part."

Chapter 6

The late afternoon sun warmed Kole's bare back. He stood at the water's edge, stripped down to his drawers, waiting for Russé, who held a hand on a rambler's trunk. Two roots slid from the damp earth. Anchors for the unruly water. One curled around Kole's ankle, while the second slithered to Russé.

Kole clenched his fists, dreading the slap of cold water against his skin. He'd gone back and forth the last two hours, deciding whether or not to go through with the ritual. It came down to him. If he refused, they would have to find someone else to go in his place. *Not an option.* He forbade himself from becoming Goren. He could do this. But Kole couldn't deny the monumental fear weighing down on him.

Even with his mind made up, as Kole stared into the oil-like liquid, about to jump, second thoughts sprouted. His breaths came in short bursts at the thought of death.

"I'll be with you the entire time."

Kole pulled his eyes from the murky depths to find Russé staring back. The Soul's calm expression seemed out of place. He held his gaze, waiting for the old man's confidence to break—for the slightest hint to tell Kole he wasn't as sure about the plan as he let on. But Russé didn't falter. It eased Kole's nerves, however slightly.

"Ready?" Russé passed off his hunting knife.

Kole clenched the blade between his teeth, then nodded. He filled his lungs and dove.

He braced for the cold this time. It didn't help. His fingers and toes grew rigid as he blindly propelled himself through the black waters.

A hand touched his arm, and Russé guided him to the bed below, where dim light pierced the murk. Drawing near, Kole recognized it from his dream.

He took the knife from his teeth, the root tethered to his ankle keeping him from floating away as he pressed the tip into the meaty part of his palm. Skin broke. A bite of pain met him, but in the numbing water, it was short lived.

Stretching his hand to the stone, he paused. His body shook, from fear or the frigid water, he didn't know. Lungs ached, hungry for a gulp of air. *No time to think. Not now. There's no going back.*

Russé's blue eyes shone in the glow of the moon-like stone. Still, the Soul held a calm air. No pressure—no anticipation—lingered in his eyes. Only patience. Kole's decision. His alone. Russé made it clear.

Now or never. Kole ground his teeth and let out a cry, bubbles tickling his nose as he thrust his hand onto the stone.

The rock broke under his palm, jagged lines running up and down the sphere, like a cracked egg. Light spilled forth, chasing away the bitter cold in his body. Wherever it touched, it left a comforting heat. But the comfort soon ended. Kole knew what came next.

He sucked in a mouthful of water as something inside him tore and drifted toward Issira's light. It felt as if she ripped his body apart, like a hunter tearing the meat from his prey, leaving behind the bones. The feeling rushed up from his feet and passed his chest. It pooled in his skull. His mouth fell open, and out of his periphery, he spotted a tiny ball of light floating past his teeth.

His senses severed.

Nothingness. Complete emptiness.

Felt nothing. Saw nothing. Heard, smelled, tasted nothing. And yet, Kole was still very much aware. He drifted in a void, unsure of where he was or how long he had been here.

The minutes felt like years. Or did the years feel like minutes?

Was this death or something else? Even confronted with his own demise, Niko's face burned into his mind. Was Niko here somewhere, waiting for Kole in the afterlife? He wanted to see that shadow of a beard his friend had been so proud of growing. Those familiar intelligent eyes that always glinted with caution when Kole suggested they break curfew. The *real* him. Not some conjuration of walking death.

The yearning fled as a force tightened around him like a lasso, yanking him back.

Ice cold water shocked him awake. Kole's eyes and mouth snapped open in a panic.

Back in the pond.

Russé had revived him like he promised. Instinctively, he gulped in a deep breath. Instead of air, water filled his lungs. Choking, he thrashed in the murk.

The current swirled around him. It tore the root from his ankle like delicate spider silk. The water took his body, tossing him and forcing its way into his mouth and nose. The weight of his filling lungs dragged him deeper. Suddenly, he was back in Solpate, flying through the air with Niko as the Black Wall drew him in. Helpless. Hopeless. Except instead of burning to death, he'd drown.

Something caught his hand. A root? No. Fingers. They entangled with his own, then tugged. Though too dark to see, warm arms wrapped around his back and drew him into an embrace. A soft, feminine chest pressed against him. Long hair wrapped around his neck, intertwining with his own.

Issira? Had he done it? He'd released her?

He relaxed in her embrace.

The water ceased its attack, letting his savior tug him back to the surface. Back to fresh air.

Kole coughed, spurting water as Issira laid him in the grass. He squinted against the blazing sun.

A silhouette with long hair knelt over him. She cradled his bleeding hand. As his vision cleared, his heart sank, only to sputter back to life at the realization. That blonde hair. Even wet, it looked like pure gold.

Vienna. He hadn't seen her for nearly two weeks since he and Russé left Socren. A member of the Liberation, she'd helped him destroy Savairo's Kayetans during the refugee rebellion.

Her freckled face drooped with concern. Kole had never been so glad to see anyone in his life.

Kole's smile faded to a frown. It made no sense, her being here. Did his eyes play tricks on him? Conjuring her up to pass the time? Maybe he still drifted through the void, awaiting Russé to return his soul to his body. Or something far worse. Kole reached up and touched Vienna's face. Soft. Warm.

She flinched at his stroke but didn't pull away.

She *was* here. *Real.*

Aware of his hand still caressing her cheek, he snapped it back to his side; the heat rising in his face chased away the frigidness from the water. Kole hoped she wouldn't notice.

Splashes came from the water. A second, curly headed figure pulled Russé, who kicked in protest, from the pond.

"Let go of me!"

The boy dropped Russé in the mud. "Sorry, mate. Thought you were drownin'."

"I am perfectly fine," Russé huffed.

Felix. The same freckles donned his cheeks as Vienna's, hinting at their shared bloodline. They had the same green eyes, as well. But where Vienna's emanated an air of confidence, her brother's held a vulpine edge. Felix had been the first person he met on his journey to find the Liberation. He'd even helped Kole rescue Russé after Savairo took him prisoner.

In an attempt to clean the mud from him, Russé only smeared it more. When his eyes landed on Kole, still laying on the ground, he hurried over and shooed Vienna aside. The Soul peered into Kole's eyes as if checking something was still there.

"I'm alive." Kole lifted to his elbows.

"Just barely." Russé's voice cracked.

Vienna leaned in, hands on her hips. "*You* might have been fine, but Kole was drowning."

Russé spun at her words. "If you hadn't interfered, he wouldn't have been drowning in the first place." Red hot anger shaded his voice. "What are you doing here? How did you find us?"

As if on cue, a hawk cried overhead. Fiona circled the sky and drifted down until finally perching on Vienna's outstretched arm.

"She knows what to look for." Vienna curled her finger and stroked the side of the bird's neck.

She ruffled her tawny feathers at the greeting, then tilted her head, setting a large, round eye on Kole and Russé.

Vienna lifted her elbow to let Fiona climb up to her shoulder. "Leo sent us."

Russé tensed beside him.

Felix folded his arms, casting a suspicious gaze between Kole and Russé. "What do ya mean, interferin'? What were you two doin' down there?"

For a moment, seeing Vienna and Felix had distracted Kole from Issira. He sat up and surveyed the water for any sign of her, but he found nothing more than the pool. The water, though, had changed from inky black to clear blue. "Where is she?"

Russé shot him a warning glare.

"Where's who?" Felix asked.

"Where is...?" Vienna turned to the water, an inquisitive look in her eye, then back at Russé. "You found one? Here?"

Kole swallowed as she exchanged a knowing look with Russé.

She knew. Kole was unsure how or how *much,* but the truth shone plainly in her eyes. Vienna knew exactly what Russé and Kole sought.

Felix turned his own questioning gaze to his sister, but he scratched his head, apparently dumbfounded. "Found what? What are ya talkin' 'bout?"

Vienna's silence made it obvious she hadn't shared her knowledge with her brother.

"What's goin' on, Vienna?" He tapped his foot impatiently in the soggy mud.

She opened her mouth to answer, but a splash silenced her.

A column of water rose from the middle of the pond like a geyser. As the water rained back down, the drops fell into the form of a woman. Though transparent, Kole made out the features of her face: angled eyes, and a long, pointed nose. Her watery form churned, constantly shifting like the ocean tide. Bare feet walked over the surface to where they stood. Her eyes, like whirlpools, fixed on Kole.

"Issira." The sight of the Soul forced the air from his lungs. Kole couldn't bring himself to say anything else.

The watery figure passed an entranced Felix and Vienna. The stranger stopped at Kole's side and knelt.

A watery hand touched his shoulder.

"Kole. Thank you." Her melodic voice rivaled the drone of a violin.

Kole finally tore his eyes away, noticing Vienna and Felix just as transfixed by her beauty.

The awe of the moment fled when Felix's cracking voice said, "The hell is that?"

A clap of thunder echoed over the hills. Rain poured down.

CHAPTER 7

Thunder boomed, vibrating the air around Piper. Only moments ago, the sky gleamed clear and blue. Rapidly blooming storm clouds dominated the serenity in an instant. She knew better than to blame it on summer storms. Nothing spread that fast. This was the work of a Soul. The work of Issira.

She'd heard many stories of the Blue Soul. Her father had been close to her. When the Souls demanded he leave Evangeline and ascend, he'd gone to Issira for help. They made a deal, and for a time, it held.

Aterus, Piper, and her mother had lived in secrecy, for if the Souls found out he disregarded their warning, they would move to more extreme measures. Piper never knew exactly what the deal entailed between the two of them — more specifically, what Issira got out of it — but it didn't matter.

In the end, she betrayed Aterus. There had been a time when Piper hated the Blue Soul for turning on her family... a time when her father's poisoned words had held influence over her every thought.

"They've released another," Piper said, keeping her eyes straight ahead as the rain pattered down on the torture tools behind her.

"Blasted rain!" Savairo's blades thumped onto the grass. He let out a frustrated grunt.

She forced herself not to look back, for she knew the scene skulking behind her: Savairo and his blood-stained tools. Those that had not been swiped away in his rage sat on the rock he used as a makeshift table. What made her keep her focus on the darkening clouds weren't Savairo or his crude instruments but rather the three mangled bodies lying a few yards away. She'd watched them die. Their horrified faces burned into her head as they begged for help.

When she'd caught up with him five days ago on horseback, she found Savairo had returned to his work. Since all of his proper materials for the ritual lay abandoned in Socren, the blood sorcerer had reverted to crude methods: a dull blade to slice the flesh and lots of blood to fuel his spell. He made his first Kayetan out of some poor unsuspecting old woman in a nearby village. Since then, his creatures had been gathering more victims from the unfortunate villages they passed.

She couldn't stop him. She wasn't strong enough. Not with him always pressing a vial of blood to his lips like a blubbering drunkard. The small ration of Aterus' blood set at the sorcerer's hip. Sometimes he gazed at it, thumb stoking the top as if tempted to drink it, but then he'd put it away and have his fill of the blood he extracted from the ritual, which seemed to hold him over. But he always needed more.

At first, Piper had tried leading Savairo from his temptations, keeping at least a mile away from inhabited towns as they tracked Kole and Russé, but she couldn't avoid the occasional farm nestled alone in the hills.

After a few days, Piper guessed Savairo had picked up on her intentions and sent his Kayetans to do his dirty work at night. If he did have suspicions, he never mentioned them. She hoped whatever stupor the blood in that vial put him in would be enough to keep her true motives undetected: keeping the sorcerer far from Kole. As promised by Aterus, one wrong move out of her and Socren and everyone in it would be reduced to a field of ash.

So she looked the other way and bottled the pain and anger and guilt as it came to her. She'd done it before: watched thousands die at her father's hands, thinking it a suitable sacrifice to preserve her mother's life. But her mind had not been her own then. Aterus molded it with stories of his ungrateful kin, who'd abandoned the planet and left it to rot.

"We should get moving." Piper sent her eyes as far behind her as she dared. They landed on her dapple-gray mare, Yanare, who grazed on the hill alongside Savairo's pale stallion.

"One more." Savairo stalked over to the villagers, grabbed one by the wrist and dragged it toward the boulder.

She turned her eyes away too late, glimpsing the sandy blond hair of a young man. Her bottled emotions burst through the wall of glass. "Enough!' Piper bellowed, her mouth twisting into a snarl. "Leave him be."

Savairo tilted his head, her outburst seeming to sober him for a moment. His black coal eyes flashed with a devilish suspicion.

Aware of his scrutiny, she leaned back, willing away the tension in her muscles. She forced her mouth in a hard line to appear more impatient than heated and tamed the quiver in her voice as she spoke. "You've spent too long playing with your toys. You've lost us precious time trying to run your experiments on the move. Now another Soul has been released, and we are no closer to finding them than when we started. I'd hate to have to tell Aterus we failed because of your twitching fingers."

Savairo dropped the young man to the ground.

Piper fought to hide her trembling lip as the man's skull cracked against the boulder.

"Because of *me*?" Beneath the thick cloak, his body shimmered like a mirage; the result of self-inflicted experiments. The essence of his shadowed servants tainted him, leaving him somewhere between flesh and ghost. Half corporeal. When he downed blood, his body shifted toward the ethereal end, then back again when the liquid's effects waned.

She lifted her nose.

"I think we both know we'd be closer to our target if we weren't weaving back and forth through the countryside," he said.

Piper narrowed her gaze. So he *had* noticed. *This isn't good.* She needed an excuse and quickly, but her mind drew a blank. She scrambled for something — anything. "If anyone is to blame, it's you."

Savairo studied her for a moment.

Her skin crawled. His eyes lingered over her body as if he contemplated making her his next victim. How could *this* be Leo's brother? Someone so far off the path of morality.

The side of Savairo's mouth lifted. "Why are you leading us in circles, girl? Did your escapade with the Liberation turn you soft? I'm sure Aterus wouldn't be pleased with that, now would he?" He strode forward, a confidence rising in him as if he could smell her weakness, like a predator.

An excuse. What was her excuse? She couldn't let him win this game of power. No telling what he would do if he found leverage over her. The mere thought sent a tingle up her spine.

Leverage. Precisely what she needed. Something to hang over his head when he got out of line — to scare him into submission. *Bend the truth.* Piper didn't bother to hide her forming smile.

Savairo paused at her changed expression.

"The only thing Aterus wouldn't be pleased with is that I have changed course nearly a dozen times to keep your focus on the Soul. You spend hours fiddling with those things." Piper jerked her chin toward the bodies. As long as she didn't look them in the eye, she'd keep her composure. "If it weren't for me, we'd still be stuck in one place night after night, bleeding out every villager in the plains. Your obsession is jeopardizing this mission. If you are of no use to me, you are of no use to my father."

Normally she avoided using that name for Aterus, but exploiting her family connection would strengthen her argument in Savairo's eyes. Make him think their bond stood stronger than it was. She needed him to believe Aterus would trust his daughter's word over his. Make Savairo think twice about using her own father against her.

"You *know* what my father does to people who serve no purpose."

A lie. Aterus had killed many people, yes, but only as a last resort to protect her mother. Savairo didn't need to know that, though. She only needed to use the reputation to her advantage.

They stared at each other, neither willing to be the first to concede. Though her jaw twitched, she kept her expression hard and unreadable.

Savairo was right. Her time with the Liberation had made her weak and left her out of practice. Seeds of worry sprouted in her gut. Had she lost more than she thought?

A drop of rain rolled down his forehead. No, not rain. *Sweat.* His mouth parted and closed again as if he didn't know how to respond. Her blood ran hot with anticipation, noticing the sheen on his skin and the quake of his hand clenched around the vial of Aterus' blood. His addiction. *That* was his weakness. Her worry melted away. *I will break you.*

"Leave them." She tested the order.

He didn't move right away—didn't respond.

Still putting up a fight? "Hopefully we can gain ground, and I won't have to report this back to my father." She gestured a hand to the bottle of blood. "He'll cut you off if he finds it a distraction."

Savairo shoved the vial into his pocket and turned on his heel. His black coat rippled behind him as he collected his equipment.

Piper let a sigh hiss through her teeth. She'd need more caution from here on out. Underestimating Savairo had been a mistake. There was a reason he'd had all of Socren under his control for more than a decade. She'd assumed her father had served a greater role in Savairo's reign over the city, but her opponent knew exactly how to play the game.

Then again, so did she.

This would stand a test of wills. Savairo's shadowless form proved he would do anything for power. Manipulate. Torture. Murder. He had cut the shadow from his very own body to perfect his experiment, which had birthed Idris, his best Kayetan creation to date. Piper recognized his current struggle. Savairo sought to replace his most prized servant after she and Kole vanquished the demon in the battle for Socren.

To an outsider, Savairo would look broken and weak. But Piper knew that man and Soul alike were the most dangerous when they had nothing to lose. When their desperation outweighed any consequence.

Piper tied back her auburn hair and wiped the slick of rain from her brow. No way around it now, she had to track down Kole. For real this time. Savairo would know if she went off course again. He'd be looking for it.

"Run. Hide," she pleaded softly into the strengthening shower. "Give me a challenge."

Give me an excuse.

CHAPTER 8

"Anyone?" Felix fidgeted with the slingshot clasped to his belt as he glanced between Russé and Kole.

A breathy laugh came from Vienna. "I can't believe it." Her head shook as in disbelief, but a smile spread across her face. "The Blue Soul." She lowered in a deep bow.

Her brother cocked his head, seemingly more surprised by his sister's response than the god standing at arm's reach.

Issira gave a warm nod of greeting to Vienna, then cast an amused look Felix's way. The water from her form splashed playfully at him. Felix jumped back in horror, and sweet notes of laughter escaped her.

"Issira." Russé stepped forward, an open palm held out.

Her eyes moved over him, inspecting him. "Risil? Is that you?" Russé nodded as she placed her transparent palm against his wrinkled cheek. "This form doesn't suit you."

"It has its uses. Unfortunately, I will have to ask you to do the same."

Issira's hand snapped back to her side. "I'll do nothing of the sort."

"You must. We can't have anyone seeing you like this. We have to keep our identities a secret for a while yet."

Issira folded her arms, causing a ripple to run through her like a stone cast into a still lake. "You free me from one prison, then ask me to put myself into another?"

"You'll still have your powers. You just won't be as... flashy."

She stuck up her nose. "Flashy?"

"I'm only asking you to take a human form. Any you'd like. You need to blend in—hide from Aterus."

Issira tilted her head. Then, a sly smile. "Very well."

Kole stepped back as her body swirled in on itself like an underwater tornado. Her skin solidified first, a pale olive. Her angular, almond-shaped eyes turned the color of a storm-ridden sky, and the liquid cascading down her back darkened into long, glossy black hair. Finally, the last drops receded, revealing billowy blue garbs of pure silk.

Russé sighed next to Kole. "That's not exactly what I meant."

Issira frowned as the rain soaked through her sleek wardrobe, dulling the sheen of the fabric. "Then maybe next time you should say what you mean. Words are notorious for misinterpretation." A darkness grew behind her eyes like a gathering storm. "You should know that better than any."

Russé swallowed, the twitch in his jaw telling Kole that he withheld a retort. "I'm glad to have you back."

"Sorry ta interrupt this little reunion, but could someone please tell me what the hell's goin' on?" Felix said, hand still latched to his weapon.

"I have questions myself." Russé peered between the Liberation members. He pulled the two aside, interrogating them on everything they knew. Vienna revealed their mission while Felix, as Kole figured, remained clueless.

Before long, Kole's mind drifted away. He found himself rubbing the spot on the base of his head where the pain had erupted when Issira first spoke to him back in Solpate.

"You're waiting for it, aren't you? The next Soul."

Kole turned to Issira.

Strange to finally see her. All this time she'd been only a voice. Now that voice had a face. It dawned on him he'd never wondered how she would look. Somehow, seeing her standing before him made her feel more eerie, where in his head, they had felt so connected.

When she spoke this time, her mouth didn't move. Her voice rang clearly in his mind. *"It's impolite to enter another consciousness without permission. But I've never claimed to be one for manners."* She ascended one of the hills encasing the pool. Her feet were hidden under the skirts of her odd, blue dress, and it appeared as if she floated over the grass like a ghost.

Kole followed, leaving Russé and the siblings to argue.

Issira waved a hand at the sky, and the storm clouds lightened, morphing into the white billowy puffs customary to a summer day. Despite witnessing Russé use his own power so many times before, the sudden change in weather caught Kole off guard. She was the Blue Soul, after all. He had long heard stories of her influence over water.

As they crested the hill, clouds parted, and the full power of the sun hit his bare chest. He embraced the warmth. A sad smile tugged at him. He thought of Niko. How his friend would have teased him about his soft body. Barely a muscle in sight. Not for lack of trying. Kole had trained hard. He and Niko practically lived the same life back in the forest, but his body had always been slow when it came to looking his age. Almost as if it refused to grow.

"Give it a few years. It'll happen. Who knows, you might even be stronger than me one day," Niko had told him.

Reality washed away the fond memory. Even if Niko had been right, he wouldn't be around to see it come to fruition.

"I was there with you when it happened," Issira reminded.

Kole flicked his eyes to her, but she set her face toward the sun, as if dozing.

"I felt it with you. Every emotion. The immobilizing fear. The pain as you burned in the Black Wall. All of your loss." She turned a fierce gaze on him.

It was Kole's turn to look away. How could she know? Maybe she felt his emotions through their connection, but she hadn't known Niko like he had. She hadn't comforted the orphans night after night, trying to rid them of their memories of Socren—of their dead parents. How could she know the nauseating horror that contorted every thread of his being when the ash of their corpses swirled around him as the Black Wall took them by the handful? When the Black Wall came for *him*. Plucked him off his feet. Pulled him into the flames. Though the wall consumed him, only Niko held his thoughts during his pass with death. How could Issira *possibly* know his guilt?

Yes, he had felt the pain. Felt his skin melting. But the greatest sorrow was knowing Niko had felt the same in that moment. Except he didn't get to live in the end.

"It still haunts you." Issira's sing-song voice pulled him back. "It always will. Some will tell you it gets better as time passes. Someone like Risil, perhaps. Russé," she corrected. "But he gives a false hope. Time will not bring Niko back, Kole. Time will not heal your soul... your mind. Only you can do that. And that is what takes time. Don't fool yourself into thinking you can be rid of it. You may heal, but you will never forget."

"*I never want to.*" He thought of Niko's laugh. His hopeless crush on Dya, though he doubted Niko even realized his own feelings for her. They always bickered, but it was plain as day to Kole. It pained him to know his friend would never get to see Socren back in the hands of its people. As a place of peace.

Niko was swept from this life as easily as a dead leaf caught on the breeze. An unfair ending for all the orphans who died that day.

"I will never forget Niko." Kole spoke the words aloud, as if saying them would make it true. Then and there, he made a promise to himself. And to Niko. None of them would die in vain. After he found the remaining Souls, he'd rid the world of the Black Wall in their honor.

Kole touched the base of his skull.

"Don't worry about him. He's blocked at the moment. I figured you'd enjoy a night alone for a change."

"Him?"

Her mouth pursed. "Obell. He and I struggled to overtake you first. I can feel him even now, trying to push his way in."

He'd first heard the whispers nearly two weeks ago under the Great Red, the tree in which Russé had been imprisoned so many years ago. With Vienna on the verge of death, Kole had pleaded for her life. And the Souls answered. All of them. From what Issira said, he now understood they had been fighting over him, desperate to take control, because whoever connected with Kole would be released next.

"Not all of us are kind."

Kole knew a warning when he heard one. She referred to Obell, the Red Soul. He chewed the inside of his cheek, wondering what the next god could possibly bring upon him.

"*I* am not kind," she said, eyes firm on Kole. "But we realize the position we have put ourselves in — that we have put everyone in — and we will not harm you. You are safe with us."

"Safe." Kole's skin tingled. Cords of melted flesh ran along his neck and chest. His entire body riddled with lumps and valleys. All elasticity gone. Where had the Souls been then? Their definition of *safe* didn't quite align with his own.

A quick movement caught his eye. He stepped back as Issira reached out a hand. It had reverted to its watery form — fingers clear as glass, drawing nearer to his neck.

"It's all right," she said. "Safe might not be the best word. Alive. I will keep you alive." Issira grazed a finger down the back of his neck. "You are the key to our freedom, Kole."

A blue light enveloped him, and the ache in his head subsided.

"A parlor trick compared to my true power."

"Thank you."

"The thanks are mine to give."

As Kole and Issira returned to the group, he noticed Vienna and Felix arguing by the pond.

"I can't believe ya didn't tell me," Felix yelled, his usual, happy-go-lucky self miles away.

Vienna stood calm and poised. Pond water still dripped from her hair as her brother rebuked her. She sent a quick glance at Kole and Issira descending the slope. Her eyes flicked down to Kole's bare chest, and he flushed. He retrieved his shirt from the water's edge and pulled it on.

When Felix stopped to catch his breath, Vienna turned back to her brother. "Leo wanted to keep this to as few people as possible. The rest of the Liberation doesn't even know."

Felix folded his arms in a huff. "Ya shoulda told me. I'm yer *brother*. Not only 'cause of that, but I have a right ta know what I'm gettin' inta. Ya told me we were gonna bring 'em back." He gestured over to Kole. "Ya coulda trusted me."

"It wasn't my place to decide. Leo gave me strict orders to—"

"Since when do his orders mean anythin' ta ya? Ya left the Liberation ta go after Lily and Etta alone. 'Member that?"

"That was different, and you know it," Vienna said.

"Do I? Leo told us ta stick together, but ya didn't. *I* followed orders. *I* stayed when all I wanted ta do was go after ya. *You* left us—left me."

"Felix...."

"I thought you were dead, V."

Vienna shook her head. "I'm sorry."

"I can't believe after all that, Leo still trusts ya more. Sets my own sister against me."

"I'm not against you, Felix. We just didn't want the information to get out. If anyone knew what we were up to, we would've put Kole and Russé in danger."

"Is that what ya think I am? A liability?"

"Of course not."

"I follow orders, and I keep my mouth shut. Ya should've told me instead of draggin' me along like an ass. I'm not some sidekick, ya know. I'm yer brother."

"You're right, okay? I should have told you."

"Damn right." Felix noticed Kole and the Souls watching them. "As for you, Blondie."

Kole's back tightened, prepared to be the victim of Felix's next scolding.

"I get why ya didn't talk, bein' new in a strange place and all. Not knowin' who ta trust. Least you and Gramps had a reason." Felix eyed Russé and Issira, a wariness behind his gaze.

After a moment of lengthening silence, Vienna moved toward her brother, a hand raised to touch his shoulder. Felix shifted away and grabbed his pack from the side of the lake, where he must have discarded it before he jumped in to save a 'drowning' Russé. "Let's get movin'."

Before they left, Issira siphoned the water from everyone's clothes with a flick of her wrist, then cast the lingering storm clouds away to make for more comfortable travel.

One by one, they ascended the ramblers Russé had anchored by the hills. Kole and the siblings mounted one while the Souls paired together on the second. It had been weeks since Kole last steered a tree. He hadn't had much energy to focus on his shepherding skills since then. More than ever he needed the distraction. Palm on the trunk, he closed his eyes. *You and me.* It swelled at his words, resistant.

Kole sighed.

Suddenly, it stirred, stretching its roots as they did when they welcomed a rider.

He pursed his lips at the drastic change, then peeked over his shoulder at Russé, who snapped around, feigning ignorance. With a huff and an eye roll, Kole took his position at the head of the rambler. It pained him — needing assistance every step of the way, especially when it came to things he should excel at.

A pair of muddy tendrils held at the ready, waiting for him. He grabbed the offered reins and thumbed away the dirt. A comfort — the familiarity calmed his nerves. The feel of the smooth wood in his hands made him think of happier times in the forest. Just what he needed. Even if it had come by a forced hand.

"Never seen ya in action before, Blondie." Felix wrapped his arms tight around the trunk, his mouth a thin line, as the tree stamped anxiously beneath.

"Scared of heights?" Kole smirked. As fearless as Felix presented himself, it pleased Kole that his friend held a weakness. Everyone did.

"Less about the height, more the fallin' off."

Vienna, on the other hand, thrived at the height. One hand casually clung to a knot on the trunk, which held the weight of her body as she leaned over to peer down at the gargantuan roots. A spark of awe flashed in her eyes. When they found Kole's, he looked away.

He cleared his throat, then nodded to a root. "If you fall, I'll catch you. Just try to stay still. The ride is smooth enough."

Without warning, Felix jumped from the trunk.

Kole's fumbling fingers jerked the reins, praying the rambler would obey. A root shot up like a whip and looped under Felix's waist. As to not hurt him, Kole lowered the root to decelerate Felix's momentum to a stop. "What the hell, Felix?"

He flashed a smile at Kole. "Not scared anymore."

While Kole's rapid heartbeat slowed, Vienna scoffed.

"Aren't you *thrilled* we're here?" She rolled her eyes at her brother.

"None of that on the move," Russé scolded from the other rambler. For once, someone else lay on the other side of his disapproving look.

Felix winked up at Kole as the root plopped him back on the trunk. "Good reflexes, mate."

"I'll throw you off myself next time," Kole clapped back.

"Oh, come off it, mate. I had ta know how this thing works, didn't I? Rather now than in a pinch, eh?"

"You'd do better to rely on yourself than me."

With barely a flick of the reins, Russé pushed his rambler off. The great tree paraded up the hill, a regalness in its stride.

Kole's rambler stood shorter, but it topped out as the biggest rambler he'd ever steered and had actual control over. The older trees required a more experienced handler. Saplings had been his specialty. In reality, if Kole attempted to tame any other rambler this size, he'd fail.

He squeezed the roots in his grip. The tree obeyed and trudged forward after Russé and Issira.

One simple command from Russé would ensure it followed without a rider—they'd been doing it all week—but Kole was glad the Soul let him do it on his own this time, even if the rambler twitched and stumbled at Kole's inexperienced hand, making for a jouncy ride. So many thoughts muddled his head. At least *this* he controlled, if poorly.

The group put as much distance between them and Issira's former prison as possible. The longer Kole controlled the tree, the more fluid his connection became, almost pleasant after a few hours. All the while they traveled in silence. Kole blamed his lack of conversation on his need for concentration. Now though, he could permit a bit of distraction.

A glance to Vienna.

Her solemn face, eyes cast down to the grass under heavy brows that seemed to droop with guilt, concerned him. He wanted to comfort her—to tell her she had only been following orders, but he worried he would be overstepping. Even though he had no siblings, he knew how Felix felt. Russé had lied to him all his life back in Solpate, claiming to be a shepherd. When the truth came out of his divine nature, Kole had never felt so betrayed—foolish even. *Still* he found it hard to completely trust the Soul.

"How are the twins?" he asked, trying to distract her from her worries.

"What?" She blinked away the concentration on her face. "Oh, they're fine. Criz is back on his feet. Boogy watches over him obsessively. They've been busy helping Leo."

"And the city?"

She shrugged. "Some are glad to see Leo back. Others remain brainwashed. They really do believe Savairo was protecting them. Some view the shift in power as mutiny. A lot of his followers abandoned the city. They think since Savairo is absent, the Black Wall will come and ravage the land."

"If we can't release the Souls in time, it may." Scolding himself for bringing back the dreary mood, he said, "Sorry, I—"

"For what? It's the truth, isn't it? No need to dilute things for me."

They crested the next hill. Grassy knolls spanned in every direction. His feet throbbed at the endeavor. If he had to walk it himself, they'd make slow progress. When Vienna turned her attention back to the scenery, he scrambled for something to say. Between steering and talking with her, his worries faded away, if only temporarily. "Any news about Piper?"

At that, she dipped her head as if it were a more troubling thought than the Black Wall. "Nothing. Tracking Savairo is impossible through the sky. We tried." Vienna tilted her head toward Fiona, who perched on a branch above. "The Liberation is spread thin."

She didn't need to finish for Kole to understand that little effort had been put into it. Too many other duties took priority after the battle: assimilating the refugees, farmers, and slaves into city life. Little time presented itself for a search party bound to fail. Savairo had taken to the skies for his retreat. What trails could they follow?

"Thomas has been taking it rough."

"Thomas and Piper were close, weren't they?"

"Sort of. Him more than her. But Thomas will come out of it. Piper—she...." A finality exuded from her voice.

She must suspect the same as Kole: Piper would not meet a happy end. He'd seen evidence that Savairo was in the process of rebuilding his army. Who was to say one of those hadn't been the product of their abducted, red-haired Liberation member?

When the sun began its dip below the horizon, Felix scouted ahead for a place to set up camp. With nothing but rolling grasslands, he settled on hunkering down between two steep hills. If they avoided making a fire, they'd blend into the tall grass well enough.

After settling down, Kole noticed Felix rolling out his bed on the opposite side of camp as his sister, clearly still holding a grudge. Kole only hoped Felix's foul mood wouldn't linger too long. It didn't suit him.

Kole collapsed into his bed, welcoming the soft furs caressing his body. Not nearly as comfortable as his hammock back in the hollowed trunk of his treehouse, but it beat the stone slab bunks of the Liberation's underground hideout. At this point, Kole would sleep on the cold ground if he had to. He just needed sleep. A long, peaceful night.

"I'll take first watch." Russé patted Felix on the shoulder. "You'll need your rest for tomorrow. It's a long trek back to Socren."

"You're leaving?" Kole asked, head whipping between Vienna and Felix.

For the first time in hours, they shared a knowing look with each other. It dawned on Kole that their departure was likely involuntary. While he had been talking to Issira, Russé must have told them they were unwelcome on their journey. Though their arrival had lifted his spirits, the next few weeks held unseen dangers. Leaving meant staying alive.

Felix ignored the question. "No offense, Gramps, but yer not very observant. Vienna and I had eyes on ya for a solid day, and ya didn't notice."

Russé's mouth twisted. The Soul's eyes flared at Kole as if questioning if he'd known the pair had been tailing and not spoken up.

Kole shook his head. He had been too incoherent to pay attention to much of anything. But Felix had a reputation for twisting the truth. A 'solid day' in his words might be a few hours in reality.

"It's true." Vienna unbuckled her belt. A dozen different pouches and bottles of muted grays and browns weighed down her sash. She placed them gently beside her blankets, which she had set up as far from Felix as possible.

"How did you find us?" Kole asked.

She raised a hand to the sky, two fingers held together as a screech graced the quiet night. A flap of wings and Fiona landed gracefully on her forearm. The bird cocked her head so one black-colored eye took in Kole and his companions.

"She's quite the tracker," Vienna gushed. "Spotted the ramblers miles off. They aren't exactly discreet."

Russé pursed his lips disapprovingly. Being bested by a bird probably took the Soul's pride down a notch.

"Though Leo's bird is credited with finding you, it was far too easy to stay on your heels. Glad we caught up before you two decided to drown yourselves in the waterhole."

"We were not drowning," said Russé, a note of annoyance still in his voice.

"Kole was," Vienna said.

"I'm sorry about that, my darling," Issira said, gliding over to him to cup a hand under his chin. "I'm afraid the water had a mind if its own."

"Like the ramblers back in Solpate," Vienna said softly, as if she hadn't meant for the group to hear. She narrowed in on Russé. "Though they've reverted back to their natural state. You have the last two."

Russé cocked his head. "The ramblers rooted for good, then?"

"They've rooted?" Kole asked. Bubbles of unease rose in his stomach. The whole forest had changed because of their departure? Impossible.

She nodded. "They're as ordinary as a tree should be. Your magic is fading from Solpate, Russé. Even the animals are changing back. That's how Leo learned the truth."

Kole lowered his head. The ramblers were no more? The beautiful stags made of vine and wood, and the exotic birds adorned with vibrant petals in place of feathers now looked normal? He felt as if he'd lost his home all over again. Solpate would never be the same without the walking trees. *An ordinary forest.* What more, it confirmed the limitations on Russé's powers: The magic moved with him.

"The point is, you're not as careful as you think you are," said Vienna, a fierce glare on Russé. "If Leo figured it out, more will too. Not only that, but we were able to track you in two days' time. You can be sure Aterus will have no problem doing the same. I'd say you need all the help you can get. Which includes us."

"We have Issira, now. Do you not think two Souls can handle this alone?" asked Russé.

Kole flicked his gaze to the Blue Soul, who'd been listening in. She clasped her hands, which barely peeked out from under the oversize sleeves of her dress and raised her chin. "I think the child is right."

Felix and Vienna flinched at the word.

"I do not feel strong, Russé." She shared a brief glance with her kin. Something unreadable passed between them. Though Kole couldn't capture what it entailed, he figured it was troublesome. Her next words confirmed his fears. "I do not feel safe in my current state. The more eyes we have on our backs, the better."

"Yer outnumbered, Gramps." A familiar sly smile lifted Felix's freckled cheeks. He looked quite pleased with himself. "Besides, nothin' fun is happenin' back in Socren. Just a bunch of errands and feedin' people and stuff."

"Which is *important*." A practiced agitation flared in Vienna's voice. Kole got the feeling she'd reminded her brother of this a thousand times before.

Felix shrugged off her comment. "I'm better with this kinda stuff."

Vienna rolled her eyes, letting it go.

"In the meantime, I'll keep watch. If ya want ta learn how ta do it properly, I can teach ya," he directed to Russé.

Russé gave a sigh. Jabbing his staff into the earth, he then hobbled to the opposite side of camp, ending the conversation. Stubborn as an ox, he propped himself on the northern hill and carried out his nightly round despite Felix's offer.

Kole lay back and pulled the blankets to his chin as the crickets composed their symphony to the stars. With Issira's promise to keep Obell at bay for the night, he sank into an absolute, death-like sleep.

CHAPTER 9

When Kole opened his eyes again, the morning sun gleamed over the tops of the rolling hills, giving a golden light to the grass as if made of tiny torches. Kole sat up, rubbing the sleep from his eyes. The night left his head heavy with a thick fog. He tried to shake it away. It clung like honey. His body urged him to lie back down—to sleep a little longer—but he fought against the desire and stood, catching a whiff of sweet meat on the air. A growl gripped his stomach.

"'Bout time," Felix sat on the base of the hill, feet propped up on his bag with his hands clasped behind his head. A long piece of grass hung from the side of his mouth, bouncing up and down as he spoke. "Eat up, Blondie. We gotta get movin'."

Kole took in the empty camp. "Where is everyone?"

"Just over the hill. Discussin' our next move. They didn't want ta wake ya. *I* would've woken ya up an hour ago, but Issira was pretty clear what she'd do ta me."

Kole grabbed the plate Felix shoved out to him. A scrap of charred meat. He bit into it. The ravenous hunger outweighed his concern to ask where it came from.

"Fiona caught it this morning. 'Fraid rats are more plenty out here than rabbits. I found if ya cook anythin' long enough, it tastes the same."

Mid-chew, Kole stopped and held back a gag. His head screamed at him, but his stomach greedily accepted it, so he forced the rat down. Meat was meat. And it had been *so long* since he had a decent meal. Not that rat was *decent*....

His concerns went to what lay ahead. If Issira had insisted on letting Kole rest, it meant he would need every ounce of energy for Obell. He tried his best to push back the worry crawling up his gut. Either worry, or the bad rat meat.

Felix put his fingers to his mouth and let out a whistle. Vienna appeared on the hill. The sun's light gave her braid a halo-like glow. She trotted down the slope, the two Souls following behind. Vienna packed up Kole's bed.

"Are you ready for the Red Soul?" Issira's sleek black hair rippled in the wind like a waterfall.

Kole nodded, but as her fingers reached up to his temples, he pulled away. "Sorry, I—"

"Russé and I will be here. Our combined power can send him back if anything happens you are uncomfortable with."

Russé leaned against his staff at Issira's shoulder. "It's something I couldn't do after I expelled my reserved power back in the forest. Issira still has a pool at her disposal." He glanced her way. "We've been discussing it, and though we need to be careful about how we use the power we have left until the others are released, we can spare some to keep your peace of mind."

Issira smiled. In the bright sun, Kole could've sworn her skin still held a blueish tint. "Tell us anytime you feel that the connection is too much."

Kole peeked over her shoulder. Finished packing, Vienna and Felix stared at him as if waiting to see how it all worked. He returned his gaze to Issira and stepped forward, closing his eyes to spare his nerves the anticipation of her touch.

He took in a long, deep breath.

Once the tips of her fingers brushed his skin, something snapped.

A wave of heat rushed from the depths of his mind where Obell had been holed away and swept through him. His body temperature spiked. At first it felt like he'd bathed in the sun too long. Then it climbed into feverish territory. The borrowed black Liberation uniform clung uncomfortably to his body.

His eyes sprang open. He stepped back from Issira. Squirming, he raked his nails over the cloth to tug it off. The heat escalated—flame-like now—yet no trace of embers arose. He glanced to the group and screamed as the eruption wrecked his eardrums. Their curious stares shifted to concern. They stood motionless, unaffected by the blaze.

Then Kole understood. Only *he* felt it. This was Obell's doing. His way of communing.

Russé's mouth moved, but the roar of flames consumed his words. When the Soul stepped forward, Kole knew the old man's intentions.

"Wait," Kole pleaded. Though he couldn't hear his own voice, Russé must've, because he paused.

No reason to let all this pain go to waste. Kole closed his eyes and reached out to Obell's presence.

"Obell?" The heat spiked at the name. *"Where are you?"*

The blood coursing through Kole seemed to thicken and overheat as if it had been replaced with molten rock. It overwhelmed him. His legs gave out. He screamed and tumbled backward down the hill.

A pair of hands hooked under his shoulders, flipped him over and held him down as he thrashed. Two hands pressed hard into his temples. Like dousing a flame, the pain extinguished.

Felix and Vienna's freckled faces bordered him. They pinned his arms to the ground as the Souls drew back their hands from Kole's temple. Russé held a pained expression. One Kole had seen many times before: the face of guilt.

Issira smiled. "All better?"

Assessing his body, Kole nodded. He half expected to be covered in blistered skin, like when Russé saved him from the Black Wall. Thankfully the fire had only been in his head, but it felt too real.

"It looks as though we will have to monitor your connection with Obell," said Issira. "What did he say to you?"

Kole swallowed, finding his throat dry and scratchy. "Nothing," he croaked. "He didn't say anything. Felt like my insides were boiling."

"The volcano," said Vienna. "Obell is the Red Soul. It makes sense, doesn't it? Aterus has been trapping the Souls in places of origin." She pointed to Russé. "The Great Red tree of Solpate." Her finger swung to Issira. "And the goddess of water at the bottom of a pond."

"It's as good of a lead as any," said Russé. "Only one volcano stands inside the perimeter of the Black Wall. Near the city of Grayfall, I believe."

"Grayfall? For the love of Souls." Felix looked to Issira, who eyed him, an amused glint in her gaze at his chosen curse. "Sorry."

"What's wrong with Grayfall?" asked Kole. For the countless stories Goren had told the orphans over the years, he couldn't recall any about the city. He knew of the active volcano at the southern border of the Black Wall, and the city nestled at its base but nothing to give reason to fear it.

"It's cursed is what it is, Blondie. People who go there don't come back. 'Only those in search of death enter the walls of Grayfall'," he said in his best imitation of the Leo.

"The curse is an old wives' tale," Vienna said, helping Kole to his feet. "No one actually believes it."

As soon as Kole stood, he pulled his clammy hand from hers and wiped it on his pants.

"Leo does," Felix said. "Don't tell me ya forgot those stories."

"Merely tales to entertain bored children."

"I haven't heard of any curse," said Russé, "but we should be cautious, nonetheless. Stories, no matter how outlandish, always hold a seed of truth."

Vienna's shoulders sagged at the Soul's words. She pursed her lips, ignoring her brother's smug 'I-told-you-so' look.

"Curse or no, we face other threats equally dangerous if we travel to the volcano," said Issira.

"Goren told us about the metal makers. The ash poisoned their lungs." Kole recalled the only story of note.

"That takes years, though. Right?" Vienna asked.

"Maybe to die from it, but yer still breathin' it in."

Goren had told the orphans the metal workers relocated every few years, traveling more northward as the falling ash of the volcano crept further from its source, to prevent breathing the concentrated fumes. Going after Obell meant traversing through poisonous air and ascending the ever-active volcano.

Kole must have held the worry on his face, because Issira reached out and trailed a thumb under his chin, then lifted it so his eyes leveled with her own.

"Don't worry, little one. We will find a way." Her soothing voice held a confidence that almost made Kole believe her.

"We can't count on the Azure River to guide us anymore. The volcano lies far south. We must cross." Russé approached his rambler. It easily carried him to the trunk.

"What about water?" Vienna asked. "We'll need a source."

Russé narrowed in on his kin. "Issira?"

"I cannot create it from nothing. Perhaps I can pull from the soil, but it will not be clean."

With a flourish, Vienna whipped out a wad of parchment. A map of Ohr scribbled on one side. "We can go as far as Cresthaven."

Kole leaned in to catch a glimpse of the marked town. It lay a third of the way from their destination.

Felix's head popped over Vienna's other shoulder. He jabbed a finger at Cresthaven, nearly poking a hole in the paper. When Vienna gave him a scornful look, Felix lifted his finger and gently dragged it further south. "Hell, we could get ourselves all the way down ta Lake Howell. Looks like only a few days travel ta the volcano from there, 'specially if we got the tree dudes."

"That path would add a week," Russé called from the trunk. "I will go no further than Cresthaven. There we will fill up on supplies— whatever we need to sustain us through the Ashland Plains. Perhaps a barrel to hold water?" He directed the question to Issira, who nodded. "Then it's settled." Russé waved a hand to Kole and the others on the ground. "Up you go."

Kole approached the second rambler. The tree lifted each one of them with a root and plopped them into position. Taking the reins, Kole set the rambler's path to fall in line behind Russé's.

He sighed. On to Cresthaven.

CHAPTER 10

Piper stared down at the still, black water. She crouched and dragged a finger over the surface. The water didn't move as it should, only parting and rippling after her finger long trailed past. She glanced over her shoulder to Savairo. Dusk had come once again, and his Kayetans began to materialize around him.

"They were here," she said.

Savairo barely acknowledged her. With a hushed word, his Kayetans shot off in the cardinal directions to scout ahead.

The stomped grass around the pool confirmed Kole and Russé's presence, and the mounds of upturned soil explained how they managed to stay ahead of her. Ramblers. The bloody things could run all day. Piper and Savairo had run their horses into the ground the last few hours, yet still lagged at least a day behind.

The strange black water could very well be the reason the two had stopped. They hadn't drunk from it; her mare assured her of that. Despite her horse's thirst, Yanare refused to draw near. If not to drink, then what?

A Soul had been imprisoned here. The timeline matched up with the sudden thunderstorm yesterday, but she rarely relied on hunches.

Aware of Savairo's watching eyes, she kept her clothes on and stepped into the pool. The water swirled mischievously around her knees. "Be gone," she muttered, as she would a fly buzzing around her ears. The water calmed as she submerged.

She drank.

Cool water filled her stomach. The added weight pulled her body to the pond floor. She sucked in more water, swallowing it to help keep herself anchored in the silt for quicker inspection. As long as she kept one hand on the soft mud, she would know exactly where she was and how to get back in the pitch.

After a while of searching the bottom, she felt something hard—sharp. Shards of rock littered the floor under her belly. She pulled past, bumping into what seemed like a large boulder and reached out.

Smooth.

Abnormally smooth in a current-less pool. Her fingers found the sharp edge of a crack, which ran down the side, splitting the sphere in two.

Piper snatched one of the shards from the mud and crawled back to the water's edge. Breaking free of the surface, she vomited up her water-logged stomach and coughed the liquid from her lungs. The heaviness left her as the squirming black water slithered back to the pool. She caught Savairo's eyes on her, a look of disgust sent her way. Smoothing the sopping hair from her face, she lifted the shard to the moonlight. Clear, blue crystal.

"She was here," Piper said. "They can't be far."

Savairo's eyes glinted with interest at the small piece of stone. "Which way have they gone?"

She tucked her prize away, concealing it from his gaze. Her eyes caught sight of what looked to be stabbed soil. Rambler tracks. The path led toward the river. "They're following the Azure."

A chilling laugh escaped Savairo. "We'll cut them off."

"You know where they're headed?"

"They follow the water out of necessity, which means their provisions are low. The closest city is—"

"Cresthaven." Piper cursed Kole and his companions. *They're not even trying to hide themselves.*

"Think of the ground we could cover with more Kayetans. With another marvel like Idris. We could reach them within a few days."

True. A Kayetan who could track in the depths of night *and* the shadows of day like Idris could greatly help speed up this chase. Which is exactly why Piper needed to get the idea out of Savairo's head. She needed to prolong the hunt until she could find a way to ditch Savairo and get Kole alone.

"Are you suggesting we leave the trail to hunt down another magic user?" she asked.

Temptation flashed over Savairo's face.

She could tell it was exactly what he wanted. Piper wrung the water from her hair and tunic. "Sorcerers are hard to come by these days. We could visit a dozen towns and still come up empty handed."

An amused smile touched his lips. "Why would we search when we have one here?"

Her. He meant *her*. "No," she said forcefully, hoping to cut off his demented fantasies. The possibility of a half-Soul, half-sorcerer Kayetan made her shiver. No way she'd let him have that.

Still he smiled.

It occurred to her he wasn't going to let this go no matter her wishes. If he must make another supercharged Kayetan like Idris, she would've been more lenient toward the notion if he were to use his *own* blood. But that ship had long sailed. Savairo had done so already. He had sacrificed his shadow for his beloved creature, and now, even in the sun, his body failed to cast the faintest shade. He would need new blood for this, and she refused to budge.

She must distract him from himself. Just the thought made her turn away and roll her eyes. *I'm nothing more than a glorified babysitter, watching over a middle-aged human.* To keep him on his leash, she may need to give him a bit more slack. Clenching her teeth, she knew she would regret this decision. "A few more Kayetans might do," she conceded. Her eyes fell hard on him. "*A few.*"

CHAPTER 11

After a week of travel along the river, Kole finally glimpsed the first signs of Cresthaven. The massive city, rival to Socren in size, sparkled with lanterns in the deepening sunset. Buildings stood on either side of the Azure. A faint line atop the water — a bridge — connected the divided city.

"Couple hours out, I reckon," Felix said. The rambler slowed on the last shallow hill before the land evened out, stretching flat and long before them. "Eh, maybe less."

"We can ride into the night or wait until morning." Russé gauged the group.

Kole managed a grunt. Every inch of his body felt the drain of travel. He could only spend so long propped against rough tree bark before it rubbed him raw. His bones ached like a bruise. Though his dreams of Savairo and Piper had faded, new ones of Obell had replaced them. Insomnia scrambled his mind. Reality and sleep bled together. Kole studied Felix's face, trying to decipher if this too was a dream.

Felix scrunched his freckled nose. "You all right, Blondie?"

Kole nodded.

"I dunno, I'm thinkin' we stay here. What 'bout you, Sis?"

"I'm fine to travel." Out of the corner of Kole's eye, Felix elbowed her side. She glanced Kole's way, then said, "Oh — uh — actually I'm pretty tired. What's one night?"

Kole took in a long, deep breath. The weight of the Souls' eyes fell on his shoulders. They'd stop purely because of him. Before he could argue, the ramblers anchored at Russé's command.

"Here," Felix reached out for Kole's bedroll. "Let me set this up for ya."

Kole let the pack slip from his shoulder.

"I think he's gone loopy," Kole heard Felix say as he slid from the trunk.

The rambler assisted him to the grass. Footsteps closed in. The wind brought the scent of honey to his nose as a hand touched his shoulder.

"Kole?"

He didn't turn.

Vienna moved around him, placing herself between him and the clouds he'd lost himself in. Her blonde curls reflected gold in the deep-red hue of the setting sun. His eyes focused on hers, and whatever fog hung over his mind lifted slightly. "Are you all right?"

"Fine."

She gave him a skeptical look but nodded. Her hand closed around his, and she led him down the slope to Felix, who currently unrolled Kole's bed beside the riverbank.

"You need to sleep," she said.

With her guidance, Kole knelt and slipped under the blanket. No reason to check if Issira and Russé watched him. Every time he turned around, he met at least one of their gazes. When night came, one of them would always stay at his side. When tossing and turning stirred him, he'd find they had switched places like on-duty guards. Monitored like a child.

The last light of day gave way to navy skies. A chill moved through camp, chasing the fleeting heat of the sun.

The brightening full moon hung like a ghost over Vienna's shoulder as she pulled the blanket up to Kole's neck, then patted his shoulder before returning to her brother's side. The siblings had barely spoken this last week, which proved quite the feat considering they'd been stuck on the same rambler for most of the journey. The tension mostly came from Felix, who seemed to maintain a grudge against his sister for keeping him in the dark about the Souls. Seeing them talk again set Kole's mind at ease.

"I think Obell is affecting you far greater than we expected," Russé said.

Kole rolled to his side. Both Souls stood over him, a wariness in their gazes. He didn't speak, only returned their stares.

Russé knelt. "You haven't been yourself this week."

"I'm tired," Kole said. He was aware of the drain on his mind, his body, his... everything, really.

Ever since Issira had set Obell loose in his head, he felt like a different person. As if his actions and thoughts originated from another source, yet more subtle than when Issira had been the one speaking to him. She had controlled his body physically, forcing him to speak and move against his will. He almost preferred Obell's way of doing things—the permanent fog over his brain. Though he might not be himself, he still *felt* in control. For the most part. On occasion over the last week, he'd found himself agitated for no reason—angry even. He'd snap at his companions in a jerk reaction to their probing questions, but then his brain would catch up a moment later, realizing what he'd done, and had apologized. Still, no matter how he treated them, the Souls and the siblings continued to care for him. For that, he felt grateful.

As he lay there in his blanket, the anger crept up again, rooting its fingers in his head. He huffed and mulled in the unwelcomed feeling. All he needed was better control. Hold the vexation inside and keep it from seeping into his actions, his words. Endure the torment.

Issira took a place next to Russé at Kole's side. "You don't have to hide from us, Kole."

Didn't he though? Kole guessed their solution to anything seemingly astray about him ended with entering his mind. He had just gotten Issira out. He didn't want her back in.

"I can help you," she said, her words long and drawn out, like the notes of a song. The way she said it, so soft and soothing, almost tempted Kole. "Let me take the burden of Obell for now. If you let me in, I can—"

Kole turned away. "I don't need your help!" Just when he thought he could tame the new beast inside him, it lashed out again.

Russé gave a heavy sigh. "At least let us help you sleep."

His muscles refused to move. Cloth rustled behind him, and Issira's long, bell-like sleeve brushed his arm. He had no desire for their help, but he was too distracted trying to reign in Obell's transferred fury to object. As her soft skin traced over Kole's temple he said, "Only take the nightmares." Maybe if they faded, sleep would come, and he could toss this anger aside for a short while.

"As you wish, young one."

Kole's mind went blank. Dark. Peaceful. But as his eyes rolled back, on the cusp of falling into sleep's embrace, Felix's voice pierced through camp. "Kayetan!"

A jolt and Kole snapped up, pulling away from the Soul's hands. His rushing heartbeat chased away any drowsiness. He found Felix darting from the riverbank with a finger pointed north, Vienna fast on her brother's heels. Both had unsheathed their sunstone daggers.

Fiona perched on Felix's outstretched arm. She squawked and flinched as if agitated.

Felix studied the hawk. "It's a scout. If we're seen ya can bet they'll be more on the way."

"*One* scout?" Russé called.

"Dunno. Birds can't count."

"Right, the bird," Russé said under his breath. "We can handle one."

"It's not a question of defeating a lone Kayetan," Vienna snapped. "Fiona reported it as a *scout*. We can't do much to fight it if it doesn't come in range."

"Right there with ya, Sis." Felix lifted his wrist, letting Fiona take to the sky again, then gathered his packs.

"Are we leaving?" Kole asked. One Kayetan proved little challenge for their group, especially when they were armed with sunstone. If more came... Kole wondered how many shadows Savairo had made. He'd seen less than a handful back in the burning village a week ago. Would there be more?

"I...." Russé shared a look with Issira, who shared the same annoyance in her expression. "This blasted bird better be right."

The Souls gathered their things, but a screech from Fiona cut them short.

Kole's eyes went to the sky, where the hawk circled their camp. "What's she doing?"

A beat, then Vienna sprinted up a nearby hill. "No, no, no...." Whatever she saw made her turn. "We're too late. Retreat!"

Kole froze. Even Russé flinched by his side.

When Vienna noticed the Souls' hesitation, she held her arms out expectantly as she ran to the nearest rambler. "There's more heading this way. They'll be here within the minute. Do you really want to argue about this?"

Arms lifted Kole from the floor. His bed roll slipped from him and fell in a wadded mass on the ground. No time for gathering what little they'd unpacked, Russé carried Kole to the ramblers, who ripped their roots up with haste. Mounds of grass and mud flew into the air at the rushed awakening. Like drunkards on their last ale, the ramblers stumbled up and grabbed Kole and his companions, hastily flinging them into position.

Kole slammed into the trunk. He teetered, nearly bouncing off before Russé's staff smacked across his chest. The strike bit his skin, but it beat falling from twenty feet up.

As soon as the ramblers reached a gallop, Kole glanced over his shoulder. Sitting on the trunk gave him sight over the hill. Finally, he glimpsed what had triggered Vienna and Felix: a small army of Kayetans streaked their way south. But their path was all wrong. They sped alongside the ramblers at a distance, some passing. Either they planned on circling in front of Kole's group or.... Kole swung his head south.

"A raid on the city?" Kole asked through the ramblers' booming strides.

Russé clenched the reins. "Then that's exactly where we'll go."

"What?" Kole snapped. "Shouldn't we force them to change course? Divert them. *Protect* the city."

Issira spoke calmly over the rush of wind. "If it's a raid like the one you spoke of before, they won't alter course. Savario is looking for people to turn. Better we alert Cresthaven before they arrive. Give them time to prepare."

"How are we going to do that?"

She smiled. "Two ramblers are hard to miss. If that doesn't work...." Her gaze shifted to the river. Raising a hand towards the water, she closed her eyes. A blue aura pulsed from her fingertips. She waved them back and forth, mimicking the current, then thrust her palm south.

Kole recoiled as a tidal wave burst from the surface. It shot forward with lighting speed, heading for the docks of Cresthaven. An alarm, for sure.

"Issira, the boats—the ships on the river." Kole motioned to the bridge.

"Will be untouched," Issira assured.

"They're gaining," Felix called from the other rambler. "Can't these things go any faster?"

It seemed some of the shadows had noticed the ramblers and peeled off from the group. Second by second, they closed the distance.

Russé cast a dark look to Kole, then urged the trees to their breaking point.

Some roots tangled with others at the excessive pace. Kole hugged the trunk in an effort to stay mounted, when a misplaced stride caught on a tangled mass of roots and hitched the rambler forward. Fortunately, the sheer quantity of legs made up for the useless clump, and the rambler continued with no more than a trip. More roots entangled around the knot. Some snapped off, left behind in the grass. The same happened to Felix and Vienna's tree. If they kept this up, it'd leave Kole and his companions grounded.

The first Kayetan reached Vienna and Felix's rambler. It swirled up through the thrashing roots and darted for the siblings. One hand on the trunk for stability, Vienna lashed out with her sunstone dagger. Her blade missed. Though the shadow shrilled, it faltered but a moment before diving back in the fray. Their rambler bucked on tangled roots. Vienna slipped, and she tumbled from the lofty trunk toward the dangerously churning roots below.

"Russé!" Kole called, hand outstretched to Vienna as she fell. But nothing could be done. Not from where Kole sat on the other rambler.

At Kole's call, Russé lashed out a hand. Four roots disengaged from the gallop. In a single motion, the veins caught Vienna, then launched her back into the air. She shot up past the trunk, where the canopy snagged her in a cage of branches. Even from this distance, the whites of her eyes flared, her features frozen in a look of panic.

Meanwhile, Felix battled the Kayetan, who swirled above his head, taunting him—toying with him. The shadow lingered just out of reach, luring Felix to take a hand from the trunk to strike.

Kole turned away for a second. "We have to do something before more close in."

"I know," Russé shot back.

Issira's stormy eyes narrowed. She set her sights west. "Lead them to the river."

"The river?" Even as Kole spoke, the tidal wave raged toward Cresthaven.

The same confusion Kole held reflected in Russé's eyes, but the Soul pulled on the reins without another word.

"Get everyone to the canopy. As high as you can," Issira instructed Russé.

A root grabbed Kole. Next thing he knew, his dropping stomach told him he was flying. Wind met his face. His arms snapped up as the branches rushed in. Twigs broke on his skin. They streaked across his delicate scars like dragging teeth. Once in the heart of the canopy, the branches twisted around him, slowing his ascent. After his breath returned, he glanced down. No one stood at the trunk. A flash of blue next to him. Issira joined him. Russé appeared beyond her—all of them enclosed inside the branches like nesting birds.

A wail echoed from the other rambler. Kole whipped around, thinking the Kayetan had snagged Felix. The veil of leaves obscured his sight. He shoved aside a young, pliable branch, then wrapped his legs around the bough and scooted along the length until the leaves thinned.

A sigh escaped him. The wail he'd heard must've been from surprise. Felix lay safely with his sister in the canopy.

Water sloshed below. The rambler trudged into the shallows, pushing deeper by the second. The waterline rose halfway up the roots, the added resistance slowing their progress. Still the water climbed; grazed the bottom of the trunk, climbed up the bark. Kole and the others moved higher into the canopy as the rambler continued to sink.

Then, a moment came where the tree lifted up—buoyant in the deep canyon of the Azure riverbed. The rambler tilted back.

Kole scrambled as his side of the tree toppled toward the river's surface. No amount of speed would've saved him against the race with gravity.

Mist hit his face as geysers shot up and hit the trunk. The force set the tree upright. He whipped his head around. A blue aura emanated from Issira. She'd set her plan in motion.

Convinced that drowning no longer posed a threat, he turned his worry to the ramblers, which floated at a near standstill, only moving with the current. Bubbling water answered him.

Issira summoned a tidal wave like before. It rose, higher and higher—twice the size of the ramblers. In a final push, she cast the wall of water at the trees.

Kole hugged the bough in anticipation. His whole body shook. The last time he was in water, he had almost drowned. *Issira better know what she's doing.* When the wave collided, the tree accelerated downstream. Kole's fingers slipped from the bark. He fell back into the arms of the canopy safety net.

The river sped them toward Cresthaven. As the city grew before him, the Kayetans shrank behind little by little. Yet still the shadows pursued, the entire raid now changing course for the ramblers and their occupants.

When Kole attempted to move, Issira snapped her gaze back to him.

Pure white eyes met his. No pupil. No iris. Only a milky fog. "Do not move. You will throw off the balance."

Kole was forced to stay pressed against the rigid twigs poking into his back and a mere arm's length away from the tidal wave riding them to safety. Near-freezing water splashed him from time to time. Coupled with the rush of wind slamming his front, violent chills plagued him until numbness took hold. He balled his fists, capturing whatever warmth he still had. He was convinced he'd turn as blue as Issira before the journey finally ended. *Better than meeting a Kayetan's claw.*

Issira's wave cut the journey to Cresthaven in half. The Kayetans had disappeared into the cover of night. No telling how far they'd fallen behind.

A few miles out from the city docks, a distant bell clanged as the first wave, the one Issira had sent as a warning, barged past the city boundaries straight for the main bridge linking Cresthaven's eastern and western sides.

A crack appeared in the center of the bridge before the wave met it. Slowly, both sides rose, lifting the gangway out of harm's way as the colossal wave neared. A needless effort, Kole realized, when the towering river collapsed in on itself and fell back into calm waters. A blink held too long, and Kole would've missed it.

The warning had done its job. More bells chimed in with the first. If the city folk hadn't noticed the floating ramblers before, they did now.

Unease bubbled in Kole's stomach, unsure if born from seasickness or the inevitable, wary welcome they'd receive once they landed.

Close now, a line of soldiers flanked either side of the river, pike-like weapons gripped overhead, prepped to throw.

Issira's wave thrust the ramblers to the bank along the outskirts of the city. At her command, the wave dispersed, leaving behind choppy waters, which harmlessly rocked the anchored boats at the river's edge.

The ramblers teetered upon release. Kole clung to the bough, bracing himself for impact. With a slam, the waterlogged tree landed on its side. A shower of river water dripped down from the leaves onto Kole and his companions.

A moan carried from the other tree. Felix lay face down in the bank where he'd apparently been flung from his rambler. Mud caked his entire front half. A broad, white smile appeared through the layer of muck. The moan morphed to a laugh. "That was... amazin'."

Russé climbed down. At the Soul's outstretched arm, a root retrieved Kole from the canopy and set him on the ground. Kole wobbled despite the stable surface.

"Get your bearings, but don't let your guard down yet. The Kayetans are still in pursuit," said Russé.

After a moment adjusting back to their land legs, Issira pointed south. "The Cresthaven guard approach."

Kole turned. A line of soldiers rushed toward them, weapons raised.

Russé moved to the front of the group and raised his hands as they closed in.

They didn't slow.

"Russé?" Kole shifted his eyes up and down the line. Two dozen armed soldiers suited in leather armor. No. Not leather, *scales*. "What do we do?"

"Fight 'em," Felix answered, but Vienna quickly shot the idea down with an elbow to the gut.

Even Russé backed up now, one hand stretched to the ramblers in case he needed to call upon their help, but the soaked trees merely twitched in response. Probably drained.

The Cresthaven soldier leading the unit flung his spear toward Kole and his companions, but it sailed overhead. A shoddy throw. Meant to intimidate? When a screech sounded at Kole's back, he understood.

More spears launched from the line. They arced past the ramblers and bore down like falling arrows onto the Kayetans who'd finally caught up.

"Move!" Kole tugged Felix into the safety of the rambler's branches when he realized the troops weren't stopping.

The others retreated to the protection of the canopy a moment before Cresthaven's forces stampeded by; no glance to the fallen trees or strangers on their doorstep. Their focus remained on the kill: the Kayetans. And to Kole's surprise, kill they did. When the weapons pierced the Kayetan's hearts, the creatures burst into a fiery light and shriveled to dust, just as they would if stuck by a sunstone dagger.

"How?" Kole posed to Felix and Vienna.

Both shook their heads, but Vienna stepped forward, head cocked to the side as she squinted to the passing soldiers, whose weapons remained in hand. "Sunstone?"

"Don't look like sunstone," Felix said.

Kole tried to scrutinize the pikes to no avail. The soldiers moved too fast.

One by one the shadows fell, vanquished. A handful remained. As if sensing defeat, the last few Kayetans retreated before they, too, met their fate at the end of a spear.

The night grew quiet.

Then the soldiers set sights on the ramblers. They encircled the fallen trees. Armor of dark scales covered the guards' bodies. Moonlight hit the material in such a way, it gave off an oily sheen, shifting back and forth between blue and yellow. Y-shaped openings in the helms revealed the eyes and hinted at the features of their wearers.

One broad-shouldered warrior stepped forward, a pike pointed out to Kole's group. "Face me."

A woman's voice.

Following Russé's lead, Kole, Issira, Vienna, and Felix all emerged. Kole pulled his hood down, further concealing his face, and peeked around the line of soldiers, who all wore hardened expressions. None so much as flinched when the rambler roots twitched.

"You have brought your warden and his minions to our doorstep." The female officer swept the point of her spear to Felix and Vienna. "Leo's confidants, I suspect?"

Vienna gave a curt nod. "Liberation members Vienna and Felix."

A bird cried overhead. Without taking her eyes off the siblings, the officer held up two fingers. Fiona landed on the offered perch. "Leo said you might stop by. I will admit, I was expecting a far less exciting visit, if any."

Expected us? It surprised Kole that Leo had been so open. What more did she know about them? Him? Their mission?

"Lady Azmali." Vienna gave a small curtsy in greeting.

Glossy black brows dipped disapprovingly. "Drop the formalities." Azmali moved Fiona to her armored shoulder. The hawk settled in. The officer jerked her chin over her shoulder, where the dust of the vanquished Kayetans sat in piles. "It's a good thing we prepared the sun incantation. I didn't think Savairo's raids would come this far south, but it seems he's had a little motivation." Eyes like venom moved over the group. "Should I ask?"

Silence answered her.

"Thought as much." Azmali slammed the butt of her spear into the ground. The mud slurped. "I was asked to give a favor, so I will carry it out for Leo's sake. Whatever business you have, deal with it tonight. You will leave my city at first light. No later. I can't have my people living in fear of Kayetan raids."

Their secret remained intact. Leo had been vague in whatever message he'd sent. All the more reason to get what they needed in the city and be on their way. Azmali made it clear her hospitality had a limit.

The group of Cresthaven soldiers circled Kole and the others. Two stayed behind by the ramblers.

"That will not be necessary." Russé motioned to the stationed guards.

Azmali gauged him with narrow eyes, then dipped her head. "Shepherd?"

With the help of his staff, Russé stood taller at the title.

"Leave them," she instructed her troops, who'd posted beside the ramblers. Turning back, she said to Russé, "Your trees are not to step near my city." A swift turn on her heel, and the battalion fell in step behind her.

Kole's group followed.

Felix slipped to the front and tailed Azmali. "What's with the pokers? Don't look like sunstone ta me."

"Pure sunstone is useless against other foes, which makes for an inferior weapon." She eyed Felix's hip, where his dagger bounced.

Felix hid it with a hand. "So what do ya use, then?"

Kole eyed them as they spoke.

"We dip our weapons in molten obsidian imbued with Leo's sun spell. Dual purpose. When the stone chips and breaks away, we still have iron points." She twirled her polearm in the moonlight. The metal tip glinted.

Kole quickened his pace to catch up for a better look. Up close now, he made out the thin cover of translucent, glass-like rock encapsulating the sharp point.

"Got any more of that stuff?" Felix asked.

She grunted.

Kole turned his attention to Cresthaven. No wall encased the city. Its lands opened freely to the surrounding hills. They traveled south along the Azure River. On the cusp of farmlands, dry, cracked mud stretched as far as his eyes allowed, an odd sight where such a grand river flowed. Stranger still, small channels diverted from the main flow, creating streams that meandered out and around the city like moats. If meant to offer protection, it would prove ineffective. Kole couldn't tell how deep they went, but they certainly sat narrow enough for someone to broad jump.

The houses they passed held a tan hue and a smooth finish, unlike the wood or stone counterparts in Solpate and Socren.

"What is that?" Kole nudged Vienna.

"Clay." She swept a hand to the dried beds in the distance. "They farm their own material by controlling the river, see? Those canals flow through the city. Makes for easy access to water for the people, crops, and they build watermills to power things like the bridge."

He spotted the giant wheel-like contraptions arcing from the river.

"Every decade or so they close down the canal and build a new one. The old ones dry up, and they use the built-up silt to make... everything really."

"How do you know all of this?"

"Leo had us read a lot of books. Felix knows, too. Well, *should* know. He doesn't retain a whole lot that doesn't apply to his interests."

"Fighting and stealing?"

She smiled, eyeing her brother, who still nagged Azmali. "The main two, for sure. Along with talking an ear off."

They shared a laugh.

CHAPTER 12

Once in the main city, Azmali dismissed her troops—all but one. She led Kole and his companions down a lively street, which seemed much too crowded for the late hour. Kole absentmindedly pulled his hood further down when a few drunken gazes lingered too long.

"They sure like their parties," Felix said.

"In Cresthaven, we pride ourselves on a hard day's labor. When the job is done, the night is ours to unwind." Azmali nodded to a group of men dressed in terracotta-stained uniforms, who raised their mugs as she passed. "I keep this city in line. A leader can't hide away. They need to be seen—in control. Something Leo finally learned. He never should've abandoned his city."

"They had him kicked out, they did," Felix countered, voice edging a bit harsh.

"Kicked out? No such thing. If pressure is put upon you, you fight back. I would sooner choose death than see my enemy prevail. Socren never would've fallen into Savairo's hands had I been there."

Felix's chewing jaw gave away his vexation. When he opened his mouth, Vienna squeezed his shoulder and put a stop to whatever retort pressed against his tongue.

Azmali stopped them at a large, brick building made from the same clay as the smooth dwellings they'd passed earlier. A chiseled, stone sign that read *Haven Inn* hung over the door. She shoved the door in, and a waft of warm, muggy air hit Kole head on.

The structure consisted of a strange mix of materials. Brick stacked high in some places like the outside, but other walls stood seamless—a similar construction to the smooth houses in the city, yet strands of grass and straw threaded through the clay, texturing the surface. Every now and then, a beam of wood sectioned off the walls.

Tobacco and ale perfumed the large, fire-lit room mixed with notes of sweat and the hint of some kind of roast. Wall to wall, a sea of people crammed the space, all consumed in their own conversations. Fits of laughter echoed every now and then. In one corner, a ring of townsfolk surrounded a woman and a man, who engaged in some sort of drinking game. A dozen mugs cluttered the table; a few had toppled over, others lay empty by the drinkers' feet. The participants swayed in their chairs as they downed mug after mug, cheered on by their small audience.

Kole tailed Russé, afraid his burns would draw attention.

"Head upstairs. I'll handle the arrangements. The fewer questions, the better." Azmali pushed through the crowd, sending those in her path stumbling.

"Buncha drunkards," Felix said under his breath as they climbed the stairs.

"I thought you liked that stuff," Kole said. As he recalled, Felix was the one who'd offered him his first sip of ale back in the Liberation hideout.

"Sure, I like it. But there's a difference between gettin' buzzed and losin' control, Blondie. Ya can't even enjoy it like that."

A thud, and then a grand cheer erupted from the bottom of the staircase. Likely the victor from the drinking game had been decided.

"*They* seem to disagree," Vienna said.

"Well *they* don't have Kayetans troublin' up their town every night. Gotta be keen enough ta fight or ya can count yourself with the dead."

Kole hadn't thought about Felix and Vienna's past too much. His own life had been filled with worry over keeping the refugee orphans away from the dangers of the ramblers. He supposed Felix and his sister had dealt with similar troubles because of the Kayetans in Socren. He noted to ask them about it when the moment allowed.

A long hallway greeted them at the top step. Doors lined either side. It reminded Kole of the Liberation hideout, with the clay walls reminiscent of stone in the repurposed mining tunnels.

"Which one?" Kole asked.

Felix tried the first door. It rattled. "Locked." When he pulled out the ring of tools Kole recognized as his lockpicks, Vienna gave him a stern glare.

"Really, Felix? If it's locked, it means it's someone's room."

"That's the point, V. They could have cool stuff in there."

"Best we keep a low profile."

He huffed and rolled his green eyes. As he returned the tools to his pocket, he gave Kole a wink and whispered. "Later, eh?"

Kole smirked and shook his head.

"How about this one?" Midway down the hall, Issira held a door open.

They all hauled into the small room; a tight fit for five people. Two lanterns hung on hooks by the door, casting light over the simple furnishings. A pair of beds shoved into opposite corners, divided by a plain cabinet. A woven rug, muddy red, lay in the center. It seemed the dull color had come from overuse. Over each bed cushion lay a frayed blanket. Straw poked from the sides of rupturing seams.

"Dibs." Felix fell into one of the cots. Dust puffed from the cushion.

A heavy sighed exuded from Vienna.

"The boys will share," Russé said. "You two can take the other. I will fare fine on the floor."

"Share... with a Soul?" Vienna's blank face made it difficult for Kole to tell if she considered it appalling or an honor.

Issira dipped her head. "You may stay with your brother if you wish. Kole and I —"

"No, it's fine. Careful, Kole. Felix kicks."

Kole shrugged off his pack and set it on the bed.

"It's true." Felix gave him a smile, as if proud of his nighttime habits.

"Am I interrupting?" Azmali stood in in the doorway, a key ring in hand. She pulled one off and handed it to Russé. "You have the room for the night. I have set a personal guard at the stairs. He will accompany you to the market."

"It's open this late?" Felix asked.

"Markets close at last call. Three hours should be plenty of time to gather supplies. After that is curfew. No one in the streets."

"What's curfew for?" Kole asked. Back in Solpate, Goren had set a strict curfew for all the orphans at dusk when the trees sprung from the soil. Too many kids had been accidentally trampled by a rambler. Only shepherds were allowed out after dark.

"Kayetans. I set the rule in place a few weeks ago when I heard word of the raids. I'm hoping once you're gone, the Kayetans will follow your party away from my city. I wish no ill will on you, of course, but I have a duty to protect my people. If they trail you, *we* are safe." With the room silent at her explanation, she cleared her throat. "Stay in the room otherwise. If you're out after curfew, I will have to rescind my hospitality and send you on your way. Clear?"

Russé spoke for the group. "We understand. Thank you."

Azmali gave everyone a once over, then took her leave.

"Sure are strict 'round here," Felix said.

"For good reason." Kole crossed to the window and peered at the bustling streets. "We're putting them in danger."

"Which is why we will make this a brief visit." A thump as Russé dropped his pack on the floor. "Issira and I will barter for supplies. You three stay here."

"Barter?" Felix snapped up and scooted to the edge of the mattress. "What kinda old timey place ya think this is, Gramps?"

When Kole spotted Russé's face, he barely held in a laugh. He'd never seen anything like it. Not on Russé. Eyes wide as saucers, one raised brow, and a slack jaw. Flabbergasted—the only word Kole thought to describe it.

"We have no coin," Russé said.

"Forgot ta take some from Leo, eh? Ya left in a hurry."

"We're not used to money," Kole piped up from his place at the window. "We didn't have it back in Solpate. I'm sure someone will trade, but what do we have of value? Labor? In one night? At this hour, too."

Felix fiddled with a pouch at his side, then pulled out a handful of copper and silver coins. "You're in luck, mate. Leo gave us a bit for the journey. Looks like we won't have ta beg or break our backs workin' for food. Last thing we need." Green eyes peered at Russé. "How much ya need?"

The Soul pursed his lips and looked to Issira, who seemed just as dumbfounded.

However small, it pleased Kole to witness Russé in such a situation. No matter how strong his magic or how infinite his wisdom, the mindless act of unpreparedness made the Soul seem almost human. *Needing help from a* child. Kole snorted.

Felix let out a long whistle. "Well your little plan's gotta change. You'll need me with ya, else you'll end up spendin' double for half what we need."

"He *is* great at bargaining." Vienna folded her arms. "Most the time, shopkeepers give him a deal solely to get him to leave."

"I believe that," Kole laughed.

Felix sent him a sly eye, then winked as if deciding to take it as a compliment.

"Very well." Russé glanced between Vienna and Kole. "I trust you both to stay here. You heard Azmali."

Vienna nodded. "I don't plan on unleashing her wrath."

"Can I borrow the journal while you're away?" Kole asked. "Might as well work on it."

Russé slid it from his belt and handed it off. "Don't get your hopes up. Here." He offered the pouch with his ink and quill. "Keep notes."

The leather had darkened in a few places where the river had splashed it. A quick pull of Kole's thumb told him the pages remained dry. He placed the journal and Russé's pouch on the clay side table.

The door closed. Kole watched from the window as his three companions exited the building. A guard accompanied them down the street.

Though he didn't mention it in front of everyone, Kole wished to go along. Wished it but knew staying was best. His scars would cause a stir no matter how well he hid them. He'd never seen a city before— well, Socren, but that didn't count. Cresthaven seemed untouched by the darkness of the world around it. No Black Wall to fear. No corrupt leadership. No famine. Its people seemed happy. Untarnished. Kole gazed at the townsfolk passing in the streets wondering what sort of lives they lived.

"Are you going to stay at the window all night?" Vienna asked.

He shrugged.

"What's going on, Kole? You've been acting strange lately. Is it Obell?"

His eyes drifted down from the window to his burned hands. "Yes... and no. Not entirely."

When he offered no explanation, Vienna crossed the room and picked up the journal. "What's in here? Something important, I suppose. It needing decoding and all."

"We're trying to figure it out. It has some stuff about the Souls. I was hoping it had more about me in there. My past. Maybe my parents."

She plopped on the bed and flipped it open to the first page, where Russé's scribbles littered the open spaces of the already crammed page. "This looks familiar."

"The code?"

"No, the runes. They're like ones I've seen Leo use except... more basic. Was Goren a magic user?"

"That's what we've found out."

"That's odd."

"What?" Kole sat beside her.

"Leo and his lists. He documented everything: the refugees in and out of the city, the supply runs to Solpate down to the pound of grain. He has a list of every sorcerer in Socren. Ever since his brother.... Well, he's been careful since then. Magic is monitored. Honestly, he might be going a bit overboard. But anyway, I've seen the document. Goren isn't on it."

"What does that mean?"

She shrugged. "He could've learned it on his own. No mentor. It'd explain the informal runes."

"You can learn magic on your own?"

"It's ill advised. You can get seriously hurt."

"But possible?"

"I guess."

"What else do you know about Goren?"

"Not much. Leo was adamant about finding a safe place to harbor the smuggled refugees. He sent Goren to scout Solpate years before the Escapes started, mostly to evaluate the threat level of the ramblers. Try to make the place livable. Goren certainly accomplished that."

Kole reached over and turned to the page Russé had deciphered by Issira's pool. "He was the one who put this whole thing in motion."

"What do you mean?"

"Goren used me as a sacrifice to release Russé."

"What? Ritualistic magic? But that's dark stuff, that's—"

"Blood magic," they said together.

"No way he learned that on his own." Vienna pulled the book back to her lap. Her eyes narrowed as she read Russé's notes, then with a sudden jerk, she straightened. "Wait. I *know* this."

"The... spell?"

"With Leo. He and I went to Solpate for clues. He looked into the past. That was *you* he saw. But he mentioned another figure in his vision... it must've been Goren." She shook her head, then looked over to him. "Why would he do that to you?"

"He chose me. Not because I was special. Because I was... disposable."

"Don't say that."

"It's true. I was meant to die. A five year old murdered for the greater good of Ohr. Does it make it worse that I was so young—that I hadn't had the chance to create a life yet? To live? Or was it a mercy pick? Someone so young wouldn't know any better. Had less to lose."

"Whatever his reasons then, it doesn't mean the same now. Look at you."

He pulled at his sleeves, trying to cover his exposed wrists. Where were his gloves? "I try not to."

"Not like that, Kole. You're meant to do something great. Without you, Ohr is doomed. We all are."

"What would you do if you were me? If this all fell to you?"

Her mouth pursed to one side. "In the beginning, I'd be shocked, sure. But I've always wanted a purpose. It's why I joined the Liberation. I need something to strive for—to focus on—or I fear...."

"What?"

A sigh. "I'm afraid if I stop to breathe, I'll succumb to pains I'd rather not relive."

Kole understood what she meant. Ever since Niko's death, he'd had something to distract him. The constant danger acted as a wall around his heart, keeping his emotions from truly playing out.

"Why did Goren have to choose me? Maybe I had a shot before, but now I'm surely the least qualified person on Ohr." He sighed at the pleasant memories of his former body. Why had he ever taken it for granted? Scrawny and short, the traits he'd loathed most about himself, seemed like blessings comparatively. "What's it like to know your life is in the hands of a cripple?"

"Stop that." Vienna's mouth twisted to the side like it always did when she got angry. "You don't need to be the strongest, or the fastest, or the smartest, or whatever else you may think. I—*we* are here to help you see this to the end."

"I don't know what I'm doing. I'm just struggling through, catching way too many breaks. Our luck *will* run out."

"The only luck we've had is that we are all still alive. All of us have been changed by this."

"I only wanted to be a shepherd. Just me and Niko."

Her eyes trailed to the floor. The slouch in her shoulders grew more prominent. "We all wanted something."

He opened his mouth. Closed it. Better not to pry. The whistling breeze from the window preoccupied him for a moment. If he closed his eyes and tried—really tried—he could imagine the wind rustling the leaves of the sleeping ramblers. But the melodic tone of the wind rose an octave, morphing into Niko's blood-curdling scream seconds before his death. His ears rang with that scream. Even the quiet had a way of reeling up the darkest parts of his mind from the depths. He couldn't bear the memory any longer. "What did you want before all of this happened?" Kole asked Vienna, hoping the conversation would distract him.

"What?" She looked at him, doe-eyed, as if taken off guard. "Me—I...." A shadow of a smile touched her lips. "It's ridiculous."

"No, come on. I wanted to ride trees. What's more ridiculous than that?"

A small laugh escaped her. That sound chased away the terrible memories. "Taming ramblers is much more interesting."

He squinted at her, trying to read her face for a clue.

"I know what you're doing. It won't work." She straightened with a sort of pride. "I'm as readable as a statue."

She was right about that. Still, he studied her. It provided an excuse to stare. The longer he did, small tells betrayed her. A twitch, and her upper lip tightened ever so slightly. He would've missed it if he blinked. "Statues don't move."

"*Most* don't."

"Don't tell me Leo has a spell for that."

"Not that I know of, but I wouldn't be surprised."

The seconds ticked by and still he stole glances her way. Something about her—just being near her—made the nightmares of his past melt away. He felt like himself. Even in this different body.

"All right, fine. But you can't laugh."

"I wouldn't."

"I wanted to be a florist."

His brows lifted. Definitely not the answer he suspected.

"I know that look. It's the look my parents gave me when I told them. It's not a useful path. I thought bringing beauty into Socren would make it a better place, but nothing can be solved with a flower." She passed the book back to Kole. "Things changed when my parents died. I put everything I had into learning combat. I can protect myself now. And Felix. A flower never could've given me that."

"Why can't you do both?"

Her laugh filled the room. "Shall I convert a wagon into a garden and pull it along on our journey?"

"We already have a traveling forest. Why not bring a garden?"

She smiled. "Thanks for that. It's absurd, but... thank you." Her eyes drifted past him. A flicker as she locked onto something, and her grin dropped to a hard line.

Before Kole could turn, she stopped him with a hand.

"Don't move."

His stomach sank. "What is it?"

Vienna came back with a forced smile. "Someone is watching us through the window."

CHAPTER 13

Kole tensed at her words. "How can they see us? We're on the second floor."

"So are they. From the window across the street."

"Who is it?"

She leaned in, face inching closer to his.

Kole froze as her arms wrapped around his torso. A hug.

"I can't tell. They're in the shadows." Her head rested on his shoulder. When she spoke, her warm breath touched his ear.

Kole's heart fluttered. Not only because it was *her* who touched him, but because he couldn't remember the last time he'd been embraced like this, even if only for show. It was nice, yet terrifying.

"This isn't convincing unless you hug me back."

"Oh, uh—" He held his breath and moved his arms around her. The moment he hugged back, a swell of insecurity overtook him. He was fully aware of her hands on his scars. Could she feel them through his shirt? He waited to feel her flinch, but the only movement came from him; the nervous tremble of his arms. This wasn't genuine, merely a ruse. No one would ever truly hold him like this. That chance had burned away with his perfect skin.

Another moment, torsos pressed together, and she released. "They're gone." She sprang from the bed and yanked the drapes over the window.

His shoulders sagged forward, glad for it to be over. A deep ache in his chest remained. He cleared his throat, ridding himself of the lingering feeling. "Maybe it's just coincidence. They could've been looking at anyone. Even if it was us, they don't know who we are. We just got into town."

"If you're implying I'm being paranoid, you're correct. It pays to be." Vienna moved to the other bed and propped herself against the wall, eyes trained on the door. "Get some rest. I'll take watch."

Get some rest. Why did everyone say that to him? It basically meant, 'I'm done talking, stay out of my way.' It was one thing hearing it from Russé, now Vienna? Kole kicked off his boots, positioned the book towards the lantern light, then delved into Goren's journal.

Kole woke with an aching neck. He'd fallen asleep, hunched over while decoding. The lanterns by the door had extinguished. With the small sliver of moonlight peeking in through the edge of the shut drapes, Kole barely made out Vienna's form in the corner. Asleep by the looks of it. How long had it been? It seemed Felix and the Souls had yet to return. An occasional cheer bellowed from the first floor of the inn, though less frequent than when they'd first arrived. *Must be coming up on curfew.*

Slow and quiet, Kole crawled from the bed and crossed to the window. He glanced at Vienna, who still slumbered, then he pulled back the curtain, allowing a flood of moonlight into the room. Road traffic had died down. Townsfolk strolled along here and there, but it appeared most of Cresthaven had surrendered to their beds.

A strange feeling enveloped him. Despite the cover of night, standing at the window gave him a sense of vulnerability. His eyes moved to the building opposite him. Dark rooms—each one. He stared at the window directly across from his. Faintly, he made out lines. The shape of a silhouette, waist up. Man or woman was unclear, but it looked large. Kole's heart jumped, but fear kept him rooted.

The stranger moved out of view.

Kole yanked the curtain closed again. The heft of his quickened lungs clouded his head, leaving him lightheaded. He leaned against the wall, closed his eyes, and focused on slow breaths. *A coincidence, that's all.* Yet he fought the urge to wake Vienna. Was it the same person who'd watched them earlier? *Stop being paranoid.* When his body calmed, he opened his eyes and took in the shadowed room. The faint light from the hallway seeped under the door.

A blink, and the shadow of two feet blocked the light.

The hammering in Kole's chest hastened. *Just a patron walking by.* The beat of his heart deafened him as whoever stood behind the door lowered to their hands and knees and peered in through the crack at the floor.

"Vienna," he whispered as loud as he dared. Kole grabbed for the hunting knife on the bedside table. Fingers bumped the leather handle.

Vienna stirred.

When he looked back to the door, the person had left. His sigh of relief cut short when a jiggle came from the handle. The door clicked and creaked open.

Kole let out a scream and chucked the knife. A thud signaled the blade had hit something, but the light of the hallway blinded Kole.

"What the bloody hell, Blondie?" Felix's voice pierced the room. "Ya tried ta kill me!"

The fierce light subdued as his eyes adjusted. His knife stuck in the wooden door level with Felix's head. The two Souls stood behind, wide-eyed.

"I-I-I'm sorry. I thought you were something else?"

"Who else would I be? We're the only ones with a key." With a grunt, Felix yanked the blade from the door. "Good thing yer a bad shot."

"You said some*thing*." Russé rushed Issira inside and closed the door. The light of his lantern trained on Kole. "Not someone."

Vienna rose from the bed. "Kole? What did you see?"

"Someone in the window across the street. They—"

"The same one from before?" Vienna moved to the curtain and eased it open a sliver.

"I think so."

"From *before*?" Russé swung the lantern to Vienna.

After she filled the rest of the group in on the incident, Russé turned back to Kole. "You saw something by the door?"

Kole nodded. "Right before you came in."

Handing back the knife, Felix said, "Didn't see no one. Ya thinkin' what I'm thinkin', Gramps?"

"They've followed us into the city," said Russé with a curse.

"I don't know." Vienna eyed the door. "A Kayetan spying like that? It's not in their nature."

"Maybe, but whatever is going on, we need to warn Azmali." The pit in Kole's stomach twisted as he spoke. They should've left the moment they arrived. Lingering meant trouble for the people here.

"It's past curfew now." Russé extinguished the lantern and joined Vienna by the window, peering out. "The people are safe in their houses. If the Kayetans haven't raided, it means they are after *us* not them."

"Ain't that peachy," Felix said. When Vienna gave him a swift glare, he held up his hands in defense. "What?" But Kole noticed her eyes set on something behind her brother. The door.

Vienna held a finger to her lips. "Look," she mouthed.

Everyone quieted and followed her extended finger to the shadowed feet at the base of the door.

Issira moved away allowing Felix to inspect. He drew his sunstone dagger and yanked the door open. A wisp of smoke lingered, but no Kayetan.

"The bastard. It's toyin' with us." Felix leaned into the hall, peering both ways.

"It's luring us," Issira said from the dim corner, her silks glimmering in the soft light streaming from the hall.

"We'll check it out," Felix whispered, nodding to Vienna.

"We'll all go," Issira spoke. Russé set a curious gaze on her. "If it is indeed luring us, we have more strength together."

Felix closed the door. "Out the window, then."

"The window?" As the question left Kole's lips, he remembered Azmali had set a guard on the inn.

"Don't ya worry, I'll help ya down."

Vienna creaked open the window. A chill breeze swept through the small room. She whistled, and Fiona, who'd she let loose to roam the city, soared down from a nearby rooftop. After a brief whisper, the hawk pushed off and took to the navy sky.

Felix went first. He climbed out and hooked his fingers around the sill while he found footing, then descended. "C'mon Kole, yer next," he said before his unruly curls dipped beyond view.

"I can't—"

Russé laid a hand on Kole's back. "No need to worry." At the words, the wooden staff slithered, snake-like, elongating into a thin root four times in length. The end coiled firmly around the clay sill and dangled down the length of the building. "Grab hold."

"Don't think ya coulda done that a bit earlier?" Felix's voice came from below.

One side of Russé's mouth lifted. "You seemed to be doing well on your own."

With the aid of the old Soul's offered arm, Kole joined Felix on the ledge and, hand under hand, slid down the smooth root, using the pressure of his ankles to control his speed.

Wings flapped and circled overhead, then soared north.

"Fiona's got sight," said Felix. A thump as he jumped the small distance to the road. "I got ya."

Hands touched Kole's waist, guiding him down the last few feet until he could jump the rest. He landed and turned to Felix with a quiet, "Thanks," then arced his eyes up.

Vienna slid down the length of the root. Her loose grip allowed for speed and ease. Why hadn't he thought of that? He hid his pursed mouth as she landed, the Souls swift on her tail.

"This way." Felix pulled Kole along the road.

They raced after the hawk, adjusting their path to Fiona, who glided between the rooftops. To Kole's surprise, the town stood completely dark. Not a single torch or lantern lit the barren streets. The waning moon peeking through the clouds cast the houses and storefronts in an eerie gray-blue.

Kole scanned the streets. "There," he whispered, spotting the distinct, long-clawed shadow slithering behind a house. Fiona must've spotted it too, because the hawk veered left down the road.

Rounding the corner, Kole and the others slowed. Guards. Watchmen, more like. Two patrolled the bisected path between them and Fiona, who'd perched atop the short house at the end of the street, beating her wings impatiently.

Felix pulled out his slingshot and prepped a pellet. The band groaned as he pulled back to fire.

"The sign. Knock it free." Kole pointed to the wooden board hung above a door a little way down the north road. "They'll blame it on the hinge. Won't suspect us."

A snort, then Felix shifted his aim. He released. A tense second passed, silent, then a satisfying ting, metal against metal. The hinge snapped. A clatter echoed in the abandoned street. The guards turned, but only one went to investigate the commotion while the other remained.

"Damn. A bit smarter than I hoped," Kole said.

"That's all right, mate. I gotta plan. Vienna," he called, pulling out a rag and a familiar bottle of clear liquid from his belt. Taliroot. With a swift stroke of his blade, he split the cloth in two, kept one, then held the other half to his sister.

"Really?" She snagged the rag from him with a sigh. "Why do you keep using this stuff? It never turns out well."

"I'm all ears for a better idea. Figure we don't wanna kill 'em, so this is second best, eh?"

"Of course we're not going to kill them." After Felix soaked her cloth, then did the same to his, she added, "Just make sure you're not seen."

Felix's brows deepened at the slight. "Make sure *you're* not seen, Sis."

"Enough," Russé snapped. "Just go."

At that, the siblings left their separate ways. They both slipped down the streets, shoulders skimming the clay walls. The sheer skill of their silent approach rocked a tinge of envy and excitement through

Kole. They moved fluidly in and out of the shadows. The guards never acknowledged their stalkers. Kole had moved like that once—before his burns. He remembered the rush it gave him sneaking up on an unsuspecting rabbit before he'd shoot it and wondered if the siblings felt that same surge as they closed in on their prey.

After Felix stepped into the north street, he fell in step with the guard, every noise of his footfalls covered by the guard's leather boots. Then he glanced back to Vienna, who circled her own target. Some unspoken signal passed between them, so subtle it eluded Kole. The siblings pounced in unison. With a hook of their arm, both shoved the soaked cloth over their guard's mouth.

Muffled protests echoed through the sleeping streets. Kole's eyes flicked back and forth from Vienna to Felix as the guards swatted behind them and struggled to free themselves. Fists slammed into the siblings so hard, the thumps reached Kole thirty yards off. Without thinking, Kole stepped forward, but an arm on his shoulder held him back.

"No need, young one." Issira's voice slipped into his ear.

The blows softened. Stopped. Only then did Vienna and Felix release their hold. An all-clear wave from Vienna gave Kole, Russé, and Issira the go ahead to emerged from the corner.

Closer now, Kole could see the guard swaying as if dizzy. When they reached Vienna, Felix was already hurrying back, leaving his guard standing still as a statue in the road.

"Went well?" Kole asked Vienna as Felix approached with a gleaming grin.

Vienna nodded, then stepped around the city guard, whose eyes, though open, had lost their glimmer, like he'd dozed off. "We have ten, maybe fifteen minutes." She turned to her brother. "What story are we going with?"

"Told mine he heard a noise, and when he went ta investigate, he found a little kitten that's so cute, he wants ta show it ta all his guard friends."

A moment went by where Kole couldn't tell if Felix was joking. Neither could his companions by their similar reaction. "You what?" Kole asked.

"Dammit, Felix." Vienna huffed. "Are you incapable of keeping things simple?"

Felix shrugged. "Thought if we're givin' him a new memory, might as well be somethin' fun. Lighten up, Sis."

A caw from the skies signaled that Fiona had eyes on the Kayetan. Vienna hurriedly whispered into the ear of her guard to connect the ridiculous story to Felix's, then they raced after the zooming form of their hawk.

The siblings took the lead while Russé and Issira flanked Kole. The remaining streets sat empty, allowing their chase to continue unhindered. Suddenly, Fiona angled down into a nosedive. After a flurry of flaps to ease her decent, she landed on a weathervane atop a petite clay building. Stairs led to the arched door of the domed abode. *A store or a residence?* No other clues hinted its purpose, but Kole hoped it lay unoccupied.

Vienna and Felix slowed and slid their sunstone blades from their belts. Out of habit, Kole reached for his own, only to be greeted with an empty space on his belt. He'd lost it days ago during his last encounter with a Kayetan.

An odd feeling bubbled in his stomach as they closed in on the building. Empty streets. Dark houses. No sign or sound of life except the soft scratch of Fiona's talons across the metal weathervane creaking in the wind. *What business would a Kayetan have here?* If anyone resided inside, Kole would have expected to hear them scream by now.

Vienna ran up the steps. She kicked the door in, then darted through. Felix followed, dagger raised and ready, while Kole and the others brought up the rear.

What little moonlight peeked through the gaps in the curtained windows and the pushed-in door revealed the faint line of a long counter at the end of the far wall. Behind it, a row of tall bottles lined the shelves. Empty chairs and tables sat around the room, neatly pushed in. The wood shone in the dim light, hinting it had been recently cleaned. Someone had been here. *Could still be here....*

Vienna and Felix checked behind the counter. After nodding to go ahead, they moved to the back door in the corner.

Vienna reached for the handle.

Movement from the floor caught Kole's eye. Like a growing puddle, darkness pooled from the small slit beneath the door. Vienna and Felix moved back as the Kayetan's smoke-like body swirled up from the dark patch. The silhouette expanded to a massive, bulky form bigger than Kole had ever seen. Though the creatures took the same shape of the body they were ripped from, no man could grow to such size, and the bulges on the arms and legs swelled larger than any muscle he'd ever seen. Kole froze in awe.

Long claws swiped at Vienna. She ducked, moved behind the creature in a flash, then swung for the shadow's back.

But the Kayetan, just as fast, swirled away, reverting to its smokey form, then shot up to the ceiling. The creature circled the room as if taking in the scene.

Felix and Vienna stalked it.

With the siblings in pursuit, the Kayetan whirled to the back door, forming its bear-sized, humanoid shape once more. The creature flexed its claws and swung its head between adversaries.

Vienna nudged her brother's arm, and they launched into a run. While she charged for the Kayetan, Felix swerved left toward the counter. He kicked off the tabletop, coming at the demon from above while Vienna covered the low ground, leaving nowhere for the shadow to escape this time.

The creature stood its ground, crouching slightly as if taking a defensive stance. The move sparked something in Kole as strange. Before, the Kayetan had retreated further into the house when it could have easily escaped through the front entrance, where Vienna had kicked the door in. Kole pushed past Russé and Issira's arms, shouting, "Wait!" but it was too late to stop the siblings' onslaught.

Felix came down on the creature as the door opened. The Kayetan disappeared in an instant, leaving Felix to fall through the now-empty space and land with a thud at Vienna's feet.

A figure stood in the doorway holding a small candle.

Vienna lowered her weapon.

Kole's jaw fell open at the humanoid staring back at them with yellow eyes. Its skin reflected like polished glass; black and slightly translucent. The sharp, angular features of the figure's face reminded Kole of a faceted gem, as if someone had carved the being from solid stone.

A Yamani.

"Guess you've never seen one of my kind before." A deep voice cut through the silence. "You're going to regret coming through my door."

Chapter 14

Kole had only heard about the Yamani from Goren's stories and faintly remembered something about them being a cursed species. Only a few remained on Ohr — or so Goren claimed. Could he trust anything his camp leader had said after learning he'd not only lied to Kole but used him as a sacrifice? Best to abandon what he *thought* he knew about the Yamani unless it came straight from the source.

"What are you doing in my house?" The Yamani stepped forward, feet solid and heavy over the creaking floorboards. She wore no clothing, leaving her chest and hardy curves exposed: the only hint to a feminine nature. Her bare body gleamed and crunched as her thick stone legs propelled her closer.

Vienna and Felix retreated, joining Kole and the Souls in the center of the room.

When no one answered, everyone apparently as awestruck as Kole, the Yamani repeated her question, a rage edging her voice.

"We were following a Kayetan," Russé said.

Yellow eyes flicked past the group, then settled on Russé. "You felt it necessary to kick in my door?"

Vienna shifted slightly.

"It's here in the house," said Russé.

"'Course it is. It's mine."

Kole felt the confusion jump through the group.

"*Yours?*" Felix asked.

The Yamani woman set the candle on the counter, then folded her arms. "That's what I said."

"So yer one of Savairo's men, then, eh?" Felix twirled the dagger in his hand. When the stone woman cocked her head at him, he shrugged. "Er, *women*, then."

Vienna gave a sharp look to her brother, then stepped forward into the light. "What do you mean it's yours?"

The woman cupped a hand over the flame, but the light passed straight through her body to the walls beyond.

"No shadow," Kole whispered. He flinched as the stone woman moved her head to him. "How is that possible?"

"It was taken from me."

"By Savairo?" Vienna asked.

The Yamani nodded.

"The ritual's 'spose ta be deadly." Felix grimaced. Tension returned to his voice. "I dunno. I smell a rat."

"You break into my house and *I'm* the one who needs to explain?" A quick snort, like an agitated bull. "Savairo captured me many years ago. I was subjected to his ritual. The removal itself isn't always fatal. He finishes the job if you survive. I feigned death and escaped when the opportunity arose."

"Then the Kayetan is your own? Under *your* control?" Kole asked.

The Yamani's mouth twisted. "It does as I wish." She closed her hand around the flame, extinguishing it.

Kole blinked as his eyes adjusted to the dark.

A silhouette appeared next to the stone woman. Kole slipped past the Souls to get a better look. Up close, he recognized the creature's broad-shouldered, wide stance. That of its master. The Kayetan's outline mimicked the Yamani's form exactly, save for the signature long claws hanging past its thighs. The shadow stood motionless.

Felix pointed his blade at the creature. "What was it doin' around town? Watchin' us and stuff?"

"I'm sure you've heard the rumors." Her yellow eyes seemed to glow more brilliantly in the dark. "People have been going missing — kidnapped. Towns raided. My Kayetan scouts the area at my command. Alerts me if strangers close in on the city."

Like a trained pet. Both ingenious and disturbing to use the Kayetan, a monster meant to kill and maim, as a tool for good. "You *knew* we were coming, didn't you?" Kole asked.

"Aye." The side of her mouth lifted at Kole's conclusion. "My Kayetan spotted your gang two miles upriver before your dramatic entrance into Cresthaven. Who do you think rang the alarm? I've had eyes on you ever since." She gave everyone a once over. "But the question remains, who are *you*? Why are you traveling so close to the Ashland Plains?"

As Kole opened his mouth to answer, he glanced to Russé, wondering if the Souls would rather their intentions remain secret.

"Azmali has allowed us to restock and leave at dawn, no questions asked." The Soul dipped his head in greeting. "I'm Russé. We apologize for intruding. We didn't intend to cause an uproar."

She squinted, as if debating whether to trust his words. "Shikar," she grunted and folded her arms over her chest. "Azmali runs the city like a turtle holed up in its shell. She keeps her people safe and cares not of the terror spreading across Ohr. You're lucky you got so close to the city before the Kayetans caught up to you, otherwise, she would've let you fend for yourselves."

"What do you mean?" Kole asked.

"She has limits to her... kindness. Especially toward outsiders. Another mile out and she would've stood by and watched you perish—only sending troops if the Kayetans directed their eyes to Cresthaven afterward."

The hem of a silk sleeve brushed Kole's arm. "You don't agree with her methods?" Issira asked Shikar.

Those yellow eyes trailed to her. "I can respect keeping a stronghold. But our resources are plenty. Azmali can afford to send protection. Since she doesn't, I do. And for weeks now, no one has come from the north, save for Kayetans. So, I ask again, which way do you travel come dawn?"

"We are heading for Grayfall," Russé said.

Shikar flinched at the name. "What purpose do you have there?"

"Our purpose is private."

The Yamani sneered. "To death then, is it? Even if you make it past the plains, you'll never survive that wretched place. It's a cursed city. All but forgotten. It *should* be forgotten. The one place I would gladly let the Black Wall swallow whole. You would do well to abandon whatever business you have there."

"How do you know so much?" Kole asked.

The sound of grinding stone filled the dark room as she set her jaw. Shikar re-lit the candle then, one by one, kindled the lanterns hanging on the walls of the tavern. Her Kayetan flashed away at the presence of the fire, and Felix's shoulders fell with a sigh.

The light revealed an assortment of decorations mounted on the walls. Bizarre masks of leather and glass stared back at him. Neither colorful nor extravagant, merely a dull, worn array of grays and browns with elongated, snout-shaped mouths and bug-like eyes of thick glass. Alongside the masks hung various rusted tools; their purposes remained unknown to Kole, but he guessed from the rust and corrosion it had been a long while since they'd seen use.

The items seemed less foreign to Vienna, though, because her green eyes lit up with excitement. "You've been to Grayfall?"

Kole looked back to Shikar, whose hand paused over the last lantern. "Not exactly."

Vienna reached out to stroke the glass eyes of a nearby mask. "Then why do you have them?"

"They belonged to my ancestors. I simply inherited junk."

"Junk, eh?" Felix scrunched his nose the way he always did when he suspected a lie. "Ya treat yer junk a bit differently than most."

"What are they?" Kole asked.

Vienna trailed a finger along one mask's snout. "They filter the air. Make it possible to trek the plains."

"Not anymore," Shikar griped. "The volcano is in a constant state of eruption. The ash is too thick nowadays, and the masks are old. They might filter soot, but they won't do much against the fumes."

Russé wandered behind the counter and lifted a mask from the wall. "Still, we may have use for them."

Shikar swiped the mask from Russé's hands and returned it to its place. "You think you can kick down my door, attack my Kayetan, *and* take my things?"

"We would compensate you, of course," said Russé.

Kole peered at the Soul. Last he knew, they'd spent whatever coin they had on supplies. What could he possibly offer as payment?

Shikar growled. "They aren't for sale."

A tense silence passed the room.

Vienna stepped from the wall. "You said your ancestors left these to you. Did they live in Grayfall?"

The Yamani's body tensed at the prying question. "The Yamani had always lived in Grayfall. Once the curse befell the city, my people were run out. No one has returned since. No one *can* return."

Kole got the feeling Shikar knew more than she let on. If they hoped to get any information out of her, they couldn't tiptoe around the subject. Direct questions led to direct answers. At least he hoped. "What sort of curse is on Grayfall?"

As he spoke the words, Issira's hand squeezed his shoulder. Her voice came to him in his head. *It would be wise not to push her too far. I sense a hatred within our Yamani hostess.*

Shikar slowly turned to Kole. The firelight glinted off her obsidian-like body, making her appear more like a piece of art than a living creature. "Those who step inside the walls forfeit their lives to the curse. They never set foot outside the city again."

The doom in her words sent a chill down Kole's spine. Of course they'd be destined for such a place. *The next Soul better be in a blessed place to balance this shit out.*

"We can protect ourselves." The line of glassware seemed to hum at Issira's sing-song voice.

Shikar's gaze snapped between Russé and Issira. A concern lay in her eye. No, not concern. Suspicion. The Yamani must have sensed something off about them. Kole shrugged from Issira's grip, breaking their connection. He could only guess what the Yamani would make of them — whether she even believed in the Souls, or if someone could tell his companions true nature at a glance. Leo hadn't known Russé was a god. Not at first. And yet, Issira was different. The form she'd taken... a lavish blue silk dress, pin-straight hair, and gray eyes that churned like angry waters. Not exactly inconspicuous. Even Kole would've gotten an otherworldly vibe from her, regardless of knowing her divine status.

Shikar swept a curtain aside and opened a window. A long rope hung from a bell above, which looked like a thread compared to her massive fist. "I'd like you to leave now. I don't need strangers in my bar, especially the ones who brought a Kayetan raid on their heels. Business is slow as it is, being a Yamani without a shadow."

"But—" Kole tried.

"I said out," she roared. "Make trouble and I'll call the guards for breaking curfew."

Kole and his companions glanced to one another, then headed for the broken door. Stepping out to the street, an eerie quiet pressed on Cresthaven, broken only by Shikar, who slammed her crooked door behind them.

When they returned to the inn, they climbed back through the window and set up for the night. Vienna and Issira took the bed opposite while Russé insisted on lying in front of the door. Kole collapsed into his own bed, grateful for the soft alternative. But the moment cut short when Felix hopped in with him and wriggled around, only settling when Kole's agitation reached its peak.

The room lay dark for a long while. Only the soft breaths of his companions filled the space. Nightmares stayed away for a time, but before long, Kole found himself wide awake. He stared out the window at the moon, which lay masked behind a thin sheet of clouds. Another drawn-out night of waiting, counting the seconds until the sun rose, and they could be on their way again. On their way to Obell. The thought of marching blind to a cursed city left him riddled with anxiety.

The bed bounced. Kole glanced sideways at the culprit. Felix had rolled over, his face next to Kole's ear.

"Can't sleep, mate."

"I can tell."

Felix's shifting jostled Kole. "We need those masks."

After checking on the others' sleeping forms, Kole lifted to his elbows. If sleep meant to evade him, he might as well humor his friend. "What are we going to do with broken masks? She said herself they only cut out the ash. A cloth around the mouth would do the same. Our liberation uniforms already have that."

"Cloth won't do. You heard Issira. 'Toxic fumes.'" Felix wriggled his fingers in the air for dramatic effect.

"But they're *broken*," Kole repeated, annoyance bubbling in his throat. "And Shikar won't sell." Through the darkness, he caught a familiar vulpine glint in Felix's eyes. "*No.*"

"Oh, come on. If we need 'em so bad, we take 'em."

"We are *not* stealing them," Kole scolded. "Besides, Shikar's Kayetan is watching the town, remember? *And* us. What about the guards? Curfew? You can't get in."

It was the worst thing to say to Felix, telling him he couldn't do something. Challenging him. Kole should've known better. He shook his head as a devious smile pulled on Felix's mouth.

"You can't use Taliroot on every single guard in the city," Kole tried, but as he spoke, Felix slipped from the blanket and tiptoed to the window.

Eyes shifting between the other bed where the girls slept and Russé's form slumped by the door, Felix gripped his fingers around the windowsill.

"*Felix*," Kole said in a low warning.

The window gave a quiet groan as it slid open. With a space big enough to allow his torso, Felix hopped up and slipped out, feet first.

Kole wriggled free of his blanket and sat up. Vienna and Russé hadn't stirred at Felix's escape, but it would be a more difficult task for himself. With the burden of his scars, stealth wasn't exactly his forte. He decided to go with the safest option and spread the blanket on the floor to mask his heavy steps. Upon poking his head into the open air, he found a readied rope. Nothing could stop the roll of his eyes. Felix knew he'd follow—probably hoped for it. He pushed a breath through his teeth, then wriggled out the window and clung to the rope. The force of his weight caught him off guard, and he slid fast. The rough fibers burned as they passed over his skin. He gritted his teeth during the short descent, then landed hard on his feet.

Catching his balance, he glanced around for Felix. The little devil had vanished. Even at a full sprint, Felix never could've made it completely out of sight. He'd at least see a retreating form. Something.

Felix's voice whispered behind him. "Not too shabby."

Kole wheeled around.

"The landin' was a little rough, but that speed." Felix gave a low whistle.

"Have you been there the whole time?"

Felix scrunched his nose. "Where else would I be? Thought ya could use a spotter."

"I'm fine." He rubbed his tender palms on his pants. "I can't believe we're doing this."

Felix folded his arms. One foot tapped the street. "Those masks aren't doin' any good in there on the walls like that. We need 'em and she won't let us have 'em. Why is that, ya think?"

"Maybe because they *are* actually broken. Either way, they're hers, and she can do with them as she pleases."

"C'mon, Blondie. They're just collectin' dust. You'd think she'd be dying ta get rid of 'em. But she's not, therefore," he lifted a finger with a flourish as he presented his conclusion, "they *do* actually work."

"That's one way to interpret it, I guess." Kole scratched his head. The more he thought it through, the more it *actually* made sense. "Still, broken or not, why are you so set on getting them?"

Felix shrugged. "I don't know about you, but I'm not dyin' by some volcanic fumes if I can help it."

"Is that the only reason?"

"Do *you* wanna die from fumes?"

"That's not what I'm talking about," Kole snapped. "You want to take a chance on masks that might not even work. *That* doesn't make sense. Tell me what's going on with you."

Felix's eyes narrowed.

"You know I'm not as stealthy as you." Kole teasingly stomped the ground, then jerked his chin to the second story window left ajar. "It'd be a shame if I tipped them off. One shout could ruin your mission."

"Stop it," Felix scolded. His eyes flicked up and down between Kole's threatening foot and his face. When he realized Kole really would wake the others, Felix held up his hands. "Okay, okay. I wanna get 'em for Vienna."

Kole stopped. A bit of pride puffed his chest now that he had some power over the situation. "Why?"

After running a hand through his curls, Felix sighed. "She didn't tell me 'bout you and the Souls and all this."

"And getting the masks will do... what exactly?"

"She doesn't trust me." Felix turned away. "If I do this, I reckon she'll remember how useful I am."

"She knows how useful you are."

"Ya don't understand, Blondie. Everyone says stealin's all I'm good at. Maybe it's true." He grimaced. "Reality is, the Liberation stands at two now. Me and Vienna." Felix kicked at the road. "Leo didn't even want me ta come, either, so I gotta prove ta Vienna I'm worthy of her confidence. Means I gotta be more than a thief. I gotta be tactical like Thomas, as strong as Griz and Boogy, and clever like Pipes."

Kole *knew* useless. He knew the pressure of living up to expectations. His only job and the sole reason he was on this mission in the first place was leveraging his connection with the Souls. Yet he couldn't even handle the pain it took to commune with them, let alone find and release them. "You really think stealing them is going to help?"

"Can't hurt." Felix shrugged. "So, what's it gonna be? Ya gonna rat me out?"

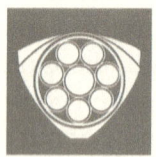

Squeezed into the shadow of a doorway three buildings away from the tavern, they scanned the street. No one had woken on their way out the window. Even if their companions cast a groggy glance to their bed, Felix and Kole had a solid head start.

The guards proved easy enough to dodge with a dwindled party. The two fit snugly between doorways and under carts. But it also made it more difficult to spot Shikar's Kayetan. Even with Felix taking the lead on their expedition, the Kayetan had the advantage.

When Felix shifted beside him, Kole took it as a sign to move. Kole rose, only to be stopped by a hand.

"Wait." Felix set a finger east.

At first, Kole thought the dark streak merely the shadow of a cloud sweeping over the city, but it moved too fast. The bulky form of Shikar's Kayetan floated along the cusp of the street.

"Wait for it ta make its round."

It zoomed past, a good hundred yards away, and continued without a glance toward the two crouched next to a storefront.

"Go," Felix pushed him into a run.

They made for the next building and slumped into the wall. Things stayed quiet, but the occasional snore drifted from an open window a few feet off. *Still in the clear.*

The light from a lantern appeared around the corner. Another guard. Following Felix's lead, Kole dove for a raised flowerbed and pressed his belly to the floor behind the cover of clay bricks. The light brightened. Footsteps moved unimpeded around the corner, and the lantern beamed a few feet from their forms. Kole glanced to Felix, whose teeth sparkled in the low glow. Palpable excitement. No mistaking Felix lived for this sort of thing. The feeling spread to Kole, and a smirk pulled at his mouth. The guard cleared his throat and moved on; none the wiser that two curfew-breakers hid at the level of his boots.

Clear, they both crept from the flowerbed and moved between houses, aiming for Shikar's dwelling at the end. The Kayetan circled around again, but they made it to the steps of the Yamani's tavern without being spotted.

Felix took out his sunstone dagger. "Stay here. Keep a look out."

"Why do you need a dagger?"

"In case things go sour."

"Do you really think you're going to do much damage to her with that? Stone on stone? What are you going to do, scratch her into submission? I thought we were going stealth, anyway. Stay quiet, and you won't need it."

"All right, all right, I get it. No reason ta be gettin' worked up, mate." He slipped the dagger back in his belt. "If her Kayetan comes, give a call like this." He puckered his lips in a shape Kole thought humanly impossible and imitated the sound of a cricket.

"Yeah, I can't do that." Kole pointed to his scarred lips, which could barely pucker without stretching the thick cord along his jaw. "How about I tap twice on the steps?"

"Knockin'?" Felix rolled his eyes. "For Soul's sake, Blondie. We ain't here for a nice visit. Ya gonna bring a loaf of bread ta the door, too? Might as well ring that blasted bell while you're at it."

"All right, bad plan. All you had to do was say no."

"Just whisper my name or somethin'. I'll keep an ear out."

Because that's discreet. "Fine," Kole said.

After a quick check down the backstreets, Felix crawled from their hidden spot, then rushed up the steps. He paused at the door Vienna had kicked in. Thankfully, in her rush to drive Kole and the others out of her house, Shikar had only pressed the cracked door against the frame, leaving a small gap near the bottom.

Felix lowered down and inched his way through, looking very much like a worm stranded on the soil after heavy rain. Somehow, he managed to wriggle in without too much noise.

Now all Kole could do was wait.

His eyes set hard on the alleys stretching from either side of the house. The Kayetan made another round. Two. Three. Still Felix hadn't returned. He tapped his foot impatiently in the dirt.

Another flash of shadow to his left as the Kayetan looped around the town once more. *What's taking him so long?* He wanted to go in after him or call out an angry whisper and tell him to stop taking his sweet time, but his lack of finesse would likely alert the guards. So he waited. Felix wanted trust, so that was exactly what Kole would give him.

Until something darted across the main street.

He brought his eyes to the slats of wood in the stairs for a better look.

The Kayetan stood in the middle of the road, apparently abandoning its normal path around the houses. *Dammit.* Maybe the shadow had heard Felix. Absurd. Nothing had come from the house, noise or otherwise.

As the demon floated toward Shikar's house, the outline of the creature grew clearer. Thin arms and legs. Scraggly. Nothing like Shikar's shadow.

Kole felt the blood drain from his face. *A different Kayetan.*

The raid had followed them to Cresthaven.

"Felix," he whispered, trying to keep quiet enough to stay hidden. When no response came, he dared a little louder.

The demon's head snapped to the stairs.

Kole scooted further into the shadows, but the Kayetan darted forward.

Before the creature reached him, another shadow shot from the alley — *Shikar's* — and he'd never been so grateful to see a Kayeten in his life. Shikar's demon locked claws with the intruder, giving Kole a chance to slip from the steps and yell a warning to Felix.

The crooked door fell to the side, landing with a crunch which rattled the windows. The time for subtlety had passed.

Felix rushed from the house; masks piled in his arms as he descended the stairs two at a time. "I thought I said whisper, Blondie."

Kole thrust a thumb over his shoulder at the battling shadows. "Plans have changed."

"Shit." Two masks slid from Felix's grip, but he left them. "Go. Hurry, before the rock lady gets up."

"Too late."

Shikar stood in the empty doorframe of her house, an annoyed glance to the remains of her front door that Felix had pushed aside, before focusing on them. "What in almighty Souls do you think—" Her eyes moved to the battling Kayetans in the street. Without a beat, she ran to the bell and rang the alarm.

The boys raced down the southern alley. Unsure if Felix planned to run or fight, Kole fumbled for the masks, collecting them one by one as they dropped from his friend's arms in the rush.

"How many did you take? We only need *five*."

"I grabbed extra in case she was tellin' the truth. Some of these are bound ta work."

More bells answered the first, and a chorus of screams pierced the air. Out of the corner of Kole's eye, a Kayetan pulled a man out of a nearby window. Before he could react, Felix ditched the masks and changed course for the demon. *Looks like we're switching to offense.*

Another scream behind. Kole whirled. A woman ran past the entry of the alley they'd just passed with another Kayetan hot on her heels. Following Felix's lead, Kole raced to help.

Kole rounded the corner, stopping at the sight of the woman, who'd fallen on hands and knees. She lifted a finger to redirect Kole's attention. He wheeled around. Only then, standing face to face with the shadowed stalker, he realized he had no weapon.

"Run," he called over his shoulder. He didn't need to kill it to keep the woman safe, just distract the thing long enough for her to escape.

The demon rose to its full height and flared its shadowed claws. Though they looked harmless, like a trail of rising smoke, one swipe could cut through flesh and bone.

Think, think. What can I use? Nothing. He had nothing. So he ran, counting on the demon to follow him down the main street instead of the woman, who had just found her feet.

A sense of victory swelled through him, if only for a moment, when the creature took the bait. His confidence quickly deflated. Kole had put himself in the same situation as last time, inserting himself as prey. Like before, his scars hindered his pace, allowing the creature to gain.

He needed a weapon. A way to retaliate until Azmali's guards answered the alarm. Kole ducked down another alley to buy himself a few seconds to think. A quick peek over his shoulder told him he'd be either dead or in the Kayetan's grasp if he didn't think of something soon.

Fire. Before Leo had developed the sunstone daggers, they'd used fire to keep Savairo's abominations at bay. *Where am I going to get a torch?*

When Kole passed under the light of a streetlamp, he smirked. An oil-fueled lamp would do nicely. But they hung too high, out of his grasp. He needed something to climb. With his tired stride, he hurried down the lane, hoping to find something to give him a boost. Then he spotted a bench snugged up against a shop window. Kole swerved toward it. *C'mon legs.* He pushed hard.

The bench less than a dozen paces off, a flicker of shadow rushed past his ear. He dove. A surge of wind riled his hair as the Kayetan's attack barely missed him. He landed hard on the cobbled road. Rolling over to his back, Kole peered up, wide-eyed, at the shadow standing over him. *Not again.*

Then, to his surprise, a bright light out of nowhere made him wince. Radiant heat swept by his head. Fire. Shikar's stone arm plunged a flaming torch into the shadow's chest. The Kayetan reeled back with a screech, then fled. The fire quelled the shadow, but it posed as a temporary solution. The demon would respawn at next dusk. Only the pierce of sunstone directly to the heart could vanquish a Kayetan.

The Yamani set her eyes on Kole. Her twitching mouth gave away her vexation, no doubt annoyed that he and Felix had broken in and stolen the masks. With a growl, she held out a hand and helped him to his feet. "Where is the slippery one?"

Kole squinted past the light of the torch down the alley where he'd last seen Felix. "He was fighting off a Kayetan down there."

A curt shake of her stone head. "I came from that way."

Shouts and clashing erupted down the street. Cresthaven guards slaughtered the raiders with their imbued weapons. The remaining shadows fled before they met their doom.

Shikar had made fast work of the intruders around her tavern, their ashen remains strewn across the street. Her own Kayetan swayed on the top step of her porch as if awaiting a command.

Guards and villagers but no Felix.

"He... must've left without me." Even as he said it, Kole knew it a lie. Felix wasn't the type to ditch a comrade. Unless his urge to please his sister got the better of him.

The Yamani swung her head side to side, eyes searching. "My masks are piled in the alley."

A pang of worry hit him. With the Kayetans dealt with, Felix should've returned. "He went after a Kayetan that was dragging a guy from the house over there."

"That man has been accounted for." Her jaw flexed as if chewing.

"Then...." The answer came to him, but he shoved it aside.

"Kole," Shikar snapped. Her tone held a grim note.

That single word confirmed what Kole had been dreading. "It's not possible. Not Felix." He was as slippery as they come. Shikar had only met him once, and even she knew that. Despite what he'd said, concern—no, a kindling flame of fear—urged his feet forward.

Kole pushed off to the edge of the road to get a good view. A sign. *Any* sign. There had to be another explanation. His ears faintly registered the sound of Shikar calling him back, but he ignored her. His head snapped back and forth down the alleys and streets. Each one empty. Then, as he rechecked the alleys with the stolen masks strewn over the cobbles, the moon peeked out from the clouds.

A glint on the road caught his eye. He ran for it. A sunstone dagger. He stared at the weapon, slack jawed. The bustle of guards tended to the spooked townspeople; Azmali's shouts carried on the wind. He cut it all out as he reached for the weapon. He turned the dagger over and over in his hand as if expecting some sort of symbol to manifest that would mark the blade as someone else's. None appeared. Denial only made the simmering dread in his gut boil over.

"They took him."

CHAPTER 15

Shikar sent her Kayetan to scan the area while she and Kole waited on the porch, their eyes alert for any lingering creatures from the raid.

"He can't be far. We can catch up to him." Kole gripped the wood post of the porch so hard, his nails dug into the grain.

"My Kayetan will bring back news. If he isn't hiding or ditched off somewhere, then you can search as you please."

Growling through gritted teeth, Kole watched helplessly as Azmali herded the concerned villagers, who'd snuck from their houses to catch a glimpse of the ruckus back to their quarters.

"Curfew is still in effect," she bellowed. Once the last of the townspeople complied and slunk away from the scene, Azmali assigned guards to assist the injured, then appointed a squad to account for any missing people. With her orders in motion, she finally took a studied look around. Her eyes landed on Kole, narrowed, and she marched over. "Shikar." She nodded in greeting. "I thank you for raising the alarm."

The Yamani answered with a single terse nod.

"I see you've met our guest." Azmali's pointed glare told Kole where she set blame for the attack. "I gave strict orders to stay at the inn until dawn."

"Yes." Too much worry clouded Kole's head to explain himself. All his energy lay with Felix. *Where is he?*

A rush of smoke billowed by Shikar, and Kole flinched, still on edge from the raid. But it was only Shikar's comrade. Out of the corner of his eye, Kole caught Azmali stiffen at the creature's arrival.

A moment passed in silence while Shikar communed. "No sign of your friend in the city."

Kole cursed.

"Friend?" Azmali asked. A tinge of fury edged her words. "You came with another?"

"Felix was with me when they raided," Kole explained. "We can't find him."

The Cresthaven leader frowned, more, it seemed, out of agitation than worry for Felix's whereabouts.

Shouts rippled down the street. Three silhouettes pushed through the guards, who'd drawn their weapons. By the outline alone, Kole recognized his mentor. Russé, Issira, and Vienna refused to heed the guards' warnings and forced past.

"Stand down," Azmali ordered.

Traveling past the remnants of the few vanquished Kayetans, Kole's companions hurried with new vigor to Shikar's stoop.

A wild expression overtook Vienna's face. "What the bloody hell happened? We've been looking everywhere for you two. When Issira heard the bell, we knew exactly where you went." Her eyes tightened, accusingly. "*And* what you were up to."

Russé prodded Kole, checking for injury. "Are you all right?"

"Fine." He shrugged him off.

Still, Russé prodded, only ceasing when he was convinced of Kole's safety.

"Kayetans raided the city," Shikar answered. "Brought here by your brothers, I presume."

"I'm not her brother," Kole muttered instinctively to the Yamani. "And we didn't *bring* them here."

"This is why I have a *curfew* in place. It was foolish to take you in," said Azmali. "They were right on your heels. No more favors to your Leo, whether I owe them or not."

"You don't know they were after us," Vienna snapped.

"You should've stayed with us, Kole," Russé whispered so only Kole could hear. "If you *must* go out, I will accompany you."

"You never would've entertained the idea," Kole snapped back. "We were only trying to help."

"And I'm only trying to keep you alive." Russé's voice turned aggressive. "What if you had been taken again? You got lucky the last time."

Thankfully, a guard came for Azmali, cutting Russé's lecture short.

"Stay where you are," Azmali commanded with a firm wave to Kole's group. "Your time in Cresthaven is over. I'll personally escort you out once we've cleaned up." A final hard stare at each of them, probably deciding how likely they were to abide her command. Then, apparently convinced, she turned and left.

Vienna's gaze passed Kole and drifted around the house. "Where is Felix?" She smirked at the Yamani. "Did you scare him away? Serves him right for trying to steal your masks."

Shikar's yellow eyes landed on Kole.

"Vienna...." Kole stepped forward. All eyes fell on him. He chewed his tongue, unable to say the words, partly because he didn't want to believe them himself.

Within a blink, her smile had faded. "Kole." Her voice quivered as she spoke, obviously deciphering Kole's bleak expression. "*Where is Felix?*"

"Gone." He held out the sunstone dagger. "He's gone."

Like in a trance, her fingers delicately wrapped around the hilt and inspected it. "How?"

"When the Kayetans came, we split up to help."

"You *split up?*" Resentment saturated her voice. "How could you let this happen?"

"I—"

She stalked toward him, venom in her eyes. "You *let* him sneak out."

Kole backed away. "I tried to talk him out of it, I swear."

"Why did you leave him? Why didn't you go after him?"

"I didn't know until he was already gone. I'm sorry."

She stopped, eyes heavy on him. The look she gave him... nothing could erase the disappointment, the anger, the betrayal oozing from not only her eyes, but every flex of her body. She stared at him as if he were Savairo himself. The look sent another punch to his already crushed spirit.

Vienna was right: he could've done more. If he had the power to go back one hour, he'd alert Issira—wake Vienna before Felix could slip a boot out the window. But in the moment, he'd been blinded by his will to help and only made a bigger mess.

"I have to go after him," she said.

An eerie silence came over the Souls. They shared an intimate look. Were they arguing?

"We'll all go after him," said Kole. "Shikar, can we use your Kayetan?"

"Kole," Russé's warning voice came behind him.

He pretended not to hear his mentor and kept his focus on the Yamani.

Shikar flicked her eyes to the Soul looming over Kole's shoulder, then back on him as she answered the question. "She is not going to be as helpful as you expect. These creatures recognize each other. If she gets too close, they will know she's not one of Savairo's."

"We just need a scout."

The Yamani tilted her head toward the road. "As does the city right now."

"Maybe Azmali will lend us some guards," Kole offered. "Some Cresthaven people might have been taken."

The Yamani shook her head. "If they are beyond city bounds, Azmali will not extend aid."

"Please. We need your help." At her sinking frown, Kole said, "I know we tried to steal from you. I'm sorry. You know what that ritual is like more than anyone. He can't go through it. If not for Felix, then to prevent creating another soldier in Savairo's army."

"Another Kayetan to raid the city." Vienna's mouth quivered. A tear broke free and streaked her freckled cheek. "Please. It's my brother. He's the reason there wasn't more casualties tonight."

Moonlight flashed off Shikar's jaw as she tightened it. A grunt, then, "Very well."

"How much time are we going to give this rescue mission?" asked Issira.

Vienna's head snapped to her. "As long as it takes to recover my brother."

Kole stepped out from Russé's looming presence behind him and turned to face him head on. Those soft blue eyes Kole had known all his childhood held a hardness. He knew the Soul wanted to continue toward Grayfall and leave this mess behind him. There had to be a way to convince him. It was *Felix* they were talking about, after all. The Felix who'd helped free Russé from Savairo's clutches when they'd last been in Socren.

Kole never blinked. He returned the same hard gaze at his mentor.

The old man's gaze faltered. His mouth lengthened to a hard line. "We can help for one night," said Russé. "After that, we need to move. If Savairo is indeed this close, we need to cover ground as soon as possible."

A small bit of worry lifted from Kole's chest, grateful.

Hand tight around the dagger, Vienna said, "If we don't find him tonight, I fear there will be nothing left to save."

CHAPTER 16

Piper knelt in the grass. Like hair on a scalp, the strands of grass poked from the soil in a distinct pattern, molded by the wind and sun. She trailed her finger around a small patch where the blades curved differently from the surrounding growth, leaning the wrong way. She grabbed the wad of grass and pulled.

A plug of earth popped up. Soil clung to the roots like someone had skinned the hill. She tossed it aside. Beneath lay a small hole. The scent of charred wood wafted to her nose. She scooped up a handful of ash and rubbed it between her fingers. Still warm. They'd taken care to hide the fire pit.

Clever Soul. But not clever enough.

She replaced the plug of grass, rotating it until it lined up how it should, then used the tip of her boot to pack the earth and blend the soft outline with the surrounding soil. No trace could remain in case Savairo actually left his experiments and decided to do his job for once. She'd pretend she had never seen it and hope Kole and his gang would use a bit more finesse when concealing their future camps. She could only do so much.

By the lingering temperature, she guessed they'd passed no more than a day ago. She'd taken every precaution to slow Savairo's progress. How could they be so close? Kole needed to pick up the pace if she hoped to keep up her charade.

Muffled cries carried over the hill—sounds she'd become familiar with. The Kayetans brought in another fresh batch of poor souls from their nightly raid. Piper ran the opposite direction, distancing herself from the noise. Though the pleas for mercy faded with each passing step, nothing spared her the torment plaguing her mind.

She knew their fate. She knew, yet she chose against interference. Aterus' threats of wiping out Socren rang clear in her head. *A few for many. A few for many.* Focusing on the words helped mask the screams. These few lives were the price paid for the thousands living in city. Still, it pained her—soured her stomach.

Then, a distinct voice rose over the hills: one that halted her retreat. "Get yer hands off me, ya filthy devils."

Felix?

Piper cursed. She turned back and crested the hill. The moment she spotted him, she dove to the cover of grass.

The Kayetans dropped a new body on the pile at the edge of Savairo's table. Felix landed on his face alongside the unconscious bodies of another man and woman. Fewer shadows had returned than Savairo had sent out. That would surely put the blood sorcerer in a rage and fuel his already unquenchable thirst to create more.

Felix jumped to his feet, spitting dirt from his mouth. Blood trickled from a freshly broken nose. "That's right. I'll kill every last one of ya. Bring it on." Despite his threat, he blinked and winced as he spoke, no doubt registering the pain of the fall.

Close your damn mouth, Piper begged. She shook her head. What were the odds the Kayetans brought back one of the few people who could derail her entire plan? *Felix* of all people. The 'stealth' of the Liberation had got himself captured.

Felix being here had to be the worst situation imageable. Not only because he sat in line to be turned and killed but because she knew the others ran hot on his trail. Vienna wouldn't let her brother be turned. If it were only Vienna, Piper might be able to handle it.

Knowing Kole's righteous ass, he'll be begging to go with her. Piper prayed the Souls took better care of their precious key than their campsites. It would be foolish for any one of them to seek out Savairo, especially in his spiraling, erratic state. They had no idea how dangerous he was with that vial of god's blood on his hip.

She needed to get Felix out of here. *And how do you suppose you're going to do that? Waltz up and take him?* A sure way to raise suspicion. Savairo already scrutinized her every move. Justifying freeing one? Impossible. Especially one he knew she had a connection to. What other option did she have?

Mid-incision in his current project, Savairo stopped and placed his tools down with shaking hands. He turned to Felix. After a once over, he fumed at the Kayetan. "You've brought the wrong child."

The shadow slunk away.

"Useless creature."

"Guess I'll be goin', then. Being the wrong one and all," Felix wheezed.

Savairo gauged him with narrow eyes. "I remember you, boy. One of my brother's lackeys." He smiled, studying his trophy. "What are you doing so far from home?"

"I could ask ya the same. Oh, wait, it's 'cause *we kicked yer ass out*." Felix spit in his face.

Savairo smeared it from his cheek. At the snap of his fingers, the Kayetans restrained Felix and pulled him to his knees. Red-faced, Savairo reached back to his belt for a vial of blood. He sipped it before returning it. Color came back to his face as he flexed his hands. A moment later, his tremors stilled. He bent down and placed a curled finger under Felix's chin. "This will be a pleasure." With the back of his hand, he smacked him across the face.

"I'm startin' ta feel unwelcome." Felix coughed up a mouthful of blood. "Gonna have ta... do better than that, mate."

"Oh, I will."

The Kayetans swirled around the hostage, engulfing him in smoke. Felix kicked and punched.

"No," Savairo commanded. His servants released Felix before he passed out. "I want this one awake." He pushed his current subject from the worktable, the body hitting the grass with a thud, then lifted Felix by his throat. Though he struggled, Savairo easily overpowered him. He strapped Felix down one limb at a time.

The vilest of curses shot through her head. Angering Savairo only made Felix more of a target. *Damn you, Felix. Why couldn't you have just laid low? Played unconscious like the others.*

She couldn't help him now. Not yet, at least. Once Savairo lost interest in his new toy, she could swoop in. But that meant....

Her stomach churned as Savairo picked up the blade.

Felix would have to go through the ritual. He'd have to survive. She thumbed the vial of Aterus' blood tucked in her pouch.

The first cut and he wailed.

Hold on, Felix. I can help you. I will. Just hold out. Stay alive.

She turned and crawled down the hill. The urge to run away consumed her. Against her instincts, she planted her feet and collapsed on the far side of the hill. His scream made her curl up, chin tucked into her knees, but she kept her ears free. If she didn't have the courage to watch, she'd force herself to listen. Leaving or staying meant no difference to Felix; he had no idea of her presence. But she vowed not to let him go through it alone. So she endured it.

Be brave, Felix. I'm with you.

His pain became hers. She silently screamed into her knees, fighting against the strengthening whispers inside, telling her she grew more like her father every day.

CHAPTER 17

An hour of searching the hills beyond the city limits and still no trace of Felix. Kole hoped Felix had somehow managed to shake his captor, but every passing minute confirmed the worst.

Vienna, who hand't so much as looked Kole's way since they left, walked side by side with Shikar at the front of the group. Anger showed in her every move; feet hard on the earth, fists clenched at her side, and her obvious avoidance of Kole. She blamed him.

Holding out a hand in warning to the group, Shikar paused on the hilltop, saying, "She is returning."

Kole followed her gaze. The darkness made it difficult to see much of anything save for the distant outline of the surrounding hills. Within a blink, the broad-shouldered Kayetan appeared at the Yamani's side. A brief moment, and she turned back to the group.

"No sign of the boy. But she spotted her kind a couple miles north."

"Like a camp?" asked Vienna. "Did she find Savairo?"

Shikar turned back to the shadow, who swayed at the question. "No camp. But there are too many Kayetans to sneak past without raising alarm."

"Useless creature." Vienna yanked two fistfuls of grass from the earth. "It can't scout. It couldn't keep him safe."

A rumble came from the Yamani. "We have spared many from unwelcome fates. No one can save everyone." She folded her arms. "The boy went out alone. His fate is his own."

"His own?" Vienna spun. "He *chose* to help protect your city, not to die."

"Death is inevitable for all mortals," Issira said coolly next to Kole.

Vienna snapped around, fuming. "*Not* today."

Kole placed a hand on Issira's elbow, sent her a look of caution, then stepped forward. "We'll find him, Vienna."

"We can only do so much." Russé stabbed his staff into the ground. "Locating him is one thing. Going in after him is another." Fingers wrapping tight around the gnarled staff, he said, "We can't risk a run in with Savairo."

"Then leave." Vienna balled her fists "I can handle this myself."

"That's insane," said Kole. "You can't take him and his Kayetans alone."

"What choice do I have?"

Silence permeated the group. All eyes set on Vienna. Finally, Russé spoke. "You don't know if your brother is there. Even if he is, there's a chance he's already gone."

"You want me to leave his corpse with Savairo?"

"All I'm saying is, don't risk it for nothing."

Vienna glared at Russé, her stoic face giving no hints as to what she was thinking. Two fingers to her mouth, she let out a low whistle. Fiona swooped down from the sky and landed on her outstretched arm. "Felix. Alive or dead. Go." With a thrust north and a flutter of wings, the hawk took off in pursuit of the command.

Kole watched after the bird long after her silhouette vanished into the dark sheet of night. Only when the swirling smoke of Shikar's Kayetan lifted a claw did he look away.

Shikar tilted her head at the creature. "Are you sure?"

"What is it saying?" asked Kole.

"Humans are near. Dozens."

Vienna peered at her. "I thought you said —"

"Not a camp," Shikar snapped. "Bodies?" She returned her attention to the Kayetan, who dipped its featureless face. "Corpses."

Kole and Vienna's eyes met. "Dumping ground," they said together.

"Felix might be in there." Vienna turned to the Kayetan. "Take me to it."

"What about Fiona?" asked Kole.

"Wait for her here."

"I'm going with you."

"Not by yourself," Russé said in a low voice.

"I will accompany them," Issira chimed in. Russé cast her a dark gaze, but she turned away and grabbed Vienna and Kole by the arms.

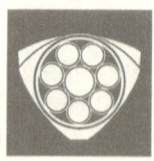

- 118 -

Shikar's Kayetan led them north. Kole knew they grew close when the smell hit his nose. Decay. But this odor differed from the basin Savairo used as his previous dumping ground Kole encountered at the mountain peak back in Socren. It lacked the caustic, chemical scent which had burned his lungs and nose with every breath. He tried to hold back a gag as they approached the rim. A glance to his left and right told him his companions possesed stronger stomachs. They didn't so much as wrinkle their noses.

This burial site—if it could even be called that—was smaller, only holding a dozen or so bodies, all naked. They'd been dumped in the valley between two hills with no attempt at concealment. *A rushed job.* It sent an eerie tingle down Kole's spine. All signs led to Savairo growing more unpredictable, which meant more danger for anyone in his path. He hoped Felix had yet to cross it.

Vienna didn't acknowledge either Issira or Kole. She walked straight into the pile, grabbing limp arms and pushing back shoulders to glimpse their faces. Knowing better than to argue, he followed her in, doing the same while the Blue Soul hung back and watched the horizon.

They worked silently. Every corpse received the same treatment. No matter how different their build to Felix, or how straight or blonde their hair, each one went through careful inspection. The cold, stiff flesh under his hands had taken on a grayish hue. Savairo's last dumping ground had been massive. Hundreds had perished, used and tossed aside for Savairo's ritual. Kole had been forced to hide in that pit after Savairo's prize Kayetan attacked Russé and meant to take Kole, too. Eight grueling hours he had sat there, waiting for dawn when the sun ensured the Kayetan couldn't return. Children, women, and men alike filled that dumpsite. He had sworn never to let Savairo make another one. Too late for that now. Did the sorcerer have more pits like this scattered around the plains? Though foolish to believe, Kole hoped the one he trudged through was the last.

Kole had only covered a quarter of the area, while Vienna had moved on to the second half. His strength had faded minutes ago. Aching arms and legs plagued him, but he pressed on, using the weight of his body to help flip the limp corpses.

He turned to the next corpse in line and froze. Small frame. Dark curls. Long scars, still slick with blood, ran along the outside arm. *Fresh from the ritual.* "Vienna?" He didn't bother to steady the quake in his voice.

She rushed over. Both hands, fingers shaking, went to the sides of her head.

Kole shook as he gripped the shoulder. Leaning into it, he let the weight of his own body take the brunt of the work. The head rolled into view. A breath escaped Kole's lips.

A beard. Not Felix.

Vienna cried out in relief and slid her head between her elbows. "Thank the Souls."

"Is everything all right?" Issira's voice came from the edge of the pile.

"Fine," Kole answered.

Vienna rose, staring at Kole straight on. "He's not here." Her lips thinned as if holding back a scream.

Kole nodded. "He's still out there. He's still...." He wanted to say *alive* but couldn't with good conscience. "We still have a chance."

"Okay," was all she said. Her eyes turned glassy and distant.

"Don't think on it. None of it will help."

Her stare moved to him and she nodded.

"I see shadows in the distance," Issira warned. "We should return to the others."

Kole went to leave, but Vienna caught his arm. He turned back.

The hardened gaze she'd held for the last hour softened to sadness.

"We'll find him," Kole said, forcing his tone to sound surer than he felt. *One way or another....*

She nodded.

As they both climbed from the pit, Issira beckoned them with a hand to follow.

"Wait," said Vienna. "We can't leave until we take care of this."

"You want to burn them?" asked Kole. "These aren't like the ones in the basin. They won't catch. They're too fresh."

"I know. But we can't leave them here. This is our chance to weaken Savairo. If we destroy his new Kayetans, the raids will stop until he can make more."

Issira squinted at her.

"There will also be fewer to track us. It's a win for us *and* the people of the plains."

The Soul cocked her head, as if considering her for a moment. "Make it quick, young one."

"Savairo or his Kayetans will see the flames before any of them burn. They'll be on us like bees to honey." Kole stopped himself and slumped his shoulders. He sounded like Russé. Though he agreed with Vienna, they might have to let Savairo have this. The bodies were just too fresh. "Unless... Issira?"

She perked up at her name.

Kole paused. The idea sounded mad, but it was worth a shot. "Can you dry them out?"

The side of the Soul's mouth lifted. "Clever. I can drain the moisture into the earth below."

"Mummify them? They'd catch like underbrush," said Vienna. "Do it."

Issira plucked back her silk sleeves and raised her hands to the bodies. "Be ready with the fire. We won't have much time once we start." When she closed her eyes, Kole understood what she meant.

A deep hum sprouted in the night air. The bodies glowed blue, illuminating the entire space between the hills. Crackling murmured over the corpses as the exposed bodies shrank. Vienna already had her flint and starter out, waiting for the signal. If the blue light hadn't caused notice, the fire would.

While Issira worked, Vienna uncorked a flask she'd had at her hip and poured its contents on the bodies near the edge of the pit. Oil. "Just in case," she said.

A faint scream echoed in the distance. Kayetans? It sounded off— deeper than the ones he'd heard before. But the hum of Issira's magic filled his ears, covering the sound. A wisp of shadow and Shikar's Kayetan formed next to him, a claw outstretched toward the hill.

"Hurry," said Kole. "I think something's coming."

Another moment, and the Soul lowered her hands. "Do it."

Vienna struck the flint and nurtured the flame until it burned steady on its own. It followed the stream of oil and caught the next body, spreading quicker than Kole imagined. Another sway from Shikar's Kayetan, and they knew they needed to move. It *had* to be enough.

They raced after the shadow, who led them back to meet with the others.

CHAPTER 18

Felix had stopped screaming a long time ago. Still, Piper didn't look back until the sound of Savairo pulling the body from the rock reached her ears. Peering out from the tall grass, she spotted Felix, bloodied and unconscious, dragging behind Savairo, who brought him to the bottom of a hill and rested him against the slope. He placed his subject's hands in two buckets to collect the remaining blood pouring from the incisions.

Piper had seen the sorcerer do this before. Now that his Kayetans had been perfected, Savairo chased a pipe dream of producing blood infused with the same benefits as Aterus'. An impossible task, but the mere thought of Savairo with an endless supply of Soul's blood made her shiver. No mercy kill for Felix. Usually a death left for the unlucky, Piper was glad for it, though, because it gave Felix a shot at survival. She just needed to get close enough.

Fate must have been on Felix's side, because a Kayetan appeared before Savairo. Whatever it conveyed to its master must've been ill news because Savairo slammed his fists into the blood-slicked table.

A burst of orange light sparked to Piper's left. The Kayetan standing watch over Felix disintegrated, leaving only a cloud of ash in its wake.

She cursed. The same thing had happened during the battle for Socren. Someone had found Savairo's dumpsite. Surely Kole and his friends had something to do with it. As far as she knew, Kole and the Liberation alone possessed the knowledge to kill Savairo's servants by the masses. *Not my idea of lying low.*

"Find them," Savairo roared. "I want the boy!"

The Kayetans dispersed.

The loss would put him into another rage. Blind rage, she hoped. For what she intended next, the angrier the better.

Savairo screamed into the night. Any sound of chirping crickets ceased. Even her own breath caught in her throat. Hands drenched in blood, he took up a knife and stomped to the fresh batch of bodies. While he snagged another victim from his pile, Vienna darted for Felix.

Just a few feet away, a whir rushed overhead, and she dove for cover behind a discarded corpse, hoping Savairo hadn't spotted her. Risking a peek, she noticed a familiar bird landing on Felix's shoulder. Fiona.

The hawk tilted her head back and forth, inspecting him. A scout. Did it mean they were near? The dumpsite must've been a distraction to pull Savairo away. Maybe Kole and his friends planned on emptying the camp before rescuing their comrade. She glanced at Savairo, who viciously stabbed the woman on his table and tore the scalpel down her side. Red light emanated from the blade as the sorcerer recited his incantation. A new fervor consumed him, as if he desperately needed to replace what he'd lost. Savairo wouldn't be lured away now. Nothing came between him and his ritual.

If Fiona spotted her — if Kole's entourage knew she was here, traveling with Savairo — it would cost Ohr more than Felix's life. Best for everyone if they thought her dead. And if the blasted bird didn't move, Felix would join that pile of corpses.

When Felix didn't respond to her pecks, the bird tugged a lock of hair from his head, leaving behind a small bald patch above his bloody ear, then flew off. After pausing a moment, ensuring Fiona was truly gone, Piper crawled over to Felix.

A dark, smoke-like vapor leaked from his wounds. She'd seen the aftermath of the ritual before. His shadow was leaving him. The moment it detached, there would be another Kayetan to deal with. She must work fast.

Felix's skin felt cold to the touch. Her heart skipped, dreading the worst, but she found a pulse, however faint, in his wrist. If she dragged him to safety, he'd be dead by the time she slipped from camp. Stabilizing him now meant risking herself. But the true question was the effect her 'help' would have on the Kayetan seeping from his body. No time to think it through.

She uncorked the vial of Aterus' blood and tipped it into his mouth. Taking his head in her hands, she tilted him back and closed his mouth, trying to activate his swallowing reflexes. It must've gone down because his fingers twitched. She allowed him one more drink, then pulled back. "Just enough for you to recover, Felix. Sorry, but the rest is meant for someone else."

Pocketing the vial, she watched the wounds tracing his skin. The blood stopped flowing. Scabs formed. A heartbeat strengthened in his wrist. *At least god's blood is good for something. Now to get you out.* She leaned around the hill just enough to catch sight of Savairo. Still preoccupied. The light from his spell doused his face in scarlet as if he'd bathed in the blood of his victim. Nowhere near finished. She hooked her arms under Felix's pits and dragged him a few yards. When she noticed what lay beneath him, she cursed and stumbled over her feet. The weight of Felix's body pinned her down.

A cloud of black smoke swelled from where Felix had been sitting. It rose, taking a humanoid shape. Even Felix's Kayetan held a mischievous air about it, with its hips shifted to one side and slinking shoulders. Long claws grew in place of fingers, and the shadow lifted up, head hung low toward Piper.

Surely Savairo would sense the completion of his new Kayetan. On edge, she waited for it to make the first move.

It swayed.

Felix groaned in her arms.

That was it. Felix remained alive, which meant he maintained power over his Kayetan. The creature had no link to Savairo until the host perished.

"You might just survive this after all," Piper whispered in his ear, then rolled him off to address the newly born Kayetan. "Take him."

The shadow leaned his hips to the side, reminiscent of how Felix responded when given a command he didn't want to follow. In that instant, the Kayetan seemed less intimidating. A pang of annoyance shot through her. "For bloody sake," she murmured under her breath. Jerking her head toward the hill, she continued, "Your master is dying. Save him or become a slave."

The Kayetan followed her gesture to Savairo, then turned back, its hip still cocked.

"This is you." Piper waved a hand over Felix. "I know you can feel it. Do as I say. Save him. Spare yourself a lifetime of servitude."

Leaning down, the shadow curled his arms around Felix and gently lifted him from Piper. She rose up to her elbows, trying to discern if the Kayetan truly understood her words, but the featureless face gave no hints.

"Find his sister. *Your* sister," she said. No sign of recognition. "Go!"

Before she huffed in frustration, the creature darted off, taking Felix with it.

CHAPTER 19

Russé charged at the trio as they returned, his staff pointed at the glow of fire over the distant hills. "What the hell is *that*?"

"We saw an opportunity, and we took it," Vienna snapped, nudging past him.

He stalked her. "More like carrying out a personal vendetta."

"We decided together," said Kole.

Russé stopped. Instead of looking his way, he directed his gaze to Issira. "You *helped* them?"

"I did."

They shared a look so intense, it sent a shiver down Kole's back. The Soul's were telepathically communicating—arguing, by their stern stances. He wondered what they were saying. Something they didn't want the group to hear. Curious, he probed the spot in his mind where Issira's presence still lingered. Once he entered, her words filled his head.

"*...has to learn we have his best interest in mind.*" A short pause, then, "*I wouldn't be so sure. I can feel the tension between the two of you. Mistrust is weakening his fortitude.*"

Kole pushed deeper, hoping to hear Russé's half of the conversation. A force weighed on him, stopping him in his tracks. Issira's eyes flicked to him in recognition. "*Our conversation is no longer a private matter.*"

Both Souls turned their chins to him. Kole severed the connection and turned away, feeling like a reprimanded child. They were in *his* head all the time. What was the difference if he did the same? If Issira really wanted to earn his trust, she wouldn't hold secret conversations about him.

Shikar stepped between them, killing the tension. A nod to her shadow swaying beside her, she said, "The fire attracted his Kayetans. They'll scout the area. If we linger here, we may be spotted."

By the flex of Russé's jaw, Kole could tell he left something unsaid. The anger in his voice turned stern. "Let's move."

They ran.

Shikar's Kayetan left as they moved out. With only a few hills under their belts, her shadow returned with news that made Shikar curse. "They've spotted us."

Vienna and the Yamani slowed. The Souls paused at their hesitation.

"I won't lure them back to Cresthaven." Shikar swiped the torch from her belt. A few strikes on her flint birthed a fire.

Vienna spun on her heel, a pulsing sunstone dagger poised in either hand. "Then let's cut them off." She nodded to the Yamani, and whatever quarrels they held against each other drifted aside.

Before the Souls could pose an argument, a rush of Kayetans whizzed over the hilltop.

When Vienna noticed Kole's empty hands, she handed off one of her daggers. He took it, then stepped close to Vienna.

The shadows blended in with the dark surroundings. The Kayetan's silhouettes moved too quickly to count. He didn't know how close they'd come until Vienna lunged in front of him, blocking a clawed hand from slicing his face. He stumbled back in shock.

As Vienna and Shikar fought off the incoming shadows, a hand caught Kole's back, keeping him on his feet. Russé. The Soul held him close. Another Kayetan darted forward. It dodged Vienna's advances, and swerved straight for Kole and Russé.

Smoking claws outstretched toward Kole. He cocked his arm to strike, but Russé yanked him back at the last second, placing himself in the creature's path.

The Kayetan stopped. Instead of attacking, it swirled back into the night.

The shadows that were locked in battle with Vienna and Shikar retreated with the others. Black smoke circled the group.

Issira grabbed Kole. She draped both her arms around him like a mama bear, yet it felt more like a restraint than an act of protection.

"What are they doing?" Vienna whipped her head back and forth as the Kayetans circled.

"A wall," Kole said. "They're corralling us."

"I will not be herded like some animal." At Shikar's command, the Yamani's shadow charged the smoking cyclone of Kayetans, but not a second later, the creature ricocheted back into the middle of the trap.

"What do they want?" Kole asked.

One enemy Kayetan shot inside from the left. It zoomed for Kole and Issira.

Shikar swatted it with her torch. A screech of pain echoed in the hills, then the Kayetan zipped back to its comrades, reintergrating into the swirling wall of shadow.

"You, Kole." Issira whispered in his ear. "They want you."

He swallowed. Had *he* been the target all along? *They took Felix in my place.*

Two Kayetans broke from the pack on opposite sides. When Shikar and Vienna raced to meet them, a third and fourth went to each of the Souls.

"They're distracting us," Russé announced. He stole the dagger from Kole's hand and stabbed one in the heart. Knowing what came next, he shielded his eyes as the shadow caught fire and disintegrated into a puff of ash. Vienna did the same to hers. "They want Kole."

Another retreat.

The wall thinned with the two deaths. At least three remained.

"They can't attack all of us at once." Vienna passed her brother's blade to Shikar. "We want them dead."

The dagger resembled a toothpick in the Yamani's grasp. Still, she wielded deftly.

Vienna peered over her shoulder. "Russé?"

"On your signal." Russé turned back to Kole, stuck in Issira's grip. "Hold still."

Before Kole could question him, Russé jammed the base of his staff into the soil. The wood sprouted into thin, rope-like roots. They encapsulated Kole and Issira. A cage of protection. Each end drilled through the earth, anchoring itself.

Kole wriggled from the Blue Soul's hold and clutched the wooden bars of his enclosure. Breaths came quick as his friends dashed to the Kayetan wall all at once.

The barrier dispersed. Four Kayetans darted forward. Three went for Russé, Vienna, and Shikar. The last came for Kole.

A shadow slipped though the gaps in the roots and materialized between him and Issira.

Kole swiped a fist at it, knowing full well its ineffectiveness.

"Down. Grab a hold of me." Issira commanded into his mind.

On the extension of his punch, he dropped to the ground, his body falling through the Kayetan's form, and landed by her feet. Blue light pulsed above. He peered up. An angry storm cloud blossomed high in the night sky.

Claws curled around his waist. Just before the creature dragged him away, Kole threw his hands around Issira's bare ankles.

"Do not be scared. I won't hurt you."

Despite her promise, he tensed.

The Kayetan wrenched at him, attempting to pull him free.

His grip strayed—loosened by the second. "Issira!" He looked over his shoulder at the shadow.

Like an answer to his call, a flash of light wreaked havoc on his eyes, and a deafening crack left his head humming. The hold on his torso vanished, and Kole's body hit the ground. The scent of singed grass tickled his nose. His vision regulated first. He scrambled up, taking in the black, star-like shape branded into the earth. The center point glowed white, slowly fading as it cooled. The cage, the Kayetan—both annihilated by the bolt of lightning. *Guess that's another way to kill a Kayetan.*

Still his ears rang. Muffled voices came, but he couldn't make out clear sounds. The hill stood empty save for him and his comrades.

Ash piled at Vienna's feet. She cupped her hands around her ears. It seemed the crack of lightning had jarred more than just Kole's eardrums.

Kole took Issira's outstretched hand and stood. Her touch settled his inner ear. One by one, she brushed a hand over the others, who shook their heads and wriggled their jaws at her touch.

Shikar eyed Issira, suspicion in her gaze. Her own Kayetan swayed safely by her side. "Best not to linger. More may be out there."

As they walked, Kole maneuvered to Vienna's side. "Are you all right?"

"Fine." She brushed off the question with a hand. "I didn't know she could do that."

"The healing or calling that bolt?"

"Both. I wonder what else she has up her sleeves."

"Probably a lot more than she'll let on."

The familiar call of a hawk cut the quiet night. Vienna perked up, then ran forward, arm outstretched for her to land. The hawk swooped down. Talons wrapped around her forearm. Something dark lay in the bird's beak.

"It's his hair," Vienna said. But as she touched it, a smear of blood rubbed off on her fingers. She turned to the group. Her contorted face gave away her next words. "He's dead."

Reality hit Kole hard in the gut. Unbelievable. He'd seen him alive and well only hours ago. It wasn't real—couldn't be. "Maybe Fiona's wrong."

Her fingers closed around the bloody hair. "She's not."

"Vienna," he started, putting a hand on her shoulder.

"Don't." She shrugged him off and stalked away.

He turned to the Souls. "Isn't there something you can do?"

"What would you have us do, Kole?" With his staff obliterated by the lightning strike, Russé rested a hand on his hip.

"Anything."

"Death cannot be fixed, young one." The Blue Soul's sugary tone irritated him. Sad or angry, she sounded the same. A sweet note unfit for the grim tidings. Almost cruel.

"You all can stay in my house tonight. I'll sneak you past Azmali if I must." Kole sensed a note of sadness in the Yamani's tone. The stone woman knew better than anyone of Felix's fate.

In a trance, Kole followed the group. The last mile back to Cresthaven felt like an eternity. No one spoke until they reached the top of the hill overlooking the clay buildings.

Shikar halted. "A Kayetan stands in the road."

Kole's body went rigid.

They all focused on the figure standing in the middle of the street. The Kayetan swayed back and forth, its arms wrapped around a human form. At first, he thought Savairo had sent out another raid party. Shikar's stiff stance told him she shared a similar concern. But the Kayetan didn't move.

With a swift command, Shikar's Kayetan darted for it.

Still, the odd shadow stayed rooted.

While Kole and the others waited for Shikar's creature to scope out the stranger, Vienna charged.

"Wait," Kole called after her. If she heard him, she ignored it. He bounded after.

Thuds came up behind him. Passed him. The Souls and Shikar easily overtook Kole. Issira, though, slowed her pace and matched his tempo while the others rushed ahead to Vienna. A hint of annoyance rolled through him. Even now he needed a babysitter.

Closing in on the strange Kayetan, Vienna slowed. She let out a rage-filled cry, which ripped through the empty streets as she sprinted to the shadow, blade raised high.

Kole finally got close enough to recognize the body in the Kayetan's arms.

Felix.

His naked body held a sheen. It glinted red. Blood. He'd been turned.

Kole pushed his feet faster, but he stumbled. Issira snagged and righted him in one swift motion. As he caught up to the scene, Vienna lunged at the Kayetan holding her brother's body.

It zoomed away. Felix's limbs violently jerked at the unnatural speed. The Kayetan's claws wrapped tighter around the body when Vienna bounded after it.

Her slashes came wild, unlike the graceful and calculated moves he'd seen her use during the battle of Socren. Madness fueled her. Kole foresaw her next attack before she made it.

The Kayetan dodged with a moment to spare. The creature didn't go far. It had every opportunity to flee but chose to stay on the road. Subtle clues gave away its intentions: the tightened grip around Felix, no retaliation, no hostility against Shikar's Kayetan, who trailed behind it. It looked like the creature was protecting Felix.

"Stop," Shikar boomed.

Vienna tripped over her own feet and landed on the dirt road. She lifted to her elbows. The Yamani's voice must've triggered something in her brain, because she hesitated.

Shikar stepped between her and the Kayetan. "It means no harm."

"No harm? It's carrying my brother's bloodied body!" In a blink, Vienna jumped to her feet and lurched at the shadow.

Shikar caught her arm mid-strike, restraining her. A nod to her Kayetan and she said, "It thinks you are trying to hurt him."

"It killed him." She dropped to her knees. Cheeks streaked, she yelled, "Put him down. Give me my brother."

After a brief silence between the Kayetans, the stranger laid Felix on the ground and stepped away.

"Kill it," Vienna begged.

"Go," Shikar commanded.

Vienna flailed against her restraints, screaming as both Kayetans faded into the night. She kicked at Shikar, who finally released her iron grip. While cursing the Yamani, she crawled to her brother and collapsed over his body.

More than anything Kole wanted to rush over, but the whole scene left him stunned. Vienna's sobs filled his soul, weighing on his already inflated guilt. He stared at the long incision trailing over Felix's hip and leg. They were too late. He was gone.

Billowing silk brushed Kole's arm as Issira stepped from Kole's side. She knelt next to Vienna and placed one hand on her back, while setting the other on Felix's bare chest.

Vienna stiffened at her intrusion.

"His heart still beats," said Issira.

She glanced at the Soul, eyes swollen and desperate. "Can you help him?"

"Yes, but... it will take most of my reservoir." Her last words were meant for Russé — not a request, a statement.

Kole snuck a glance at Russé, whose grinding jaw gave away his true feelings as blue light glowed under Issira's hands. Giving up her power might cause them trouble down the road. The alternative, though... too horrific for Kole to entertain.

The dull glow spread down the incisions like a downpour filling a dried riverbed. The streams of her power thinned as the sliced skin closed in on itself, stitching together. A faint scar remained.

Issira removed her hands, her back rising and falling with heavy breaths. "He will live."

The words made Kole's body shake. He grabbed the sides of his head as Vienna gathered her brother in a tight embrace.

No one was safe. Not Felix. Not Cresthaven. Not the Souls. Not even himself. No matter how careful or strong, there was no escaping the danger surrounding their mission. One had been saved today. Countless others hadn't been so lucky. And what of Piper? If Savairo had turned Felix this quickly, could he hold out hope for *her*? He knew the answer before he posed the question. Piper had long passed. A Kayetan herself. The only sure way to end this was killing Savairo. But how could they do that with two Souls drained of power?

"What is that?" Vienna asked.

Kole followed her pointed finger to a black wisp, flicking like a flame from Felix's wrist. A shadow?

After gentle touch over the spot, Issira said, "This is not my doing. Something from the ritual, perhaps?"

"Nothing I've seen," offered Shikar. When curious stares appeared in the nearby windows, she bent and gathered Felix in her arms as easily as a bear would a cub. "Let's get him inside. He can use my bed."

Azmali and a small squadron stood post at Shikar's tavern.

"Where have you — what happened?" Azmali's hardened brows lifted at the sight of Felix's bloodied body.

"He's been turned," Shikar said at Kole and the others' silence.

Azmali frowned. "You found him? The blood sorcerer?"

"No. The boy's Kayetan brought him here."

"What about the others? We have two missing."

"I'm sorry, Lady Azmali, but I cannot discuss this with you now. The boy needs my attention." Without another word, Shikar ascended the steps to her house and disappeared inside, Vienna close on her heels.

"Russé," The Cresthaven leader's voice turned stern. "You can't stay here."

"Very well," he nodded. "We'll gather our things and be on our way."

"No need. My guards have brought your goods from the inn. I will give you enough time to pack, then I will personally escort you out. Until then, you will be closely watched." She pointed a hand to her squadron, which moved to form a barricade around the tavern. "One hour."

They all filed into the small house. The Souls stayed in the front room, which acted as a tavern, while Kole found Vienna and Shikar in the backroom. Sparsely furnished with a bed in the corner, a table at its side, and a single cabinet shoved against the far wall, the room appeared cramped for such a large Yamani.

Shikar laid Felix on the bed, then left the room, either unaware or indifferent to the blood from his closed wounds smearing her blanket. Vienna sat on the mattress, a finger brushing her brother's plastered curls from his face.

Upon returning, the Yamani handed Kole a bucket of water and a rag. "Clean him up," she said, then joined the Souls in the tavern.

Kole set the bucket on the bed. As he wrung the extra water from the rag, Vienna grasped his wrist. He glanced up at her bloodshot gaze. Nothing shone behind them, like looking into the face of a sleepwalker.

"I'll do it." She slid the rag from his open hand and wiped Felix's face clean. The clear water took on a pink hue as she worked.

Thinking it best to give her some privacy, he made his way to join the others. Shikar's voice, low and sharp, drifted to his ears as he passed through the doorframe.

"You've almost lost one. Do you want to risk another?"

"We have no choice. Our business requires it," came Russé.

Kole peeked out. The Souls sat with their backs to the door. The wood floor creaked as the Yamani rounded the table with two mugs of amber liquid. She placed them before the Souls, then grabbed a full bottle for herself. After a long drink, she wiped her lips and leaned back in her chair. "What sort of business requires three children to suffer a blackened lung? You know what the ash does to fleshkind, yet you are still determined to travel there."

"The masks will help them," said Russé.

"A mask can only do so much. Prolonged exposure—anything more than a few days—will weigh on their health. If you think ash and fumes are the only dangers, you are sorely mistaken."

"What do you know?"

"A lot more than you." Another chug. She slammed the bottle on the table. Her yellow eyes trailed back and forth between the Souls as if gauging them. "There are monsters there. They crave flesh and bone. You will be hunted and slaughtered before you reach the city wall."

Russé thumbed the glass handle. "We can handle it."

"Is that right?"

Silence.

Wood groaned as Shikar leaned into the table. "You need a guide."

"Are you willing?" Issira's voice made the glass around the bar hum.

"No." Shikar rocked back in her chair, her stone arms scraping as they folded across her chest. "I will not voluntarily walk into that cursed land without incentive."

"We have nothing to offer," said Issira.

"Now see. I think you do, sorceress."

Issira moved her hands to her lap. "We don't—"

"Don't play me for a fool." The legs of Shikar's chair slammed into the floor as she leaned in. "I saw your call to the skies. What you did to the boy's wounds. And you two smell different from the others." Her nose twitched. "You *and* the burned one you travel with." Her head turned to the door.

Kole leaned behind the safety of the doorframe, hoping she hadn't seen him. He *smelled* different? What did that mean?

"Less human, that one," she continued. "A mixed breed. But not an offspring of yours. Something different than I've encountered before."

Goren had mentioned the Yamani's keen sense of smell. He thought it meant they could track things, similar to a hunter following a trail. Could she really tell they were Souls by their scent? Maybe not Souls. She never said that. But different than human. Even *he* held a different odor. Could she smell the Souls in his head? He risked another peek.

"Leave Kole out of this," Russé growled.

The Yamani's lips ground together.

Issira touched Russé's forearm, and he relaxed. She turned to the Yamani, whose mouth had upturned to a grin. "What do you seek?"

"A favor." Shikar grabbed Russé's untouched mug and downed it. She wiped the dripping alcohol from her chin. "Of the magical kind."

"She's spent of magic," Russé protested.

"Then get it back."

Russé and Issira tilted their heads toward each other. Kole saw the chance and took it. After a few times, he'd gotten used to connecting his mind with hers. This time, when he found her walls, they crumbled on contact. Too easy. Maybe her drained power had weakened the barrier between their minds. As he entered, though, her consciousness enveloped him like a warm blanket. Not a weakened barrier at all. An invitation.

Unlike the time before, he heard both sides of the conversation.

"*Should we trust her?*" Russé's voice came.

"*I don't know if we have a choice. We must protect the boy at all costs. If it means entering a deal with — *"

"*We don't have the means to uphold this kind of deal. Even if we did, we can't afford to spare it on mortal issues.*"

"*Mortals are the only help we have at the moment.*"

Silence from Russé.

"*Do you know of the curse? The beasts of which she speaks in the city?*" Issira asked.

"*No. I would have easily played it off as a ruse to manipulate us, but Goren spoke of cursed beasts, too. Rumors. Nothing concrete. They may be something we can handle. Or it could prove the undoing of my pride.*"

"*For Kole's safety, I think we should accept.*"

"*Figure out what she wants first.*"

Issira's voice broke the silence in the bar. "What sort of favor do you have in mind?"

A sadness weighed on Shikar's eyes. "I'll know it when I see it. Don't worry, sorceress. It won't be beyond what I've already seen. Promise."

By the deepened arch of Russé's back alone, Kole could read his skepticism. "A favor for *safe* passage to the volcano." He held out a hand.

"Safely *to* the volcano. Yes." She closed her hand over his, her fingers curling halfway up his forearm. "What of the others? The boy and his sister? They will slow us down, but I would advise against leaving them. They need protection."

"I doubt Azmali will let them stay. She wants us out."

"Aye," the Yamani agreed.

"Can you ensure their safety if they come with us?" asked Russé, turning in his seat toward the door. Kole hid behind the wall again, ear pressed to the clay, straining to listen.

"The extra Kayetan will be useful. The boy.... It depends on how he takes it when he wakes. His mind may be broken. He will need looking after."

Back against the wall, Kole stared at Vienna, who hunched over her brother's chest, scrubbing the dirt from his skin. No way she'd leave him. For good reason.

They never should've come. Death followed him and the Souls on their journey. Best if they both returned to Socren and forgot about him. At least they'd be safe there. Safer than traveling to a cursed city, home to flesh-eating beasts, as Shikar claimed.

Kole let his worry for Felix and Vienna reach Issira. Instead of responding directly to him, she spoke aloud.

"Let Vienna decide for them both. She is his guardian now."

Anger bloomed in Kole's gut. That wasn't what he meant, and Issira knew it. *"Send them back. Russé will heed your word over mine,"* Kole urged through his connection. *"We have to spare them from any more danger."* In his anger, he pounded a fist on the doorframe.

Vienna looked up at the sound, curiosity in her swollen eyes. Kole held Vienna's gaze as Issira's voice came to him once more.

"Calm yourself, young one. Your head is thinking in the moment. Felix will not wake the same as he was before. Who best to guide him through this change than one who has lived through it herself? Shikar is the key to his sanity and our only way to the city." With that, she severed their connection.

He swallowed.

"Are you all right?" Vienna wrung the rust-colored water from the rag, eyes lingering on Kole. When he remained silent, she placed the damp cloth on Felix's stomach and leaned in enough to peer out the door. Her lips pursed. "They're deciding what to do with us, aren't they?"

Kole nodded.

"They want us to leave."

"They want *you* to decide," Kole corrected.

"My duty is to aid you and the Souls." Vienna grabbed the rag again and wiped the dried blood from Felix's neck.

"Forget Leo." Kole pushed from the wall. "He doesn't understand what aiding us means."

"He does. That's why he handpicked me. *I* was the careless one." She scrubbed harder at a stubborn patch of blood. "I didn't want to be parted from Felix, so I convinced Leo to let him come along." New tears fell down her cheeks, but her eyes stayed firm on her work. "And look what it's done. My selfishness. My secrecy. If I'd only been honest, he wouldn't have felt the need to prove himself to me."

Kole fiddled with the hem of his shirt in the silence.

Finally, Vienna looked up at him. "I'm sorry for blaming you."

"It's all ri—"

"No, it's not. This isn't your fault. I never should've put this on you." She sighed and shook her head. "I was just angry. I still am." She slumped her head. "This is my fault."

He crossed the room to her side and laid a hand on hers, stopping the scrubbing which had left Felix's skin an angry red. When her hand tensed beneath his, he released her and lowered onto the bed. "Felix acted on his own. There was no talking him down. You know how he is. Tell him he can't do something, and he'll prove you wrong. It's no one's fault, Vienna. Only Savairo's. *He* did this to him. Not you."

Her jaw locked. She sat back from Felix and hugged her knees. "I don't know what to do. How do I fix this?"

Seeing her this way, weak and vulnerable, drove his frustration over the edge. Issira was right. How much help could Leo offer if Vienna took her brother back to the city? Felix needed guidance, and Shikar was the only one with experience.

"Shikar," he told her. "She can't fix it, but she's been through it. She'll know what's to come—what to expect—better than we do. It's his best shot."

Her eyes, brimmed with tears, found his. "I want my Felix back."

"I know." The pain in her gaze struck him like a dagger through the chest. He wished to scoop her up and hold her until all the grief faded away. But the courage he'd need to do such a thing hid too deep within him—out of reach. Instead, he inhaled a shaking breath and let it go. "We all do."

CHAPTER 20

Within an hour, Kole and the others had packed one of Shikar's old carts with supplies: food, blankets, cookware, tools, weapons, and anything else they might need for their journey to the volcano. The Yamani said it'd be a week's travel if they kept a hard pace—a feat Kole could only manage with the addition of a cart. If they only brought it for him, he'd be embarrassed, but the cart was necessary for Felix, too. And supplies. Something Kole and Russé hadn't worried about until now. A bigger group forced them to carry more. Despite their size, the ramblers only held so much.

Kole helped Russé lay canvas over the frame they'd constructed out of wood scraps to act as a makeshift cover, giving him a place to escape the sun when his body overheated. Satisfied with its sturdiness, Kole stacked blankets in the middle of the covered wagon for Felix to rest on until he recovered. A covered space best suited them both. They headed to the Ashland Plains, after all.

As Kole finished rolling out the last layer, Shikar turned the corner of the far road with a stout donkey at her side. The sheer size of the Yamani made the animal appear no bigger than a foal, despite its shoulder reaching the top of the cart.

"Who's this?" Vienna rounded the wagon.

Kole crawled from the cramped space and sat on the ledge, letting his legs dangle over the edge.

"Old Jin." Shikar steered the donkey around, turning its rump to the cart.

The speckled, dulling coat and protruding shoulders disclosed the donkey's age. By the way Shikar guided it, he guessed the beast was partially blind.

"She can pull this thing?" he asked.

With a single hand, Shikar lifted the front of the cart and rolled it to the animal. Kole braced himself on the sides before the steep angle sent him rolling out the back end. She let it drop with a thud, a smirk on her face as Kole lurched forward. "She'd old but strong."

Vienna ran a hand down the donkey's nose. "Of course she is," she cooed. For a brief moment, the pain in her face dissolved. She even smiled as the old animal nuzzled her palm in search of food.

It set a warmth in Kole's stomach. He forced back a smile.

"All set?" Russé walked down the steps with an unconscious Felix in his arms.

With a final tug, Shikar secured Old Jin to the yoke. "As ready as we can be."

The Soul laid Felix on the bedding Kole had set up.

Vienna hurried to her brother's side and pulled a blanket over his sweat-drenched body. "Any change?"

"Not since the fever," Issira answered behind them. "He's burning hotter by the hour."

"And that's how it'll be until the boy decides to fight it off," said Shikar. "Give him a day or two. He'll come around. You should be more worried about the nightmares to come."

"Nightmares?" Vienna asked.

The Yamani grunted, then stalked toward the house. "I better bring something to tie him down."

With Azmali and four guards as their escort, they returned to the river, where their ramblers waited. The guards gawked as Russé woke the trees. No exchange of farewells. No wish of safe travels or blessings. Azmali stood tense while Kole and his companions mounted the roots and set on their way toward the distant hills. Despite her coldness, Azmali watched their departure until her form blended with the night. At first, Kole assumed she sought to see them safely away from Cresthaven. More likely, though, she waited to ensure they never returned.

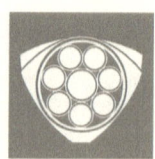

After sixteen grueling hours of travel, and Kole endlessly switching between rambler, walking, and the cart, the bottom of the sun dipped below the horizon. Kole had never been so thankful for a sunset in all his life. Even with several long rests in the cart, squeezed up next to Felix's feet, his body ached. Every muscle burned, every joint throbbed, and his delicate skin, protected from sunburn by a layer of fabric, felt feverish from overexertion.

Fiona, who Vienna had sent out a few minutes prior in search of a campsite, returned and led them to a deep valley between a set of hills. While everyone unloaded the bed rolls and food from the cart, Kole plopped down to the cold grass, his breath coming quick and shallow.

A pair of feet stopped next to him, and a waterskin lowered into view. No need to look up to know it was Russé. The Soul had kept a constant eye on him all day.

"You're dehydrated."

"Nothing gets by you," Kole said sourly.

"How are you feeling?"

"Like I got trampled by a rambler."

Russé shifted from foot to foot, then settled against his newly made staff. The rambler had given one of its branches willingly to Russé, who'd shaped it in the exact form of its obliterated predecessor. He could tell the Soul wanted to talk, but Kole wasn't in the mood. When he refused the waterskin, Russé wedged it into the tall grass beside him.

Kole's thirst overpowered his stubbornness. With a dejected sigh, he swiped the container and guzzled its contents. The water passed his throat, but a dryness remained. No amount of liquid seemed to quench his thirst.

"I want to show you something." Russé walked off before Kole could decline.

Begrudgingly, Kole waddled in pursuit, rubbing the tender patch on his upper back where the tree bark had left him raw from leaning against it.

"You need to learn how to anchor a rambler."

"Don't you think I need to be able to steer one first?" He gave Russé a pointed look. "*Without* your help?"

"You have that knowledge. Saplings may be easier to gain control and trust, but it's all the same. Give them time. They are gentle giants. They'll come around on their own."

"Not soon enough," Kole muttered under his breath.

Russé pursed his lips but ignored the comment. "If you master this, you're one step closer to gaining trust. Place your hand on the root."

He hesitated. "What's the point? We're not in Solpate anymore and the ramblers are... gone. There's no need for shepherds or apprentices. Just do what you've been doing and control it for me."

"I haven't been controlling them for you, Kole. I only tell them to listen. Everything else has come from you." Russé sighed, closed his eyes for a moment, then returned his attention to Kole. "I want you to finish learning. I know there's no official title to work for any longer, but is that all you wanted when you entered the trials?"

The Shepherd's Trials seemed so long ago. Becoming a shepherd had been his only goal for as long as he remembered. His and Niko's. They had lived it. Kole had longed to connect with the magic of the forest, but the forest had perished. If not from the destruction of the Black Wall, then from the waning magic. Sure, technically it still lived, but not in the way it did before. Not truly alive. *The great forest rooted forever? It may as well be dead.* Kole jabbed the toe of his boot at the ground.

"It wasn't for the title," Kole confessed. "It's just now... after everything...."

"There may come a time when you need them."

He glanced up at Russé, catching the underlying meaning. Moving his focus back to the rambler, he placed his scarred palm upon a tree root as instructed, then closed his eyes.

"Rooting takes more finesse than awakening. You need to calm the heart of the rambler. Let me show you." Russé laid his hand over Kole's on the root.

An energy deep within the rambler revealed itself to Kole. The Soul had summoned it—let Kole feel what he couldn't on his own. It felt... like spring. The same feeling that bubbled in Kole's core when he spotted the first sign of green on the edge of winter.

"Do you have hold of it? Can you feel it?"

"Yes."

Russé took his hand away. "To anchor an awakened rambler, you must settle its spirit. Bring it to dormancy. Will it to hide its roots." He stepped back and waved Kole to try it on his own.

Kole flexed his fingers on the soft bark, then closed his eyes. *Make it sleep.* He channeled his thoughts and willed the tree to rest. When nothing happened, he changed tactics and asked the rambler to drive its roots into the ground. After all, that *was* the first step to grounding it. Maybe if he could get the tree into his desired position it'd be easier to quell the thing. But the tree only stomped, more restless than before.

"Gently, Kole. Tell it to sleep."

"I did," he snapped back. "It's not listening." Kole pulled his hand away before his frustrations seeped into the rambler. "Did you have to practice to get them to follow your command?"

Russé cocked his head.

"That's what I thought." Kole huffed. "Telling them doesn't work for me the way it does for you because... because — well, you're the one who created them. They're a part of you in a way, right?"

"I suppose so."

"They don't understand me. It's like...." Kole searched for the right words. "We have a language barrier."

Those kind blue eyes softened. "Worry not. It will come to you with practice." When the Soul reached for the rambler to anchor it, Kole grabbed his hand.

"Wait." That language barrier thought gave him an idea. "Let me try something else."

Russé gave him some space.

Again, Kole placed his hand on the soil-crusted root. He thought back to what he felt before — the energy of the awakened rambler. Like spring. If awake meant spring, dormant meant winter. He focused his thoughts to autumn. Pushed the rambler to see falling leaves of color — the creeping chill of winter winds coursing through empty branches. The vigorous energy of the rambler shifted to drowsiness.

The root under his hand twitched.

"That's it. Keep strong," Russé said.

Kole focused on the changing season. Imagined the dew on the grass hardening. Frost-covered earth. The first powder of snow, light and pillowy.

The root slid from his hand.

Kole opened his eyes and stepped back in awe.

All at once, the rambler drove its tendrils into the earth. The trunk lowered down and nestled atop the grass.

He'd done it. Anchored the behemoth.

"Very good. How did you do it?"

"I made it feel the seasons."

Russé gave a subtle smile. "Interesting." His eyes twinkled. "I want you to practice. It'll be easier next time. From now on, this will be your nightly duty. Can you handle it?"

Eyeing the second rambler, Kole nodded. The work left him even more fatigued, but an old spark flared inside him — hooked him. He allowed himself this moment of accomplishment. This pride.

"One is enough for a first try. Go get some food." Russé waved him off as he anchored the other rambler.

As the others bustled around camp, Kole plopped to the cold grass.

The hawk brought back a small rabbit, fresh from the hunt. Vienna left the head aside for the bird to pick at, then cleaned the animal and added it to the simmering pot.

One by one, the rest of the group settled by the fire.

"Fish head?" The Yamani held a murky jar toward him.

Kole and Vienna promptly declined. Even the Souls refused, opting to wait for a small share of Fiona's catch.

The acidic scent of vinegar hit Kole's nose as Shikar twisted the lid open. She wedged two giant stone fingers into the jar, plucked out a fish head, whose black eyes shone a silver-green in the firelight. When she popped it in her mouth, the crunch of bones made Kole gag. He lost his appetite for rabbit and grabbed a loaf of bread instead.

Finishing a bite, he asked, "Do all Yamani eat like you?"

"Do they eat like me?" Shikar smiled between chews. "Spit it out, lad. No need to be shy."

"Do they eat food?"

"Ah, you want to know why I don't eat rocks."

Kole peered at Vienna, who tended the pot of rabbit stew bubbling over the fire. She paused, mid-stir. "Yamani eat rocks?"

"They do if they want to keep up appearances."

"What do you mean?" Kole asked.

Another fish head slipped in her mouth. She licked her fingers clean. "Rocks keep us strong. Without it, our bodies soften." A tap to her leg. "I was once hard as a diamond. More consistent with quartz now."

Kole fiddled with the half-stale bread. "Do *you* eat rocks?"

"Not anymore."

"Why not?"

"Two reasons." She raised the jar to her mouth and sipped the brine. "First, the taste. Have you ever tried it?"

He shook his head. "Why would—"

"Try licking one sometime. You'll see what I mean. Horrible stuff."

Kole gnawed on the thick piece of bread, hoping the saliva in his mouth would soften it. "I'll take your word for it."

"And second?" Vienna ladled the finished stew into the line of bowls, then passed them out.

Issira took one graciously, saying, "I believe Shikar is trying to die."

"What?" Kole stopped mid-bite, swinging his head back to the stone giant. "Is that true?"

The Yamani closed the jar and set it aside. Whatever playful tone she held before fled. "Yes."

"Why?"

Silence. She leaned back, crossing her massive arms as if debating whether to answer. "My world was taken from me centuries ago. There is nothing left for me to live for."

Centuries? The way she said it made Kole wonder if the Yamani spoke of the Black Wall or something else.

"How old are you?" Vienna asked beside him.

"All Yamani on Ohr are the same age. I'm as old as the earth. We don't count sunrises or seasons."

"Wait—so, you're immortal, or something?" Kole neglected his stew to Vienna's dismay. Her stern look forced him to take up the bowl. If nothing else, it warmed his hands.

"In a way. We die when we please. If I do not eat to sustain myself, erosion will desecrate my body, and I will return to the earth. Some do choose to end their life. Our death is not like humans. We never cease. We become the living earth."

Kole idly stirred his supper. His appetite for meat eluded him while the fish eyes stared through the glass jar next to Shikar's ankle. Still, if he were to travel tomorrow, he'd need his strength. "Why do you choose to die now? Is it the ritual? Your Kayetan?"

"No. The Kayetan I can live with."

"I don't quite understand. If your body is as hard as a diamond, how did Savairo... cut it off?" Vienna asked.

"I abandoned my ways long before I was captured." Shikar nodded to the jar. "Quartz is soft enough."

An unlucky coincidence? Had Savairo grabbed the Yamani on a whim to see if he could conquer a Kayetan from her species? Or had he watched her beforehand and knew the weakness she'd set on herself? Kole would never know. But what he did know was if eating rocks made *him* near invincible, he'd shove them down his throat without hesitation. Still, he knew not the reason behind Shikar's choices. "If not the ritual, then...." Kole pried. "Why?"

"The curse." Shikar's gaze moved to the fire. "It's taken all I have left to live for."

"Grayfall?" Kole guessed. The same feeling of despair had washed through him when he'd lost his home and family. He'd wanted to die then and there—pleaded for Russé to give him the same fate as the orphans. "Is that why you came with us? You want to see home again before—"

"I'm going for my daughter."

"Daughter?" Vienna perked up. "But I thought you said Yamani were all the same age. If you have a daughter, she'd be younger."

Without warning, Shikar grabbed the jar and retreated into the darkness over the hill.

A tense quiet lay over the four of them.

"It's best not to pry. I sense an instability when she speaks of her past," Issira warned. Pulling back her delicate sleeves one at a time, she tipped the bowl to her lips and sipped.

Kole and Vienna's eyes found each other. She shrugged. Neither spoke until they'd finished eating and returned their dinnerware to the wagon.

Vienna hopped up on the back of the cart, her legs swinging over the edge as she stroked her brother's face.

"How is he?" Kole asked.

"No different. At least not that I can see. Shikar said he could be like this for days. Longer even." Worry overtook her expression with a sigh. "I wish he'd wake."

"He will."

"So she says." Though skepticism hid deep in her voice, her face betrayed her true feelings.

Kole folded his arms. "You don't believe her?"

"It's not that." She pulled her knees to her chest. "I don't know what to think. Guess I'm playing the overprotective sister, eh?"

The inflection at the end of her sentence made him smile. Whatever dialect Vienna fought off—the city slang Kole guessed the siblings had learned on the streets before the Liberation took them in—peeked through, telling him it never truly left. She merely concealed it. His first instinct was to tease her about it, but he caught himself. Maybe not the best thing to say in her current state. "Felix is lucky to have someone watch over him like you do."

"Even luckier, he has two *Souls* willing to help. And a Yamani." Resting her chin on her knees, she said, "He's in the best hands, yet I'm still scared."

Unsure of what to say to that, he stuffed his hands into his pockets.

She peered up. "Do you feel safe?"

"I—uh, what do you mean?"

"With the Souls."

He shrugged. "I stopped feeling safe the day I met you."

Her brows furrowed.

He cleared his throat. "When Idris came to Solpate," he clarified, worried she'd taken it the wrong way.

Savairo's prime Kayetan kept a permanent spot in Kole's past despite his best efforts to rid himself of the grievous memories. The moment that Kayetan stepped foot in Kole's forest, everything changed.

"Idris is gone now," she reminded.

"I know. It's not just him — it's everything. The wall. Savairo. Piper. Now Aterus and this curse Shikar talks about. Nothing is easy. It feels like the whole world is against us. Every time we try to do something right, something else goes wrong. Like back in the village." He looked to Felix's unconscious body tucked under a blanket. "We wanted to help, and it cost us... him. I couldn't *do* anything." Kole clenched his fists. Skin pulled taut over his knuckles. "I'm tired of letting people down."

"You didn't let him down."

"I was the only one there. You said it yourself, I should've talked him out of it. Should've stayed with him instead of splitting up." He blinked back the rising heat in his eyes. "You know, even if I was there — right beside him the moment the Kayetan grabbed him — there was nothing I could've done to change the outcome." Staring down at his burned arms, he said, "I'm useless like this."

A strained emptiness filled his gut. Guilt piled onto guilt. No way of ridding himself of it. And sure as the sky was blue, more waited in his future.

"I know what will help." Vienna leaned back, sifted through the pile of equipment in the corner, then pulled out a familiar weapon: Felix's slingshot. One arm grabbed a pot and flask, tucking them securely under her arm while her other hand wrapped around Kole's wrist.

He flinched at the unexpected contact. Her cold fingers sent a shiver up his arm as she pulled him from the cart and up the hill. "Where are we going?"

"Not far."

He glanced over his shoulder to Russé, who tended the campfire. Issira looked up in time to see them crest the hill. She gave no reaction and instead pointed to a darkened spot in the flames, baiting Russé so his back turned to Vienna and Kole as they slipped from view.

He was grateful for the escape. Still, they had company. Fiona circled overhead. Better a distant chaperone than Russé's claustrophobic approach.

Once the campsite was out of view, she dropped his hand and laid the cast iron pot and flask at the bottom of the slope.

"Target practice?" he asked.

"For you."

"Me? I don't know how to—"

"I'm going to teach you."

"But it's Felix's. I can't—"

"He isn't using it right now," she dismissed. "Plus, it'll give us both a distraction." A rattle came from her hip as she produced a small metal ball from Felix's pouch. Though he'd seen it before, Kole never noticed the intricate design embroidered onto the worn hide. The Seven Soul's symbol was stitched on the front, each circle sewn with a different color to represent the gods. A sun and crescent moon flanked the sides of the pouch. Lines of stars connected the three pictures, and thin, delicate threads curved and swooped into script too tiny for him to make out without closer inspection.

Vienna caught him looking and smiled. "He's skilled, isn't he?"

"*Felix* did that?"

"He's good with a needle. Our mother taught him. She was disappointed when I didn't take a fancy to it, but Felix's interest was more than enough to lift her spirits." Her thumb rubbed over the design. "Don't tell him I told you. Thomas teased him about it once, and he's never owned up to it since."

Attention refocused to the slingshot, she set the ammunition and pulled the band back. A sharp note echoed over the hill as she hit her target dead center. The metallic ball bounced into the grass. "A bit rusty, but I reckon I can teach you a thing or two."

Vienna came to his side and placed the handle in his hand. She turned Kole by the shoulders so his left hip faced the pot and flask.

"Square your hips."

He shifted. A gentle kick to the inside of his boots made him open his stance.

"Good. Two fingers like this."

Kole gulped as Vienna shaped his hand around the wood so his pointer finger and thumb wrapped around the Y shape of the slingshot. The scent of her hair hit his nose: a mix of honey and sweat. Her closeness sent a warmth through him, negating the chill night breeze.

She handed him a pellet. "Pinch it between the pouch."

He took the small, silver sphere, set it in the fold of the short strip of leather at the end of the string, then pinched the ends as instructed.

"Now to your face." She circled him. A shiver ran through Kole as Vienna stropped at his right shoulder and rested her arms around his. Her hand wrapped around his wrist and lifted it to his cheek, while the other set over the handle to hold him steady.

The tension in the taut band made his arms shake, but surprisingly, his scars gave no argument in the ready position. His hand hurt the most—the one wrapped around the narrow handle. The tighter he gripped, the more his skin protested.

"That's how you'll aim. Lean your head into it and line up the target with your eye. Go for the pot first."

He adjusted and took aim. Her body pressed against his back made his head spin. He pushed down the part of himself that wished the touches meant something more. Only target practice. Nothing more. *How could it ever be?* He cursed himself and concentrated.

"Release when you're ready." She slowly stepped away, and his mind settled.

He chewed his lip, willing his muscles to hold out. A small adjustment and the pouch slipped from his fingers prematurely. The pellet flew. A soft thud told him it hit the hill.

"Not bad for a first timer," she said, but a small laugh betrayed her.

Kole switched the weapon to his other hand and flexed away the pain.

"Does it hurt?"

"The handle's a bit narrow."

"Give it here." She took it from him and pulled a strip of cloth from a sack set on her hip. After wrapping it around the handle, she tied it off with a knot and returned it. "Try that."

This time his hand fit comfortably.

"Have another go."

He tried again.

She touched his right elbow. "Little higher."

This time he nicked the edge of the pot. That sweet *ping* swelled his confidence.

"Nice."

Nearly half an hour went by and Russé hadn't tracked them down. Issira must've intercepted him and convinced the Soul to leave them be. For that, Kole was grateful. Focusing on his aim distracted him from their mission—relieved his stress.

His aim improved with every shot. After hitting dead center on the pot three consecutive times, he moved to the smaller target. Some of the skills he used with his bow translated to the slingshot; the same deep inhale on the pull, tightening the core throughout the aim, and the swift exhale on the release.

Kole pulled back for another shot. "Why don't you trust Shikar?"

She shifted in the corner of his eye. "Have you seen the way she looks at him? I think she's more interested in having another person like her than helping Felix."

The pellet hit the hill. He loaded another, pausing before taking aim to look her in the eye. "Does it matter that her motive comes from a different place? You both want the same thing."

"She wants him to be like her. You see how she treats those creatures. She'll want him to embrace his Kayetan." Vienna turned, eyes following Fiona in the sky. "I want him to be like he was. I just want my brother back."

"He'll still be himself."

A moment passed with no answer.

Thinking her done with the conversation, Kole raised the slingshot for another attempt, but her voice made him pause.

"Are *you* still yourself?"

His eyes fell to the knotted skin of his fingers. He lowered the weapon to his side. "Not on the outside." Her question ignited a sense of foreboding. He'd never thought about it before.

The Black Wall had changed how he looked and moved. It left his green innocence charred. But the deaths. The loss. The aftermath is what changed him most. No longer the naive, adventure-seeking boy of the forest. That died along with Niko. But the core of him still remained. "Not entirely on the inside, either. But I'm still me."

Her features remained cold.

"Shikar is the only one we know of who's lived through the ritual," Kole said. "If there was someone who survived the Black Wall like me to help me adjust, I wouldn't object. Let Felix decide when the time comes."

"It's not Shikar herself, it's her insistence to keep his Kayetan alive. To keep it near like some demonic pet."

"Except that 'pet' brought him back to us. It protected him."

She sighed at that. "You're on her side."

"Just give it a chance."

She moved to the hill and gathered the targets. "Probably good for one night."

After searching the grass and collecting what pellets they could, Kole and Vienna climbed over the hill. She froze at the top.

Kole looked back to see her fiery gaze set on something in the distance. Turning his head, he followed it to the cart where a Kayetan—Felix's Kayetan—stood over her brother's sleeping form.

The shadow raised a clawed hand, the razor-sharp edges sinking ever closer to the blanket draped over Felix.

Vienna darted down the hill. The campfire set off a glint in her hand. Her sunstone dagger sat ready, poised in her pumping fist as the decline granted speed to her legs.

"Vienna," Kole called, trying to run after her.

Before he'd managed a few strides, Shikar's massive form appeared from the side of the cart and tackled her.

She struggled against the hold, shouting curses at the Yamani.

With a swift command from Shikar, Felix's Kayetan flashed over the hill.

As Kole reached the cart, he glimpsed the fire in Vienna's eyes, which trained on the hill where the Kayetan had disappeared. Even though she ceased her struggle, Shikar kept her pinned.

"Get off me!" she demanded, her hand still tight around the hilt of her weapon.

"Only when you've returned to your senses, girl."

A moment went by, followed by a deep huff, then Vienna relaxed.

Slowly, Shikar lifted and offered a hand, but Vienna refused it, saying, "Don't get between me and my brother."

"Then control your temper." Shikar's low voice rattled Kole's bones.

"That *thing* attacked him."

"His Kayetan has been watching over him for the last twenty minutes while you two were away. If it was going to attack him, it would've done it already."

"You let it come into camp? Stand next to my brother?" Anger flared in her green eyes.

"Vienna." Kole stretched out a hand, recoiling when her venomous gaze darted to him. Fearing his insertion would escalate things, he slumped back.

"That Kayetan *is* your brother. A piece of him torn from his soul. Why can't you see that?" Shikar stepped toward her, arching her massive stone head down.

Eyes back on the Yamani, Vienna held her ground.

"It hasn't harmed your brother, only protected him when you couldn't."

Vienna flinched at the accusation.

Even Kole felt the blow from Shikar's words. It would be like someone accusing him of not doing enough to save Niko. Though he may feel it true, he didn't need the reminder. He wished they'd both cool off before either said something too far to come back from.

"You only endanger him further with your savage attacks. Have you stopped to think what will happen to your brother if his Kayetan is killed?"

Caught off guard by the inquiry, Kole turned to Vienna, whose jaw clenched, clearly as dumbfounded as him.

"A Kayetan lives without its host." Shikar gestured to herself. "And I am proof of co-habitation. Even if the Kayetan is killed, the host may survive. But has your Liberation encountered such a thing as this? A host who leaks his own shadow?"

"No," Vienna croaked.

"What do you think it means?" Kole asked.

Yellow eyes slid to him. "Something happened during the ritual. He's not fully disconnected from his shadow. His connection is going to differ from the one I hold with my Kayetan, but if I had to guess it'll be more potent. I don't know what that means for Felix yet, and we won't know until he wakes. A death sentence to one may mean the other's demise. No way of knowing exactly without experimentation." Shikar turned to address Vienna. "So unless you want to gamble with your brother's life because of your prejudice, I'd steer clear of his Kayetan."

Vienna remained silent. Her eyes drifted from the Yamani to Felix, unconscious in the cart.

"It's your choice. I will not stop you again." With a long look up and down Vienna, Shikar stalked back to the campfire.

A sigh pulled Kole's attention back to Vienna. "Are you okay?"

"The brute is right. I need better control."

"Don't be so hard on yourself."

"I have to be. I said I'd try, and I will. I *am*." She sunk next to Felix and wrapped an arm over his shoulder. "We've been hunting them our whole lives. Every time I see a Kayetan, I have these...," her fists clenched, "*instincts*. It's what's kept us alive all these years." She shifted and held out her arm. The sunstone dagger lay in her open palm. "Take it."

"I can't do much with it. It's better in your hands."

"I don't want it on me in case...." She shoved it in his lap.

"What if Savairo's Kayetans show up again?"

"The Liberation fended off the shadows decades before Leo created the daggers. I can manage."

"Are you sure?"

"Just take it and be done," Vienna snapped. She buried her head in Felix's shoulder.

Kole flinched. The last thing he wanted to do was anger her. He tucked the dagger in his belt and left the cart to give her some space.

CHAPTER 21

After two days, the hills finally smoothed into open fields. Kole's muscles delighted. The strain of the constant up and downhill climbing exhausted him, not only because of the effort, but each step pulled the skin on the backside of his legs. Flat lands meant easy going. So he hoped.

The sun beat down. Kole's skin warmed under the heavy cloth draped over his burns. Though meant to protect his sensitive skin, it suffocated him. He walked in the shade of the lead rambler for relief. Unable to sweat, he relied on pouring water over himself to cool down his core temperature. This worked for a time, but with the constant damp clothing rubbing against skin, whether from walking or atop the rambler, rashes formed. His inner thighs and underarms stung. He kept his grimace inward—or tried to—but Russé watched him like a hawk. One whimper escaped through his clamped lips, and the Soul closed in.

"Take a break."

"I'm fine."

"Then why are you wincing at every stride?" Russé waved down Shikar. "Hold."

A tug on the lead, and the donkey stopped.

Kole sighed. The group paused, waiting for him to jump into the cart. He pushed himself when he could, not entirely out of stubbornness, though his ego did play a role, but because the added weight in the cart slowed progress. Old Jin could only handle so much. How could they expect a donkey to pull the same load as an ox? Eyes cast down, he scooted in, refusing Russé's outstretched hand of assistance. The wheels creaked as Old Jin trudged forward.

Kole pulled the flap closed after him to keep anyone from seeing the pain on his face as he leaned against the side and peeled off the damp clothes. Digging around the pile in the corner, careful not to disturb Felix, he found the only spare clothing, borrowed from Shikar, and pulled them on. A dark-green tunic embellished with silver trim, too fancy for his taste, and a pair of baggy black trousers. The pants weren't so bad. The loose cut gave his angry sores space. He had no idea where the Yamani had gotten this outfit; she herself wore no clothes, and even if she had gathered them for some odd occasion, they were entirely too small for her broad frame. Whether to his liking or not, he swallowed any complaint. Anything dry was a godsend. He kicked off his boots and socks, then slipped them beyond the flap to dry in the sun along with his Liberation uniform.

Alone with nothing but the groan of wood to focus on, fatigue caught up to him. He sprawled out in the small space between Felix and the cluttered supplies, using the side of a bedroll as a pillow. The gentle bounce of the cart lulled him to sleep.

Whispers woke him. Kole peeled his eyes open, still heavy from exhaustion. No matter how much sleep he managed, it never seemed enough. He lifted up and stretched his arms. His eyes perked open when he spotted the curled-up figure in the corner. "Felix?"

Felix sat, back to Kole against the far edge. At his name, his head slowly turned.

"You're awake." Kole leaned forward to crawl over, but something in Felix's eyes—or rather, the nothingness in them—made him pause. "Felix?"

"Where am I?" The monotone of Felix's voice gave Kole a chill.

"You're in the cart." When no recognition flickered, Kole added, "We're on our way to Grayfall, remember?"

"Remember? Oh."

"You've been asleep for days. Since the... well, you know."

"Know what?"

"The Kayetan?" Kole offered.

Felix's vacant eyes continued to stare.

Kole cocked his head, unsure how to respond. He expected anger—an outburst or something. It was like Felix had no idea what had happened. Did Felix not remember? How could he not? *The fevers.* Maybe they had something to do with his friend's strange, empty state. "You were taken. Savairo...." He couldn't bring himself to do it—to tell him what had happened. "Who were you talking to before?" Kole asked, remembering what had awoken him.

"There's whisperin' inside my head."

"What whispers? What are they saying?" Could it be the Kayetan? Maybe Savairo himself? Kole knew little about how the transition worked. Shikar would know better. He opened his mouth to call for the Yamani, but suddenly Felix's face contorted in—Pain? Confusion?

"It wants somethin' from me," Felix said.

"What does it want?"

Felix shook his head, his features twisted, almost unrecognizable. "No, no, no, no," he begged. "No, I won't. Never." Tears streamed down his freckled cheeks as his body shook. Small shakes, at first. As he repeated 'no,' over and over, Kole crawled over to comfort him.

The moment Kole's hand touched him, Felix's trembles burst into convulsions, and he screamed, sending a jolt of panic down Kole's body. Any remaining fog of sleep evaporated in an instant as Felix flailed before him.

"Calm down, you're all right," Kole called as the cart lurched to a stop.

But Felix didn't calm. His incoherent shrieks surged as if oblivious to Kole's presence. Felix clawed at his own arms and legs, scratching and tearing flesh.

Kole lunged for him. He grabbed one of Felix's hands and pinned it down. As Kole reached for the other, which had just carved a strip of flesh from his thigh, Felix slipped free. Unable to match Felix's strength, Kole tackled him, using the weight of his body to keep him restrained. "Stop it, Felix."

It worked for a moment. Then, like a cornered animal, Felix turned the attacks on his captor.

Fingernails, though dull and short, came down on Kole's back, nicking the scarred skin of his neck before dragging over the protective layer of his tunic. Hot pain erupted from the wounds. Kole roared.

The back flap of the cart whipped open. A beam of sun blinded Kole, and a cacophony of voices filled his ears. He couldn't tell whose was whose in the fray.

"What's happening?"

"Felix!"

"Release him, Kole. I've got him."

Only when a hand touched Kole's shoulder did he relax. Russé's arms wrapped around his waist and dragged him out of Felix's reach as Vienna, Issira, and Shikar rushed in.

"Felix. Stop, please!" Vienna urged, but no recognition came. Felix swiped at her. There was enough time for Vienna to dodge, but she planted herself, letting him hit her shoulder.

"It's pointless. He's still asleep," said Shikar.

That's when Kole focused on Felix's eyes: half rolled up in the sockets, twitching side to side. He'd seen episodes like this many times before amoung the orphans of Solpate.

Vienna shook her brother's shoulders.

"Let him ride it out," Shikar barked.

"But he's hurting himself. We have to stop him."

An annoyed grunt. "Move." Shikar tried to force her away, but Vienna wouldn't go without resistance. "He'll have less effect on me," the Yamani insisted as she wrapped her arms around Felix, who squirmed like a worm caught in a bird's beak—the same hold Russé currently used on Kole, as if the Soul thought he would dive back into the fray if left unchecked.

Issira lifted her hands to Felix's temples. Blue light flared from her fingertips. Whatever magic she used made his head roll forward. Felix's arms and legs dangled from the Yamani.

Quiet returned to the hills.

Issira tucked a curl behind Felix's ear. "He will be calm for now."

"What was that?" Vienna asked.

"A night terror," said Kole. Russé's arms dropped from around him. "The orphans had them back in Solpate."

Vienna looked back at her brother. "Night terror?"

"He's reliving the event in his dream. The ritual." Kole shrugged, testing the damage to his back. Definitely bleeding, though the fresh adrenaline veiled the true severity of his injury.

"Aye. I had many of those through the height of the fever." Shikar laid Felix back on the cart. "Only I had no one to watch over me to know how destructive they are." The Yamani pursed her lips at Vienna's fallen features. "This is good news, girl. The mind is on the mend. It shouldn't be long now."

As Vienna doted on her brother, Russé called Issira over. Her dark brows furrowed at Kole's wound. When she tried to touch it, Kole slid away. "I'm fine."

Issira turned to Russé. "Set up camp. We've gone far enough today. I think everyone could use the extra rest."

A tense silence blossomed between the Souls. With an agitated sigh, Russé left.

"Let me heal you, Kole."

"It's not that bad."

"You're right. In normal conditions you'd heal up fine. But the air grows thicker by the day. I won't allow anyone of us to go into the ash with an open wound. Best not risk infection."

He relented.

She rounded him, pulled down his collar, and placed a hand over the scratches. The same blue light pulsed from her palm. A cool sensation encompassed his back. His skin itched, from shoulder to shoulder, as the scratches mended.

"You shouldn't waste your powers on me."

"It is never a waste with you."

When she finished, her hand dropped, and he rolled his shoulders. Though his tight skin pulled, the pain had left. "Thank you."

"If you want to thank me, I'd have you act with more caution in the future."

He turned on her. "What would you have had me do?"

"Let *us* take care of things."

"Wait and watch him mutilate himself?"

"If you had, I'd only be healing one body tonight."

Kole's eyes drifted down. Maybe she was right. Another bad call. But in the moment, he'd only cared about Felix. Was that so wrong? "Do you always think in those terms?"

She pushed her silk-like hair over her shoulder. "In what terms?"

"Logically."

Issira leaned back for a moment as if weighing his question. "Isn't that best?"

His turn to think on it. Though her reasoning sounded just, it seemed the Soul regarded the situation like a puzzle in need of solving, which struck him as odd. "I guess it depends on who you ask."

She gazed at him. "I'm asking you."

"Maybe it was a bad call, and I made things worse, but doing nothing... standing back and watching something bad happen without interfering... it feels wrong."

"Sometimes standing back is the best way to combat destruction. Especially if the one trying to help doesn't know how."

Kole shook his head. Though the Soul looked human, he kept forgetting it was all a façade—that a god dwelled beneath that skin. "You don't understand."

"I shared your belief at one time: strive to save, not thinking of the cost. But by acting and letting my impulses drive me, I let thousands die. Never again."

"What are you talking about?"

Issira side-eyed Russé, who began prepping a fire a dozen paces away, then guided Kole away from the cart so the others were out of earshot. Eyes cast down, she laced her fingers. It was odd seeing her like this. Fidgeting. Nervous. Her voice softened. "Has Russé told you about Aterus? How he came to fall from us?"

"He told me he fell in love with a human."

"Evangeline." The sides of her mouth pressed down.

He noted the name. "You knew her?"

"I never met her, but I knew *of* her. Before my kin learned of her." A beat, then, "I kept Aterus' affair from the others."

"Why?"

"Because they would not have approved. Neither did I, but his instability frightened me. He stayed level-headed with her at his side. At least for a while." She smoothed a wrinkle on her blue sleeve. "When Russé and the others discovered Aterus had a lover, I agreed to help hide Evangeline until the child came."

"Child? Whose child?"

"Aterus'."

"He had a kid? With a human?" Was it possible for a god and a mortal to conceive? If they created life—Ohr—surely siring their own baby lay within their scope. The child concerned him. Would it be mortal? Curiosity took hold of his vocal cords. "What becomes of a child with mixed-mortal parents?"

"Demigod." Her voice barely carried over the waking crickets. "Half Soul, half human."

"I didn't know that was possible."

"Neither did I. Half of me wanted to destroy the babe. I thought its very existence would shift the balance and reign destruction on Ohr."

"You let it live, then?"

She nodded after a glance over Kole's shoulder.

He followed her gaze to Russé, who doted over a birthing fire. "Wait." He snapped back to Issira. "Russé doesn't know, does he?"

Her hands fidgeted in front of her belly. "He knows I helped Atreus. He knows of the deal I made, but I'm not sure he knows of the child."

"What deal?"

"I...." Her eyelids drooped for a moment. "I agreed to hide Evangeline and the child. Agreed to convince my kin Aterus had seen his errors and separated himself from the human so we wouldn't need to ascend."

"In exchange for what?"

She leaned back, face solemn. "I was not ready to leave Ohr. I had many other entities I wanted to gift the world." A sigh. "Aterus agreed to help me in exchange for my deceit."

The story grew more complicated by the second. Kole barely kept things straight. It dawned on him the presence of the Black Wall had been more preventable than he'd guessed. Not a mistake or happenstance, but a consequence to the Souls' selfish agenda.

Aterus risked the world for love. Issira for greed.

The Souls proved as manipulative as Savairo, except they possessed more power. It made sense. A blood sorcerer's poor choices could poison an entire city, whereas a god's could do the same to all of Ohr.

"I acted when I shouldn't have." Issira waved a hand to Felix in the cart, where Vienna cradled her brother's head in her lap, combing her fingers through his matted curls.

When he understood what she implied, he barked back, "That's not the same."

The Blue Soul's curious gaze set on him.

"What I did for Felix and what you did for Aterus.... They're *not* the same. You acted for yourself. You gained something in that deal." He shook his head. "I only wanted Felix's pain to stop. You can't pretend selflessness and selfishness are the same."

"You miss the point, Kole." Something flashed over her features. An expression Kole couldn't pinpoint. Not anger but of a similar nature. A split second and it vanished. "I speak not of the motivation, but of the outcome. Rushing in without thinking yields avoidable consequences. We are more alike than you think, young one." She spun on her heel, and her silken dress billowed around her as she stormed off. The faint rumble of thunder boomed overhead despite the cloudless evening sky.

She'd left him more confused than when they'd started. After anchoring the ramblers, Kole decided to spend the evening alone to sort out his thoughts. Finding privacy proved a simpler feat than anticipated. With Vienna and Shikar secluded to the cart in case Felix woke in another fit and the Souls leaving him after dinner to take watch, he had plenty of time to think things through.

It bothered him how the Souls had been presented to him all his life: intertwined gods serving a singular purpose. Moving, acting as one. Peaceful and wise. A minute alone with Russé and Issira had demolished the concept. The Souls were at constant war with one another. When Kole first released Issira, the two Souls had displayed a sense of camaraderie. Kole'd go as far to say it seemed they'd missed each other. But Russé and Issira only spoke when needed. A means to an end. Even the snippets of their telepathic conversation Kole eavesdropped on had been arguments.

And Obell. Kole shivered against the heat of the campfire as he shoveled the last spoonful of porridge into his mouth. No doubt the Red Soul, based on their brief interaction, would prove just as temperamental.

After wiping his bowl clean with a rag and returning it to its place in the cart, quietly as to not disturb Vienna and Felix, he curled up in his bedroll and tried to think of anything but the Souls until dawn.

Crying babies fueled his dreams. Sons and daughters of Souls. New rivers flowed forth over Ohr as their tears fell to the earth. Pounding fists and stomping feet made the land quake and shift until the entire land crumbled into itself. True destruction. The ultimate death of Ohr and its people.

CHAPTER 22

Felix had yet to show any sign of improvement. He remained unresponsive while awake and restless at night. His frequent outbursts kept Russé and Issira on their toes, racing to calm and cut off his screams before the noise drew unwanted attention. The scenery, though, changed drastically.

Within a day's travel, finally shifting westward, green plains transformed to dead, barren land, much like Kole had seen on the overworked farmlands on the outskirts of Socren. Instead of a chalky brown though, the dirt held a tone of dreary gray, and a thin layer of soot coated the field—remnants of the volcanic ash carried miles on the wind. Clear blue skies lay beyond Kole's back, but ahead loomed a dark curtain of ash. They closed in on the volcano day by day, so said Shikar, yet the mountain never showed.

Kole tugged at the strap digging into the back of his neck. Though the air remained relatively fresh with only small, burned particles floating here and there, Shikar insisted they all wear the masks Felix had tried to pilfer from her. The long filter jutted beyond Kole's jaw, cutting off his vision to the ground. It may have caused more problems if he walked, but having chosen to ride the rambler today, it merely served as a slight annoyance, cutting off his view to the ground far below. Worse, the bug-like lenses fogged from the inside with every breath. He'd lost count how many times he'd removed the mask to wipe them clean, just to do it again a few minutes later. At this point, with how often he removed it, he wondered if the thing was even worth wearing.

Only Shikar traveled without a mask. She claimed the volcanic air didn't affect her, but her ever-growing cough the last few hours made him believe her refusal had more to do with her death wish than a pair of iron lungs. Despite their immortal status, the Souls wore the masks. At first it surprised Kole, but likely the human forms they'd taken meant they shared the same vulnerabilities.

When the wind shifted, Shikar, trekking on foot at the front of their group, held out a hand.

Kole and Russé halted their ramblers.

Vienna peeked her head through the flaps of the cart and tugged Old Jin's reins. "What's going on?" A look to the Yamani, who lifted her nose into the oncoming wind, quieted her.

Squinting through the foggy lenses, Kole found nothing out of the ordinary.

Seconds ticked by. No one dared move until Shikar gave the all clear. The longer he waited for her command, the more insane possibilities popped up in Kole's head. Another Kayetan? Maybe Savairo. Or worse, Aterus himself. Icy fear shot through his veins. He cursed himself for such thoughts.

A faint sound perked his ears. Low. Gritty. Similar to the noise Kole and Niko used to make as children, when they competed to see how deep they could make their voices. Except this sound clicked and skipped like the rhythm of a cackle.

"What is—"

A growl from Shikar cut him off.

The strange sound stopped.

"Get in the cart," the Yamani roared.

The ferocity in the Yamani's command forced Kole to jump from the trunk. The rambler caught him and dropped him by the cart. He climbed in and slid in next to Vienna, who still held the flap open, ushering him past.

"If it's a threat, our ramblers can handle it," Russé said.

"I said in the cart. All of you," Shikar ordered the Souls when they didn't budge. "Your ramblers will only draw more attention with their heavy stomps."

Russé and Issria cast a look at each other, then conceded. The Yamani followed them closely, only pausing to blindfold Old Jin before yanking the curtain from Vienna's grip. Yellow eyes set on Kole. "Give me your shirt, boy."

"My shirt?"

"I need the blood."

Kole looked to the others crowded in the cart. The Souls and Vienna gave a nod of encouragement, though they appeared just as oblivious for its purpose. Vienna held his mask as he slipped off his blood-crusted shirt, torn where Felix had attacked him earlier. Kole handed it over.

Balling the shirt in her giant hands, the Yamani said, "Stay quiet until I return. Don't leave the cart." Then she left, the flap closing after her. Her heavy steps faded in the strengthening wind.

Though midday, the curtains left the cart doused in shadow. Kole could barely make out the outlines of his comrades stuffed beside him. Once his eyes adjusted, he spotted Felix curled in the corner, unaware of the cramped space or the danger outside. His eyes never lifted, nor did his features, stoic as ever.

Shoulder to shoulder, they sat in silence, the small enclosure warming by the minute. His burned body couldn't regulate his core temperature, and it quickly grew uncomfortably hot. He remained quiet at first, only removing his mask for fresher air. No use complaining when Shikar could return any moment.

Time passed. More than he anticipated. What was Shikar up to?

To preoccupy himself, he counted the minutes and focused on his breathing, stopping when he reached his final finger. Ten minutes and still nothing. By now, he felt faint. On the brink of passing out, something built in his head. A wave of lava rose in the depths of his mind.

Obell.

The Soul's presence grew on the opposite side of the barrier in his mind, stalking the crumbling walls of Kole's consciousness as it weakened with the rising heat of the cart. Kole knew the Soul was waiting to strike at the opportune moment.

Kole held against Obell. If he could just stay awake—stay strong. But how long could he hold out? Even now, his eyes drooped. He shook his head and looked to his companions.

"What's going on?" Kole whispered. To his surprise, no one hushed him.

"I don't know," Russé answered.

"It sounded like an animal." Vienna shifted next to Kole's shoulder. He didn't know if her proximity made his heart skip or if the heat was to blame. Either way, it kept his eyelids open.

"Are you all right, Kole?" Issira touched his knee.

"I need air."

A small stream of gray light streaked down the middle of the cart as Vienna slowly pulled back the flap. "A little shouldn't hurt."

A breeze wafted through the cart, billowing the back flap as it left. The small gust provided a moment of relief. Clarity returned.

But so did the strange, clicking growl.

Vienna tensed beside him and shut the flap. Their echoed breaths in the cart ceased as heavy footfalls closed in.

Kole pressed his back into the wooden half-wall of the cart. Stale air crowded his nose and mouth again, flowing into his lungs like molasses. Obell swelled against the outer wall of his mind as the cart shook from the colossal gait of whatever creature stalked out there. The sheer heft reminded Kole of the walking trees. An animal could never reach such a size. The warmth must be messing with his perception. How big could the creature be?

A low click like before, then a guttural sniff no more than a dozen feet from the cart by the sound of it.

The chime of soft metal and a tug to his belt loop told Kole that Vienna had unsheathed the blade she'd given him for safe keeping. Taking the cue from her, he fumbled for the slingshot at his hip.

Only fear kept Kole awake. It coursed through his veins, alerting his senses. But the heat of Obell's presence clung to him like a fever — lulled him away. He pressed his fingernails into the handle of the slingshot, hoping the pinch of pain would keep him aware. One blink, though, he held too long, and Obell struck like a wolf lying in wait.

"Obell," was the only warning he managed to utter before the Red Soul took his mind.

Kole gritted his teeth to keep from screaming. Magma crawled beneath his skin like before, scorching his flesh. *It's not real. It's not real.* The thoughts didn't abate the torment. His body seized.

Next thing he knew, Issira was on top of him, hand to his temple, fighting back Obell's heat with her cool touch. She washed him away like a tsunami flooding the coast.

Obell retreated, but he did not leave.

"He's still here," Kole wheezed, feeling the god's presence slip to the dark corners of his head.

"Stay calm." Issira's melodic voice hit a dark octave. "I'll find —"

Outside, the pounding of a dead sprint bounded toward them. Every footfall sent a shock through the cart.

The creature had heard them.

Vienna cursed. Out of the corner of his eye, Kole saw her open the flap.

Russé caught her before she jumped out.

The low-pitched clicks of the animal hastened.

"I will *not* be an easy kill," Vienna fumed and tore from Russé's grasp. As she poked her head out again, a flash of black rushed past the open curtain.

Claps of colliding rock reached Kole's ears.

Shikar's grunts circled the cart as she tussled with the animal.

"And she worried about the rambler's noise," Russé muttered after the sound.

Whatever Vienna had witnessed sent her crawling back to the safety of the cart, her mouth hanging open in terror.

Meanwhile, Obell lashed out at Issira, leaving a trail of embers across Kole's brain. He screamed as it sizzled away. The blue light pulsing from the Soul's hands brightened. Cool relief tingled across his mind. Half his head swirled in a ruthless fever while the other side felt numb as frostbite. The Souls battled for his mind.

"Don't pour all you have into him," Russé warned. "Obell is trying to deplete you."

"What would you have me do?" Issira snapped. Her hands trembled against Kole's forehead. The mix of extreme temperatures made him dizzy.

Russé leaned into view. "Kole, you have to fight him. Push him beyond your walls. It's too much power for us to spare. We'll have nothing left."

Between the commotion outside and the ever-rising fever within him, any chance at focusing had fled.

"You have to learn to do it on your own, or you will forever be at his mercy." Russé's aggressive tone brought Kole back to reality.

Kole snapped his eyes open, breaths coming in spurts. Muscles spasmed against his will as Obell sunk into his limbs and flexed his power over his new vessel. Kole would be at his mercy soon—a mere puppet like Issira had made of him once before. Except Issira never exuded an urge for domination like this. A shudder pierced Kole's core, and he knew if Obell took control, he'd never give it up.

"How do I get him out?" Kole croaked.

"Stand your ground. Reclaim your mind. Set a border he cannot cross. You've done well handling the ramblers. This is within your power."

Set a border. What kind of border could keep out a god?

The cart jerked as Shikar and her assailant rammed into the side. Kole toppled forward into Issira, who caught him and wrapped her arms tight around him, pulling him into her lap.

The wagon slammed back to all fours. On impact, wood snapped, and the bed tilted toward the back-right wheel. Broken for sure.

"This is ridiculous," Russé growled.

"I'm here with you." Issira squeezed him reassuringly. "We can do this together, young one."

A border. He needed a border. A wall. Something to keep Obell at bay.

No. That wouldn't be enough. Building a wall would only make the Soul retaliate. He needed to make the Soul never want to return, and he knew exactly how to do it. If Obell could inflict pain telepathically, so could he.

You want fire? I'll give you fire. He closed his eyes, and the memories of the Black Wall propelled to the forefront. The night Kole obtained his scars filled his thoughts; the harsh gale pulling him into the air like a leaf on the wind, sucking him toward the blistering heat from the wall of black flames. He put himself back there—forced Obell to relive it with him. As his skin prickled at the memory—blistered, peeled, and charred—so did Obell's. As flesh dripped from him, fingers and toes curling from the singed muscles, so did Obell's.

It worked. The Soul screamed along with the memory. But Kole continued his onslaught. He set his misery on the Red Soul, filling every nook and corner with raw agony, so the god was left exposed no matter where he cowered.

A surge of heat arose in Kole's hands. Obell's last-ditch effort to hang on. Kole clenched his fingers, embracing the blaze. No threat of fire came close to the ferocity of the Black Wall. Not even a god's.

Another push, and Obell fled.

Outside the cart, a crunch came, followed by a yelp.

Other than Kole's arduous breathing and the slight whine of a breeze drifting through the flaps, silence returned.

"He's gone." Kole swallowed, lifting his eyes to the others.

Vienna shifted, rustling the crooked cart. Her tightened jaw told him thoughts of the creature she'd glimpsed preoccupied her attention.

"Stay put," Shikar called from outside. A wheeze cracked her voice.

No one moved. Kole glanced to Felix, who hadn't so much as flinched through the entire encounter. *Just a vacant body.* The thought left Kole helpless. When would Felix come back to them?

After a moment of receding footsteps, Kole caught Vienna's attention with a nudge. "What did you see?"

Her wide green eyes found his. "I'm not sure I want to know."

Curiosity got the better of him. He scooted out of Issira's arms and leaned out to peer through the wind-blown gap between the flaps.

"We should do as Shikar says," Vienna warned with a touch to Kole's shoulder.

He possessed no strength to fight her. With little room in the cramped cart, Issira let him rest on her until Shikar returned.

"You did well, Kole," Issira whispered.

Russé nodded in agreement. A shift to the side of his mouth conveyed a sense of pride. Any other time, Kole would've reveled in it. Strange how he still craved Russé's approval. Even after their rocky past—their disagreements—there was no escaping that need to please his mentor.

A giant rock hand pulled the front flap aside. "Get out. One at a time." Instead of waiting for a volunteer, Shikar grabbed Vienna's arm, who yelped in surprise, and yanked her out of the cart. The Yamani's other hand clenched a fistful of ash. She rubbed it over Vienna's arms before she could protest.

Vienna's mouth fell open as stone fingers brushed soot through her long, blonde locks. "What are you doing?"

"Getting rid of your scent. They smell flesh-kind miles off."

Every inch of exposed skin, clothing, and hair received a thick coating. When Shikar finished, she nudged Vienna, now a gray ghost, aside and reached for Kole.

"What are they?" He climbed from the cart. Only then did he notice the ramblers had closed in on the cart, entangling their roots around it like a cage.

Turning Kole around with a push, Shikar said, "The cursed." Her heavy hands pulled his tender skin, but the stone of her fingers, cool and smooth, chased away the lingering heat of the Red Soul's presence. After a few winces and bites of his tongue to keep from voicing his pain as she worked, Shikar must've caught on to his sensitivities, because she lightened her touch on the more severe scars of his neck. Soon, his reddened skin blended in with the dreary scenery.

"I told you the ramblers weren't needed," Shikar huffed at Russé.

"We lost one wheel, I wasn't about to make it two. Or worse, us."

Shikar grumbled at his response.

The Souls received the same treatment with the ash, as did a sleeping Felix. Issira put up a bit of resistance but relented in the end, frowning as the powder dulled the sheen of her silk dress. Shikar went a little rougher applying the soot to Russé, clearly annoyed by his disobedience with the ramblers.

While everyone tended to themselves, wiping and shaking off excess soot, Kole investigated the aftermath of Shikar's fight with 'the cursed,' as she called it.

Deep channels in the ash and soil disrupted the ground around the cart, as if something heavy had slid past them. He knelt next to one, measuring the width with his arms. Bigger than his arm-span by a foot or two, which meant whatever had made it stood well over six feet. But what animal—*thing*—could've produced it? Maybe Shikar had made the channel. The size seemed comparable. Had she been thrown? He mocked his own thought. *She's too heavy to be thrown. Shikar shakes the ground when she walks.* Then again, so had the creature. It must be larger than he guessed. How could something that big sneak up on them?

A grunt of frustration came from over his shoulder as the Yamani tended to the broken wagon wheel. Unsure how long the fix would take, he used the time to his advantage.

Kole stepped into the channel. More like a ditch to him, as it came up to his hip. He followed it to the end, eyes scanning the curved bottom for a tuft of hair, blood, or claw marks—anything to hint at the source's identity. Nothing came of his search until he reached the end of the trail. Scuff marks marred the earth, and beyond the channel, a set of crisp footprints led away. Two pairs: one Shikar's—he could tell by the girth—and the other... *bigger*. Six holes pierced the compacted ash at the end of each elongated toe: four claws in the front, one in the back, reminiscent of the talons of a bird. If these prints belonged to some kind of bird, why the absence of feathers?

Then he saw it. The green shirt he gave to Shikar hung on the branch of a dead shrub. He picked it up. A hole sullied the fabric of the upper back where his dried blood had been. The ripped edges of cloth frayed as if torn out. Or chewed out. He fingered the shredded perimeter. No saliva. Odd as it may be, he found it stranger still why his shirt was left behind sans the bloodied spot. Shikar mentioned she needed the blood when she took it from him. Had she pulled off the piece? Or had the creature? Only one way to find out.

Kole pulled the tattered shirt over his head, then returned to the cart. Undeterred by the gaping hole in the back, he felt more comfortable than going bare-chested with his scars out for everyone to see.

From the looks of it, Shikar had mended the broken wheel. Only she possessed enough strength to bend and wrap their metal tools into the shape of one of the annihilated dowels. At the front of the cart, their salt-and-pepper donkey had turned a ghostly gray.

Shikar carefully brushed Old Jin's nose in ash, then removed the blindfold from the anxiously stamping animal. "Just be grateful you weren't eaten." He heard Shikar say with a pat to the donkey's rump.

"Eaten by what, exactly?" Kole pried.

The Yamani's head turned ever so slightly over her shoulder in Kole's direction, a vacant expression on her face. Bored or evasive, he couldn't tell. Given the situation, he guessed the latter.

He rounded on her, a thumb directed over his shoulder to the hole in his shirt. "It bit the blood from my shirt and ran. What creature does that?"

"I ripped it out myself."

Kole was ready for the deflection. "You tore it in a circle? That's pretty hard to do to woven fabric."

Shikar adjusted Old Jin's reins, then nonchalantly said, "I am stronger than fabric."

"It's too perfect. Look," he turned so the hole faced her, "no linear tears. What was that thing, Shikar?"

"Why all the questions?"

He crossed his arms. "Why all the deflection?"

She growled. "I already told you what it was."

"I don't want its name. I want to know what they are. Birds? I saw talon marks."

A thunderous laughter shook her body.

Kole felt the vibrations through his feet.

"Yes, boy. They are *birds*." Warmth pooled in his cheeks as she tugged the donkey into a walk. "Best leave it alone, little flesh-kind. I've heard what you speak of while you sleep. No more fuel for the fire, yeah?"

He balled his fists as the Souls and Shikar took to their usual travel formation: Shikar in the lead, Souls perched on the trunk of one of the ramblers, which flanked the cart. The front seat of the cart, Vienna's post, was left vacant. No doubt she'd holed herself up with her brother. If he could only get her to talk.

Russé squinted his way as Kole left his rambler for the wagon. *The old man knows me too well.* But the Soul didn't question him, only eyed Kole until he stepped up and closed the curtain.

Through the dim interior, he spotted Vienna hunched in the corner, inspecting something in her hands. The moment she noticed Kole, her hands closed, hiding whatever she'd been enthralled with.

"What's that?"

She stared at him for a long second as if debating whether to change the subject or fess up. With the trepidation of a child caught stealing, she opened her shaking hand and extended it toward him. A small, reddish-black stone lay in the crease of her palm.

"Oh," he said.

It must not have been the reaction she'd hoped because she rolled her eyes and placed it between two fingers. "*Look.*" She brought it to the sliver of light shining through the crack in the curtain. It appeared ordinary at first, but when the slightest bit of sun touched it, Kole realized where the reddish hue came from.

Translucent black stone, or at least what looked like stone, stared back at him. It reminded him of obsidian, the material Leo pumped some sort of spell into to create the sunstone daggers used to kill the Kayetans. Inside swirled a red liquid. Not a pocket of fluid—still and encased—but free-flowing, dancing throughout the rock like a fish navigating a pond. Impossible. *Unless touched by magic.*

"What is that?"

"I don't know. I found it in the ash."

"Just now? After Shikar's fight?"

Vienna nodded, concealing the stone in her palm. "A piece of the monster."

"The cursed." Kole swallowed. "That stuff in there. Is that blood?"

"No clue. I'm not even sure Leo's seen such a thing."

"Come on, Vienna. What did you see? What sort of creature?"

"I told you, *I don't know.*" She sighed. "I want to tell you, Kole—it's just—I don't know how to even begin to describe it."

"Was it... bird-like?" he asked hesitantly.

A cocked head told him the answer.

Way off-base with the bird theory, got it. But the talon marks had to mean something. "Claws?" he tried one more time.

"Not that I saw. Honestly, the only thing I got a good look at was the eyes." Her face scrunched. Goosebumps crawled down her arms. "They were red. And the pupil—it spiraled around the eye like the red liquid in this rock. At least I think it was a pupil." Fishing through a pouch at her side, she pulled the foreign piece out once more and inspected it. "I remember the eyes. And I remember the feeling that came over me when it looked at me." She peered up at him, a glint of terror behind her gaze. "I wanted to die."

"What are you talking about?"

Vienna shook her head, and her eyes fell to the floor of the cart. "The feeling wasn't mine. I know that. It came from the creature. Projected from it or something. But it felt so real. This overwhelming urge to drop my weapons and fling myself at it consumed me. I thought I was going to do it, too, until Shikar tackled it."

"Like hypnotism? Is that even real?"

She shrugged, returning the stone to her pouch. "I don't want to feel like that again. Shikar was right to put us in the cart. I... I think we should trust her. With this, at least. And with Felix, too. Whatever hell beasts prowl here, whatever curse she claims... I think our only hope to reach Grayfall lies with her."

A rustle from Felix pulled their attention. Though still passed out, he tossed and turned.

"He's not going to—"

"Attack?" She gave a side smirk. "No. He's been getting restless. Even when he does wake, it's brief. And he's delirious. Shikar says he's coming around, but I fear it will take longer than my nerves can handle."

"It'll be all right."

"That's what everyone keeps saying. I'll believe it when it is." With a swipe of her hand, she pulled her rope-like braid over her shoulder, shoved the bulbous-nosed mask over her head, then leaned back, settling in for the long ride ahead. When she closed her eyes, ending the conversation, Kole did the same.

Sleep came in patches. Whether the humidity in the mask, choking him awake, the pitch of the crudely mended wheel, or the dreams of a river of magma swallowing him whole, he never truly rested.

CHAPTER 23

Twenty-four hours later, the scenery took a drastic change for the worse. Savage winds brought a blizzard of ash. Each step from the tree took twice the effort in the pounding wind. Kole sat atop the crawling rambler with Vienna, who had emerged from the cart for a few hours: a rare occurrence.

Shikar had wrapped Old Jin's muzzle in cloth to keep her from inhaling clouds of dust, even bringing it up over the animal's eyes to act as blinders when she planted her hooves and refused to move.

Fiona had pushed through an hour of flight, but the poor bird exhausted herself. A rest upon a rambler branch provided no comfort as the wind threatened to push her clear off despite her talons locked around the limb. Vienna called her and placed her in the cart for a rest.

They pressed long into the night, only setting up camp when the winds had died. No warm supper this time. Shikar had cautioned against anything needing prep, as the small cinders, drifting down like powdered snow, were likely fresh from the volcano and ripe with toxins. They took turns nibbling on stale bread and cheese in the confines of the cart.

With only a few hours until sunrise, everyone turned in, save for Russé.

The Green Soul stood, shin deep in the ash drift. Body still covered in soot to keep his scent at bay, Russé looked very much like some forgotten statue left to bow to the winds of the plains. Ghost-like.

Kole approached, but the Soul remained still. "A chill roots in my bones. One I haven't felt before. I fear it lies ahead in Grayfell. It grows stronger the closer we get." The mask gave Russé's voice a subdued muffle.

"Obell?" Kole guessed. "Or the cursed ones?"

"They may be the same."

"Wait." He thought back to Solpate. Before Aterus imprisoned Russé within the forest, the trees had been ordinary. Normal size.

Rooted. But a Soul's presence, the sheer proximity to power like that, had changed them. The trees had grown three, four times as large and pulled themselves from the earth to walk atop their roots and roam the grounds like human and beast alike. Even Issira had changed the nature of the water of the pool where her prison sat. Could something similar happen with Obell and the volcano? "Is this like the ramblers? Are the cursed... parts of the volcano coming to life?"

"If we were talking about Braxus I'd say you were right."

Braxus. The Soul of Earth and Moon. Russé mentioned the Souls so freely. As casually as Kole would bring up Niko or Goren. Like nothing more than friends or family. Maybe to *Russé*. To the rest of the world, they were the creators. All-powerful forces deserving of praise and worship.

Russé looked down the long nose of his mask. "I think Obell is the curse. I'm not sure *how* it's all connected — or why — but the fact that all of this links together begs no coincidence."

But which had come first? Shikar had said the Yamani were as old as the earth. Was Grayfall cursed from the beginning, too? Or maybe the Souls' imprisonment had birthed the bane on the city. Perhaps something else. It occurred to Kole that Shikar could be thousands of years old. Would she look at the passing of time the same way he did? A day could be a blink of her eye. Her memories of things could be... off. One thing he knew for certain from his journey thus far, he agreed with Russé: coincidences were never just that.

"What does that mean for us?" Kole asked.

"It means we best be on our guard. If this is a product of Obell, not even Shikar can save us from it. Neither can two spent Souls."

Kole glanced to the cart with its stubby, half-broken wheel. "How are we going to get to the volcano like this?"

"*We* won't."

The hair raised on Kole's neck. "Russé?"

"Look inside yourself, Kole. Unless things change, we will have to go it alone."

"You mean...." The nuance of Russé's words registered. "We're *not* ditching Felix and Vienna out here. Why are they even coming this far if that's the case?"

"If it comes down to it, Obell's freedom takes priority."

"You sound like *him*."

"Can you not feel him? Even now as we speak, he writhes. My connection to him has been severed. I shouldn't feel him. But I can. The thickness of his anger rattles me. The ground quakes. He's *in* there, Kole."

In there? The scenes he'd witnessed in his trance-like state while tracking Issira had been clues to her whereabouts—a map straight to her. But Obell sent Kole more than pictures. He burned and scorched. Intentional or not, it served as another clue. The realization made his stomach twist. "He's inside the volcano," the words slipped out, trance-like.

Russé gripped the top of his staff. "He must be freed before his rage causes...."

It clicked in Kole's head. "Before he erupts? Before he makes the *volcano* erupt?"

The downward wrinkles around the Soul's eyes, visible through the bug-like goggles, gave away a frown. "Obell grows more unstable each passing day. If we take too long...."

"But—wait. How do we know when it's coming? We're heading straight to the rim of the volcano. What if we're there when it—"

Russé grabbed hold of Kole's shoulders. "That's why I need you. If you can connect with him again—calm him, then maybe."

"I can't calm him. You were there last time I tried. And again, in the cart. He doesn't want to talk. He wants *control*." Kole didn't mean to snarl the last word.

"I can teach you. You've done it once."

"That wasn't calming. I forced him out."

"With Issira, then, back when the Kayetan took you. She took over your body. You nearly merged with her, but you broke away."

"This is different. Issira wasn't attacking me. She saw reason."

"We can make him see reason." Desperation lit his eyes. Russé blinked, and it faded. He slid his hands from Kole's shoulders. "It's been too long since our last training."

A groan escaped Kole. "I'm no good at it."

"You'll need to be. If not in time for Obell, then for the three Souls after. This is your power, Kole. You need to learn to wield it."

Some power. Russé controlled plants. Issira manipulated water and weather. And *Kole*? He'd lucked out with agony and splitting headaches. "You act like I chose this. Like I was born to do this."

"Maybe not born, but you were chosen."

"I was chosen to die," Kole snapped, venom in his voice. "If Goren knew I would survive his ritual, he would've picked someone more worthy. This isn't some granted power—some blessing. It's a curse, and

I never wanted it." The brightness in the Soul's eyes dulled. For some reason, that reaction only angered Kole more. "Look at me," he hissed, holding out his arms to show off his reddened scars. "Is this going to save anything?"

"You are more than your body, Kole. You are your mind."

Kole gave a manic laugh. "Well, that's scarred, too." Only after did he think on his own words, then mumbled, "Maybe more than my skin." The ache in his throat threatened to reach up to his eyes. He could feel the tears brewing. Kole curled his upper lip and forced it all away. Nothing Russé could say would make things better. Apparently, the Soul sensed that, because he remained silent for a time until Kole's heart settled.

"In the meantime, we keep our focus on the mission," Russé whispered, firm. "That's all we can do. We have little control left. There is no plan from here. There's never been a plan on how to do any of this, only that it needs to be done. You have me. You have Issira. And once you release the rest of us, you'll have Ohr back. All of it."

The lump caught in Kole's throat again as he swallowed. "If we make it that far."

"Yes...." Russé's voice turned grave. "If, indeed." He returned to his post and set his statuesque stare on the swirling gray abyss. "You should—"

"Get some sleep. I know," Kole finished for him. Lately, it was the go-to cue the Souls used for 'this conversation is over.' In the past, he'd resist out of spite, but the events of the day had his lids weighing heavy.

He trudged down the hill, kicking at the fluffy soot with every step. It bothered him how pristine the ash looked. Something so poisonous shouldn't look so beautiful. As he continued his destruction down the hill, a wisp of movement caught his eye. He glanced to the cart, not bothering to stop, and expected to see a restless Vienna. Nothing but the cart and falling ash. He blinked back the haze of sleep, then rubbed the fog from his googles. *These blasted things are a nightmare.* On his way past the cart to his tent, a shape pressed into the ash made him pause. A footprint—no, *footprints* leading away from the back of the wagon to....

His eyes trailed up just in time to spot a silhouette disappearing beyond the veil of ash. Felix's Kayetan came to mind. The creature must be lingering around, keeping close watch on its host. Then again, Kayetans left no footprints. Kole pulled back the curtain and peered in.

A form lay in a heap, snuggled up next to the food crate. The sides of Kole's mouth tugged into a smile. *Figures.* Even subconsciously Felix was drawn to food. No sign of Vienna, but a discarded mask lay in the corner. She'd gone off without it, he supposed. Good to know someone else was fed up with them, too. He grabbed it, peeked at Russé, whose back faced him, and followed the trail. No one wanted to wear it, but a 'poisoned lung' as Shikar called it, stood as the alternative.

Two figures lingered at the end of the footprints, neither one Vienna. Only now did Kole realize the dark cart had fooled him. He'd seen *Vienna* asleep there, not Felix.

Instead, he found Felix at the end of the trail, whose grown-out brown curls hung below his ears. Next to him, stood the silhouette of his Kayetan a few paces off. The outline of the disconnected shadow mimicked every curve of Felix's body, from his tousled hair and short stature, to his precise lean, hip favored to the right. Everything identical, save for the hands. Where fingers should be, long, smoking claws hung.

Kole froze as Felix and his Kayetan stared each other down. Felix clutched a dagger in his fist. "Felix?"

The wind tugged at Felix's messy curls.

"What are you doing out here without a mask? It isn't safe to breathe the ash. Here, put this on."

Felix only stared at the shadow before him.

"Felix?" he tried again, fighting the sinking feeling overwhelming his gut. This wasn't Felix. Not as he knew him: sly, with a face meant for a smile. Something within him was off. Terribly so. "You really should put a mask on." His words barely came out as a whisper.

"I can hear it. Whispers in my head."

Kole swallowed. At least he got a response this time, even if it wasn't what he wanted to hear. "Your... Kayetan?"

"Yes, I felt it. *Him*. He called ta me in my dreams. Woke me. Lured me here."

"What is it saying?"

No answer.

Then, Felix's hand tightened around the sunstone dagger. "I want it outta my head."

"You can't kill your Kayetan, Felix. Shikar doesn't know what will happen if your shadow dies. Destroying it might do the same to you."

"It needs ta end."

Ice shot through his veins at Felix's monotone remark. "What needs to end?" Kole prodded.

"All of it."

In that moment, reality hit Kole like a kick to the stomach. He knew this feeling—the dark wheels turning in his friend's head, for he lived through it once. With cautious steps, he made his way closer, taking a rounded path to steer away from Felix's line of sight. "Nothing needs to end, Felix." It was the only thing he could think to say to buy time—distract Felix while he inched closer.

"I know what you're doin', mate. I see through demon eyes now. I'm the shadow."

Kole paused mid-step.

"Good choice," Felix said, though his eyes never left the Kayetan swaying an arm's length from its master.

Kole switched his gaze to the Kayetan. The creature had swiveled its head, following his every move. If he got close enough, he had a fighting chance to wrestle the blade away before Felix could do the unthinkable. But it seemed the demon's watchful eyes somehow connected back to Felix. Anything the creature saw, so did its master? Only one way to find out for sure. Kole took a step.

"Ya won't stop me in time. There's no other end ta this. Thought you'd understand more than anyone."

Kole's body sagged at that. Desperation clung to his heart. The moment wouldn't last much longer despite his effort to extend it—to give him time to think, to act while he still had a chance to save Felix. He hadn't done enough back in the village, but he could do something now. Maybe not stop him physically but convince him to abandon this suicide mission. Then, his hand brushed by something cold at his hip. The slingshot.

"You're right, I'm not fast enough to stop you." While he spoke, Kole angled his body away to conceal the weapon. He ran one hand through his hair and grunted, feigning frustration, while the other reached around and slipped the slingshot from his belt. "Your Kayetan saved you when we couldn't. It brought you back to us." Each passing second felt like an eternity as Kole loosened the pouch and plucked out a pellet. "What about Vienna? Are you going to leave her?"

"She'll understand."

"Then you don't know her well enough. She wants you back, Felix. We all do."

"Ya want back what I *was*. Not this."

"That's not true."

Felix pulled back his sleeve. A long scar traced both sides of his arm. "Savairo took my shadow. Made me inta a monster. Merged me with one a them." One of his hands snapped to his head and pulled at his curls. "Gotta get it out."

"It's not a monster. I doesn't have to be. You saw Shikar. She went through the ritual same as you. You can use it how you wish. She'll teach you to control it." His hand shook around the slingshot. If Felix really could see through his Kayetan's eyes, Kole wouldn't manage to draw back the band before the dagger plunged into the shadow's heart.

"Kayetans slaughtered my people. They're destruction, they are." Felix held onto the hilt so tightly, Kole thought the veins of his arm might pop. "They raided my house. Did ya know that, Blondie? Vienna hid me under the bed while they took my ma and pa. Slit Ma's throat and dragged her out the front door like it was nothin'. We lay under there a whole day 'fore Leo found us." His jaw quivered as he spoke, voice shaking. "I was bred for this. Trained ta kill these bastards. No way I'm gonna let this one live. Not even ta save me."

"Then don't do it for yourself. Do it to save your sister. For the Liberation. Ohr. Your ma and pa—they wouldn't want this." Shifting his other hand behind his back, he slipped the pellet in the pouch, ready to strike if Felix didn't stand down.

"Don't care anymore. It's me or the monster."

When Felix raised the blade to attack, Kole whipped out the loaded slingshot and aimed for the sunstone dagger. As he released, black smoke whizzed through the falling ash.

Felix growled when his mark slipped away and streaked toward Kole.

The Kayetan deftly swatted Kole's projectile away. Another swirl of shadow and the Kayetan closed in on Kole, claw raised for a strike. It all happened so quick, Kole never had a chance to run.

A fresh dose of fear coursed through Kole's veins. His eyes widened at the oncoming attack.

"No!" Felix's shout ripped through the night.

The Kayetan halted.

The claw hung in the air, a hand's length from Kole's head. Still, Kole held his breath, unsure what was happening.

The Kayetan lowered its arm and looked back to its master as if awaiting the next command.

Kole gasped and stumbled back. Only now did his heart hasten, finally catching up.

Wide-eyed, Felix faced him. "It didn't—didn't hurt ya? I thought...." A dull thud, and a puff of ash as he dropped the blade and fell to his knees. "I can't do this, mate. I can't."

"You can. You made it stop." Kole tested a step. The Kayetan eyed him but made no move to intervene. Kole took it as a sign he could approach and bent down, draping an arm over a sobbing Felix. "You won't have to do it alone."

Minutes passed. The Kayetan stayed frozen while they sat there.

When Felix finally calmed, his pink face lifted, swollen eyes taking in the demon. "It'll listen ta me?"

Kole shrugged. "It already has, right?"

"If anythin' happens... if it goes and does somethin' foolish, I'm puttin' it down. No matter what happens after, ya hear? And I won't let anyone stop me then."

"It won't come to that."

Felix grunted. "Get outta here," he directed his Kayetan. "Stay outta my head."

The shadow swirled away.

The tension building in Kole's body dissolved all at once with a sigh, but his eyes stayed on Felix, whose gaze had gone to the new scars marring the sides of his own body. Scars from Savairo. The scars that signified Felix's shadow had been removed.

"Tell me, mate. Did ya wanna die after what happened ta ya? After ya burned?"

The question made him release Felix and lean away. He found his friend's green eyes staring at him, waiting for an answer: one he did not want to give. "Yes," he admitted. "I did want to."

"Why didn't ya do it?"

"I... don't know." He searched himself, homing in on the moments after he learned of Niko's death—of the annihilation of his home. Remembered the carnage of the aftermath: toppled trees ripped from the soil, plains of ash just like the ones surrounding them now, but even crueler, the scent of his people's burned flesh hanging in the air. "Russé stopped me. After that, I guess I realized things wouldn't be over or better because of it. It'd only be gone. Done."

"Done...."

Suppressed rage trickled back to Kole as he spoke of the past. It raised the hairs of his neck. "I couldn't have that. Leave things unfinished. And if I had gone through with it Ohr would be—well, it'd be—"

"Shit outta luck."

"Something like that."

Felix slumped forward and traced a finger down the raised line of scar tissue along the tender side of his arm. His hand stopped at the wisp of shadow wrapping his wrists like a bracelet. "Guess I'mma bit like ya now."

Fleeting thoughts of meeting someone disfigured like him lay in the chasms of his mind. To have someone to relate to. But *this*? Never what he wanted. By the way Felix flexed his hands and tested his legs, stretching them out, it seemed his limitations weren't as severe as Kole initially thought. The power Issira used on Felix must be far superior than the ambrosia Russé had used on Kole when he had his encounter with death. For that, Kole was grateful. It would be too painful to watch his dear friend go through the same thing he had.

Felix twisted his hands, inspecting the shadow dancing at the base of his wrists. "Don't suppose ya know what these are, do ya?"

Kole shook his head. "Obviously something to do with the ritual, but Shikar doesn't know either."

After a nod and a long stretch of silence, Felix asked, "Does it get better?" Emptiness lay behind his eyes as he spoke. "This." He signaled to his changed body lined in faint scars.

"No. Not really." *Better* wouldn't be the word he'd use to describe the last month since surviving the Black Wall. "It gets... different. Things change. You adapt. But it won't be like before."

"The blasted thing saved me, eh?"

"It was holding you when we returned from our search party." Kole shrugged. "Do you remember anything?"

"Not after." Felix rose on wobbly feet, using Kole's shoulder to balance himself. "How long's it been?"

"Nearly a week." After fetching the mask he'd dropped earlier, Kole handed it over.

"How did I—"

"Issira healed you," he added at Felix's hanging jaw. "Put this on. I'm not going to pretend to know if she's able to mend our lungs from the fumes. They're both trying to conserve energy for now."

Felix pulled on the mask. The bottled lenses made his eyes appear slightly larger. He took in Kole in for a moment, then examined himself. "One more thing."

"Yeah?"

"Why are we covered in soot?"

"There's monsters trying to eat us."

"Right." A slow nod, then, "Wait, what?"

"We'll catch you up on everything. But right now, you should go see Vienna. She'll be cross if she finds you missing."

Russé looked their way as they returned to camp. The Soul nodded, then reverted to his scouting duties. No questions tonight, it seemed.

Kole brough Felix back to the cart to where his sister slept.

With a hand over the blanket-covered lump in the cart, Felix hesitated, as if uncertain the black wisps emanating from his wrist would hurt her. A soft test. He nudged her. Then another, when she didn't wake.

After a groan, she stirred and lifted to her elbows, lids heavy under her brow. Kole could pinpoint the moment recognition sparked in her sleepy gaze. Like a jolt, she squealed and leapt into Felix's outstretched arms. "You're awake." Vienna pulled back and peered into the mask's bulbous lenses as if checking it truly *was* him.

"Yeah, I'm awake."

She tucked her face in the crook of her brother's neck, yet he still held his hands away from her.

Kole slunk away. His first urge was to hang around and talk. He wanted to be near them, but it wasn't his place. After everything, they needed privacy.

Likely Russé felt the same, because he didn't move from his position to alert Shikar and Issira or offer a 'welcome back' to their Liberation member.

Kole went to bed knowing no matter what tomorrow had in store, it would be better now that Felix had returned to them.

CHAPTER 24

Shikar pointed a stone finger south. "We're close now."

The sun had become a fuzzy ball beyond the veil over the last few days, as if someone had tossed a fur over it. It left the plains doused in an eerie gray glow. A dark shadow loomed overhead, shrouded by the thick cloak of ash. The volcano.

"Grayfall sits at the base," said Shikar, turning her watchful eye up to Felix, who'd insisted on riding the tree along with the others. Since morning, she'd been doting on him like a wolf would a pup. "Pack on more ash. We're in their territory now."

They all obeyed, slathering handfuls of cinder over every crevice of their bodies, even going so far as stuffing it in their shoes when Shikar still caught their scent. The Yamani finally satisfied, they continued. Though Kole understood the need, he hated applying the soot. Over the days, his tender skin had developed rashes in high-friction areas; his armpits and upper thighs, the place on his neck where the hem of his shirt touched, and the perimeter of his mask on his face all sprouted small, itching bumps. He tried his best to refrain from scratching—a short-lived relief. The others too, suffered the same. Well, the siblings, at least.

Vienna sat close to Felix. Between her and Shikar's persistent concern, Kole sensed his friend felt a bit smothered. They'd practically been flanking him since breakfast. Though Shikar and Vienna both questioned him throughout the morning with 'How are you feeling?' 'Do you need anything?' and 'Are you okay?', Felix remained terse.

Kole walked alongside the rambler to stretch his legs a bit. He was unsure if Felix had shared with Vienna the details of their encounter last night. By the looks of it, with his gaze permanently affixed to the roots and his hands tucked away in his pockets, it seemed Felix had retreated within himself again: a reflection of how he'd acted in the presence of his Kayetan the other night.

Could Felix hear the shadow right now? See through its eyes like he mentioned? Feel its presence? Kole gave him a once over. No hand to his head. No shifting eyes like before. The Kayetan must be keeping its distance as commanded. Or maybe, whatever pain Felix had experienced merely resulted from the high fever. He *had* been unwell — comatose — for days. Kole hoped to blame it on illness. At least then the odd behavior would go away. Otherwise, it meant a possible side effect of Felix's botched ritual: something Shikar may not know how to help.

While deep in thought, trudging through the knee-high ash, movement to the left caught Kole's eye. He wiped the glass goggles with a finger, but the powder on his skin smeared more dirt in his vision. A shadow moving through the falling ash stopped his growl of frustration short. So the Kayetan had returned to torment Felix. Kole opened his mouth, about to give warning, but the silhouette grew as it drew near: a massive humanoid — too massive to be a Kayetan.

"The cursed!" Kole had meant to yell. His voice cut short as something cold and hard slammed into him. An arm wrapped around his body, another swiftly closed over his mouth.

"Quiet, flesh-kind," a deep, raucous voice barked in his ear.

The tight restraint over Kole's upper body made it difficult for him to turn his head, but a shout from Shikar, followed by the aggressive war cry of Vienna and a braying donkey, plagued his ears.

His captor shifted, and the scene revealed itself.

Yamani. Six of them, including his abductor. They'd snagged Kole and his companions from the ramblers too easily and clamped stone hands over their mouths save for Shikar, who stood her ground before the tallest.

"Why are you here, she-rock?" The Yamani man looked like one of the divine interpretations Kole had seen sketched in one of Goren's old books, except even more intimidating. A picture of pure strength, the stone of his body flashed with the subtlest of movements despite the low light. Solid black. Polished, yet faceted around the arms, legs, and stomach as if muscles beneath forced the smooth surface to jut and shift.

"I've come to see the city."

"You bring soft bodies with you. Flesh-kind," he accused. "You knowingly endanger the land. Invite a frenzy. Careless, *she-rock*," he drew out the name, as if a vulgar slang.

Shikar flinched and growled back so low, Kole felt the ground shake through his captor's arms.

"For that, the penalty is death," the massive Yamani said.

"They have business here, Mikal," Shikar fired back with her own venom. "Do what you must after we're through. Until then, I will remain alive."

"What business could humans have here except slaughter?"

A muffled voice came from Kole's right. Russé. After a nod from Mikal, the Soul's mouth was freed. "We seek the volcano. Safe passage to the rim."

The arms around Kole tensed.

"*Into* the hive?" Mikal's steel gaze narrowed back on Shikar. "I will not allow it. You've already endangered the plains with your carelessness."

"I've taken precautions."

"No amount of dirt can cover their stink. Their smell reaches the wall."

A head lowered down to Kole's ear, nose poking into his peripheral. He tensed as his captor sniffed him, then made a gagging noise.

Shikar grunted. "Then it's only a matter of time before they come to feast. Bring us in. We're too close to the city. If you send us away, we will lure a pack mainland. Isn't that why you're here?"

"My oath is to the city. I don't protect blood-kin."

"You protect the cursed. One taste is all it takes."

A stuttered, throaty cry pierced the air from somewhere beyond in the gray landscape. The same sound of the beast who'd attack them previously. The cursed lurked out there.

"Morkaas, she-rock," Mikal said, a finger pointed her way. It must've been a Yamani curse by the way Shikar puffed her chest. "You bring death on your heels."

Mikal and Shikar stared each other down as more calls joined the first, like a pack of howling wolves. Finally, he broke away and moved to the cart. "Take them," he commanded. Two hands on the yoke, he snapped the wood as if were a twig.

"What are you doing?" Vienna asked. She'd wiggled her mouth free from her Yamani's grip.

Mikal snarled at her.

Shikar answered instead. "A distraction." The way she said it, a knowing sadness in her tone, made Kole think the animal's fate had been decided when Shikar first loaded the donkey back in Cresthaven.

Mikal slapped the donkey's rear. Old Jin took off north. No more than a few seconds, and the thick cover of ash swallowed her.

The hand over Kole's mouth dropped. Before he could react, the hulking Yamani behind him hauled Kole onto his back. The rest of their group received the same treatment. Issira rolled her eyes, while the lines around Felix's deepened, hinting that someplace deep within him, his humor still existed.

"Hang on, pup," Kole's captor ordered over his shoulder.

Kole locked his arms around the thick Yamani neck. Kole found the skin—or stone—slick and difficult to hang onto with his ash-coated garments. Unable to cross his ankles around the front of his captor's stomach due to the sheer girth of the torso, Kole's legs slipped until hands grabbed them, pinning them in place.

"Stop squirming," the Yamani growled to Kole, then lurched into a sprint after Mikal, who led the pack.

Calls of the cursed closed in, but from which direction proved indiscernible. Kole gritted his teeth against the Yamani's heavy stride. Every footfall sent a bone-shaking vibration through his core. If he didn't keep his mouth clamped shut, he found his teeth chattered.

No more than a few minutes had passed when he spotted the black city wall. The only thing Kole had to compare it to was Socren's crumbling stone border. Yet this, though apparently abandoned, stood in immaculate condition other than the dusting of soot. He wished to see how a structure so close to an active volcano could stand. The mystery would have to wait, for Mikal took a hard left, and the pack pursued.

As they came up to a puddle, the water a thick, murky black, a distant squeal penetrated the air. Old Jin.

Brutish growls overtook the brays, and Kole understood what Mikal referred to when he had said 'frenzy.' Kole gulped. A cacophony of snarls and wails chorused. He'd seen wolves hunt back home, but *this* sounded like a war zone. If they'd stayed much longer, that would've been them.

Mikal stepped into the puddle. Surprisingly deep, the water level reached his waist. The Yamani stepped further still. Elbows. Shoulders. Then his head dipped beneath the surface.

Kole's Yamani stepped up next.

"Take deep breath when I command."

"What?"

"Mask keeps lungs safe from ash, not water."

Well, duh, I know that. Kole flinched when his toes pricked the water. Warm. Almost bath-like. And boy did he need a good bath.

Ideally, any water but this. When his chin touched down, his host signaled him to inhale.

He did. The biggest breath his lungs allowed.

Dark waters clouded his goggles, so grimy and viscous that the back of the Yamani's head, less than a finger length from his face, disappeared. The murk seeped up Kole's neck, crawling between his skin and the leather. It flooded his lenses. He hadn't bet on the mask repelling water, but he'd hoped it'd hold it off a little longer. Apparently not. He shut his eyes, too afraid to risk a peek for fear of getting Souls-know-what in his vision.

But his host never dove—never swam. The tempoed thuds told Kole the Yamani, weighed down by his stone body, walked on the water's bed. Kole squeezed his legs tighter when his body buoyed toward the surface. A burn kindled in his lungs. Small at first, but the blaze seared hotter with each passing second underwater. If he could only see their destination, he might be able to hold out. Uncertainty weighed on his stamina.

At one hard step from the Yamani, Kole swallowed water. Like the breaking of a dam, the gritty murk filled his mouth and nose as his reflexes took control, and he gagged. He writhed on the Yamani's back, desperate for breath. Even an ash-filled one. In his panic, he let go of his captor.

Arms snagged him before he drifted too far and pulled him into the solid chest of the Yamani. His escort hastened his pace.

Kole shivered when they broke the surface. Fresh air bombarded his body, sending goosebumps over every inch of skin. He vomited water, but it had nowhere to go within the waterlogged mask. Still drowning. He clawed at the leather, but another hand ripped it away.

His eyes opened to the face of the Yamani, who cradled him like an infant. Kole turned his head to the side and drained his stomach. "Thank you," Kole croaked. A film of bile laced his tongue.

"You have weak lungs."

"I—sorry?" Kole finally got a good look at the Yamani who'd been carrying him. His coloring differed from Mikal. Though dark, he was a smokey brown tone. Dapple-gray specks covered his collar bone and poured down the top of his chest and shoulders until dissipating at the elbow, as if draped in a clipped cape. Shorter in stature than Mikal, his physique compared to his leader: mountainous. No doubt the stone guy could squash him with a squeeze of his fist. Kole truly felt like an infant in his grip.

Like a river masking footprints in the forest, the pond acted as a plug for their scent. It may also be the reason the Yamani had insisted on carrying Kole and his group, preventing their scent from touching the ground. The wind carried away any lingering trace of them.

A gasp came behind him. Kole used what little energy he possessed to peek around the stone giant's bicep. Russé emerged from the pond. He'd swam on his own, closely followed by his own Yamani chaperone. Other than a heaving chest, the Soul seemed composed. One by one, Vienna, Felix, Issira, and Shikar filed out, drenched in black liquid and flanked by their bodyguards.

Even Felix, in his weakened state, survived the underwater journey with a mere cough. The old glimmer returned to his friend's eyes as if amused by the whole situation.

"Let them walk," Mikal ordered.

Before Kole's escort lowered him like the rest of the group, he asked, "Does weak lungs have weak legs?"

"Umm, I'm fine to walk."

A pause, then the Yamani released him. "No need for mask here." The Yamani handed back the soggy lump of leather.

"Thanks for the ride, mate," Felix said with forced enthusiasm when he touched down. His own escort grunted, likely more out of annoyance than acknowledgment.

"Follow," Mikal said, leading the way. That's when Kole noticed the Yamani leader's hand had brightened, lit from within and casting a fiery warm light around him. The other Yamani, including Kole's escort, touched their hands to the cave floor and walls, and their hands too ignited with that same glow. The temperature rose around their group as if their rock bodies held the warmth of torches. Shikar hadn't joined in the act.

The puddle had spit them into a cool underground cave. Stalactites jutted from the roof, dripping water onto their counterparts below like salivating canines. A blue-green river, pristine as crystal, wound along the path ahead. If not for the ever-raining pollution, the waterway leading to this place might've looked the same. They traveled single file, Kole and his host at the head behind Mikal, while the rest trailed after. Silence cast over the group, save for the trickle of falling droplets diving to the river, disturbing the surface with growing rings. The echo made it sound like a summer rainstorm.

Every so often, a rumble jostled the cavern. Kole glanced up as dust and pebbles shook free and landed on the party. For a passing moment, his heart spiked, thinking of the last encounter with a cursed one in the cart. It had rattled the plains with its stride and Kole's bones with its growl. No matter the source, the Yamani men's unperturbed strides told him it was a normal occurrence.

Kole peeked over his shoulder, trying to catch Vienna's or Felix's eye, but their focus dwelled on the cave beyond. A glimpse to the Souls, and he found their own escorts lingered close — too close. The stone men kept narrowed eyes on Russé and Issira, with their chiseled noses fixed in a permanent crinkle. The Yamani suspected something. Though Kole remained oblivious as to what, it appeared they had picked out the same odd scent Shikar mentioned back in her tavern. The Souls... inhuman essence.

Not five minutes later, Mikal turned right at a fork and steered the party away from the river. The path bottlenecked, then opened into a large room. Kole's lips parted in awe.

Round nubs dotted the ceiling and floor, footprints of removed stalagmites and stalactites. A black stone table — round — rested in the center, polished and faceted like a glittering jewel. Every piece of furniture had been carved from stone. A pair of blue chairs with white-and-gray veins weaving down the sides like a cracked egg flanked a small peridot table in the corner. Swirling bronze cabinets of agate with color-shifting opal knobs lined the far wall. Plates and utensils ranged from smokey, to rose, to colorless quartz. The familiar obsidian, like the blade in Kole's pocket, dominated the space; chairs, shelves along the walls, and in some areas, atop the floor like grand rugs. Chiseled to perfection — everything. It made for a beautiful picture, yet the space held a cold and uninviting feeling compared to the worn, lived-in spaces Kole was so used to in the forest.

Mikal offered them no seat and instead turned and leaned against the table, arms crossed over his wide chest. Where his hand touched his elbow and stomach, the light of his fist bled into his body, making a piece of his torso glow, too. "Grarstein, cover the air."

Kole's chaperone left his side and opened one of the ornate drawers of the cabinet. His hands clanked, rock on rock as he rummaged through. Every stone he touched pulled some of the light away from his hand.

The other Yamani moved around the room and touched places on the walls. The orange glow transferred into the cave walls and soon the room was spotted in light.

"Your stay is temporary. Out of necessity." Mikal's amber eyes studied Kole's party one at a time. The two Yamani who had escorted

Issira and Russé approached their leader and whispered something in his ear. Mikal's nose flinched. His eyes moved like daggers between the Souls. "You will be escorted back to your lands once the cursed ones have settled. Until then, you will stay under heavy supervision."

"We cannot leave," Russé challenged.

"Right. You have business here." Mikal mocked with a shift of his weight. Another twitch of his nose. "Tell me, *human*, why do you seek the volcano?"

Even Shikar perked up, waiting for the answer.

The sound of scraping flint forced Kole's eyes to Grarstein, who held a bouquet of reed-like plants. Smoke floated from the tips and clouded the air with a bitter, earthy scent.

"There is something there we need," said Russé.

"Which is...?"

Russé glanced to Issira, then flicked his eyes to Kole, an uncertainty within them as if, for a moment, he'd hoped Kole would answer. "We're not sure."

A growl resonated in the air, which thickened with smoke by the minute. "My patience is weak." Mikal pushed from the table. Thuds rattled Kole's bones as the great Yamani approached Russé. "I am charged with keeping this city. Nothing goes on within it—*can* go on—without my knowledge. If you want something in my city, be clear. Keep up with your secrets and I will ensure you never step foot in Grayfall again." Yellow eyes flicked to Shikar, then he leaned down to Russé, voice a whisper, "With or without help."

"We seek the Red Soul," Kole said. The weight of every eye turned on him; some curious, some bewildered, but the most intense came from Russé. They burned holes in his sopping tunic.

Mikal turned, taking in Kole as if really seeing him for the first time. "The Red Soul?"

"He's in the volcano. Somewhere. We don't know much else. But if we can find him, we can release him and—"

"I know where Obell rests."

Kole gaped.

"Even these guys knew? C'mon," Felix whined. "They're in the middle of nowhere." A look from Russé hushed him, but his mouth weighed heavy to the side in a defiant frown.

"Of course we know," Mikal spat as if insulted. "Yamani are of earth. We feel his presence trapped within. Why else do you think the cursed have made the volcano their home? They crave him."

"What are the numbers now?" Shikar asked, breaking her silence.

"Our hand has been forced. Three have been slain this year. Their bloodlust grew too manic to keep under control. The others follow that path by the day."

"Names? Do you have names?" A deep desperation seeped from Shikar's words.

Mikal sneered, then turned back to Russé, ignoring her inquiry. "What plans do you have to release the Soul?"

Kole's party slowly turned their heads to him. Every Yamani followed their gazes to scrawny, scarred Kole. He shivered under the scrutiny. Even Grarstein, waving the incense near an upward-leading stairway at the far end of the room, paused.

Mikal crossed the room. "Two humans, litter mates," he directed at the siblings. "A Yamani. Two...," his gaze lingered on the Souls, "*divine*." Then he planted before Kole and leaned in for a second sniff. "And a damaged mixed-breed?"

Back in the village, Shikar had implied the same thing. Kole's scent was off, conjugated with the Souls in his head. The 'damaged' part cut deeper than Kole liked. Through the conversation, he'd almost forgotten his angry red scars. A reminder never ceased to present itself.

"He's not damaged," Felix growled under his breath.

Kole allowed a glance to his friend, who stroked his own scars lining the outside of his hand.

"And he's just a boy," Vienna added.

Although Kole recognized it as an attempt to defend him, her statement left a heaviness in his chest. *Just a boy.*

Mikal ignored the siblings and lowered down, hands on his knees so his eyes dropped in line with Kole's. "How did you burn?"

The question left a simmering rage at the base of Kole's spine. He tried to vanquish it, but it surged up and painted his words venomous as he seethed, "The Black Wall."

Yellow eyes flashed. "A survivor." Mikal rose, folding his arms over his sculpted chest as if satisfied by the answer. "The Soulstone has been excavated, but you'll never reach it. Its energy attracts our cursed. They swarm it like scavengers to a carcass."

"Soulstone?" Vienna asked.

"When the cursed first grew out of control, we sought the Red Soul. We dug him out, but our tools cannot penetrate the Soulstone. Obell sits in the heart of our volcano." Mikal squinted to Kole. "Awaiting the burned one, it seems."

Kole returned the Yamani's mocking stare.

"We can release him," Russé assured. "We just need a way in."

"The lava tubes are the only way," said Mikal. "Anyone unfamiliar will lose their way."

"We're used ta mazes," Felix said.

"Then you will have no problem." A rumble around the room as Mikal's men laughed.

Kole remembered the way to the Liberation hideout, an abandoned mine beneath the Poleer mountains. 'The Cobweb,' as Felix called it. Though Kole doubted mine shafts would hold the slightest similarity to help navigate a path through lava tubes. The Yamani's help, if they would offer it, would be the key to finding the Soulstone.

"Lead us there." Issira's voice echoed eerily within the cavern.

"I will not risk my people on a death mission. We have duties here in the city. A job that will become more difficult the longer flesh-kind stay. Here is my proposition." Mikal raised a hand to Grarstein.

With the cavern now completely veiled in thick, pungent smog, Grarstein pinched the smoldering herbs and squelched the smoke. He crossed the room to the Yamani leader's side.

Mikal nodded his way as he approached. "Grarstein will show you the entrance of the volcano. No further. We will equip you with weapons." He looked over Kole and his group. "You'll need proper attire and a map of the tubes. The tunnels have not been explored for two decades. Many have collapsed. New ones may have formed—the cursed drill the earth like ants. There may be no clear path left to the Soulstone, but that is your problem. You will have two days to do this. Fail or not, we will escort you out."

"Two days?" Kole cried.

Mikal's piercing eyes landed back on him. "If your comrades are who I think they are, it should pose no problem. You will have expert guidance in the volcano." He sneered. "All Yamani can read the earth, and you have your very own." He nodded to Shikar. "You can still do that can't you? Or has living among humans dulled your senses?"

When Kole studied Shikar, who snarled in response, he did a double-take. Her Kayetan had returned. Not standing to the side, claws out, ready for a command but spread long over the cave wall, blending in with the shadows of the rest of the group. She hid her true nature from Mikal. A moment of confusion swept through Kole. It dawned on him that Shikar already seemed lesser in Mikal's eyes because she'd abandoned her kind. No doubt he'd think more poorly if he knew she'd been tainted by Savairo.

Russé dipped his head. "Two days will suffice."

"Good." Mikal nodded. "What of you, she-rock? Why have you returned home? Don't tell me you escorted them here out of the kindness of your heart. What's in it for you?"

Shikar swelled, stone jaw flexing. "I seek my daughter."

The sound of grinding rock thrummed from Mikal and his men.

The leader's eyes seemed to glow with anger. His voice rumbled low. "You know the laws. I forbade it."

Shiakr's body deflated, and she stepped back.

"What? Why?" Kole fumed. "She just wants to say goodbye before—"

Mikal's obsidian head snapped to Kole. "Don't speak of what you don't know, burned one."

"But—"

Russé squeezed Kole's shoulder in warning.

He shrugged it off with a glare to the Soul. Not the time or place to argue with Russé or Mikal, who could still refuse their request to go into the volcano. Still, what law forbade Shikar from her own child? Was she here somewhere? One of Mikal's troops? Then again, as he scanned the Yamani in the room, no other female stood present. He'd have a better chance of getting answers by grilling Shikar.

Mikal turned to his line of men, who blocked the exit as if they expected their visitors to run. "Take your posts. No one in or out." They scattered, save for one lumbering form who guarded the passage to the tunnels. "Grarstein, take Shikar and the pups upstairs. They'll need rest. As for our divine, you will stay with me for the time being."

The Souls eyed each other as Grarstein summoned the rest of their group. Shikar's Kayetan mimicked her every move so as to not draw suspicion. But Kole knew what to look for. The long claws, though curled into fists to look more like a Yamani hand, still poked through like spiked knuckles.

Russé caught Kole's eye. "We will be up in a moment." Which translated to 'don't get into any trouble.'

"Up you go," Grarstein barked at Kole, who'd lingered behind.

He followed Vienna, Felix, and Shikar up the steps, Grarstein hovering behind like a glorified cattle dog.

"What was big boy's name, again? Gary?" Felix called back, his voice just loud enough to carry back to the hulking Yamani.

"I am Grarstein."

"I like Gary better. Can we call ya Gary?"

"I think Gary suits him," Shikar mocked from the top of the stairs.

"She-rock suits *you*," Grarstein clapped back.

"Ah, he's a feisty one." Felix turned, walking backwards up the steps as he waved a finger at their chaperone. "I like ya, Gary."

Vienna grabbed her brother's shoulder and pulled him back around. "Felix, please. Don't start anything."

They hiked up the twisting staircase for what seemed like ten minutes with only the light from Grarstein's candle to guide them. When exhaustion forced Kole to fall behind, Grarstein wordlessly scooped him up in one arm and carried him the remainder. Fortunately, Vienna and Felix appeared too preoccupied with their own climb to turn around, else he swore they'd see his vibrant red face through the dim light. Finally, the path widened into an egg-shaped chasm. Grarstein released Kole on the top step.

Less ornate than the previous room, with plain walls curling into a dome, this area stood above ground as determined by the sight beyond the single window cut from the rock. The faint, ghost-like outline of a building, blurred by swirling ash, told Kole they were in the city. The urge to see the infamous cursed Grayfall drove his feet forward, but he stopped at the bizarre floor. Large, humanoid-shaped depressions dotted the length. It reminded Kole of casts used to make statues, but Yamani-sized.

Before Kole could question about them, Grarstein waved a hand to the right half of the room. "These beds taken. Other side free."

"Beds?" Felix walked to the edge of one, which could have easily fit four grown men. "Ya want us ta sleep in this?"

"Yamani slumber in the earth. It helps rekindle our connection," Shikar answered.

"Wait. Didn't ya have a bed, Shikar?"

Grarstein gave a rumbling laugh. "Soft bed for soft body. You will toughen up here."

They all settled in. Grarstein's eyes trailed them as they picked a row of 'beds' next to one another. But Shikar moved to the end of the room without a word and sank into one of the depressions. Her kin had given no gracious welcoming. He'd need time to cool off, too, he supposed, if he faced that sort of greeting.

"Look at this," Vienna beckoned from the window.

Felix and Kole flanked her.

A few more details of the city revealed themselves at closer inspection. Their own building stood a mere story tall. As for the adjacent building, he couldn't quite tell with the gray haze's interference, but no visible roof meant it reached three or four stories, at least. Stone walls, stone ledges and doors. Even the window, he noticed with a tap of his knuckle, promised thin quartz opposed to glass.

After their fill of gazing at the city, Kole, Vienna, and Felix, exhausted from the day, changed into drier clothes (Kole had picked the full sleeve and pants Liberation uniform to fight off the cool underground air), then curled up in their basin-like beds. They stuffed blankets, pillows, extra clothes, and emptied sacks beneath them to buffer their bones from the chill rock.

"Anyone else feel like we're sleepin' six feet under?" Felix had said as they lowered themselves into the holes, yet minutes later, his faint snores drifted around the room.

Despite several layers of cushion, pangs from his scarred skin kept Kole awake. That and Felix's comparison of the Yamani bed to graves aided in his restlessness.

Russé and Issira had yet to return. Kole wished to look over Goren's journal while he had a semi-peaceful moment, but the Soul had kept his pack. If not for the lengthy climb back to the main room, he may have been tempted to retrieve it. Instead, he practiced the mind exercises Russé had taught him after they started their journey to find Issira. Calm and clear. "Focus on your breaths, long and steady. Slow your heart rate. Reach the state of a waking dream." Kole pondered the old Soul's words and tried to meditate.

A gentle wind tickled the hairs on his neck. He opened an eye. Nothing. Still, he scrambled to his feet. The Yamani bed, or rather bowl-like impression in the floor, sunk so low, even at full height the top of his eyes barely reached the floor. He curled his fingers over the ledge and peered at the window.

It stood open. Barely a crack wide enough for a finger to slide through, if that. Unnoticeable unless you knew what to look for. A shadow slipped through and darted in. After a quick look to Grarstein standing—well, sitting—guard at the staircase reading a book, Kole swiveled his head to the opposite side of the room where Shikar had holed up. Shikar's Kayetan always came and went in the night. Whether fulfilling Shikar's orders or free to roam, Kole couldn't be sure. Maybe Shikar had sent it to look for Felix's Kayetan. Kole hadn't seen his friend's shadow since the night it almost attacked him.

Movement stopped his thoughts. Shikar rose with such silence, Kole would've thought his ears were plugged. She tugged on the window, but it refused to budge. As her Kayetan darted to the stair, Kole ducked and snuggled against the sloping wall of his bed trying to feign sleep. *Yeah, 'cause you sleep standing up. Great job.* It proved enough, fore the shadow slipped by without a passing glance and slithered to the ceiling of the stairwell. A moment later, it disappeared into the dark hall.

The screech of scraping metal on rock emerged from below. Grarstein perked up and tossed his book aside. Kole ducked in case the Yamani guard did a sweep, only rising once heavy footfalls descended the stair. The noise must've covered up Shikar's escape, because when he glanced back to the window, it sat closed and his companion was gone. A diversion. The Yamani and her Kayetan had planned the whole thing. But why?

Kole climbed out of the stone bowl and rushed to the window. Ash swallowed a dull silhouette behind its curtain. Where was she going? His fingers curled around the sill, then paused. He shouldn't go. At least not alone. But the one person he'd think to share the chase had been hurt the last time. Felix was out. And Vienna? She wouldn't let him go, let alone leave Felix behind.

Rumors of the dangers of the city plagued his subconscious. He pushed them aside. If he caught up to Shikar, he'd be safe. She'd handled herself against the cursed in the plains. This was no different.

Grarstein's agitated growls traveled up the stairs.

Now or never.

He thrust the window open and climbed out, feet first. A six-foot drop. He landed firmly, then jumped to close the window. Only when he turned to face the haze did he remember he'd forgotten to take his bulbous mask. He untucked the Liberation mask from his neck and pulled the thin cloth over his mouth. No goggles to protect his eyes, but his lungs would be safe. *Safe-ish.* Didn't matter. He wouldn't be gone long.

CHAPTER 25

"The stone beasts have taken them in." Savairo dismissed his Kayetan scout, then pressed an open vial to his lips, chugging the contents. The bottle marked the third he'd emptied today. Neck veins swelled, knuckles popped, and he rolled his shoulders with a deep inhale. "We can cut them off before they enter the city."

"No." The force in her own voice surprised her. Piper had kept close tabs on his stash of blood. That bottle had been the last from the rituals. In a few hours, Savairo's manic self would return—too short of time to pull off the kidnapping. No telling what chaos he'd cause in a city like Grayfall. He'd draw every cursed beast's attention. *There's no coming back from that.*

Savairo turned to her, his coal-like eyes glinting through the low light.

She stepped forward and put just enough distance between them so the swirling ash might hide her clenching jaw. A slow breath to keep from snapping again, then she tried her best to backtrack. "We can't see any better than them. It's best if we follow—*I* follow."

"My Kayetans can swipe the boy from under their noses."

"You have three shadows to your name. Do you really think they can stand up to two Souls and half a dozen Yamani? And the cursed— how do your Kayetans measure up against those creatures? For all you've lost, I thought you'd want to save what's left of your precious slaves. There'll be no more towns to replenish your demons. Not in this Soul-forsaken place." Piper dusted the ash from her shoulder with a swipe of her hand, but more replaced it.

Silence met her.

At least he can still see reason. For now, anyway.

"Let them go inside where they think they're safe," Piper said. "Once their guards are down, I'll grab the boy." Her fingers tucked into the pouch at her hip and fondled the half-empty vial of Aterus' blood.

"In the meantime, don't draw attention to yourself unless you want to be eaten."

A wailing animal cried in the distance, but the savage snarls and growls from what Piper could only guess was the cursed catching their prey drowned it out. The proximity of the beasts sprouted a foul thought. As she turned for the wretched city, she pulled her dagger and made a small incision in her left forearm, enough to maintain a slow drip. A trail for the cursed to find. A trail to Savairo. She hoped they'd do her dirty work for her. After half a mile, she closed the wound so they wouldn't track her instead.

CHAPTER 26

The wind howled in Kole's ear. Ash and dirt slapped the bare skin around his eyes. His mask kept the grit from entering his mouth, but if fumes hung in the air, they'd surely find his lungs. He wiped his watering eyes out of habit, each time expecting it'd clear his vision, but to no avail.

Though gray soot washed out the stone buildings along the road, giving their edges a blurred, watercolor effect, his path stood clear ahead. Shikar's heavy footprints lay stamped into the fresh powder. New winds swept the depressions away every now and then, but he kept pace and found the next easily enough.

All along, Russé's condemning voice harassed his thoughts. The Soul would be livid upon his return. Rightly so. He'd disobeyed. *Again.* But something about the Yamani reared his suspicion. Since Mikal and Shikar refused to fess up, he'd find out himself. Plus, how much trouble could he get into with a Yamani around? Shikar knew her own city.

When he veered too close to the side of the street, details of the building revealed themselves. A door stood open to his right. Did he dare peek inside? The footprints continued straight ahead. He paused, giving it a thought. The wind had slowed for a moment, leaving the path unsullied. *A peek won't hurt.*

Kole counted his steps to the door so he knew how far away the trail lay from the entrance, then stepped through the double-wide threshold. Remnants of the door lay crumbled across the room as if a mighty blow had kicked it in. His eyes adjusted to the low light.

Long lines of cabinets and finely carved pedestals declared the room as a former shop. Missing chunks of stone walls and toppled furniture made the place look like it had been ransacked long ago. The claw marks scarring the stone gave away the culprit. From the looks of it, the cursed had been up and down this city ten times over. *When* was the real question. The thick buildup of ash draping every surface calmed the bubbling nerves of his stomach. This building had lay untouched for at least a little while, as did the entire city, he guessed by the eerie absence of any signs of life.

A shimmer from the corner caught his eye, and he wandered over. He wiped a hand over the only surviving glass box in the shop. Years of residue drifted to the floor. A blue crystal necklace stared up at him. Five roughly cut shards pointed out from the middle acting as petals, while the central stone consisted of a swirling opal the size of his thumbnail.

Kole lifted the fragile box and took the trinket. *No one will miss it.* It'd been lost for Souls-knew how long. If he hadn't come along, it'd remain that way. Knowing he'd been off the path too long, he tucked the pendant into his pocket and hurried to the door.

A growl stopped him dead.

Fear surged up Kole's spine. The noise came from the road, somewhere nearby.

He slid up to the wall and let one eye peer beyond the door frame. Nothing but gray winds in sight. His fingers glided along the wall, feeling his way out of the building and around the corner for a glimpse of the source.

Shikar's voice carried to him. The muscles of his neck relaxed a bit at the familiar sound. But she was speaking to someone. Hands held out ahead of him, he blindly felt his way along the side of the building.

Shikar stood in the middle of an alley, back to him and slightly hunched over as if inspecting something. A sweetness hung in her tone. The kind of voice Kole saved for comforting the younger orphans in camp when they woke with hideous nightmares: reassuring and soothing.

Kole stepped from the wall. "Shikar? Who are you talking to?"

The moment his words passed his lips, the Yamani spun, her yellow eyes wide like a full harvest moon. A small, dark figure stood next to her.

His eyes trailed the strange new creature; rough stone skin the color of a starless sky, a round, youthful face, and golden eyes. A mini Yamani. A child. But not just *a* child. Shikar's. It must be.

Those eyes. Those gilded, innocent eyes turned red and trained on Kole.

Shikar dropped to her knees, her hands clasped together. "No, Liara. Resist."

Kole took a step back as the young Yamani's skin cracked like fissures in an earthquake. The small body expanded, doubled, then tripled in size, her back solidifying to a sickly arch. Foam spewed from her lopsided mouth. Disjointed limbs popped back into in place. Within the gem-like body, red dots of liquid churned. Vienna's stone came to mind. The one she'd found right after they'd been attacked in the plains.

This. This was what Vienna had seen. No wonder she wouldn't speak of it.

Kole remembered her words. "This overwhelming urge to drop my weapons and fling myself at it consumed me."

He blinked and forced his attention to Shikar, who rose. At full height, she barely came up to the monster's waist. A haze of anger veiled her eyes.

"Run, Kole. For your sake, I hope you're faster than you look."

The cursed lifted, arms reaching wide as that low-pitched click Kole had heard in the plains boomed from its throat. A battle-cry or a hunting call, Kole didn't know. No way he'd stay to find out.

Kole spun on his heel. The momentum threw him off balance for a brief second, but he gripped the building wall, kicked off, and forced his feet to move. The path leading back to the window proved difficult to find in his adrenaline-fueled scramble. A footprint here. One there. Then the trail ended.

A booming crash echoed in the alley over his shoulder. Even a glance back gave him no hints of its origin, for the ash hung so thick, it'd cutoff line of sight to Shikar in the few yards he'd stumbled. Another crash resounded, and Kole assumed Shikar must be entangled in battle with the creature—her own child.

Bounding down the street, he found a faded footprint. At first thought, he meant to follow it, but clarity hit him: luring one of those things to base might not be the best call. Where to go? Further into the city? Before he could properly think it through, Kole lurched at the next corner. If he wanted to keep everyone at base safe, he'd need a decoy path.

So he ran blindly, stretching his stride as wide as he dared. Risking a tear in his scars certainly meant bad news. Soot clouded his already watering eyes as the wind bashed him head on. He zigzagged between the stone buildings when he could, touching everything in arms-reach to spread his odor, and hoped the chaos he'd wrought wouldn't attract any more attention.

For a minute or two, it seemed his plan had worked. The further he went, the softer Shikar's sounds of battle became.

Then, quiet descended.

A tingle spiraled up his spine. A victor had prevailed. Now a growing rumble, like thunder on the horizon, preyed upon him. Either Shikar was coming to retrieve him or....

He knew the answer.

His eyes darted back and forth down the street. They landed on an ash drift piled up in the corner. As he beelined for it, he yanked the waterskin from his belt, doused himself, then dove for the soot.

The soft powder enveloped his body and clung to the damp patches. Taking two handfuls into wet palms, he jumped to his feet and emulsified it into a runny, gray paste. Quick swipes to his underarms, groin, and neck to conceal his scent, and he continued his path to....

He hesitated. He'd only gone a block, yet each direction he turned looked the same, washed out by the gray veiled wind. The drum of his heart deafened him and fogged his brain. Back-tracking would help regain his bearings. It'd also put him directly in the creature's path. He'd have to bank on stealth—the one thing he'd excelled at before obtaining his burns. *I don't need to be quick. I just need to be quiet... and downwind.* If he followed his same trail back for a bit, he'd prevent creating a new line of scent for the cursed to track. Hopefully that would would throw the beast off his tail.

After a hard swallow, he commanded his feet toward the sounds of the oncoming monster. He held the path until his limbs shivered in fear before breaking away. Sheer courage outweighed his instincts enough to get him a couple dozen yards back the way he'd come—enough distance to sneak by once the cursed passed.

A frantic look to the left revealed the looming silhouette of a building. He rushed over. Crumbled stone containers littered the adjacent alley. The shards trembled as a rumble strengthened to the likes of an earthquake. He sank behind a box big enough to conceal most of his body and peered over the top. Despite all his concentration, he failed to slow his breathing. Instead, he forced it out his nose to prevent the scent of his mouth from drifting into the airstream.

He waited.

Loose shingles rained down in the alley. One crashed an arm's reach away—too close for comfort. Kole inched closer to the building, wedged between the wall and stone box for cover. Less than a second after he pulled his feet in, a rock slammed down like a meteor, cracking the cobbles below. Shrapnel from the exploding stone shot toward him. He flung his arms up to protect his face, but one slid through and clipped his temple. The incessant clicks of the nearing creature drowned out his string of curses as a pearl of blood ballooned through the caked soot.

He cupped handfuls of ash and patted it on the open wound. After the third wipe, he shimmied back into his hiding spot.

The scent of his blood surely mingled with the current. Nothing he did now could fix that. *Just hope it's moving too fast to catch it.*

A hulking form broke through the shroud. The black-stoned creature stampeded past the mouth of the alley in a blink of an eye. At that speed, Kole only had a moment before the cursed reached the end of his decoy trail and rounded back.

He went to move, but his legs shook too violently to gain traction. On hands and knees, he crawled out from behind the stone container, then used it to pull himself to his feet. *Go! Come on, legs. Please.* One foot pounded in front of the other. Stride by stride, he expanded the distance between him and the cursed.

The quake stopped. A roar ripped through the city. The beast had reached the end of the trail.

Terror seeped through Kole's veins, sabotaging his getaway. His steps faltered. Toes caught on the uneven road hiding beneath the blanket of ash. His flailing arms kept him upright, but every move diminished his energy. The exhaustion of his prolonged heightened nerves took a toll—slowed his pace, though he fought against it.

Tremors shook the earth again, signaling the cursed was on the move. Its strides closed in.

The time for discretion had passed. A warm stream of blood trailed down Kole's cheek and neck where his efforts to suppress his wound fell short.

The cursed hunted him.

"Shikar!" Kole called out, but it came out as a wheezed moan. Dizziness overtook him, either from overheating, succumbing to the toxic fumes, or a mix of both. He staggered and lurched.

Hot breath, like the smoke from a bonfire, panted on his back.

It had found him.

Kole didn't dare look back. Not even when what felt like a solid wall of stone crushed into his side.

Weightlessness. His stomach dropped as the impact threw him a dozen yards up the road. He tumbled and rolled, bouncing off the ground four times before he finally skidded to a stop.

For a moment, pain didn't register. A numbness coursed through him. Like thawing ice, it melted away, and searing jolts bellowed from every inch of his body. The taste of iron coated his tongue, choking him.

Kole barely caught a glimpse of the cursed beast as it closed in and towered over him, its crooked mouth opening to consume. Rows upon rows of sharp teeth filled the entirety of the beast's mouth. No tongue or uvula, only a black hole of canines.

But something made it stop abruptly... and turn away. Not just turn away — flee.

A stabbing pang in his neck met him when he tried to lift to his elbows. He surrendered to the pain and collapsed on his side, waiting for the cursed to return to its meal.

Someone, human-sized, flashed in his peripheral.

"Shikar?" he wanted to say but gargled on blood instead.

A wail came from the cursed, wherever it had run.

The next thing Kole knew, a pair of arms dragged him up and flung him over a shoulder. The whiplash knocked him out for a moment, but color returned to his vision once again. His body ached as it bounced against his rescuer's back.

Not Shikar. Too small — soft.

The blood from his mouth drained to his nose. "Vienna?" he croaked.

"Quiet."

Something about the voice sparked a faint recollection. Not *quite* a memory. No face came to mind. But a *feeling*. Something good. Though Kole couldn't pinpoint where it came from or who the voice belonged to, his heart told him he was safe.

Another rush to his head as his rescuer shrugged Kole off, and his rump hit hard floor — back reclining onto something soft. Kole blinked, taming his spinning vision.

A hooded figure stood over him; the fabric pulled so far down, Kole only glimpsed a chin. Pale. Wide hips suggested a female.

She fiddled with something in her hands, then knelt next to him.

"Who are — "

"I'm sorry." Like a striking viper, she grabbed his chin, titled it back, and shoved a vial to his open mouth.

The tang of blood ran down his throat before he could fight it back. He kicked and writhed, his hands grabbing at the feeding arm, but she pushed harder until he'd consumed the lot.

As he spit the residual onto the ground, footsteps clicked away.

"Wait. Where are you going? Who are — " An explosion of cramps wrecked Kole's stomach. It felt as if a hand grew in his gut and clawed at the fleshy lining in attempts to rupture the organ. Feverish heat burst from his abdomen, and his eyes forcibly rolled back in his head as the convulsions came.

CHAPTER 27

Kole peeled open his heavy lids.

Thundering red clouds dominated the sky. Not the delicate hue of a sunset but a deep, rusty maroon. The air, though clean of ash, left a sharp, bitterness on his tongue. Like... *like the smell of a fresh kill.*

He eased from the floor and climbed to his feet.

The landscape held no sign of Grayfall or the volcano. Flat horizons spanned every direction. And the ground—not soil but liquid. Ruby ripples spread from his feet, yet when he checked his clothing and boot bottoms, not a single drop had transferred.

"So, this is what you think of me?"

Kole whipped around at the voice.

A man stood a dozen yards away, his hands held out to the ghastly landscape. Salt-and-pepper hair graced his head, and his clothes, though plain and white, stretched snug across shoulders and a chest, a physique that could only have been acquired through hard labor. He tutted. "They have misled you, boy."

"Who are you? Where are we?"

The man lifted his chin and gave a slow blink as if agitated by the question. "We are in your head."

"What?"

"It isn't ideal. I wanted to speak with you in person, so I could ensure you see... *we* see... eye to eye. But what's done is done. Consequences will be dealt with later."

"Who *are* you?"

"I am your enemy, as my brothers and sisters would have you believe." Gray streaked brows set heavy over blue eyes.

Breath caught in Kole's throat. "Aterus." The name came out as a whisper.

"It's cruel the way they've twisted your mind." He leaned down and dragged a finger over the crimson ocean beneath his feet. New waves of ripples flourished, expanding out to Kole. Aterus inspected his hand. "Is this supposed to be blood? Hmm, you see me as a murderer." He tilted his head. "Fair. Death has come from my hand. But the others aren't so innocent, either. They've done their share."

"The Black Wall has killed thousands."

"There are far worse things than death. The Yamani know that most intimately. Their children turned to monsters. I warned Obell. Told him to take his time. A botched job leads to a problematic creation. The pain he's caused rocked all of Ohr. When a life lasts for an eternity, the suffering walks along with it." A weak smile. "And then there's Issira. I know you've met. Her Kayetans brought out the evil in humanity."

"*Issira's?*"

"They really tell you nothing." Aterus' eyes narrowed. "Yes, *Issira's* Kayetans. The creatures she wanted to bestow upon the earth. All my kin sought to create a rival to my humans, the superior lifeform, but the others created for amusement. That's why they never matched what I did with humanity. Issira knew it. It's the reason she sought my help."

Kole's earlier conversation with Issira played back in his head. The deal she had made. The Kayetans were the payment for her secrecy about Aterus' child. "But they were under Savairo's rule. *You* trained him to use them against us."

"I am not here to compare death tolls. I have come to enlighten you. Lay the truth before your feet and let you decide your own fate. Something Russé is too scared to do."

"What are you talking about?"

"He's told you his side of the story, twisted it to his narrative. Now I'll tell you mine, and how this whole mess came to rest on your shoulders." Aterus turned his gaze to the ocean beneath.

Kole stepped back as the blood churned. The face of a young woman appeared in the red liquid. Her mouth upturned into a smile and she laughed.

"The moment I saw her, I knew she was something special. Something I never could've created. Not only her beauty but her soul. My Evangeline."

Kole recognized the name.

The scene changed. Now, the woman walked through a meadow, her hand intertwined in another's just out of view. She tugged, and a younger version of Aterus joined the replaying memory. "I began to develop human feelings. Love. After a time, I knew I couldn't lose her. I granted her immortality so we'd never have to part. Mine forever."

Like a breaking dam, blood poured over the serene meadow, and it shifted to black. Angry faces emerged. Some Kole recognized—Issira and Russé—others, he guessed, were Souls he had yet to meet.

"My kin felt differently. They didn't see love. They didn't see how I'd developed, changed from a god to something more... humble. I wanted to do good for her and everything she touched."

The vision flashed. Evangeline held a hand over her swelling stomach. In the image, young Aterus appeared behind her and rested his chin on her shoulder. The cries of a baby echoed around the landscape.

Aterus waved a hand, and the picture faded. Piercing eyes fell to Kole. "Have you ever cared about someone so dearly, you'd do anything in your power to keep them safe?"

Kole swallowed the lump in his dry throat. Niko. Memories of his friend jotting notes and scribbles in his dear journal. The way he'd tease Kole about his baby face and flaunt his chin of stubble. Late nights they'd lay awake and talk of their plans to become the greatest shepherds Solpate had ever seen—rivals to Russé even.

Not two months had passed since the night the Black Wall took him. Yet it seemed so long ago. He pursed his lips, fighting back the wave of grief. But it gripped him hard when he realized he could no longer recall the sound of Niko's voice.

"Maybe you're too young to know of love." Aterus sighed. "There are other things I can offer. Money, power... but you desire something else do you not? All you have to do is ask and I will give it, Kole."

"What are you playing at? You think you can entice me with promises and gifts? And for what? Why do you waste your time? What do you want from me?"

"I've already proven my power over the Souls. Escaping their prisons won't change a thing. I can throw them back in whenever I wish. It's you, Kole. I need *you*."

Kole forced a laugh. "A new puppet to replace Savairo? Are you sick of your old toy and want a new one?" Once the words left his lips, a sense of dread fell over him. In times before his burns, he'd considered himself brave. But this? Antagonizing a god? He swallowed, eyes taking in the Soul's every reaction. "If you want the Souls take them." Kole gestured to his body. "I'm just a burned kid, right? It's not like I can stop you."

"No. Not a replacement for Savairo." Aterus remained poised as if aware of Kole's scrutiny. "You have something I seek. Leverage over my kin. And a means of communication."

"You want to *use* me," Kole accused.

"I want to give you your life back. Your former body."

Despite himself, he repeated those last words aloud. "My body?" Kole looked to the angry red blotched skin of his hands, scarred forever. "You can fix me?"

"Easily, when I achieve full power. You can be what you were before the flames touched you."

A pregnant pause.

Kole blinked. The temptation of regaining his former body left him unfocused. No more limitations. He could run again. Climb and fight. He could quit hiding behind his hood and have his old face back. Those round chubby cheeks that he'd once hated seemed like a blessing now. No more odd looks. No more pity cast his way. He could be *him* again. Unashamed. Free to live. To love....

Aterus must've sensed his chance to strike, for he began to pace, circling Kole as he spoke. "I will not ascend. I will not abandon humanity. Convince my kin to let me stay. I have witnessed what your kind is capable of. I granted you free will, and with it you've built great cities, garnered families and love. But there's also a darkness that needs to be kept in check. Love swings the other way on the pendulum. To war and hate. *I* can protect Ohr from that. I am the only Soul interested in saving you from yourselves."

The hope of reversing the burns over his body consumed nearly every thought. It took a moment for Kole to digest Aterus' words. "Where were you during the rebellion? You didn't protect the refugees from war; you brought it on us. *Russé* was there, not you."

"I can't distract myself with small squabbles. Too much is at stake in my current state." With sickening speed, Aterus flung out his hands. The air above shimmered. Floating above one palm was the figure of a sleeping woman, and above the other, familiar black flames. "My powers are split between Evangeline and holding back the Black Wall. If I continue to deplete myself," he clenched his fists, extinguishing the images, "both will perish. Intervening in the rebellion would have done the same. The only way everyone wins is if my dear brothers and sisters comply. They get what they want: ascension. And I get what I desire."

"What about the Black Wall? It exists because of an imbalance of power, right? What happens when six gods leave and one stays?"

"Destruction. But that is not what I'm proposing. They will bestow their powers to me. Balance will reside in one Soul, and the wall departs from Ohr." Aterus tilted his head slightly, eyes firm on Kole. "You will have a new body, free of this burden you carry. Isn't that what you want?"

"Yes," Kole admitted. "And the Black Wall gone."

"So we have a deal." The Soul walked forward and stopped an arm's length away. "You convince the Souls to relinquish their power and ascend. In return, I will heal your body and destroy the Black Wall." He offered a calloused hand.

Kole stared at it. Another outstanding deal lay between him and Russé. He'd agreed to release the Souls for Russé's help at translating Goren's journal. But what did that journal have to offer any longer? More answers about his family—where he came from? Did it matter, though? His true family lay in Niko and Solpate. The journal would only cause pain. Aterus' deal... it would heal him.

But at what cost?

"Something is preoccupying your mind." Aterus lowered his hand and folded his arms, slightly leaned back as if studying Kole. "I can see it—him. Is this what you want?"

The red ocean bubbled between Aterus and Kole. From it, rose a pillar of blood. It molded itself into a life-like red statue resembling Niko.

"Ah, yes. A friend of yours? What happened to him?"

"He burned in your wall," Kole spat with venom, though his sight never faltered from his friend. He'd forgotten about the scar on Niko's chin. Why had it slipped from his memory?

"The best thing about being the creator of your kind is having control over your living and dead. Would you like your dear friend back?" A flick of his wrist, and the blood fell from Niko, leaving flesh, hair, and clothes.

Niko's mouth opened. He gasped.

"Niko?" Kole's heart stuttered.

His friend's head turned at the name. "Kole? Is that you—really you?" Niko staggered forward.

Kole ran up to meet him. They wrapped their arms around each other in a long embrace. A real hug. One that meant everything. Niko *felt real*. His flesh warm—chest pressed into Kole's with each breath—and a faint heartbeat pulsed through his shirt. The scent of the forest clung to him.

Niko pulled away to study him at arm's length. "Kole, what's happened? Last I saw you; we were... the Black Wall... must've been some crazy dream."

Before Kole could answer, a finger snapped. Niko morphed back to red liquid and fell to a puddle at Kole's feet.

"Niko!" He dropped to his knees and swiped and punched the floor where he'd disappeared. "What did you do to him?"

"We are in your head, remember? Things aren't real here."

"Bring him back."

"You can have Niko back if you so choose."

The sight of Niko had made him abandon all caution. Kole pointed a finger to the Soul. "*Don't* say his name. He died because of you and your Kayetans." Kole's breath shuddered as he exhaled.

Aterus' voice came gentle. "And he can live again because of me."

Kole forced his reproving hand to his side.

The Soul offered up his hand again. "The deal."

The god's hand held still, waiting for Kole to shake it. Would the deal be bound by magic? Irreversible?

"How do I know you won't go back on your word once you get what you want?" Kole peered up at Aterus, who stood a full two feet taller.

"We are bound by blood now, Kole. I will not betray you."

Kole swallowed. It only now dawned on him the blood he'd been force fed belonged to Aterus. A chill ran through him, quaking his bones at the reality of what that meant.

Slowly, his hand rose from his side. His fingertips reached for the Soul's.

Kole's stomach churned for considering the offer. If there's one thing he knew about the Souls, it's that none could be trusted. Not fully. Aterus' story confirmed it. The gods created out of amusement, careless as to what became of their failed attempts, like the Yamani and Kayetans. *The Yamani.* The curse on their children triggered with the birth of the Black Wall — with the Souls imprisonment. *Aterus* had caused that.

And here the Soul claimed to be different. But he sought to control all power, no matter the cost. If Kole had learned anything from Savairo, he knew total power turned those who wielded it into tyrants. The rebellion had barely managed to dethrone a blood sorcerer. What could mankind do against a Soul if the same happened? The very fail-safe built into seven separate gods sharing equal power would be void. All on Ohr would be helpless to one all-powerful being.

And Niko.... A bargaining chip. Nothing more. Aterus cared not for him. The Soul merely waved gifts before Kole's face — gifts his heart so deeply desired. He closed his eyes imagining what it could be like going back to the forest in his new body with Niko by his side. Like old times.

When Kole opened his eyes, he found his hand had swayed so close to Aterus', he could feel the heat radiating from the god's skin.

All these thoughts... in his head they seemed perfect. But Kole would know. He'd know the cost. He'd know the truth. All the magic in the world could never erase the trauma, the tragedy. The past could never return to how it was.

Before he touched Aterus' skin, Kole curled his hand into a fist.

"I won't do it."

"A poor choice." Aterus' voice came unnervingly calm. Pulling back his hand, he said, "You will regret this moment, Kole."

"I won't be used. Not anymore."

"Are they not using you? Do you even know *what* you are?"

"I'm the key to releasing the Souls." Kole swallowed, unsure of what else to say.

"And the reason why you are the key? Do you know why you can communicate with them?" He stalked forward. "The gods cannot commune with one another in their imprisoned state. That only comes to them through you."

Kole balked at Aterus' growing rage, though the empty scenery left nowhere to escape. He wished this dream would end. *Wake yourself up!* But his trembling jaw told him Aterus controlled this encounter.

"You died the day you released Risil. He accepted the offering— used your blood to break from my prison. The only reason you are alive is because he needed to find the others. What happens to one happens to all." A flick of his hand and another vision appeared: seven orbs floated, colors ranging from red to violet, resembling the corresponding gods. "Risil ripped out a piece of his soul and laid it in you." A sliver of green detached from Russé's orb and moved to the center. "Therefore a shard of every god's soul now resides within you, too." The rest followed suit as a hint of light from every orb seeped to the middle, fusing into a conglomerate of color. A new orb generated. "You know what that means don't you?"

Kole wanted to run, but his feet wouldn't move.

"You are a creation of the gods. Your life is forfeit. Every time you release a Soul," he plucked the blue light from the new orb and returned it to the original source, "you lose that piece. And once they are all gone...." Aterus thrust his hands at the image. The colors dispersed. "You lose your life source."

"My life source?"

"You die, Kole."

"What?" His head reeled.

"You are a risen corpse living on borrowed time. Yet your loyalty resides with those who'd see you to your grave. Risil killed you once for his freedom, and he'll do it again to quell me."

The red clouds above thundered. A sheet of blood poured down. Kole blocked his face to the gruesome liquid, but it ran down his hands and neck, soaking through his clothes.

Aterus tilted his chin toward it. The rain coated his face. When he set his sights back on Kole, his jaw clenched, eyebrows downturned in anger. "So they've come to rescue their puppet." Blood ran past his open mouth and coated his teeth as he sneered. "Ask them for yourself. I'll be here when you change your mind. My offer, though, may not be as kind."

Kole glanced up to the building storm overhead, blurred by the wash of red, then back at a waiting Aterus.

Then the Gray Soul vanished in a blink.

Kole found himself alone in the eerie space of his head.

With a crack, the barrier over the ocean dissipated. Kole fell full force into the sea of ichor. No matter how hard he kicked, the current dragged him under until his vision went red.

CHAPTER 28

A pair of hands shook him awake.

Kole bolted up, nearly smacking his head into Issira's. He forced deep breaths into his lungs. The moment he recognized the Yamani room, the extravagant stone pieces glittering in the dull light, he calmed. Safe from the cursed creatures. Safe from his own head and Aterus.

"Kole? Are you all right?" Issira's soft voice drew his focus.

"I...." He glanced down his body, clad in the tattered Liberation uniform. The last he remembered, he'd been struck by the cursed beast, yet not a stroke of pain lingered. Burn scars peeked through the holes where the cloth had torn. Instinctively, his hand snapped to his temple. Dry to the touch. Only the cord-like knots of scar tissue pressed into his fingers. No wound. "I'm fine."

He lay on the stone table. Silhouettes of others, too far from the light to distinguish, stood around the room.

Turning to Issira, he said, "Thank you for healing me. I'm sorry I—"

"It was not my doing. They found you like this." She nodded her head to Mikal, who stood at the head of the table, arms crossed over his chest and a grim expression set on his stone face.

"We pulled you from a mind-link." Russé stepped into the light behind Issira, leaning heavily into his staff. "Who were you talking to?"

"Aterus."

Issira pulled back. "What?"

His old mentor's face hardened. "How did he get to you?"

"Someone in the city. A woman saved me from the cursed. Not Shikar. Someone else. I didn't get a good look at her. Her face was covered."

Mikal mumbled to his men at the ready around the room, then the Yamani leader turned and said, "No one else was at the scene. No trace. No scent."

"She was there. She forced a vial of blood down my throat."

"It is unlikely someone entered the city without us knowing. But I will send scouts to take a second look."

While Mikal beckoned for one of his men and gave instruction, Russé leaned in with a hushed whisper. "He knows where we are, Issira. We cannot linger here."

She nodded, and Kole knew they were right.

"You realize, young flesh-kind, you brought havoc to our front door." Mikal thrust a finger toward the stairs. "My men fight a horde of cursed out there as we speak. Your spilled blood drew fifteen beasts."

"Where's Shikar? Is she ok?"

"The she-rock is alive for now. We've taken her into custody."

"What? Why?"

"She broke Yamani law. As did you. Your group is no longer welcome. The moment you step out of Grayfall will mark the last you ever see of it."

Banished? Not that it mattered much to Kole; he'd be happy never to return, but his worry lay with Shikar. "What will happen to her?"

"She will get what she desires most." Darkness underlined his voice.

Defiance rose to Kole's vocal cords, despite his efforts to keep it at bay. "To see her daughter? You wouldn't let her so she did it herself. That's why she went out there."

"What are you talking about, Kole?" Russé asked.

"The cursed. They're the children. *Yamani children*. Shikar found her daughter out there. The kid got one whiff of me and turned into this giant creature like the one that attacked us."

Issira slipped off the table, her hands clasped over her stomach. "Mikal. Is this true?"

The Yamani leader ordered his men out. Once the room had cleared, he sat hard into the head chair. "It's not something we share with the outside world. Not something we like to remind ourselves of. Yes, the boy speaks truth. The cursed are our children."

"How did this happen?" Russé asked.

"We know not how but when. The Black Wall marked the first cursed infant. They develop a taste for meat—flesh and blood. A deformity, we thought. But babe after babe, they turned, each as vicious as the last. We outlawed reproduction, but we never agreed upon a true solution. We cannot kill them. We won't. So we keep them. They destroyed the city. Our race disbanded over it. Me and my men are the only ones left here as I'm sure your burned one noticed out there. We keep the children contained and fed to prevent them from doing to Ohr what they did to our people. They are our burden. Our curse."

Aterus' mind-link made more sense now. A careless creation caused problems. But what Aterus failed to mention was the curse upon the Yamani people only triggered when the Black Wall appeared. When the Souls were imprisoned. This all came back to Aterus. "If we release Obell, maybe he can fix them." Both Souls gave Kole a curious stare. "He created the Yamani, right?"

"Well, yes." Russé shifted into his staff, clasping his hands over the weathered top.

"He has a reservoir of power like you both did when you were released. He can use it to fix their children. Remove whatever defect makes them change into those monsters—make them just Yamani again."

Mikal perked up at his words. "So it is true. The great divines stand before me. I knew you smelled odd. You've come to collect your kin, no?"

A nod from Russé. "We wish to keep our presence unknown."

"Kole." Issira touched his arm. "What you speak of takes quite a lot of energy. More than Obell may possess."

"It's worth a shot," Kole persisted. "Obell is the best chance they have. If nothing else, we need to try. It's only right."

The Souls eyed each other.

Russé's pursed lips betrayed his uncertainty. Leaning in close, he whispered to Kole and Issira, "We will be three drained Souls against Aterus if we should be caught."

As if sensing the disagreement, Mikal rose from the chair. "If this is possible, we will provide protection through the volcano. We lead you to the soulstone."

The Souls looked to Kole, then back to each other.

"I saw it up close, Russé," said Kole. "They're too strong for us alone. *This* is our plan to get Obell."

"A quick retrieval can get us out of here faster," Issira added. "We will do this."

"So be it," Russé said, a bit dejected. He turned to the Yamani. "There are no guarantees to what Obell can do. But we agree to it; he will do whatever is in his power."

Mikal nodded. "Ready yourselves. We leave in one hour."

"So soon?" Issira asked.

The Yamani nodded to Kole. "We'll use the burned one's distraction to our advantage — enter while some of our children's numbers are preoccupied."

"What about Shikar?" Kole asked. "We'll need all the help we can get."

Yellow Yamani eyes narrowed on Kole. "The she-rock will be released when we leave, no sooner." With that, he exited into the caves.

The Souls turned on Kole.

"What did Aterus say to you?" Russé asked.

The mind-link burned bright in Kole's head, Aterus' words echoing through his core. He met Russé with a daggered stare. "What you wouldn't."

The moment Russé digested his words, the Soul's face drained to white. "You can't trust him. His lies are what caused this mess in the first place."

"Tell me this — the truth, Russé." Kole gritted his teeth to compose himself. "He told me that every one of *you* I release takes a piece of me. I'm — I'm living on borrowed life. Through blood magic! We know Goren sacrificed me," he gestured at the journal tied to Russé's belt, "but you accepted it."

Russé's jaw flexed. "I didn't know what I was doing, but yes, I accepted the offering. Kole. It was out of necessity. I saw an opportunity to escape, and I took it. Once I realized the cost, I revived you."

"Revived how? You put a piece of your soul into me, right?"

A hesitant nod.

"And what happens to one happens to all. Isn't that how it works?" Kole's voice quivered, betraying the hardened front he tried to put on. "Every Soul has a piece in me?"

"Yes, that's why you can commune with them. You are part Soul, so to speak." Russé shook his head. "It's complicated."

"Then *un*complicate it. Tell me the truth. What happens when I release them?"

"Calm your heart, young one." Issira stroked his arm.

A soothing tingle washed over him, sprouting from her touch. Kole knew it for a fake feeling. "No." He shrugged away, cutting off her sedative.

Issira opened her mouth to respond, but Russé placed a hand on her shoulder.

"It is important I talk to my kin through you before you release them. That's why I went into the pool first when we found Issira." The crow's feet around Russé's eyes deepened as he continued. "They suck their life essence from you to come back — the energy maintaining you.

You die for a moment as mentioned in Goren's journal. You *knew* that going into Issira's prison."

Kole remembered the blue light at the bottom of the pond after he touched Issira's soulstone. It had drifted from his mouth. The absence of time. The nothingness. Death. Then, it had returned to him.

With a shake of his head, Russé said, "But I won't let you go through with the ritual until they agree to replace that energy after they are freed. We come back as lesser gods because a piece of us remains with you, but you will not sustain permanent harm."

A cool trickle of relief washed Kole's worry down. But it stopped in his gut, pooling and churning when his mind finally caught the complication. "Except... when all the Souls are released. What happens then? Can six of you—fragmented like that—take on Aterus?"

A long pause conquered the room. Even Issira, whose body and hair always seemed to be swaying like a current, kept stone still.

Finally, Russé spoke. "We don't know. That's why I'm so hell-bent on keeping our powers in check. There may be a chance if we do that. But keeping you safe has proven far more difficult than I expected. Issira used her reservoir on Felix, mine on reviving you from the Black Wall, and Obell will use his on the Yamani when the time comes."

"If your powers aren't enough in the end, what happens to me?"

Both Souls removed their gaze from Kole. Neither, judging by their paled faces, wanted to voice the truth. That reaction alone shed light to it.

Aterus was right.

Kole pushed off the table, shoved past Russé and Issira, then ran up the long spiral stairs to the Yamani sleeping quarters. Boiling anger fueled his climb. By the time he reached the top, heavy breaths overwhelmed him. He stumbled into the room and crawled into the first Yamani-sized hole.

He didn't care to hide his wheezes as they morphed into sobs. Warm streaks ran down his cheeks and neck. His mind raced, yet his thoughts came back blank. Only the image of his own limp corpse lingered. It was all he saw when he closed his eyes.

No wonder why Russé protected him so. He needed him alive.

... Until they needed him dead.

If it came down to it, the world or him, Kole's execution stood as the solution. But what of *him*? Did they think he'd willingly go through with it?

Would I?

"Kole?"

Every muscle tightened at his name. He'd been so wrapped up in rage, he hadn't noticed Vienna and Felix climbing down into the bowl— hadn't noticed them in the room at all. He swallowed and wiped his eyes on his tattered sleeve before meeting her gaze.

"What's going on?" Vienna asked, taking a seat before him. "They said you'd been out in the city. You caused quite a ruckus." She reached for a torn hole on his pant leg. "Are you all right?"

"I'm fine."

Felix curled up next to his sister. A small spark shone through the dull stare he'd had since the last encounter with his Kayetan.

"You don't look all that fine," she said. "What is it, Kole?"

Though he wanted to tell them everything, Kole held back. What if they agreed with the Souls? His heart tugged deeper in his chest at the thought.

He opened his mouth, unsure of what to say, but Felix spoke for him, "What'd Aterus look like?"

Vienna hushed her brother.

The question sobered him. "What? How do you—"

"Felix used his Kayetan to eavesdrop," Vienna confessed. "Not the most valiant way to use it."

"It was yer idea!"

"I was getting to that. Let me finish." She sighed, then patted her brother's leg apologetically. "We're tired of being left in the dark. The Souls don't use us like they could. We are soldiers, not children. We just want to know what's going on. We *are* putting our lives at risk here. Then again... so are you."

"You heard that part?"

They nodded.

"We're not gonna let it happen, mate," Felix croaked. Failure to use his voice these last few days seemed to have left it hoarse. "The Souls aren't the only buggers who know how ta use magic. There's a lot more allies we can gather against Aterus."

Like a breath held too long, cool relief flowed from Kole's core. He didn't care that they had eavesdropped—he'd have done the same. Instead, he was glad for it. No need to explain and relive the conversation.

"How long ya figure it takes take recharge a Soul's powers?" Felix asked.

Kole shrugged. "Russé said he'd been saving up his resources since he'd been imprisoned. He doesn't even know exactly. A millennia, however long that is. Would Leo have records?"

"That far back? I dunno."

"Even if he did, how would that help us? We don't have that kind of time," said Vienna. She took up his hand. "Our mission is to protect the Souls *and* you. Don't forget that. We'll find another way."

Even at the small touch, Kole's heart fluttered. He remembered what he'd given up when he refused Aterus' deal: a chance to look her in the face without shame. His eyes drifted from hers.

"I've trained him on ya," Felix said, barely a whisper, as he nodded to the corner.

Kole shifted, following his gaze.

Felix's Kayetan lurked in the shadows, face aimed at Kole.

"His Kayetan followed you into the city. Felix saw the whole thing through its eyes. He told the Yamani where you were."

"He'll be useful," Felix said as if he'd muttered it a thousand times before, then went back to rubbing his wrists where black wisps still emanated—a habit he'd picked up, it seemed.

"Did you see the girl?"

Felix nodded, then shared a glance with Vienna before saying, "I think it's Piper."

"What?" Kole sat stunned. The voice. That familiar voice. The last thing she'd said to him on the battlefield before Savairo kidnapped her had been the same word. *"Quiet!"* She'd said to him before sacrificing herself. But then why was she here, force-feeding him blood? "How do you know it's her?"

"Livin' with her for a year got her voice pretty carved inta my brain."

"You think she escaped Savairo?"

"Kole," Vienna said sternly. "She *caused* the mind-link."

"What are you saying?" They stared at Kole, waiting for him to make the connection. "She's working for Savairo? But why—how? She saved me during the battle. *And* in the prison. If that's the case, why help me?"

"We don't know the hows or whys, but I sent Fiona back with a message for Leo. At least we know she's alive."

"And she's nippin' at our tails," Felix added.

"You think she's been working with him from the start?"

"It would explain how Savairo knew about our ambush the night of the rebellion."

Felix cocked his head. "She was the last one gettin' back from the prison break, too, mate. Not a scratch on her. Sounds fishy ta me."

It didn't settle well with Kole. Someone working for the enemy never would have let Kole and the Liberation live during the prison break. The setup had been too perfect for a full sweep—the Liberation killed off in a single night. And the fact she *helped* retrieve Russé from Savairo's clutches. "Think she could be under his control or something? It just doesn't seem like her."

"Possible. But everyone has secrets." Vienna looked up at Kole with a sorrowful gaze. "Even ones we didn't know we possessed."

"Lies, you mean. That's all they are. Hidden lies. Russé says he keeps things from me to protect me." Kole scoffed, remembering the night Russé first told him about his connection with the Souls. Though overwhelming, things had finally made sense. This sprinkling of truth, here and there as the situation called for it... no longer would he stand for it. "How am I supposed to go headfirst into all of this knowing half the story? I don't need saving. I need the truth."

Vienna leaned back. Something he couldn't quite place flashed behind her eyes. "You never told us the truth. You and Russé left Socren without a goodbye."

"I... I didn't want to. I thought if I told you, you'd want to come with us. I didn't want anyone else to get hurt."

A sad smile curled her lips. "You sound like Russé to me."

She's right. His anger turned inward. Was he that similar? All this talk about letting people make their own choices, yet he went against his own rule. Never again.

"We gotta make a pact," Felix murmured. "If we can't trust these old geezers, then we trust us. Vienna can kill just about anythin', I gotta new shadow servant, and Blondie here's got gods in his head. It's a super team if I've ever hearda one. Whaddya say, mates?" With a shaking hand, Felix released his smoking wrist and offered a pinky to the group.

"We all need saving," Vienna said, curling her finger around her brother's. "Kole?"

They looked to him expectantly.

Kole nodded and intertwined his own.

CHAPTER 29

Feathers flapped overhead. Knowing no wildlife traversed this close to the Volcano, Piper paired two fingers to her lips and whistled.

Leo's pet answered the call.

Piper held out her arm to receive the hawk. Rust-colored feathers held a silvery hue from flying in the gray winds. "Hello, Fiona. What do you have there?"

The twine around the bird's leg secured a small, rolled parchment the size of her thumb.

She tugged it free, unfurled it, and read what could only be Vienna's message by the fine-looped script. "A traitor, huh? Oh, Vienna, if you only knew." Kole must've recognized her despite the disguise.

Searching through her pack, she found a quill and shred of parchment. No ink. A prick to her thumb, and she twirled the end of the feather into the dot of blood. "I have a new message for you, dear Fiona."

She tossed Vienna's message into the wind and replaced it with her own. Once secure around the hawk's leg, she whispered orders. "Socren. Leonardo. With haste. Now fly."

Fiona jumped off her arm and opened her wings, letting the wind carry her out of sight.

To her disappointment, Piper returned to find Savairo alive and well. The chaos Kole had provoked in the city must have proven more enticing than the blood trail she'd set up for the sorcerer. *What a shame.* When Savairo turned, she faltered and gasped under her breath.

His mirage-like body had solidified back to flesh. But the sleek sweat coating his face and purple veins dark over his pale neck triggered alarm.

"What took you so long? Where is the boy?"

"There were complications." She kept her distance, even moving back when he tried to approach. "I couldn't capture him. I created a link instead."

"A link?" His fists clenched, and he took another step closer. "Aterus wants the boy, not a conversation."

"I gave him an opportunity to settle things how they should be done."

"He will have our heads if we don't return with him."

"Your head, not mine. I'm not going back." It pleased her picturing Savairo on his knees, enduring her father's wrath.

Savairo's eyes narrowed. "You bitch. You set me up."

"You set yourself up. I don't know what he ever saw in you. You're just a parasite leeching off my father's arm."

Savairo roared, a mix of desperation and anger, as he kicked the knee-high ash.

Bloodshot eyes leveled with Piper's. By his maroon face and heaving breaths, he seemed on the verge of charging.

She pulled her blade, ready for him.

But he straightened and said, "Die by Aterus' hands if you like. I'm bringing him the boy." He turned for the white stallion, stained gray from the ash.

Oh no you don't. No way she'd let him ruin the motions she'd only just put in place. Without another thought, Piper rushed him and lunged, her dagger aimed at his back. The sweet sight of metal piercing flesh made her shudder. Out of his blood-induced state, she could touch him—make him bleed. The force of her arm sunk the short dagger to the hilt.

Savairo grunted at the stab, then whirled, casting Piper into the pillow of ash.

She scrambled up, coughing away the film of soot drifting into her mouth and nostrils. For a second, the thick puff of disturbed ash clouded her vision. As the dust settled, she caught a glimpse of Savairo hobbling to his horse.

The horse whinnied and stomped as Savairo neared.

End this now. Piper found her last blade, rose to her knees for leverage, and chucked it at the sorcerer. It thumped into the small of his back.

A cry of agony pierced the droning wind. Savairo staggered. Two more steps, and he fell face first into the ash.

A smile played on Piper's lips.

But her victory was short lived. The sorcerer's back rose above the drift as he crawled toward the stallion.

She cursed and chased him down, forcing each stride longer, faster. Halfway to her target, she knew she'd failed.

Savairo grabbed the horse's hock. Embers erupted on contact, spreading up the leg and across the horse's back. Bright-red muscle and flesh burned away, revealing ivory bones. The stallion's flesh fell into the wind until a skeleton stood in its place.

Piper stopped dead in her tracks. The same trick he'd pulled to escape the rebellion.

The daggers embedded into Savairo's back popped out and fell out of sight into the ash, leaving healed wounds in their wake. One hand on his knee, he pushed up from the ground and turned to face Piper. Quenched by the soul of his horse, his body shimmered once more, taking on its mirage-like state. "Too timid to take me on now?"

She backed away. Her powers could only go so far.

"Daughter or not, if you get in my way again, I will drain you of every drop and take your soul for my own."

Rage flooded her throat like hot bile. Her jaw clenched despite herself, but she dared not move. Even if she went for the daggers lying somewhere at the horse's feet—even with all the powers of a demigod running through her veins, Piper knew victory was slim if she acted here and now, alone. Wounds she inflicted would heal with that blood in his veins, and it would only make her look weak in his eyes. Piper waited as he climbed the bones of his horse.

The ribs cracked, sprouting long, finger-like bones, which rose into colossal wings. At a kick from Savairo, the steed sprang into a gallop. A trail of ash lifted behind the animal as it leapt up and flew into the sky.

Piper let her fury out in a scream and fell to her knees. She'd forgotten about the stupid horse until it was too late. *Those daggers should've been for the wretched beast.*

She whistled and her mare trotted over. Piper hauled herself on the horse's back. Even with the wind and haze, Savairo would make quick time to the volcano. Yet here she stood two miles from the city wall, stranded on horseback. Whether she wanted to follow or turn back, the choice was made for her. Savairo still possessed one vial of blood. Aterus' blood. The one he meant to drink to take down the Souls, which he'd easily manage without intervention.

But the blood sorcerer wasn't the only one with a trick up his sleeve.

She fondled the vial she'd fed Kole. Streaks of rust-red stained the side. A drop, maybe two, settled at the bottom.

CHAPTER 30

Kole shoved his leg into the pants of the silver suit the Yamani had provided. The thin, metallic fabric supposedly protected against the intense heat of the volcano. The Yamani had no use for them, but Kole and his companions each donned one. How such delicate material could stand against the sweltering magma baffled him, but he pulled the wide torso up over his tattered clothes. *Souls know I don't need more burns.*

"You're tellin' me we gotta wear the bug mask *and* this?" Felix complained. He held the air filtering mask they'd used to traverse the Ashland Plains in one hand and the silver one in the other. "Seems a bit overkill."

Grarstein, who had been put in charge of chaperoning the party, gave an annoyed grunt. "Filter for weak lungs. Suit for weak skin. You have both, you wear both."

Felix made a face when the Yamani turned, then pulled the goggled, snout-mask over his face. Once he topped his attire off with the heat-protectant helmet, Vienna laughed. Through the lenses and screen of the suit, Felix's squinted eyes barely showed.

"You look like a metal marshmallow," she said.

"And whaddya think *you* look like?" Felix snapped back at his sister.

Vienna placed the final piece of her suit atop her head like a crown. "A *taller* marshmallow." Snark oozed from her voice like she knew it was a touchy subject.

Meanwhile, Kole finished pulling his arms through. By the pucker of fabric at his waist and the cuff of the hem grazing the floor, it seemed apparent these were meant for someone much taller. Universal-sized suits, perhaps, given to those visiting the city centuries ago when humans had been welcome. He felt like a kid wearing his father's armor. He looked to Felix and Vienna and noticed theirs were just as ill-fitting.

Vienna stood taller, so it lay smooth, but the stiff form of the fabric made her look like a caricature of herself. And Felix, a similar build to Kole, looked just as Vienna described: a wrinkled, silver marshmallow.

Once Kole fit his own mask on, a slow-growing warmth encompassed his body. The material trapped his breath and body heat, stifling the air like a muggy summer day. It didn't bode well for someone unable to sweat. He stared at the bright sheen of the suit. *At least if I pass out, I'll be easy to find.*

"Anyone else hot as hell?" Felix's voice came muffled behind his getup. "I thought this thing was suppose ta keep us cool."

"It will feel cool when flesh-kinds stand by lava," Grarstein mocked.

Issira and Russé joined them, their borrowed garbs better fitting due to their taller stature.

Russé's eyes found Kole. Sorrow held behind them. Maybe he felt guilty for another lie—something he promised against weeks ago. He approached Kole and offered his waterskin. "Drink as much as you can before we go. I know how you get with the heat."

Though reluctant to accept the Soul's olive branch, Kole relented. The last thing he needed was to overheat. It'd weaken him and leave him an easy target for Obell. If Russé thought the small gesture meant forgiveness, he was wrong.

After downing a long swig, Kole handed it back.

"Keep it with you."

Kole patted the lump on his hip. "I already have one."

"You might need two." Russé walked away before Kole could protest.

Grarstein unraveled a bundle of weapons: a variety of spiked maces, morning stars, flails, war hammers, and a maul with a head as big as his skull. "Blades no good against cursed. Blunt strikes crack and shatter rock. Take one."

The siblings' eyes widened at the choices. They both carefully picked one out, weighing an option in their hands before putting it back and testing out the next in the lineup. Eventually, Vienna decided on the massive maul which took both hands to operate, while Felix chose two lightweight war hammers with pointed pick-like heads.

Vienna and Felix practiced holding their weapons while wearing the thick hide gloves. The maul proved cumbersome. Vienna used the weight of her body to propel it around. A low whoosh echoed throughout the room as she spun.

Meanwhile, Felix twirled the two picks with his wrists. They suited his fighting style. After all, Felix had always battled with a pair of daggers. His steps and quickness transferred well into the hardier weapons.

After a few wobbly practice swings, compensating for the slick, heat-resistant material, their aim and battle grace returned.

Kole retrieved the slingshot Felix had insisted he keep but found using it difficult. The pouch of pellets hung on the inside of his suit. He'd either have to pull his hand through the sleeve and grab a pellet each time or affix his ammo to the outside somehow. When he reached for a pellet, he found the gloves too cumbersome to pull a single ammunition. His finger stuck in the small opening of the pouch. A frustrated shake and he freed his hand.

Issira came to Kole's side. "Are you ready?"

Kole stuffed his hand back through the sleeve. "To die, possibly permanently this time if Obell doesn't agree?" he quipped, with no effort to hide the sarcasm. "Sure. Why wouldn't I be?"

"We won't let that happen to you."

"Because you need me for later, I know." Immediately after he said it, a ball of remorse weighed him down.

A sad smile pressed on Issira's lips. She turned away without another word.

The old him never would've said such things. Not to a friend *or* a god. Sure, he'd always been stubborn. Sometimes a bit cocky, especially before his burns. But contempt? Was this him now? One side of his brain scorned him. The other side fed off it, posing the question, "*Why should I feel guilty?*" He held no responsibility for the Black Wall—for Aterus. Why should he be okay with any of this? And it wasn't like he had a choice in the matter. The conflicting thoughts gave him a headache. Kole downed more water and pushed the cacophony aside.

The Souls took no weapons: Issira apparently fine unarmed and Russé content with his staff.

Grarstein herded them all down the stairs to the underground caves, where they met up with Mikal and the rest of his men.

Kole caught sight of Shikar and recoiled, bumping into Vienna, who followed behind.

"Whoa, what is it?" she asked.

He mouthed 'Shikar.'

Vienna's mouth opened when she spotted the Yamani, then nudged her brother.

Cracks ran down Shikar's arm. A chunk of her torso, above her right hip, had been ripped out, a gouge big enough for Kole to fit a balled fist. Other less severe nicks and chips scattered across her body. Like newly added facets in a gem, she glittered in the low light of Mikal's torch, but for all the wrong reasons.

Kole's jaw tightened. Shikar's own daughter had done this. A moment before her daughter transformed into the cursed beast, mother and child had been face to face. Maybe not conversing or touching but connecting nonetheless. Looking at each other for the first time since Shikar had abandoned her. Decades? Centuries? Shikar alone knew.

When Shikar's eyes flicked to their group, they darted to each face until finally landing on Kole.

Through the blur of the double masks, he met her gaze, thankful for the barrier between them. He expected seething hatred.

Instead, her body hunched forward slightly, as if letting out a held breath.

Relief, Kole realized. He felt the same: glad their Yamani friend still stood after the encounter in the city. For the life of him, he wondered why no fury held in her stare. He'd forced her hand against her own child. Her beaten state was *his* doing.

She dipped her head at him, then looked away.

Grarstein directed Kole and his companions before Mikal.

"Armed and ready, I see," the lead Yamani said with an amused glance to the maul resting over Vienna's shoulder. "Three-dozen cursed are licking blood off the city streets as we speak. The rest returned to the hive. We make our move before the blood is cleaned. Flesh-kind stay together, my men and she-rock will keep a barrier. If we are discovered, we will split into two: Grarstein and Shikar with me and the humans. Understood?"

Like an earthquake, the Yamani grumbled in unison.

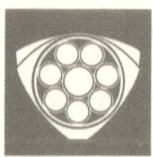

The Yamani surrounded Kole's group like a ring as they traveled through the caves. Both Shikar and Felix's Kayetans slid overhead, unnoticed across the ceiling.

Every now and then, Felix mumbled to himself, shaking his head. He'd told Kole before that the creature whispered things to him. Now must have been one of those moments. What sort of things did it say? Could the shadow inflict pain like the imprisoned Souls did to Kole?

The connection between Felix and his Kayetan appeared different than Shikar's. Not only because of the lack of shadow wisps anywhere on the Yamani, but also because she never mentioned seeing through its eyes or having it whisper things. She spoke to it on multiple occasions — communed — but the relationship came off as one-sided. Shikar gave the commands and her Kayetan obeyed, reporting when necessary. A simple transaction. She did say Felix's ritual had been botched somehow: Felix remained connected to the creature. Maybe that attachment made for a more intense bond. Kole itched for answers. Curious as he may be, traveling underground toward his next death probably wasn't the best time to pry.

Shikar shrugged past her kin and fell in line with Kole. "I am glad to see you alive."

"You, too." Kole glanced over, then shifted his eyes to the ground. The height difference put his line of sight directly on the massive wound in Shikar's side. "I shouldn't have followed you."

Quiet stretched. Only the trickle of water, plopping down from the hanging stalactites, and the crunch of the Yamani's rock-on-rock footsteps echoed in the caves.

"I am glad you did."

He looked up to her, aware of his own gaping mouth, and for the first time, he appreciated the cover of two masks.

Her voice came hushed. "I was there to say my last goodbye. She isn't the same. Time has ruined her mind. She has succumbed to the beast now. No flicker left in her eyes. The last time I saw her, she still remembered my face. Not who I was or my name, but I sensed hesitation in her when she looked at me." Her head dipped. "No longer. When I saw her there... she just stared at me. Empty. Then the moment she spotted flesh, the beast took over."

"I'm sorry."

Shikar's topaz-like eyes turned to him. "I've heard my kin talking. I know who I protect, though I've always had a hunch. But you are something of a mutt, Kole. Not a true divine."

Unsure of what to say, he swallowed, avoiding her stare.

Shikar must've sensed his discomfort because she patted his head like a wolf pup. "I will watch over you, boy."

He winced under her touch, the hard stone of her hand knocking against his skull.

"The moment my daughter turned on you, I knew my duties had shifted. Promise of powers or gifts no longer bind me," she said with a nod to the Souls a few paces ahead.

"Why?" The change in her seemed sudden. She hadn't agreed to bring them to Grayfall for anything less than a favor from Issira.

"My daughter isn't the only one lost. All the magic of the Souls can't change that, try as they might. It's time I forget." Her hoarse voice held a trace of grief. "Death is merely one solution. I will choose another."

Though he knew she couldn't see it behind his masks, Kole smiled. "I'm glad to have you here."

Words never truer. The more allies they acquired, the better chance Kole had at surviving. Not just today, but when they faced down Aterus.

They walked until the path steepened underfoot. The uphill climb normally would've bothered him, but since the mind-link, Kole's muscles felt stronger. Fatigue couldn't touch him. Even his body, sweltering inside the suit, somehow regulated its internal temperature. He dared say, he felt a bit like his old self before his encounter with the Black Wall. The change surprised, and he almost let himself feel grateful for it until he realized the cause. *Aterus' blood at work.* He gulped from his waterskin, preparing for the sure moment when this new feeling faded.

The spikes on the cave's ceiling and floor grew sparse. Surrounding rock shifted from grays and browns to porous black stone. More and more alcoves and tunnels sprouted from the main path. Mikal had mentioned taking old lava tubes to the soulstone. They must be getting close.

"We approach cursed territory. No one speaks," Mikal said, confirming Kole's suspicions.

The temperature spiked as they climbed, but the Yamani trudged on, exhibiting no discomfort. Kole, on the other hand, began to pant. He told himself that the rest of his group felt the weight of the heat, too. The thought alone made him feel better, regardless of the truth.

Distant, low clicks echoed down the tunnel: the call of the cursed. Scratches and slams came from above, not the ceiling, but a different, adjacent tunnel. The underground system reminded him of an ant's colony. Paths broke off from the roof, leading into a dark abyss. Mikal ordered them into a single-file line and led them around a hole in the ground, whose end never met the light of their torches. Amidst the growing and fading racket of the creatures, the Yamani remained calm, like hardened soldiers.

A deep rumble ripped through the tunnel walls. Kole stopped and braced himself, thinking it an earthquake. But no one else reacted.

Shikar's heavy hand found his back and nudged him on. "No slowing."

"Carry the burned one if he breaks pace," Mikal hissed over his shoulder.

With reluctant feet, Kole moved on. "You didn't feel that?"

"Feel what?"

A screech blared from further up their tunnel.

Mikal lifted an open hand, and the group held.

Tension built through the silence. Kole swore he could hear Felix's heartbeat next to him.

Out of the corner of his eye, Kole saw Shikar tap two fingers toward her Kayetan, who slithered across the ceiling, then disappeared into the darkness ahead to scout. Two breaths later, it returned. "It took the eastern path," she whispered.

Mikal turned to her, giving her a steely glare, then waved his hand in a signal to proceed.

Another rumble shook Kole, this one stronger. But he shrugged it off, crediting it to a cursed in a nearby tunnel.

Like a branding iron, white-hot pain erupted from the back of his skull. He bit his tongue against the rising scream pushing from his throat.

Someone nudged his side, urging him on, but the affliction planted him.

Obell had come for him again.

A feral urge coursed through Kole. The bile in his stomach spiked to boiling levels as if he'd chugged a glass of lava. The scream broke through.

A hand slammed over his mouth, muffling his cry, but he rode it out until his lungs ached for more air.

Russé stared him down, one hand silencing Kole while the other hooked under his arm, keeping him on his feet. A cross between fury and concern lay behind his blue gaze. "Obell?"

Unwilling to open his mouth in case another scream pushed out, Kole nodded when Russé released him.

Around them, Mikal and his men faced out from their formation, watching and listening down the adjoining tunnels.

Felix and Vienna stood back-to-back, a fighting style Kole had seen the Liberation utilize in the rebellion, and fidgeted with their weapons.

Issira circled into view and placed a cool hand over Kole's head. A short second later, she looked to Russé. "Obell knows not what he does," warned Issira. "He senses Kole's proximity. We must get to him before he blows the volcano."

Another earthquake-like thunder shook the lava tube, and the guttural click of a cursed beast hastened.

"Two stay. Block the way. Don't let it by," Mikal ordered, and two Yamani broke from the group and raced down the tunnel toward the incoming beast. "The rest, this way."

"Keep Obell at bay as best you can," Issira whispered in Kole's ear. "We will stay with you if he lashes out again."

Kole nodded while more chaos ensued around him.

"She-rock, carry the burned one," Mikal called.

On Kole's second step, stone arms swept him off the tunnel floor. Shikar cradled him to her chest. "I mean you no shame."

Kole averted his chin to the path ahead. The Yamani had split ranks, half to the front, half bringing up the rear. Two of Mikal's men squeezed along either side of the siblings and the Souls, protecting the flanks.

Felix ran, unhindered despite his recent scars—swift like his sister, but his former grace had gone—and Vienna trudged next to him, the massive weapon slowing her usual stride. She compensated by lengthening her gait, stag-like.

A crash came from behind. Kole peeked over Shikar's shoulder. Beyond the Yamani guards tailing Shikar, an object flew toward them, rolling to a stop on the cusp of the moving light of their torches. Long and dark. Kole thought it a stalagmite until his eyes spotted the hand at one end. He gasped and flipped around, realizing the cursed had ripped one of the guard's arms from his body.

"Can two Yamani take down a cursed?" he whispered in Shikar's ear.

Stone arms wrapped tighter around his body. "No."

The ruckus behind them must've caught the attention of the hive because Mikal signaled two more of his men down the adjoining tunnel as they passed. Another pair, and then another, until only a dozen Yamani remained.

Kole's group steered left then right, climbed up and leapt down a deceivingly shallow tunnel to avoid the growing battle cries closing in. The rough terrain made it clear why Mikal had insisted that Kole hitch a ride.

Then, the light of Mikal's torch exposed a dead end where the cave had collapsed in on itself. Mikal stopped the group and turned as if intending to backtrack and take a different tunnel around, but a shadow bounded toward the rear, the form so large the edges scraped the tunnel walls.

Trapped.

"Clear the way," Mikal commanded the four men at his side.

They dove at the crumbled pile of rubble and got to work, scrapping, clawing, and rolling the rock away to clear the cave-in.

Mikal pushed through Kole and his companions and took his place at the front of their depleted force.

Eight Yamani. One cursed.

Kole *hoped* for only one.

In a blink, and the beast was upon them.

Red pupils shone when the light of Mikal's torch hit them. Teeth glittered as they bit down on the head of the Yamani to Mikal's right. With a flick of the creature's head, a nauseating crack resounded in the lava tube as rock snapped from the torso. The Yamani crumpled to the floor, no more than a pile of rubble, while the cursed flung the head into the side of the tunnel like a cannonball.

Mikal let out a war cry so intense, it forced Kole's heart to skip. The Yamani all sprang at the cursed—some at the feet, others at the arms, and Mikal around the neck. Their added weight restrained the monster.

It clicked and whined, shaking its body to rid the newly attached parasites.

Mikal climbed up the cursed's muzzle and clawed out one red eye.

The monster flung itself into the wall, crushing two Yamani along with it. They fell from the beast, dazed.

Kole glanced back to the cave-in, where they'd made significant progress. The ceiling had been cleared out; a small gap, but big enough for a human to crawl through. When he looked back to the battle, Mikal had succeeded at blinding the creature.

"The neck." Mikal wrapped his massive stone arms around the head. A grunt and he pulled back, exposing the throat. "Now!"

His men converged and attacked the throat, breaking away chunks of stone with their bare fists until they reached a hollow.

Several struggled breaths and the cursed beast fell limp, the impact launching Mikal from its head. The Yamani leader curled his body before landing, taking on a boulder-like shape, then safely rolled to a stop.

"Through the tunnel," he barked, climbing to his feet.

The two Yamani who'd been thrown into the wall found their bearings, but after a long look from Mikal and a final nod, they left their decapitated kin behind.

Felix and Vienna went through first, the Souls trailing close.

Shikar, with Kole in tow, climbed up the slope of crumbled rocks, which shifted and slid underfoot. Once near the small opening, she sat him down and helped him through the small gap.

When Kole's heat-protectant suit caught on a rock, Russé took his hand and pulled Kole to his feet. After tugging free, Kole inspected the new tear in the suit while the rest of the Yamani squeezed through.

Thankfully, it was small. The extra fabric of the ill-fitting garb came in handy. He folded the hole shut and tucked it into his belt to form a new seal. He worried his scent would escape and draw more cursed, but fussing about it would only slow progress. It would have to do.

The last Yamani who emerged from the cave-in pushed the cleared sediment back over the opening to fill it. Enough to block the way but simple to remove should they backtrack.

Shikar eyed Kole's folded suit as she lifted him but said nothing.

The ache in Kole's head built again. This time, he prepared himself. "Russé," he called as the group settled into their formation. "He's reaching out."

Both Souls came to his aid.

"Again? Already?" Russé's frown deepened, and he cast Issira a worried look.

The pain skyrocketed to its climax quicker this time. It forced Kole's eyes shut. Russé and Issira ran on either side as everyone continued. Their touch subdued the agony enough for Kole to keep his scream at bay this time.

The escape through the collapsed tunnel gave them a solid minute of peace.

Then the clicks and snarls started up again, advancing. Their echoes made it seem like monsters flooded in from every tunnel they passed. No telling which tunnel paths carried the cursed and which sat empty.

Mikal dove when a cursed sprang out from a lava tube on the right.

The creature cut off the party, landing in the center of the group, directly before Felix and Vienna. Without hesitation, the siblings attacked.

Felix circled the monster, clearing the reach of its colossal stone arms. The movement caught the beast's attention. As it turned to swipe, Vienna spun and swung her maul, letting the force of her turn give it strength. She pulled back at the last moment, changing the plane of her weapon's trajectory. It arced up and slammed into the exposed neck of the beast's turned head.

The cursed cried out, a sharp piercing whine, then the Yamani shot into action and quelled the noise.

Before Kole could register what just happened, another creature burst from the tunnel behind them. He shouted a warning too late. One Yamani split in two under the force of the cursed's strike.

"Go," Mikal shouted to the Souls. "The soulstone is close. Follow the heat. We will protect the rear."

Kole had no choice in the matter as Shikar stepped off into a dead sprint after the Souls, Vienna and Felix in tow.

"Felix, send your Kayetan with mine to scout ahead," Shikar directed. "Command it, and it will follow."

"Ya heard her," Felix shouted to his shadow speeding on the tunnel wall. "Get outta here." The Kayetan swirled, then darted after Shikar's.

Mikal and Grarstein followed at a distance, Grarstein soon breaking off down a tunnel to grapple a cursed, then Mikal veered a moment later.

Russé led them, turning down tunnels left and right as directed by the two Kayetans. Each path proved more sweltering than the last.

Kole's body shook from the rising temperature. He managed to free and finish off one of the waterskins tucked away at his belt. Downing the warm liquid helped little. Gradually, his body reached its limit. Apparently Aterus' blood could only do so much. Short gasps and a heightened heartbeat made Kole woozy. If he had been on foot like the rest, he'd have already passed out.

Obell swelled inside him again, purring like a cougar about to pounce on wounded prey.

Kole opened his mouth to alarm the Souls. Instead of a yell, a slurred gurgle came out, too quiet to hear above the soft roar in the distance. Not the click of a cursed, a different sound, one which vaguely reminded him of a gushing river. A faint orange glow pulsing from the far end of the lava tube gave a hint to the origin.

They all rounded the curve where the tunnel opened into a giant cavern.

Kole squinted his eyes against the brilliance. Heat hit him like a slap to the face.

A river indeed. Of pure lava.

"The lava rises." Shikar nodded down to the molten rock below. "We must find higher ground."

"It's Obell. He's doing this. He can feel me," Kole groaned. The orange fluid bubbled and sprayed liquid fire into the air as it belched up displaced gases.

"Worry not, small one." Shikar greeted her Kayetan as it returned. After a brief exchange between them, she said, "My Kayetan sees the soulstone. Follow the ledge."

Kole turned and eyed the path she motioned toward. His gut shriveled at the sight. An outcrop so thin it barely stuck out an arm's length from the wall led around the curve of the cave.

"I will not be able to fit. You go on your own from here." She lowered Kole to the ground. "No cursed will get past me. You have my promise."

His knees buckled the moment he touched down, but he caught the wall and righted himself.

Russé came to his aid, hooking an arm around his waist to keep him balanced. "Remember how we climbed Poleer?" Hands wrapped tight around the center of his staff. Russé pulled, and the wood split in two.

Kole nodded. "I'm going to need a bit more help this time," he admitted as his eyes moved from the rising magma to the precarious rocky shelf. *Figures the benefits of Aterus' blood would wear off right when I need it most.*

"I won't let you fall. Arms out."

Kole obeyed.

After slamming the butt of his staff on the ground, the rigid wood grew long and thin, stretching into two malleable roots. One end of the transformed staff wrapped around Kole's torso, while the other root slung around his arm, the end flicking like a snake tongue.

Issira grabbed Kole's hand and led him to the ledge. Her touch cooled him and flushed Obell to the chasms where he belonged. The moment he stepped up to the outcropping, the root around Kole's torso pierced the wall, anchoring itself, while the other secured around his torso released. Like a giant earthworm, it slithered into the wall out of view. Stone cracked from the borrowed hole, and a small chunk fell away, bounced off the ledge, and sizzled as it hit the top film of lava. The two roots took turns fixing Kole to the wall as he shuffled along.

"Felix," Shikar called from the tunnel.

Felix snapped his head around, back pressed to the wall.

"Use your Kayetan to find a path. Listen to it as it listens to you."

His friend glanced above where his Kayetan hovered: right over Kole. It seemed the shadow still followed the original command Felix had given it to train on Kole. Felix nodded to Shikar.

"Make it quick." Shikar shouted above the bubbling magma. "My kin can only hold the cursed for so long."

CHAPTER 31

Kole and the others followed the ledge around the cave. The lava far below left them mostly undisturbed. Every now and then, a splash of orange shot up to their height, but none close enough to the walls to touch them. The heat-protectant suits seemed less about keeping the user at a comfortable temperature and more about preventing the skin from melting away. Worry multiplied with each shuffled step, and he hoped the hole he'd concealed in his suit held up. If not for Issira's constant touch with her fingers curled around his wrist, and the roots tethering him to the wall, he'd fall headfirst to his demise—the kind of death the Souls couldn't bring him back from.

As Kole stared at the boiling lava, Felix's Kayetan swooped into view. It stopped before its master.

Felix grabbed his head and squirmed, so much so that Vienna slapped a hand over her brother's chest to steady him. It seemed communing with his Kayetan pained him. After a moment, Felix's drained voice informed the group, "The stone's at the top." Felix pointed up the incline, where the outcropping widened.

A moment later, they'd climbed high enough to see what lay beyond. Kole gasped at the sight.

At the peak of the rocky stair, a large ruby-colored stone hung like an egg sack from the curved ceiling. Light seemed to pulse from within, though Kole found it hard to tell if it emanated from the stone itself or rather an effect of the churning magma at the base of the cavern. Either way, the pulsing light reminded Kole of a beating heart.

One at a time, they climbed to more solid footing. The roots around Kole's waist slithered down his leg and reformed into the old familiar staff. He retrieved it and passed it to Russé, whose hardened gaze set on the soulstone.

Kole's nervous stomach bubbled as violently as the liquid fire below. It took all his courage to bring his eyes to Obell's prison. When he locked onto it, a deep-rooted shudder scaled his spine, shaking him as it crawled past the base of his neck to the spot in his head where the Red Soul resided. His eyes burned and watered. He blinked back the growing moisture, but he was unable to dismiss the feeling that Obell returned his stare—felt the fear consuming his muscles, the hitch in his breath, the erratic tempo of his heart. Kole shied away and buried his head in Issira's shoulder.

The Blue Soul wrapped an arm around him. Even through two layers of fabric, her cool touch reached him. "We are with you, Kole."

Russé cut a slit in the arms of his suit and slipped his bare hands into the open air. "Stay back until he's ready."

They all watched him approach and place his palms on the stone's surface.

A brilliance of red light burst on contact. Blistering winds hit Kole and his companions. Kole latched onto Issira, who held him strong. Another hand, then another graced his shoulder and his back: Felix and Vienna stood by him.

Russé hunched forward in a lunge, digging his heels into the ground as if bracing himself from being thrown back. The suit covered his body, but his freed hands, paling against the soulstone, trembled.

The moment lasted an eternity. Kole looked to Issira.

She shot him a nod meant to sooth his worries, but unease lingered behind her stormy stare. For a brief second, her eyes churned like raging whirlpools just as they did when he first saw her on the pond.

On instinct, he flinched away. In a moment of weakness, he'd almost forgotten a god stood behind that human facade.

"He accepts the terms," an out-of-breath Russé said. He held his hunting knife in one hand and offered his other arm to Kole. The Soul meant to escort him. "Are you ready?"

Vienna's and Felix's hands slid from Kole's back. The same grim look peeked through the window of their masks, somewhere between worry and sympathy.

Kole cast Russé a pointed stare and stepped into the Soul's space. "I'll never be ready." Instead of taking his old mentor's hand, he grabbed the knife and marched past, his elbow clipping the old man's side.

The moment he lost physical contact with Issira, the protective barrier gave way and Obell's presence weighed on him. He expected the Soul to attack him like before, but the god showed restraint, obviously aware now of the ritual. Still, the air thickened, so much so, each step landed hard and sluggish over the bluff. He fought for every swing of his arm, every inhale, like traversing through a pool of molasses. That thick air rolled down his throat as he swallowed: hot, sticky, and reluctant to conform to his will. As if Obell owned this very space and everything in it, merely allowing Kole to enter.

Kole took in a shaking breath as he stood before the soulstone. Twice his size, its translucent surface allowed him to witness the licking flames of its core. Dangerous heat radiated through Kole's suit. His skin tightened. *It's not the Black Wall. It can't burn me.* He repeated the mantra until the involuntary reaction subsided.

Mind trained on the mission, Kole sliced the base of one sleeve open and pulled back the metallic fabric to expose his marred hand. He forced cold thoughts to center stage—icy winters, frost-burned fingertips—hoping to compete with the part of his brain warning him against the exposure. He clenched his jaw and dragged the knife over the tender skin of his palm.

When blood met air, the soulstone vibrated, seeping anticipation.

Aterus' words writhed in the depths of his mind. His promise to return Niko. To rid Kole of this broken body. Could he really?

Kole thought he knew his decision when he had severed the mind-link with Aterus. He had been so sure then. Even now, his every intention had been to release Obell... up until this moment. He hesitated. A new will birthed inside him. *I will have you back, Niko. I will have everything back*, Kole promised himself. But it was too late to stop the ritual while he stood within the heart of the temperamental volcano, surrounded by those who could easily overpower him. He gritted his teeth and gave in.

"Get out, you bastard," Kole growled, then thrust his hand onto the soulstone.

The heat branded his palm, and his body seized.

Vermilion light consumed his vision. A split second of pain registered as a blast of fiery air burst from the soulstone. Then it died.

And so did he.

Familiar nothingness greeted Kole. Thoughts scrambled and drifted in the void. Coming and going, coming and going. He began to count, but the numbers abandoned him. Only a matter of time until he returned. A matter of....

Time. A slave to it. A slave to the Souls and their graces.

His rage encompassed him. No, not rage. Hate. Latching onto it, his thoughts cleared. Numbers came back. His task came back. How long would it take this time? Had Obell sensed Kole's new intentions?

Would he leave him out here, stranded in the abyss as punishment for Kole's thoughts of betrayal?

Finally, a soft red sphere bloomed, banishing the dark. Kole threw himself at it—clung to it as it vacuumed him back to Ohr.

His eyes burst open. He lay cradled in fiery arms. A scream escaped him. In a panic, he wriggled to free himself from the flames.

White-hot orbs peered down on him. Eyes.

A breath caught in Kole's throat.

The eyes held a commanding presence that drilled to the depths of Kole's core.

He froze, letting the fire lick his skin, only now realizing the flames produced no heat.

Obell held him. The Soul had no mouth or body, simply a bulk of flicking fire. His center, though, offered a more corporeal form. A globule of lava churned beyond the shroud of flame. His true center. A heart, perhaps.

"You have done me a great deed," Obell said.

To Kole's ears, the roaring of a wildfire omitted from the Soul, but the words branded his mind.

"*I am in your debt.*" The white orbs shifted and looked beyond Kole.

Russé and Issira strode forward. Both gave a nod to the Red Soul.

Felix and Vienna hung back. What little of their faces Kole could make out through the small window of their masks held expressions of awe mixed with horror.

"Give us the boy. We need to seal his mind from the others until we can get out of this wretched place." Russé stretched his staff out to Obell. The wood groaned as it lengthened.

A tendril coiled around Kole's torso and gently lifted him from Obell's grasp.

The Red Soul offered no protest, only gazed at Kole as he drifted away and said, "Our key."

Kole found his feet next to Russé.

"He'll remain this way as long as you and the others cooperate." Russé reverted his staff to its original form, then fussed over Kole. "Are you all right? Do you need Issira to heal you?"

"I'm fine." The truth for once. The initial blast of heat had pained him, but as he rolled his shoulders, checking for injury, he found nothing. The stuffiness of the suit had subsided. Even the fiery atmosphere of the lava-filled cavern seemed less intense. Surely a product of Obell's control over the element.

Russé and Issira each lay a hand on Kole.

Energy flowed through him, fortifying the crumbled walls Obell had left when he tore his soul from Kole's lifeforce. The piece had been returned, but a dull throb lingered in the back of his head like a fresh wound. The power of the Blue and Green Souls surrounded the tear, mended it, then locked it safely away. When they withdrew, he felt a little more like himself again.

"How long has it been? Where is Aterus?" Obell asked.

"Too long," Russé answered. "Aterus is far from here. For now."

"He knows where we are." Kole's hoarse voice surprised him. His throat rubbed together like he'd swallowed a handful of sand. A gulp of water ended up depleting the last of Russé's borrowed waterskin, yet his tongue yearned for more.

"He mind-linked with Kole," Russé added at Obell's curious stare. "We have a lot to discuss. Most will have to wait." He followed Obell's stare, which had landed on Felix and Vienna. A sigh, then, "Take a human form before you burn their eyes."

"Risil, the recluse. What do you care of mortal eyes?"

Russé gave no response. Not the slightest shift in his expression to hint at Obell's meaning: a trait Kole had once admired.

The fire of Obell's body shrunk like a dying campfire until only the lava core remained. The molten rock morphed and hardened to a thick, muscular form. Skin cooled to a rich brown. A wide, stern jaw settled, covered in a neatly trimmed beard. Eyes the color of dancing flame burned under bristly brows, which flicked up at the ends. Muted fabric of rust wrapped his waist and billowed down into loose-fitting pants, leaving his chest and back exposed.

A sudden yell echoed over the murmuring lava, drawing everyone's attention to the tunnel opening Shikar guarded.

The Yamani dove from the tunnel mouth and hugged the cavern wall. A blur of glinting rock shot past her.

A cursed. It ran so fast it charged beyond the ledge and plummeted down to the molten lake. Like a cannonball hitting water, the magma geysered on impact and sprayed Shikar's back. She roared, slapping it off. Small divots appeared in her stone skin where the rock had melted away.

Kole couldn't help but watch the cursed sink to the depths, clawing and clicking as its body liquified. The last-minute dodge had saved Shikar from the same fate.

Obell moved to the tip of the ledge, his head turning from the melted cursed to Shikar and the other Yamani emerging from the tunnel mouth. "What is going on?"

"The monsters have us cornered," Felix answered. "But ya know all about 'em, I reckon." He grunted when Vienna nudged him with an elbow.

His flaming eyes searched Russé and Issira. "Monsters?"

"The Yamani children." Issira stepped forward and laced her fingers with the Red Soul's.

Obell closed his eyes. His stoic expression hardened.

A moment later, Issira released his hand, saying, "This is your burden."

The Red Soul merely nodded, then raised an open hand. "Aid me."

The lava below thrust up like a backward waterfall. Where Obell's hand moved, it followed, creating a bridge between the platform where they stood to the Yamani's small ledge.

Issira squared herself to the new bridge and flourished her fingers in a beckoning call. Steam rose from the lava. It sizzled and snapped as she extracted water and vapor. With its core temperature dropping, the brilliant orange bridge faded to black and solidified.

Once done, Obell walked across. Kole and the others followed.

After seeing what happened to the cursed, Kole stuck to the center, careful not to look down for fear he'd lose balance. He kept his eyes on the tunnel, noticing Shikar, Mikal, Grarstein, and four others had made it out. Their grim looks meant ill fates had met their companions.

Mikal stepped up when Obell descended. "Red One."

Obell's burly form compared to the Yamani. He met Mikal's gaze straight on. "My child."

The Yamani flinched at that. He opened his mouth to speak, but the call of another cursed pierced the tunnel.

"Seal the door," Obell called back to Issira as he guided Mikal aside with a simple touch of his hand.

An orb of magma emerged from the ledge. It reshaped into a disc and covered the entrance. Issira hardened the edges like she had done with the bridge. A moment later, a solid stone wall stared back.

Kole stumbled as a crash came from the opposite side of the tunnel. A cursed had hit the new wall head on. A small crack fractured the edge where the fresh and old rock merged. Another slam. Rock scraped rock. It was trying to dig its way through.

"Will it hold?" Kole asked Russé.

"Not for long. You heard Mikal. They dig through the volcano."

With the tunnel closed off, Obell turned back to the Yamani people who'd gathered together; Shikar at the back, eyeing the cracking door. "Issira has made me aware of your plight."

"We made a deal." Mikal stood tall, but his thin voice gave away an uneasiness. "Our side is upheld. It's your turn to do the same. Remove the curse over the Yamani."

Obell beckoned the lead Yamani with a finger.

Mikal drew near—a slow, hesitant walk. Yellow eyes took in the Red Soul, who reached out and placed his hands on either side of Mikal's head.

More growls added to the cacophony of sounds behind the sealed door. Kole inched away, positioning himself firmly behind the siblings, their weapons held ready. At this rate, if they lingered too long, every cursed in the hive would sit between them and escape.

Grarstein stepped before the growing fissures in the barricade. A shard of stone the size of a fist crumbled away. He shoved his hand over it before a cursed could stick a talon through. Shikar rushed to his aid. They held the wall while Obell worked.

The Red Soul's hands moved to Mikal's chest. A frown, then, "I cannot do it."

"What?" Mikal shoved the Soul's hand away. "You created us. You fix us."

"I can, but not you—any of you. Not in my current state," said Obell.

"What does he mean?" Mikal snapped at Russé.

"We are not at full power." Russé's eyes shifted between the Yamani. "There are limitations."

Mikal's top lip curled into a snarl. "Then fix *them*." He motioned to the collapsing barricade. "If you can't fix the root, then save the children. Return them to us. Save them from the monstrosities they've become."

The air around Obell spiked to sweltering temperatures. It seemed rage stimulated his powers, something Kole should've guessed by their earlier encounters. "The abnormality in the children derives from a flaw in the reproductive system. My imprisonment must've sparked the flaw. It drove them to devolve into the earlier prototypes I made of your species. Feral creatures." He shook his head. "The fix can only be made in new beings. I can remake your species without the reproductive flaw, but such a feat requires centuries of work and full power. Nothing can be done now."

Mikal backed away, a dejected, glazed-over expression on his face. "Foolish Soul." His head swung from his men to Grarstein and Shikar holding back the cursed Yamani children. "If they cannot be fixed... they must be slain."

Every Yamani looked on him with hardened faces.

"We've wasted our lives to protect them," said Mikal. "I had hoped their curse would break. Fade. But it hasn't—it won't—and our creator can't cure. We've lost too many numbers to contain them. No... it must end here. Or our children will bring destruction on Ohr."

When no one moved, Mikal's stone fists tightened, and he cast his furious stare to Russé. "We want our miracle. End their suffering one way or another."

None of the Souls answered.

A large chunk of rock broke free from the barrier. Teeth snapped at the edges, chipping it away. Mikal landed a punch to the creature's jaw, and it flinched away, but another maw replaced it, snapping back at the Yamani's hand. Mikal scowled at Obell's silence. "Kill them!"

"If that is what you wish." Obell took Issira's hand, walked her to the ledge, then called to Russé. "Retreat to the bridge, my brother."

Russé ushered Kole, Vienna, and Felix up the incline. Though Kole withheld his protest, he failed to see how Obell expected to get them out when monsters swarmed their only exit.

When Mikal refused to move, Obell cast him a glare. "*Everyone.* Remove your people from the mouth."

Mikal urged Shikar and Grarstein away and followed the six surviving Yamani over the bridge.

"Leave the suits," Russé ordered as he tugged his mask off.

"Take them off?" Vienna objected.

"I imagine it'll be a foot race from here. We can't have any of you falling behind."

"Don't have ta tell me twice, Gramps."

Kole removed the metallic suit, happy to be rid of it. Apparently, Obell's possessed the ability to cancel the pain from all heat sources. Though still uncomfortably hot, it compared to a muggy summer day rather than the flesh-melting sort. Tired of the claustrophobic leather over his face, he also unbuckled the ash-filtering mask and tossed it to the ground. If Russé disapproved, he suppressed it. Already Kole felt a little stronger—more agile. And *by the Souls* could he breathe better.

Vienna and Felix followed suit, casting their discarded layers to the floor, then planted themselves beside Kole.

The Red and Blue Souls called forth the lava. A twister of molten liquid arced up and touched down a few yards from the top of the tunnel. Another and another swirled up, connecting in the same way until a cage formed.

Issira coaxed the water and vapor from the magma. Steam rose. The form dulled and hardened, cracking as it cooled into a giant stone enclosure.

Once finished, Obell brought forth a massive globe from the bubbling lake below. With a thrust of his hands, it launched toward Kole and the others.

Kole flinched as it soared overhead.

At the last moment, the globe hardened into a boulder and crashed through the cavern wall. Rocks rained down, and gray light streamed in. Their escape route.

Her job done, Issira joined them on the platform where the soulstone once resided. "He wants everyone out." She pointed to the hole. "Hurry now. He's going to lure the creatures, then trigger an eruption."

"We'll be killed." Vienna sprinted alongside as they all moved toward the exit.

"Only if we're still in range. Now, go!" Issira stopped at the opening and helped Kole through. "I'll stay at the rear. If the lava spreads too fast, I'll solidify what I can. Call the ramblers."

"They're already scaling the volcano," Russé answered.

Kole climbed up the jagged hole. The freshly pulverized rock poked like sharp teeth against his palms and boots. A gust hit his face as he emerged. Gray winds blocked out the sky. The presence of Felix's Kayetan, drifting next to him, meant the moon lay somewhere beyond the veil.

One by one, Felix, Vienna, and Russé emerged, followed by the Yamani.

A thundering boom sounded from the cavern. Kole peered back, squinting against bright lava rising like an ocean tide. The cursed creatures had barreled through the barricade. They streamed in like a colony of giant ants, filling the cage to the brink as more pushed in behind. Some gnawed the bars of the stone enclosure, chipping it away, while others bashed headfirst like charging rams. A large chunk gave way, clearing a hole big enough for a cursed to squeeze through. Once one wriggled free, another followed. The cage would only last for a short while longer.

Obell met the escaping beast head on. He grappled it. Their arms intertwined in a contest of strength. Though the cursed dwarfed him, they appeared evenly matched. Obell flicked a wrist to the lava. A jet of burning liquid hit the monster in the chest. It fell back with a massive cavity melted from its torso.

Dead.

Before the next creature came in range, Obell thrust his hands at the magma, then arced his arms over his head toward the busting cage of cursed beasts. A tsunami of lava rose and crashed down on the trapped monsters. Their cries and the sound of sizzling rock blared over the side of the volcano.

The lava swelled beyond the cage. It rose, up and up, consuming the bridge they'd escaped over, the platform, and Obell himself. Still it rose, creeping toward the opening the Yamani climbed through.

"It's not stopping," Kole said, trance-like.

"Move!" Russé tugged him into a run.

Kole stumbled down the slope, only staying on his feet because of Russé's tight, painful grip around his elbow. For the first time in a long while, he felt fast. Gravity worked with him, giving him the speed he needed to keep up—even with his limited stride. A short-lived triumph.

Felix's Kayetan rammed into his side, knocking him to his hands. The force ripped him from Russé's grasp, and he tumbled down the side of the volcano. His vision spun. The gray sky blended with the cover of ash on the slope. He lost track of which way was up until his back hit a rock. Instinctively, he thrust his legs forward and flexed his heels, which carved a trench through the ash and slowed his decent. Echoes of his name called from somewhere uphill, beyond the thick curtain of pyroclastic sediment. He opened his mouth to answer but stopped when a silhouette cut through the opaque wind. He blinked.

A Kayetan stood over him. Only it *wasn't* Felix's. Or Shikar's.

Hooves clambered from below. A skeletal horse with massive bone wings folded at its sides emerged from the haze. On its back sat Savairo.

Bloodshot eyes fixed on Kole.

CHAPTER 32

Exhaustion slowed Piper's horse. Sweat slicked Yanare's coat, and she felt the horse's heaving breaths become erratic beneath her seat. Though she urged her mare faster, nothing would give her horse the speed and stamina needed to catch up to Savairo. For all Piper knew, the blood sorcerer had already found Kole. *He could have carried him halfway to Aterus by now.* The shroud of ash gave her hope. Spotting anything from the air would be difficult. If nothing else, the ash would at least slow his search. It gave her more time.

Piper thumbed the corked vial of her father's blood tight in her sweaty fist. The urge to drink it increased with every sluggish step of her mount. A drink would make her faster than her horse—maybe enough to catch up.

Only a few drops coated the bottom. With so little, the affect would wear off by the time she faced Savairo again. The true battle.

No. She clenched the tiny bottle. *Not now.*

To her surprise, the ground below steepened. She'd reached the volcano, though she couldn't see it.

Her horse gave up on the incline and slowed.

"You've gotten me far enough. Thank you, friend. You're on your own now."

Piper jumped from the mare's back and sprinted up the volcano alone. Soon, her aching quads made her regret her decision to save the blood.

She rolled her eyes. *You're a demigod, Piper. Are you really going to let uphill sprinting get the best of you?* She managed another burst of speed. "Aterus will have Kole all because you... can't... push yourself... up a hill." Nausea bloomed in her stomach. She gave in and stopped, lashing at the ash with a kick.

The ground shook. Not an earthquake, for it never subsided. Instead, it grew. Louder. Stronger.

She shrugged. She did stand on a volcano. But as it strengthened, she realized it came from... downhill. Surely not her horse.

Piper turned to the noise, which seemed to race straight for her. A shape cleared through the soot. Giant. Spider-like. She retreated a step. Whatever it was closed in fast. Out of the question to outrun it. She dove aside, catching a better look as it passed.

Roots. A whole tangled mess of them.

Rambler. She curled her lips into a grin. *My ride.*

Piper threw herself at the tree. Once a root rushed by within range, she leapt on. The ash-covered tendril made for a slippery climb. Every stride up the volcano sent her sliding down a few inches, but she continued her slow crawl to the trunk. It beat climbing the monstrous volcano herself. More importantly, she knew where the little bugger was headed: Russé.

CHAPTER 33

"Grab him," Savairo ordered.

Kole scrambled back when the Kayetan who'd tackled him clamped its claws around his arms. The sharp edges sliced his skin as he struggled within the vice-like grip. The more Kole fought, the more he weakened himself, so he stilled and let the shadow take him. Russé and the others were near. They only needed a hint as to where he'd landed.

"Russé!" He willed his voice to carry over the chaos.

The Kayetan's smoke rushed down Kole's open mouth at once, gagging him.

Kole coughed and heaved, but the smoke only yielded when the Kayetan lay him belly down on the horse's exposed vertebrae. They pressed uncomfortably into his stomach.

Cold hands pulled at his cheek as Savairo wrenched a gag taut over his mouth. Next, his hands and feet—bound like a hunter's prize.

When Savairo shifted away, Kole thought about wriggling off. *And go where?* How far could he go tied up like this? He hoped Russé had heard his call over the rising rumble of the volcano on the brink of eruption.

Wait. The ramblers! Russé had called for them.

The horse lurched into a gallop.

As it picked up speed, Kole reached out to the place where Russé's shard of soul lay hidden away in his mind. Like he'd done before when speaking to Issira and Obell, he pushed through the barrier and siphoned a bit of Russé's power into his body. He felt Russé tense.

A hesitant moment passed where Russé fought against the transfer.

"*Savairo,*" Kole warned.

The Soul relented at the name, revealing his own feelings of panic as Kole absorbed his energy.

Kole thrust the Soul's concerns aside. The last time he'd tapped into a Soul's power, Issira had nearly taken over his body, but he knew better now. *I can do this. I have to.* This time he practiced restraint and only took what he needed.

When faint green energy started radiating from his skin, he cut himself from Russé's mind. He clenched his fists and focused on locating the ramblers. The Green Soul's borrowed power had awakened a new sense within him, one so foreign it took him off guard. The flickering energy of the rambler's life source tickled his mind. He homed in on the ramblers using Russé's power. Both trees climbed up the volcano, less than a quarter mile off.

The horse hitched beneath him. Kole's stomach dropped as they lifted off the ground and soared up into the gray winds.

Kole called to the nearest rambler, relaying his location like a beacon. A hand yanked his collar.

The blood sorcerer's eyes searched Kole. He sneered at the green energy radiating off Kole's body. "No one will save you this time." Savairo punched him.

Sharp pain bit as Kole's nose snapped. Darkness flooded his vision. It waned. Kole blinked, slow and heavy. He shook the confusion from his head. Blood poured from his broken nose into his mouth.

The hit had severed his connection with the ramblers. His only hope lost.

He collapsed over the horse's neck. Whirling ash spanned below — no way of knowing how far they'd climbed or where they headed. No one would spot them.

The horse squealed. Its hindquarters dropped, sending Kole rolling into Savairo's torso. Skeletal wings beat the wind. Kole glanced to the animal's thrashing bone legs. Something held its hind leg, dragging it down.

Kole's breath caught in his throat.

A root.

Savairo jammed his heels into the horse's ribs, urging it away.

With his captor preoccupied, Kole took in a long, deep breath of courage, then rocked back and flung himself off the animal's back.

He fell away from Savairo, whose head whipped around at the last second, rage-filled eyes locked on to Kole's.

A blink later, the skeletal horse and its rider faded into the gray abyss.

Kole plummeted. Doubt swelled with each passing moment. Though he descended back first, he knew the rocky volcano waited close below — a fatal landing from this high up. As his body cut through the wind, the blood from his broken nose left him in a stream. *Oh, Souls, what was I thinking?*

The whir of something moving fast closed in on him. Dozens of roots burst through the veil and tangled around Kole with the agility of a frog's tongue. They slowed his descent, then reeled him in.

The rambler set him down on the base of its trunk. Two roots glided within Kole's reach, offering themselves for him to steer.

"Not exactly who I was looking for," a familiar voice said as a form rounded the trunk. "But it'll do for now."

Kole snapped his head to his red-headed friend. "Piper?" he gasped. Remembering Felix's hunch, he tugged one root. Wood groaned. Tendrils slammed into Piper, pinning her to the trunk.

"What's the deal?" She squirmed, but the rambler held firm.

"What are—you're working with Savairo!"

She frowned. "I'm trying to protect you."

"You put me in a mind-link with Aterus." Kole squeezed the root and the rambler pressed harder into its victim.

The veins in Piper's face bulged. "That blood healed you," she wheezed. "You're alive because I... intervened. Better than taking you straight to him."

The angry trumpet of a horse neared the rambler.

"He's coming for you," Piper said, breathless.

"I know that."

"He won't stop until he has you."

Kole lifted the rambler's roots. "I'm not easy prey anymore."

"He's taken blood, Kole. Too much. The ramblers—the Souls—they can't protect you. He's too powerful."

Her mention of the Souls surprised him at first. Of course she knew, she'd linked him with one. The way she talked, though, gave him a feeling she knew much more than even he did. He smeared the blood from his face on his sleeve. "How do you know all this?"

Piper shook her head as if to say, *not now*. "I can put him down."

"You?"

"Yes." When Kole gave her a suspicious look, she added, "Trust me. You need all the allies you can get."

"More than you realize," Kole muttered to himself. He spit up the blood congealing in the back of his throat, then signaled the rambler to release her. The tendrils lifted away. "One wrong move...," he warned.

Her shoulders lifted as if holding back a laugh. Piper opened her palm. A glass bottle lay within. "Ground Savairo. I need him off his bloody horse."

"What are you going to do?" Kole peered up to the rambler's canopy. No sign of Savairo yet.

Her open mouth poised under the uncorked bottle. Two, three—four drops landed on her tongue. When Piper noticed him staring, she gave him a sinister grin, then licked the rim clean. "Just ground him, Kole," she repeated.

Closing his eyes, Kole focused on the rambler. He cleared his head of the violent booms coming from the top of the erupting volcano and let his thoughts sync with the tree. "Follow my lead," he whispered to the tree as he clenched a root in either hand. The rambler rattled its leaves in response.

Before he gave a command, a gale rushed down the slope, hitting them head on. Kole and Piper fell back from the blast, but a rambler root flicked up with lightning speed and anchored them to the trunk. He buried his head into the bark, protecting his skin from the residue flying by. When the tempest subsided, he peeked out.

For the first time in more than a week, clear skies met him. The volcano showed itself. Despite the rising sun to the east casting a soft blue over the scene, the peak lit up like a beacon. Lava spewed over the sides and rolled down the slope in fiery rivers. His eyes trailed down to his companions and the Yamani, who sprinted down, the magma fast on their heels. Issira ran at the front, her hands held out the way she always did when she used her power. She had done that—cleared the sky by casting away the ash with the gale. The other rambler Russé had summoned lumbered slightly behind the group. It dragged its roots through the soil, creating valleys and divots in its wake.

Lava poured into the rambler-made trench. The stream diverted from the path and filled the crevasse before overflowing and streaming down to Russé and his escaping companions. Though the rambler's efforts slowed the lava's progression, it failed to halt it.

Russé must have spotted Kole and his rambler, because he broke from the group and bounded his way.

"Kole, there!" Piper's shout pulled Kole's attention back toward the sky.

The skeletal horse dove for the rambler.

Kole pulled on the reins. The rambler acted. Its branches flicked at the flying beast but missed at the last second when Savairo nudged his horse into a death spiral.

The skeletal horse circled close to the trunk, wings stretched out flat to reduce speed. It glided halfway up the trunk; low enough so the branches couldn't smash it down and too far for the roots' reach. As Savairo rounded toward Kole, black, shadowy tentacles burst from his back like his own pair of wings and shot out for Kole.

"Watch out," Piper called.

Kole yanked the reins.

The rambler drilled its roots into the soil.

Kole and Piper braced themselves as the trunk slammed down fifty feet. Now well within striking range, a bough swung for Savairo's back. Before it made contact, Savairo vanished from off the horse and reappeared on the trunk next to Kole.

Kole should have seen it coming—he'd witnessed the sorcerer teleport like his Kayetans before—but it happened so suddenly, it caught him off guard. Kole reeled and dropped the reins. Eight shadow-like arms curled around Kole's body and lifted him. The icy touch of the tentacles seared his skin.

"You're lucky Aterus wants you alive." A wildness consumed Savairo's eyes as he took in Kole's body. "But one can survive without a limb or two."

Fire shot down Kole's arm as a shadowed tentacle attempted to wrench it from its socket.

Piper jumped on Savairo's back and dragged a blade across his neck. Black ooze poured from the wound.

A manic laugh gurgled from the sorcerer, sprouting bubbles in the tar-like ichor. The slice across his throat stitched and healed. "I knew you couldn't be trusted."

The grip on Kole loosened. He slipped through the tentacles and landed on the trunk, back against the bark. He rubbed his tender shoulder, thankful it remained attached.

Savairo's black tentacles arced around, removed Piper, and brought her flailing body before him. "I can't wait to tell Aterus of your betrayal. He will gift me with his power when he learns I've rid him of a traitor."

Kole fumbled for a rambler root.

The sorcerer's eyes shot to him. "No more." He placed a palm on the trunk. The bark darkened around his hand.

As the discoloration spread, the rambler groaned. A sickening tremor rocked Kole's core. He sensed the rambler's distress. It was as if a drought sapped every ounce of liquid from the tree. The dry and brittle pain intensified until Kole could handle it no longer. He broke his connection with the rambler for fear that whatever spell Savairo had cast on the tree would link to him.

The rambler stiffened. Leaves fell from the canopy in a solid sheet. Not one remained on the rigid branches.

When the sorcerer's body swelled, Kole realized Savairo had sucked the life from the tree and claimed it for himself.

"No!" Kole kicked the sorcerer's knee, but his boot bounced off, ineffective.

Piper struggled in her restraints.

"Let her go," Kole begged. "You want me, not her."

Savairo's eyes turned to him. "I want both." One of his tendrils unleashed from Piper and shot toward him.

It stopped a foot from Kole's face.

Piper's skin glowed. Not from sweat but an internal light of some sort. Where Savairo's skin shifted gray and black like a mirage, Piper's burned with a brilliant opalescent ripple. Her fingers wrapped tight around the tentacle reaching for Kole.

Russé's voice sprang in Kole's head. *"Get away while you can."*

Kole glanced from the approaching Soul to Piper. He couldn't ditch her.

"Do as he says," Piper said.

"How do you...?" The rest of the sentence died on his lips. She'd heard Russé's order. But how?

"Go, Kole!"

Kole jumped from the trunk and landed in the soft ash. Bumbling up the slope, he caught up with Russé.

Russé surveyed his broken nose.

"Enough with me." Kole waved him off. "You have to help Piper."

The Soul's eyes drifted over Kole's shoulder. His voice came grim. "She can handle herself. We have to get away from the volcano before it erupts."

"It's already erupting."

"No. Obell is filling the lava tubes, killing what he can. It's only a matter of time until—"

Soil exploded into the air twenty yards away. Kole flinched, bracing Russé's arms to maintain balance. Guttural clicks echoed as a cursed crawled from the depths of the volcano. Another explosion, not far off, then another. One by one, the monsters broke free and bounded down the slope, orange streams oozing from their exit tunnels.

"...until the rest are driven from the hive," Russé finished.

CHAPTER 34

Finally, the blood hit Piper's system. *Took long enough.*

Warmth surged through her veins—a power she'd never felt before. The hairs on her body stood on end as her skin glowed. With Kole out of the picture, she needn't worry about casualties.

Piper smirked. "Let's see how we measure up." She wrenched her arm free and sent a punch to Savairo's jaw. Her knuckles struck true, but he barely flinched. *The blood in his system must block out pain.* Fortunately for her, she wielded the same power now. Her knuckles tingled, almost as if invigorated by the strike.

Savairo bared his teeth and roared, "I will deliver you to Aterus in pieces."

The shadowy tentacles wrapped around her free arm once more. Once her arms and legs were fully restrained, Savairo's tentacles pulled apart all at once.

Her limbs stretched. Shoulders and hips popped and cracked. She flexed against the building pressure. If she didn't do something soon, the sorcerer would indeed carry her back in parts.

Gathering strength, she inhaled, then wrapped her hands around her bindings and pulled her knees to her chest. She drove flexed feet straight into his chest with such force that the tentacles ripped from his back, and he launched off the trunk. Piper caught herself on the dead rambler trunk as Savairo's back slammed into the ground twenty feet below. The shadowy tendrils around her arms and legs dissipated.

The sorcerer bellowed, more from the loss of his shadowy arms, it seemed, than the impact itself.

Before he had the chance to regain himself, Piper sprang after him, an elbow lifted and ready to smash into his neck. The killing blow. But when she landed and arced it toward her target, he stopped it with a hand. *Damn.* She knew what came next. Savairo grabbed her by the shoulders quicker than she could react and thrust her up the slope.

She had underestimated his strength. Piper soared through the air, twisting and turning thirty feet up. The ground rushed up fast. Curling into a ball made the impact more bearable. She rolled to her knees, covered in soot. Heat blared on her back. She glanced over her shoulder. The main river of lava sluggishly approached. She'd have to veer the fight away. Not even god's blood could protect her from lava. *That's it!*

When she looked back, Savairo had risen and was barreling toward her at breakneck speed.

Piper retreated to the boiling stream. If she met him strength versus strength, she couldn't hope to win—not after the force he put behind that throw. But she could use that strength to her advantage.

A sidestep, and she veered her path along the red-hot river, as close as she dared. Even at this distance, and with the pain-reducing agent of Aterus' blood, the heat burned her skin.

To her relief, Savairo followed.

Her eyes focused on a break in the lava flow where it had split at the base of a rock: a steppingstone in the inferno.

Soul's blood had devoured Savairo's mind. The more he drank, the more he acted on instinct. Rash. Reckless. She'd use his instability against him.

Piper stepped onto the rock, then turned to face her oncoming opponent. Precision was key. Too early and he may catch on. Too late and... she'd go down with him. She screamed at him, taunting him.

He ran faster.

She only needed to jump when the moment came. Her heart drummed in her ears. Suddenly, the heat behind her intensified. Realization hit her when she took in the dulling light of her skin. The blood faded from her system. *Already?* She swallowed and clenched her fists as Savairo closed in.

I am the daughter of Aterus. Daughter of the Souls. You will not take me.

Closer now.

The whites of his eyes. The sweat dripping down his rage-fueled scowl. His lips pulled back, exposing red-stained teeth.

Finally, she jumped.

And so did he.

Savairo snagged her ankles and yanked her back on the boulder, ruining her escape.

Her back cracked on the rock. Shooting pain blasted from limb to limb, so intense, numbness seized her. She blinked up at Savairo, her mouth half open in shock.

He leaned over, pressing his body into her.

Yet she didn't feel it. Not the pressure of him crushing her. Not the heat of the lava pooling inches away from the rock.

Savairo must have seen the confusion on her face, because he lifted and flicked her arm. It wobbled.

She didn't feel it. Any of it. Nothing below her neck registered any sort of sense. The impact had paralyzed her.

If not for her eyes watching his every move, she wouldn't have known he'd touched her. She was at his complete mercy.

A gruesome smile spread on the sorcerer's face. "It would be easy to take you back like this, but I have other plans."

Piper spat in his face.

Is this it? After all she'd fought for, she'd die before her mother. She couldn't. Not yet. Who else would fight for Evangeline? Who else would give her mother the mercy of death? She couldn't let her mother be the bartering chip for Ohr forever. Piper was her only chance, and she was determined to stay alive and see it through.

She delved deep into her mind and followed the road down, past the barriers she'd raised long ago to block out the only thing in Ohr that truly terrified her: a piece of her father's soul. Their link. The connection she'd hidden—forced herself to forget. She grasped the energy and directed it to her spine.

Anger flooded her. Not hers, but her father's. Aterus knew she was leeching his power source. He fought against her, but she refused to let up.

Consequences would come from stealing Aterus' power. She'd make him unstable again. The Black Wall would move, or Evangeline would dive toward death. She hoped for the latter and took the risk.

Piper siphoned more and more, draining her father until a snap resounded in her back, and the nerves in her limbs revived. Finished, she retreated to her own mind, raising and securing the gates she'd traveled through.

Savairo's hand had moved around her neck. He squeezed, collapsing her airway.

Now healed, she twitched her fingers to be sure. It took all of her will not to smile. She moved quickly, taking the sorcerer off-guard. In one smooth motion, Piper jammed her thumbs into his eyes.

Savairo wailed in pain.

Still she pressed. When her thumbs hit the back of his sockets, she pulled away, red flowing down her palms and wrists. Then, she pounced.

Piper heaved and rolled Savairo to his back as the sorcerer scratched at his bloodied eyes. Gripping a hand on either shoulder, she lowered his head toward the flowing lava.

But his eyes... the mangled holes shifted—changed. His face morphed; nose grew long and pointed, jaw widened and squared, and a salt-and-pepper beard poked through the skin. A familiar image.

She looked upon the face of her father.

Aterus.

The lips moved. Instead of Savairo's scream, her father's voice came forth. "Don't do this, my Piper. Stay with me."

The gentle plea of his voice—a tone he'd solely reserved for her mother—sprouted a warmth deep in her heart. It caught her off guard. Her fingers softened around the sorcerer's shoulders. "Daddy?"

The slightest hint of a smile pressed upon Aterus' lips. "You've strayed too far, my darling."

Darling? How she'd longed to hear him say those words again. Sincere. He'd called her that long ago—decades before when her mother had still been well. 'My darling Piper,' he would say every morning when she woke and in the evening after he kissed her and her mother goodnight. When there had been love and joy in their family... up until the day Evangeline began to weaken.

The old memories sent a stab of longing through Piper. How she wanted them back. Wanted them to be real and pure. He had cared *then*. Did he now?

Searing pain touched her knee. She winced and pulled her leg from the rising lava, which inched up the rock to swallow it whole. The burn cleared her head and gave her a brief sense of clarity. Her father's presence had distracted her. She thought she'd severed him off after she'd healed herself with his power. Somehow, he'd found a breach.

Piper blinked. While she had fantasized, Aterus had gotten a firm grip on every crevice of her mind. He worked his way through her, slowly taking over. Her right hand released Savairo's shoulder, though she hadn't intended to move it.

Aterus used her like a puppet. His words had merely served as a distraction. He held no love for her.

I've always been a tool.

"Come back to me, my darling Piper. All will be forgiven." His syrup-sweet voice swept through her.

So badly she wished it to be real, but she'd never be a puppet again. *Never.*

Piper bared her teeth and glared straight into Aterus' eyes. "I will come back to you, *dear Father*," she spat, mocking the endearment. "And when I do, it'll be *me* who drives a sword through your heart."

She grabbed Savairo's neck. With a barbaric cry, she plunged his head into the river of lava.

The body thrashed beneath her for a moment, fueling her rage. She pushed his head deeper. Skin melted from the skull. The musk of burning flesh, hair, and sulfur mixed in her nostrils. Still she screamed — throat rubbed raw. Blind rage blocked all pain. Drops of molten rock, sizzling off the burning corpse, sprayed her hands and wrists. She held Savairo down long after life had left his body.

When a hand touched her back, her thumbs pressed harder. The sorcerer's neck snapped.

"It's done. Let go," the feminine voice pleaded.

Pale hands reached around and stroked Piper's forearms, coaxing them to release. The stranger tugged at Piper until she finally surrendered. Soft arms looped around her torso and dragged her away from Savairo's burning body.

Adrenaline faded. Piper's voice cracked away. Whimpers replaced her screams as the sting of her scorched hands became unbearable. Her caretaker swooped her up and carried her away from the blazing rivers of magma.

Through her watery vision, Piper gazed upon the stranger.

Eyes the color of a raging storm set under fine black brows.

She knew who they belonged to.

Piper ceased her fight against the pain and let it draw her into darkness.

CHAPTER 35

The monster bolted toward Kole and Russé.

The Soul hurled his staff into the air like a javelin. It arced and stabbed the soil at the cursed's feet.

Unfazed, the beast charged past. On its next step, the creature stumbled.

The staff had rooted itself into the soil at one end while the other coiled around the giant rock ankle, tethering it in place.

"It won't hold long. Go!" Russé pushed Kole into a run. "Toward the group." The Soul pointed to Vienna, Felix, and Shikar a little ways up the slope, flanked by Mikal and his Yamani men. "We'll have a better chance."

They directed their course west, running straight along the volcano rather than down in order to meet up with the others sooner.

Another explosion wreaked havoc on the volcano. This one different. Stronger. It shook Kole's feet and vibrated up his spine. It rattled the blanket of soot beneath their feet so hard, the top layer of ash lifted into the air, creating a waist-high fog.

A quick look up the slope revealed a menacing geyser shooting from the main vent. Orange lit up the brightening dawn sky as if the sun had already reached its apex. From the crater spilled a wave of fresh lava.

"Russé!"

"I see it. There's nothing I can do. Just run."

More cursed popped up from the volcano, above and below, some blocking their path to safety. If they had any chance of outrunning all of this, they needed a ride.

"The rambler," Kole said through labored breaths.

"I've already called for it."

"Where the bloody hell is it?"

Specks of red fire rained down on Kole's thin uniform, burning holes down to his skin. Most cooled before the pain registered, but the bigger embers nipped his scarred flesh. Adrenaline kept him on his feet. He charged forward, resisting the urge to glance back at the destruction over his shoulder, even when clicks rushed up behind.

Russé's efforts to delay the cursed had expired. The beast came up fast.

A yelp sounded not five yards behind them. The deep clicks ceased. Something had taken it out.

Shuddering relief rushed through Kole's body when a crescendo of roots stabbed the earth. The rambler. *Finally.*

A soft, soil-crusted root wrapped around his waist. Kole lifted his arms, letting the rambler hoist him off the slope and set him on the trunk. The tree offered two roots. Kole held them out to Russé, who dropped down next to him.

The Soul nudged them away. "I'm moving to the rear." Their eyes locked and held. "This is you, Kole."

Kole gazed at him as the rambler carried them toward the group. Only a few days ago, Russé had fretted over him walking alongside the cart, straying too far, and diving into frays well over his head. Yet now he offered control. Maybe the Soul finally realized Kole refused to take a passive role in this whole mess. He dipped his head to Russé and curled his fingers around the roots.

Back in the saddle. He had power here. Not with his body but through the rambler. As a shepherd. New strength charged him.

"When you catch up, take who you can. Felix, Vienna, any injured Yamani. Too many, and it'll slow the rambler," Russé warned. "Get them as far away as possible. Drive the tree into the ground."

"What about you? Issira and Obell?"

"We'll manage. I need you away from the volcano." Russé side-eyed the crater. "The eruption isn't done yet. There's no telling how far the lava will reach. Just go and keep going, Kole. Understand?"

Kole nodded.

Russé grabbed Kole's face with trembling hands. "Promise me. I can't leave you unless I have your word."

The intensity of the Soul's gaze pierced through Kole. Desperation. Fear. Seeing the Soul like this triggered a fresh wave of fear through his bones. "I won't come back for you," Kole vowed.

The tense lines around Russé's mouth softened. "I'll find you when it's over." He released Kole and made for the opposite side of the trunk. A root lifted, forming a shallow decline to the ground below. With the grace of a stag, Russé ran down, jumped from the rambler, and fled up the slope toward the cascading lava.

PARRIS SHEETS

It took all his effort to tear his eyes away from Russé, who grew smaller—more distant—by the second. New determination ignited Kole's core. He had a mission. A job. Save who he could. Get out. He clenched the roots and urged the rambler faster.

Felix and Vienna ran at the head.

Swerving the rambler toward his targets, Kole prepared the roots to grab the two once in range. As he closed in, a buffet of ash shot up beneath their feet. Felix and Vienna launched into the air. Below, a cursed pounced from the volcano.

A twist to the reins, and the rambler snatched Kole's tumbling friends from the air, then guided them to the safety of the trunk. While the rambler heeded the command, Kole tugged the other rein and dozens of roots slammed into the cursed, pinning it to the floor.

The restraints allowed the Yamani to make quick work of the creature. Grarstein slammed the force of his massive stone body on the head. A crack sounded as its neck snapped under his weight.

At a slight squeeze from Kole, the rambler reeled in its roots, leaving the lifeless corpse for the lava river snaking its way downhill.

Felix touched down on the trunk beside him. "Nice save, Blondie." He nodded to the rising sun. "My Kayetan ditched me. Woulda been a rough landin'."

"Grab on." At Kole's words, the rambler curled a root around Felix's waist, harnessing him to the trunk.

A root lowered Vienna down. She nodded to Kole, the maul still affixed to her back. "What's the plan?"

"Get the hell out of here." Kole slowed the rambler to match pace with the Yamani. He scanned the group. Four remained. All in fairly good condition. Now that Felix and Vienna had been removed, Grarstein and Mikal took the lead at a quicker pace.

One glaring absence.

"Wait. Where's Shikar?"

Vienna, freshly leashed to the trunk like her brother, snapped her head to the Yamani group. "She was right behind us. I saw her just before the—oh, no!—Kole, up there."

He followed her finger up the slope to a dark dot trudging through the knee-high ash. Shikar, doubled over, clutched the injured side of her torso. A river of lava closed in on her heels.

"Hang on," Kole instructed. Felix and Vienna hugged the trunk as he whipped the rambler around and urged it double-time up the volcano.

- 258 -

Shikar must've noticed the incoming magma because her hobble hastened.

To no avail.

The molten rock surged in fast behind her. It raced underfoot and lapped at her ankles. Her cry carried down the slope, penetrating Kole's ears.

He jerked the roots.

The rambler darted to the lava's edge and stopped.

Hesitant energy emitted from the roots squeezed within Kole's grasp. The rambler knew just as well as Kole that entering the lava would mark their deaths. As much as he wanted to ignore the tree's warning, Vienna and Felix stood beside him. He couldn't put them in danger.

Instead, he urged a rambler root from the ground and extended it over the magma to the stranded Yamani, who'd scrambled to safety on the edge of a crag. Safe for the time being.

"Shikar," Kole called out over the blasting volcano.

She glanced around, eyes wide and fearful. They locked onto the outstretched root, which fell a couple yards short from her, then eyed Kole on the trunk. Her brows furrowed. "What are you doing? Get out of here."

The steady flow of lava crept up the crag, inching closer. Shikar scooted further from her rescuers.

"Jump, Shikar."

"I can't." The Yamani swiveled around, exposing throbbing orange nubs where her feet should be. They had melted off.

"I can climb to the edge," Vienna offered.

"If ya fall yer as good as gone."

"I know that. But I'm the best option out of the three of us."

"No, Vienna. He's right. Even if you made it out there, you can't hold her weight. I'm not sure if the root can either."

"We can't leave her," Vienna protested.

"We won't." Kole pushed the reins. The rambler leaned in. Another yard closer to the crag. An idea came to him. "I need you two to climb down to the roots on the opposite side."

"What're ya thinkin', mate?"

"Counterweight."

Vienna nodded. They both did as he said, and climbed down, positioning themselves on the bottom of the roots farthest away from Shikar.

A flicker of dread passed through Kole as he glanced at the lava. He gulped. If this failed, he'd not only doom Shikar, but the rambler, too: a tragic end to maybe the only walking tree left on Ohr. Not to mention the rambler remained their only means of escape. Nothing could grant Kole the speed he needed to get out of this on foot. Not alive, anyhow. Here he stood with two species on the cusp of extinction. Neither could succumb to the volcano.

With Felix and Vienna in place, waiting for his command, Kole locked eyes with his Yamani friend. He'd save them both.

Kole bit his bottom lip, determined, and added two more roots to the one stretched to Shikar. They twisted around the first, fortifying it into one thick braid. His friends in place, he egged the rambler forward. Another yard closer. All Shikar had to do was throw herself far enough to touch the root. He could do the rest.

The Yamani wearily glanced at the teetering tree and shook her head. "Leave me, Kole. I've done what I came to do."

"It's not over yet."

Shikar turned away. "You heard what Obell said. We are a doomed species. It's over for us."

The lava swelled an arm's length from her hip. This time, she didn't scoot away.

She was giving up.

Kole deflated. Back in the tunnels, Shikar had sounded so sure of herself. He thought she'd abandoned her death wish. Kole would never forgive himself if he left her stranded here, whether by her request or not. "Choose a different path, Shikar. You did it once, do it again. Don't die here with the cursed."

The rambler shuddered as he forced the root closer. A warning from the tree shot into his head. The wood of the roots blackened from the heat. Much longer and they'd burn away. A crippled rambler wouldn't get them far.

Shikar lifted to hands and knees. Her head turned to the erupting peak, then swiveled back. She surveyed Vienna and Felix, clinging to the rambler roots. Finally, her tired gaze rested on Kole.

"Grab the root. I've got you."

The Yamani winced as she touched her melted ankles to the crag, then braced herself. She sprang off, arms outstretched and aimed for the root. Lava belched and hissed beneath her, but she soared over.

When her hands closed around the braided root, Kole forced the tree back. It reared like a horse. The burden of Shikar's stone body dragged the twisted rope down. She descended toward the molten river. The obsidian of her chest glowed hot as it skimmed the lava.

Just when Kole thought his plan had failed, the sudden momentum of the rambler's tug hauled her up. She soared. The root launched her to the canopy where a net of branches broke away but caught her nonetheless. They lowered her down.

Felix and Vienna climbed up to meet the Yamani, who collapsed against the trunk, unable to stand.

Kole had a root secure her. "Are you all right?"

"No. Neither will any of you be if you don't get this damn tree moving. Go, Kole. Another blast builds. I can feel it."

Her words barely made it to his ears when an earth-shaking thunder boomed beneath their rambler. Kole reeled and squeezed the roots on instinct. Both hands preoccupied with the reins, he slammed into the trunk quicker than he could react. His face scraped the rough bark. Fresh pain jolted from his already broken nose and spread to the base of his skull. He stumbled back, delirious, but a soft tendril touched his shoulder, steadying him. Globs of warm blood trickled past his upper lip, half dried from the first break.

"Kole!" Vienna cried, at his busted face.

"I'm okay." He blinked back the dots in his vision, then wiped his nose. Though he hadn't had enough time to catch himself, his reflexes had saved the others. Roots coiled tight around their waists.

"We'll get ya fixed up when we—shit!" Felix pointed to the crater.

What was left of it.

Chunks of the volcanic crater shot into the sky, a plume of magma and ash hot unfurling behind it. The boulders rained back down to the slope and rolled down the lava streams, coating in molten rock. One struck like a comet fifty yards away.

"Go, Kole," Vienna shouted.

He took the reins as smaller rocks, pebble to skull-sized, battered the canopy like flaming rain drops. Kole drove the rambler down the volcano.

The roots strained against the load of their new passenger. The trunk's altitude sank, leaving Kole and the others a bit closer to the ground than before, but the decline of the terrain aided their speed.

Earlier, on the way up to rescue Shikar, the path had been relatively clear—few rivers of lava had yet slithered down—but in the short time they'd spent retrieving their Yamani friend, the land had changed. No longer a straight shot, Kole weaved the rambler around the scorching currents.

Bodies of the cursed littered the slope. Sludge crept over and consumed the corpses. Once the lava cooled and hardened, their bodies would forever be welded into the volcano. The thought made Kole tear his eyes away and focus on the course ahead.

From the eruption came an advancing tide of lava and rolling clouds of ash. They plummeted down, closing in on the rambler faster than Kole could force their escape.

Soon, they caught up to Mikal and Grarstein. Their group had dwindled by one.

Two cursed trailed them.

Kole wiped the crust of blood from his mouth, then pulled on the roots. The tree veered toward the monsters. Carefully, he inched closer until they came in range. He thrust a tendril at each of their feet and flung them back into the incoming magma. Piercing shrieks told him he'd hit his mark.

When Kole went to grab the fleeing Yamani, intending to bring them aboard the rambler, Shikar grabbed his ankle.

"Leave them," she said weakly.

"They'll be overrun," Kole protested.

"The added weight will ground the rambler."

"She's right, mate." Felix pointed his borrowed weapon at the singed holes in the canopy. "This thing ain't lookin' so good."

Shikar released her smooth hand from Kole's leg. "They only need to make it to the pools. They'll be safe in the caverns."

"Should we go in after them? To the pools, I mean," Vienna took a worried glance over her shoulder at the nearing lava.

"Their bodies can survive a tunnel collapse. Can yours?"

"Russé wanted us to run." Kole studied the Ashland Plains stretching out from the bottom of the volcano. No shelter. No water or animals to hunt. Only flat, exposed land.

Shikar rested her head on the bark. Groggy eyes rolled to Kole. "Then you run. I'll watch over you in their absence."

The rambler galloped off the volcano and trudged through the built-up ash. Every stride of its roots kicked up more soot, leaving a trail of gray in their wake.

Kole only slowed the pace at Shikar's command. She seemed to think them safe on the plains.

They endured another hour of travel before Kole halted the tree. Its leaves had burned away from the falling embers. Shaking branches rattled overhead. Exhaustion poured from the tree, but a sliver of urgency held as if it, too, still sensed the danger behind them. The rambler would continue on if asked.

Kole dropped the reins. His hands trembled and cramped. Even after he'd released them, the feel of the roots lingered on his skin.

A communal sigh washed over the rambler and its occupants.

Vienna and Felix slipped from the rambler's hold and joined Kole on the ledge of the trunk.

After the last quake, which tore off the crater, the eruptions had slowed. Orange pulsed at the top like a torch and streamed down. Shikar had been right. Halfway down the slope, the brilliant streaks of lava dulled and faded away. And the sky. Gray clouds billowed up and out, blocking out the sun. Nothing new for the Ashland Plains.

No sign of the Souls or the Yamani—Piper or Savairo. Knowing who survived lay well beyond his guess. One thing he knew for sure: Issira lived. The energy she'd used to blow the ash away and clear the air remained. Plus, a Soul couldn't die. Right? The more he thought on it, the less sure he became.

"Do you think...?" Vienna began.

"There's no telling," Kole said.

"We can't be the only survivors." Her voice came raw.

"The Souls'll be all right. They're gods, they are. Wouldn't mean much if a volcano could kill 'em. Well, not *just* a volcano. I mean— like—they're eternal and all that, eh?"

Kole nodded. "They can heal." He remembered the last time Russé had been horribly wounded. A Kayetan had driven a claw straight through his chest and he'd survived without so much as a scar. "But Piper can't."

"Piper?" Vienna turned to him. "She's here? You saw her?"

Everything had happened so fast, Kole had forgotten to fill them in. "Savairo, too." He told them of his encounter.

"Whose side is Pipes on?" Felix asked.

"Ours," Kole said without a shred of doubt. He'd seen the venom in Piper's eyes when she went for Savairo. Had she succeeded? Even if she had—killed him for good—where was she now?

Vienna cast him a wary, unconvinced look.

Kole didn't blame Vienna's trepidation. What with Piper's strange appearances, popping in and out so conveniently, and her connection to Savairo and Aterus. Nothing added up. Especially what had happened back on the volcano right before she took on Savairo. Piper had heard Russé speaking to him. *Telepathically.* How did she know? How had she heard? Better yet, what did it mean?

PARRIS SHEETS

Then it clicked.

Issira's conversation with him days ago. Talk of a child. Aterus'. Half human. Half god.

"Shit." Kole glanced between the siblings. "It's her. Piper is the demigod."

"Aterus' daughter?" Vienna leaned in, concern in her green eyes.

"I don't know, mate. Think you're way off."

"No—think about it. During the rebellion, she made a blood magic-fueled weapon with Russé's blood. She knew what he was from the beginning. *She* was the one captured." A beat as more of the piece became clear, then, "... she *wanted* to be captured. Why would she want that?"

"To protect you," Vienna answered.

"We all would've done the same," Felix argued. "She knows a little magic, so what? So does Leo."

"Piper gave me the mind-link with Aterus, has super strength, just *happens* to know where we are. *And* she got inside my head! No one else can do that. Only the Souls." He bit his blood-crusted lip. "It adds up."

Vienna unslung the maul from her back and set it on the tree. "So we know what she is. How does that help us?"

"Knowin' a secret means leverage," said Felix. "And I reckon she'll know a lot more about Aterus. Maybe she knows a way ta help Blondie."

Kole sighed. "Wishful thinking."

"Hate ta sour yer milk, but that's all we got, mate."

Vienna shrugged. "So, what do we do now?"

"Russé said he'd find us."

Felix scratched his head. "Like a few hours? I dunno if I wanna stay here. What if some of the cursed survived and decide we're dinner?"

"I don't mean to stay long." Kole turned to Shikar.

"As well you shouldn't." The Yamani's closed eyes and slumped back made it look as though she were sleeping, but she held a hand up. "You saw the cursed escaping. It's not far-fetched to assume some have fled to the plains for safety as we have."

"Well, that's just peachy, now ain't it? We're as good as a paddle-less boat."

"We have weapons." Kole jerked his chin to the maul and Felix's picks. "And a rambler. Don't forget about your Kayetan, too."

"What goods havin' a shadow servant if it up and leaves ya half the time?"

- 264 -

"Your Kayetan will return at dusk," said Shikar. "As will mine."

"I'm not worried about being armed." Vienna waved to the dreary landscape. "We have no food or water, and it takes days to get out of the plains. We should move as soon and fast as possible. The Souls will find us no matter where we are, but they can't help us if we starve to death."

"Aye." Felix dipped his head.

"We're all exhausted, the rambler, too. We should rest a bit or we won't have the strength to protect ourselves out there anyway. A few hours at most," Kole suggested. He was amazed by the authority in his own voice, and more so, when his companions put up no resistance.

"Then in the meantime, I suggest lying low." Shikar patted the trunk. "Can this thing lay down or something? It stands out like a beacon. Anything out here will come straight for us."

Kole placed a palm on the rambler's trunk and relayed his wishes. Once he and the others dismounted, the roots lowered the trunk and the rambler gently laid itself down like a felled tree in a forest.

They all moved to the base and huddled within the tangled mess of roots, which closed around them acting as a cage.

The Yamani crawled through the ash and collapsed next to the heart of the tree, resting her head on the wood like a pillow.

"Shikar...." Vienna knelt next to her. "Is there anything we can do?"

"No, girl. I just need some rest."

"The rambler will carry you when we move out." Kole adjusted his seat so the volcano and the others sat well within his line of sight. "Your feet... can you...?"

Shikar opened one yellow eye. "Grow them back? No. But I can replace them."

"How? What do you need?" As Kole spoke, Felix plopped in front of him. "You're blocking my view," Kole snapped.

The left side of Felix's mouth lifted. "Won't be much of a scout with two black eyes, Blondie."

"What?"

"Yer nose. It's broke."

"I know that."

"Gonna have ta align it."

"Align it?"

"Felix has had a broken nose before." Amusement laced Vienna's voice as if an old memory popped in her head. "He knows what he's doing. Go on, Shikar. What do you need? Is it something we can help you with?"

"I need rock. I can make new feet, but it has to be the material I am made from."

"Obsidian," Kole said as Felix lined his thumbs on either side of his swelled nose. "The rock on the volcano."

"Yes, but it takes time. Longer than we have," said Shikar.

"How long?" Vienna asked.

"I have been off a normal Yamani diet for years. The process would be longer."

"How long, Shikar?" Kole winced when Felix's thumbs grazed his skin.

"Weeks. Maybe a month."

Without warning, Felix squeezed.

White hot pain pierced Kole's skull. He cried out and scooted back. "Bloody Souls, Felix. A countdown would've been nice."

"Ya woulda tensed up," Felix accused.

A string of curses left Kole. Water poured from his eyes. It hurt to blink. His eyes, his nose—even his cheeks—everything pulsed and ached.

"That'll have ta do for now. Don't ya touch it." Felix swatted Kole's hand away from his swollen face. "Ya kinda look like a chipmunk with yer puffed-up cheeks. It's pretty damn adorable. Don'tcha think, V?"

"Oh, leave him be," she chastised her brother.

Kole grumbled. Sitting on his hands to keep from messing with it, he cast his attention back to the Yamani. "We can get you back to the volcano."

"No. The volcano won't be safe until it cools. Ash covers the molten rock now. One wrong step and you'll be in my same situation. Best to sit tight. All of you small ones need rest."

Felix ducked through the roots. "Let's split up watch."

"I'll go next," Vienna volunteered. She offered Kole a sympathetic smile. "You're in for a rough day with that nose."

Kole gladly accepted the chance to rest and settled into the thick cushion of ash, which he found surprisingly comfortable. Remembering her amused look earlier, he asked. "How'd Felix break his nose? Thomas?" The cranky Liberation member seemed like the best guess.

She gave a smug smile. "Me."

His brows drew together. Immediately, he regretted it. The movement angered his nose. "What did he do?" he asked through gritted teeth.

"It wasn't like that. We were training hand-to-hand combat. My right hook was faster than we both thought." The smile tugging on her mouth warmed his heart. Even covered in ash and grime, her green eyes pierced straight through him — gave him peace and anxiety all at once.

Kole moved to pull the mask of his Liberation uniform over his face, then stopped himself. What difference did it make out here, drenched in filth and blood? She knew what he looked like. No use hiding now, after all they'd been through. Instead, he detached the mask and shoved it in the waist of his pants. "You'll have to teach me that right hook sometime."

"Sure."

Kole settled in. Heavy lids weighed on him, but he stared at Vienna a little while longer. Shikar had laid her head on Vienna's shoulder, fast asleep. She nestled back, too, letting her own head tilt against the Yamani. For the moment, all was peaceful. But as Vienna's clear, content eyes stared down at their Yamani companion, a sudden bolt of fear clouded them.

"No, no, no...." Vienna wriggled free from Shikar's weight.

The Yamani fell wordlessly to the ground.

Kole perked up. "What?"

"Shikar? Shikar!" Vienna screamed.

Felix climbed through the roots. "What's the ruckus for, V?"

"She's not breathing." With a great push, she tried to roll Shikar to her back.

Kole and Felix rushed over to aid. It took their combined strength to roll her over. Kole assessed her. The Yamani's chest had stopped rising and falling. No matter how hard they shook and shoved, her limbs remained still. Nothing more than a fallen statue.

"Please, Shikar." Kole's fist pounded harder into the stone chest until his knuckles stung. "You can't be dead. Wake up!"

"Mate." Felix grabbed Kole's wrist. "It ain't gonna help any."

Vienna fell back, panting. "I don't understand. She seemed okay, didn't she? She was talking to us like... like she was fine. Wasn't she?" She glanced between Kole and Felix. "*Wasn't she?*"

"I reckon her injuries were worse than she thought."

Kole only stared at the dead Yamani. He'd been a fool to think she'd be all right after such severe injuries. Only a Soul could've saved her. Now that she'd passed, even divine powers couldn't help. Just when she'd broken free from her death wish and truly chosen to move on.

Death. Destruction. Misery. It's what Kole's mission brought. Everyone with him risked it.

Shikar had been their only chance at survival. She knew the cursed, the land, the volcano—everything. If anything other than the Souls found them first, they only had the rambler. They only had *him*.

"What do we do?" Vienna's eyes fixed on Shikar's body.

"Doesn't change the plan. We wait for the Souls ta find us, 'least a little while, then get ta movin'."

"No." Kole leaned against the roots. As much as he longed for rest, he'd have to resist. "Without Shikar, there's no chance of us finding food or water here. Some cursed may be out there. It's best we get as far away as we can while the confusion holds."

"Leave? Are you sure?" Vienna asked.

"The Souls need me more than I need them. That's the only thing I'm sure of. They'll find us eventually, with or without a head start." Tapping a root, Kole ordered the rambler up. Like an overturned bug righting itself, the tree crawled to its root legs. Three tendrils curled around Kole and the siblings' waists.

"What about Shikar?" Vienna asked.

Kole's lungs pushed out a heavy sigh. They couldn't take her along. Leaving her felt wrong—out in the open, subjected to the weather and the eyes of any passerby. A proper burial. He could give her that.

Remembering the grave site back in Solpate forest, he had the tree push aside the drift of ash and scrape up the soil. Two roots lifted Shikar's body and lowered her into the shallow grave.

The siblings stood by his side. They stared at their Yamani friend for a long while.

More than anything, Kole wished Obell could've done something about the Yamani curse. If her daughter had been healed, none of this would've come to pass. So many families would have been reunited. Children given a second chance at life. It pained him that Shikar never found peace. Acceptance, maybe. But true peace? That had been robbed from her long ago. Now she lay dead in the middle of the Ashland Plains in an unmarked grave.

Kole commanded the roots to cover the body. "She deserves better."

A rustle of paper filled the silence as Vienna rummaged through her pack. She pulled out a scroll of parchment and a quill. A map of Ohr lay sketched on the unraveled parchment. "We'll come back for her." Vienna marked their spot on the map. "After this is all over, we'll come back."

After this is all over. The words preyed on Kole's mind. He longed for and dreaded the end. Up until now, he'd been a puppet—his fate inevitable. Things had changed when he'd released Obell. He'd realized what truly mattered. *I'll have you back, Niko. I promise.*

"Kole?"

A touch to his elbow disrupted his thoughts.

Vienna leaned in, concern on her scrunched face. "Are you ready?"

He nodded and followed her and Felix to the rambler's trunk. Two roots poised themselves over Kole's open palms. He took hold and urged the tree forward, away from the volcano.

After Vienna and Felix settled in, sat at the base of the trunk with their legs dangling over the edge, a strange urge arose from the back of his mind. The overwhelming itch forced him to glance back to the grave.

There, standing over the disturbed soil of Shikar's grave, stood her Kayetan. It slowly sank into the grave with its master.

CHAPTER 36

Leo gripped the rope at the front of the line. "One, two, three, pull!" he called over his shoulder. The strength of a dozen men and women tugged on cue; the second group, hands on their own rope, followed the command, too.

The statue groaned as it leaned. Leo had made sure to keep enough empty space between the front pullers and the statue so that, when it fell, they'd be clear from injury. Still, the front positions held the most danger, which is why he headed the first rope and the twins, Criz and Boogy, handled the second. Even for teenagers, their massive bodies, thick and muscular like bulls, proved extraordinarily hardy. Their eyes flicked between the statue's progress and their Liberation leader for instruction.

Only a little further. Leo braced his heels between a crack in the cobblestone and thrust back, adding the strength of his legs to the rope. Gasps and grunts sounded behind him. The townspeople who'd volunteered with the extraction wanted the effigy toppled as much as Leo.

Finally, the statue passed the point where gravity took over.

"Retreat," Leo yelled.

The rope went slack. Everyone ran for cover save for Leo, Criz, and Boogy, who all held their ground and watched it fall.

As the statue closed in on the stone courtyard, Leo took one last look at the carved face—one nearly identical to his own. His brother's reign was over. For good. Leo'd make sure of that. No more hiding in the dark, fighting a losing battle. Socren was free again, and Leo promised himself, as long as he lived, it would remain that way. A place of peace.

The statue crashed down, cracking and chipping the cobbles beneath. Crumbled pieces shot out to the edge of the courtyard. The head rolled to Leo's feet. He shoved it over with a heave of his foot. Even carved in stone, those eyes held a thirst. "Savairo," Leo whispered.

The crowd cheered at the destruction. Nearly the whole town had gathered around the square, waiting for them to pull down the last mark of Savairo left in Socren. Since the rebellion when they took back Socren from Savairo and his Kayetans, Leo had scrubbed the city clean of every trace; burned what he could, repurposed things of importance — mostly metals and other precious resources they couldn't afford to waste. With each removal, a heaviness seemed to disappear from the people. Now they clanked glasses together, celebrating the moment, the last stain of the warden's reign gone.

A strange sense bubbled in Leo's stomach. Not sadness, never that. But a sense of finality. Whatever the feeling, it washed over him, setting goosebumps over his skin. As he stared at his brother's face, he sensed this would be the last time he ever saw it. He sensed... his end.

Criz and Boogy flanked him.

"That thing creeps me out," Criz said, breaking Leo from his thoughts. "Eh, it's still looking at me."

Boogy leaned around Leo. "Just close your eyes and it'll go away," he said to his brother.

"*Or*, we could smash it to bits. That'd be less dumb."

"Dumb?" Boogy growled at the insult.

"You know how the saying goes about twins, 'one has the brains, one has the looks.'" Criz lifted his chin.

A sly smile played at the corners of Boogy's mouth. "Are you saying I'm pretty?"

"Ah, shut it, Boogy."

"Enough, boys." Leo held out a hand and they both dipped their heads obediently. How he missed Vienna and Felix. *At least those two saved their bickering until they were out of my presence... well, mostly.* The thought of his long-gone Liberation members sent a bittersweet sigh through him. Weeks had passed. Still no word. Leo had yet to determine if that meant trouble or victory. "You boys have done quite enough today. Clean this up, then consider yourselves off duty until morning."

Another nod from them, then he turned and set his sights on the former prison. As he walked, the twins muttered behind him, arguing over which was the smart one.

"Leo!" A voice carried through the square. The urgent tone pierced through the joyous chorus of the townspeople's celebration.

Leo turned toward the voice, yet by the continual cheers, no one else seemed to have heard it. His eyes scanned the crowd, wondering the source. Then, a group to his left stumbled and cursed as a tall, lanky boy with string-like black hair pushed through them.

Thomas sprinted for Leo, a piece of paper slipped in his hand.

Panic jolted Leo's heart when he spotted the hawk gliding after Thomas. Leo lifted his arm for his beloved bird. Fiona reached him before Thomas. "There, there, my love, it is so nice to see you," he cooed, trying to calm the tawny hawk who flapped her wings impatiently, claws a bit too tight around his forearm for comfort. He ground his teeth and bore the sharp talons scraping his skin.

Her head swooped to the side. One dark eye landed on Leo. Something—an image—shown in her pupil. A face stared back at him. The last one the hawk had seen before returning to Socren.

"Piper?" he whispered loud enough for only Fiona to hear.

The hawk cocked her head and snapped her beak in response.

Footsteps pounded near. Leo set his jaw as Thomas closed in and handed over the message.

Leo unrolled it:

The wall will move on you. Prepare.

He studied the note, or rather, the handwriting. Exaggerated loops. *Hesitance....* At a glance, he'd think it Vienna's. But after Fiona's hint, he knew the message had been sent by another. *Meant* to look like Vienna's, but off just enough to reveal the forgery.

A look back to his hawk. Piper's face had faded from the bird's eye. Leo knew the possibility of her being killed was slim. If Savairo wanted her dead, the warden would've killed Piper during the battle. Instead Savairo had kidnapped her. Since that day, Leo had wondered why. Piper held some kind of importance. He brushed the thought away. *A puzzle for another time.*

Somehow, Piper and Vienna's paths had crossed—of that he could be certain—and all he had to go on was the message in his hand.

"It's from Vienna and Felix, right?" Thomas asked, breathless from his run. "Their mission?"

"No. It is from Piper."

Thomas' jaw dropped. "What? She's alive?" The shock morphed to bliss. "What does the note mean?"

Leo tucked the paper into his breast pocket. "Gather the Liberation. Gather the shepherds and the ramblers. We prepare for war."

THE END

ACKNOWLEDGEMENTS

Thank you to all my beta readers, who helped me figure out this sequel. To my mother and dad, who continuously encourage me to follows my dreams no matter how impossible they may seem. I never would've started writing to begin with if it hadn't been for your early support.

I give all the thanks in the world to the amazing editor, Darren Todd. You continue to help me grow in this profession and challenge my story by asking all the questions I never thought to answer.

Sam Keiser has done it again. Another fantastic book cover, this time featuring the Yamani. I couldn't be more pleased with the art.

And finally, a great big thank you to David Lane (aka Lane Diamond), who is responsible for this story in your hands. I will forever be grateful for the chance you've given me and for welcoming me into the Evolved Publishing family.

ABOUT THE AUTHOR

Parris lives in Mesa, Arizona with her husband and two golden retrievers. She discovered her love for reading when a middle-school reading assignment led her to the fantasy section of the library. This passion sparked stories of her own imagination, yet she never put pen to paper until after college. When she's not consumed in her writing, she enjoys Olympic weightlifting, playing Dungeons & Dragons, and coaching color guard.

For more, please visit Parris online at:
Website: www.ParrisSheetsAuthor.com
Facebook: @AuthorParrisSheets
Twitter: @Parris_Sheets

MORE FROM EVOLVED PUBLISHING

We offer great books across multiple genres, featuring high-quality editing (which we believe is second-to-none) and fantastic covers.

As a hybrid small press, your support as loyal readers is so important to us, and we have strived, with tireless dedication and sheer determination, to deliver on the promise of our motto:
QUALITY IS PRIORITY #1!

Please check out all of our great books,
which you can find at this link:
www.EvolvedPub.com/Catalog/

Thank you!